THE
NIGHT
SHE
WENT
MISSING

THE NIGHT SHE WENT MISSING

KRISTEN BIRD

mira

ISBN-13: 978-0-7783-3210-7

The Night She Went Missing

Copyright © 2022 by Kristen Bird

Recycling programs
for this product may
not exist in your area.

This edition published by arrangement with Harlequin Books S.A.

For questions and comments about the quality of this book, please contact us at
CustomerService@Harlequin.com.

Mira
22 Adelaide St. West, 41st Floor
Toronto, Ontario M5H 4E3, Canada
BookClubbish.com

Printed in U.S.A.

For Mom & Dad,
who read *I Am a Bunny* too many times to count

THE
NIGHT
SHE
WENT
MISSING

PART I:
THE MISSING

"A mother's love for her child is like
nothing else in the world.
It knows no laws, no pity.
It dares all things and crushes down
remorselessly all that stands in its path."

—Agatha Christie

PROLOGUE
Emily

They find me faceup in the murky water of the harbor on the day of my funeral. Or memorial service. Whatever. It's not like there's much difference. Dead is dead.

Except I'm not. I. Am. Not. Dead. I would pinch myself if I could move.

"Can you hear me? Hey, what's your name? Can you open your eyes?"

My eyes are as dense and heavy as basalt. *Basalt: rich in iron and magnesium*, Mr. Schwartz penned on the board during our volcanic rock unit in eighth grade. I fight to come out of the emptiness that has held me for the past…the past what? Hours? Days? Weeks?

I attempt to whisper my name even though my eyelids remain anchored. *Emily.* That's right. Emily. I can't remember the last time I voiced those three syllables.

"Pull her up."

Hands yank at me, jerking me from the arms of the water. Two hands wander up my body—over my feet, my legs, the arch of my hips, my arms, onto my neck, stopping at my forehead. This touch is not like the familiar plying of the boy I love, so fiery that it almost stings. This touch is necessary, cold, perfunctory. *Perfunctory*, Mrs. Abbot, my sophomore English teacher had pronounced for us students as we learned the word for the first time. *P-E-R-F-U*—

The voice cuts in. "Tell them we have a girl, a teenager. No broken bones as far as I can tell but looks like she's been out here for hours. Unconscious, but breathing on her own." His voice muffles as he turns his head. "I think she might be Emily."

Suddenly, a brilliant choir of tenors and baritones and basses burst forth. "The Emily?"

Emily. Yes, that's me. What a comforting thing to hear one's name spoken by those who can point the way home. I breathe in gratitude and descend into the lightness of sleep before a hand touches my cheek again.

"You awake, Emily?"

The swooshing of the waves calls to me, a reminder that the song of the deep is steady despite all the new sounds: The bustle of work boots, the hum of the boat waiting to churn to life and set out across the open sea.

"Your mama's been looking for you, Ms. Emily. You gave us all a fright. You hear me?" The man seems to sense that I can hear his words while my body remains frozen despite the warmth of the water and the sun overhead. "You're gonna be okay, sweetheart. Yes, ma'am, you're gonna make it just fine. Got a daughter about your age, and I woulda been worried sick if my girl had gone missing for weeks on end. Your mama sure is gonna be happy."

A nasally voice now. "Where you think she's been all this time? Turned into a mermaid?" The boy chuckles.

"Hush, Beau."

The man's hand touches my forehead, his fingers sandpapery with callouses. "Now, sweetheart, if you can open your eyes for a sec, I can introduce you properly to the crew. We're getting you help as fast as we can, but you can go ahead and open them eyes before all the medics arrive. They'd be good and relieved to see you looking around."

I try. Oh, how I want to flicker them open, but my head aches and oblivion pulls harder. The siren call of the void is too tempting to resist.

1
September
Catherine

Catherine Rubisi patted the wilted feathers sprouting from her headdress and frowned.

"You look fine," her husband whispered for the third time, his fingers pressing into the small of her back to remind her that he was by her side despite the crowd of strangers and the wet warmth of the night air. Another thing she did not like about Galveston Island: even on the short walk into The Grand Hall, she was dripping with sweat and swatting at a host of gnats and a swarm of mosquitoes. Did it bother other residents that there were only two ways out of this town? By boat or by causeway, that was it. Unless one felt like swimming, she supposed.

"This is just like the PTA fundraisers you helped organize back in Woodhaven," Carter attempted.

Catherine shot him a look. Gift cards to Woodhaven Diner, a stack of novels from the only bookstore in town and a photo shoot by a senior photography major couldn't compete with Hawaiian vacations, Italian villas and puppies. Yes, puppies. Who gives away a living creature to a drunk couple in the corner at the end of an evening? Apparently, Callahan Preparatory Academy, the only private school on this twenty-seven-mile strip of land.

As she crossed the threshold behind her husband, her eyes fell to the sparkles and silk adorning the women. She had not realized that when one attended the illustrious Callahan Preparatory Senior Auction, one did not just dress according to theme but also according to designer label. Her costume would've had potential if she'd worn the black Dior gown Rosalyn had suggested *and* if she'd allowed Rosalyn's makeup artist to affix to her head actual peacock feathers with emeralds for eyes. Back home in Woodhaven, Oregon, with her group of girlfriends who'd taught at the university for years, she might've joined in just for fun. But not here, not with these people in this place. No, Catherine had happily ignored her mother-in-law's advice, instead grabbing an old Ann Taylor dress from her closet and an assortment of florals and feathers from the discount bin at Hobby Lobby. She crossed her arms. She would not let these ridiculous women throwing air kisses and finger waves at Rosalyn make her feel inferior.

"It's easy to say that I look fine when all you had to do was put on a tux," Catherine lobbed at Carter.

He wrapped his arms around her waist. "Hey, lady, penguins are birds too."

"Touché." She wriggled away from him. "I swear, though, I'm about to tear off these Spanx."

"Yes, please," Carter breathed as he squeezed her love handles. She almost pushed away his hands, not wanting to be reminded of the way her clothes hugged her midsection these days.

Once again, her husband ignored her protests, and in the

dark, his palm wandered down her back, to her hip, the top of her thigh.

"Really, Carter." But Catherine couldn't help smiling even as her eyes accidentally landed on Rosalyn with her pointed chin and high cheekbones. Her mother-in-law nodded curtly. That woman was like…like a mantis shrimp. Yes, that was it. Just the other day, Emily had been talking about her new fascination with this sea creature whose eyes move independently of one another, giving the crustacean a wide field of vision. That's what Carter's mother was like, a creepy little crustacean. Always watching.

Catherine shuddered and removed her husband's hands again, but not before pressing herself into him. "You behave for two minutes. Grab a drink with your insufferable alumni friends, and I'll be back."

She exited the floor and ducked under the yellow and green and purple and orange swaths of fabric cascading around the Birds of a Feather sign—the theme of the evening. Pointy birds of paradise poked at her, their orange heads appraising her undignified apparel.

As she opened a door, a voice squawked, startling her. "Welcome, r-r-r-awk." A cockatoo. In the bathroom. Catherine's hand flew to her chest.

"I know. I almost jumped out of my skin, too, when I walked in," tittered a tall, thin woman wearing a black sequined number with a fabulous white-feathered cape. Her hair was darker than most of the other moms—almost as dark as Catherine's—and she stood in front of a floor-to-ceiling mirror, her eyes staring as she applied mascara. "I'm not sure which woman's idea it was to put a bird in the bathroom, but I'm guessing she didn't think about all the weak lady bladders in the fortysomething crowd." The woman smirked. "But what am I saying? Everyone is so nipped and tucked that there's not a chance anything is leaking."

Catherine tried a polite smile as she scooted into the stall to tear off the tight fabric sucking her into this dress. Not worth it. She emerged moments later, victorious, to find the same woman now working on her lips.

"Just fixing my face." The timbre of her contralto voice was inviting; the cadence, waves at low tide. "You're Emily's mom, right? Dr. Callahan?" she said.

Catherine almost corrected her. *Dr. Rubisi*, she would've answered a few months earlier. *I kept my maiden name.* But here, on the island where she was trying to hide, she preferred the veil of the patriarchy. Catherine examined herself in the mirror and immediately spotted two recurring strands of gray. She hid them under a feather. "Callahan. That's right."

"I've heard about Emily from my son." The woman clarified, "I'm Alex Frasier's mom—Morgan Frasier." She said the name as if everyone already knew it.

"Oh." Catherine didn't know what to say. Emily hadn't mentioned spending time with an Alex, had she? Not that Emily had said much since Catherine and Carter dragged her here. *Alex Frasier. Alex Frasier.* There was something about that name.

Morgan was already tall and lithe, but in heels, the woman had a good six inches on her, and Catherine could feel her eyes peering down, monitoring her reaction. "You know teenagers," Morgan said. "Enthralled one minute and uninterested the next."

Catherine frowned. *That* did not describe Emily.

"Don't worry. Alex is a good boy, and this is a good school. Graduated nearly a dozen Ivy-league-bound kids last year, haven't you heard?" Morgan smirked and held out a tube. "Lipstick?"

"No, thanks." Catherine attempted to hide her repulsion as she wiped her hands with the fluffy white hand towel and turned to leave.

Morgan put out a hand to stop her and leaned in with a conspiratorial whisper. Her lips were thick and bright red. "I'm sorry, but I have to ask. Is it true that your mother-in-law actually paid thousands of dollars of her own money for the falconer when she was told he wasn't available for this evening? Doesn't she realize she's supposed to be raising money, not spending it?"

The cockatoo shifted to eyeball both of them.

Catherine closed her eyes for a moment too long. Yes, it was true. Why? Because that's what Rosalyn Callahan did. She took control, she got what she wanted, and she managed Callahan Prep in the way her grandfather—the founder of the school more than a hundred years earlier—would have intended, or at least that was her excuse.

Catherine pasted on what Carter called her *rich-lady-face*, lips pouted and eyebrows furrowed as if she cared. She pinched her voice and demurred, "I'm not actually privy to the details, but isn't Rosalyn just the… Oh, I don't even know *how* to describe her." Manipulative? Petty? Superficial?

"Oh, you can cut the crap with me, sweetheart," Morgan chuckled, putting away her lipstick and lifting a flask that had been biding time in her purse. "Look, I grew up around here, went to school here, have spent my life here. I know that everyone on this island adores Rosalyn, and I know that she runs every detail of the school, but I, for one, am not a fan. Not that I'd be brave enough to say that to her face. God. Never."

Catherine was struck. She had yet to meet anyone who didn't endlessly and gratuitously praise her mother-in-law. Even Carter rarely said a negative word about his mother. Catherine let the smile fall, her face relaxing for the first time

since she'd put on this stupid costume. "That is the most re-
freshing thing I've heard all evening."

"You want a sip? It's liquid courage for me at these events."
Morgan raised the flask, took a swig and offered it to Catherine. "You're lucky you came when you did—you only have to
endure one year of this crowd with Emily graduating in May."

Gin. The warmth quickly spread, the tip of her nose already turning pink. "Thanks, but I have the twins too. Lucy
and Olivia are just in third grade, so we've got many, many
years here." *A lifetime*, she almost said, taking one more gulp
before handing the flask back.

"Oh, that's right, you poor dear. I was hoping you'd be
spared. Now I remember Leslie mentioning all three of the
Callahan kids at the first Senior Moms meeting during the
summer."

"Leslie?" Catherine recognized that name. She was the
only Callahan Prep mother that Rosalyn had mentioned as
the movers pulled out of the driveway a few months ago. *Of
course, you'll want to join the Merry Moms*, Rosalyn had said. *They
are the heart and soul of Callahan Prep, and you'll adore their chair-
woman, Leslie Steele. Maybe you and Emily can begin helping Leslie
and her daughter plan the senior events. Wouldn't that be lovely?* A
light—or a fire—had gleamed in Rosalyn's gaze.

That first night, Catherine had brought up the conversation
to Carter as they stretched clean sheets over their mattress.
"Do you know someone named Leslie Steele?"

Carter half grinned. "That's Mother's second-in-command."
He rubbed his head as if recalling an onslaught of memories.
"Leslie and I were in school together, but she was a few years
behind me—in Andrew's class. The daughter Mother always
wanted. I'm sure if you check the mail, we already have a
gold-embossed invitation from her, calling on us to attend
some function or other."

"Yep. I already opened it. It was addressed to *Mrs. Carter Callahan*," Catherine said in a singsong voice.

"I bet you just loved that."

Catherine shrugged. "At least people won't find anything when they Google *that* name."

Carter gave her a pitying expression he reserved only for her. She didn't like it. "Leslie took over coordinating most of the school's social scene from Mother a few years back." He put on the Southern drawl typical of the old-monied Callahan Prep parents. "I'm sure Leslie would absolutely love for you to help her with all the party planning."

Morgan brought Catherine back to the present. "Yes, Leslie Steele. She's the one hanging on Rosalyn's every word, doing her bidding without a second thought. She planned this event tonight, though Rosalyn will probably still get most of the credit, at least until she officially passes the mantle. Which, let's be honest, may not be until she's six feet under." Morgan gathered her purse and smoothed her own feathers—jewel clad—before turning to run her fingers across Catherine's flimsy headdress. She leaned in a bit too closely and lilted her finale, the evergreen scent of gin hanging in the air between them. "I like you. You seem almost normal, not the typical Callahan Mummy Dearest. Though it could cost you if you don't figure out fast how things work around here." Morgan narrowed her eyes. "Seems like you might be a quick study, though. I'll see you around?"

The words carried weight. Catherine felt certain there was a streak of rebellion in this woman despite her ability to adorn herself and laugh and play along with Leslie, Rosalyn and the other women in The Grand Hall.

"Yeah, I'll see you around," Catherine echoed.

"R-r-r-awk…*see you*," the cockatoo screeched as it eyed both women one last time.

★ ★ ★

When Catherine returned to Carter, standing with his buddies from the Class of '94, he made excuses and extricated himself. "You decided to get something from the bar after all?" He kissed the tip of her nose.

Catherine closed one eye and showed him the tiny amount with her fingers. "Only a smidge."

"Enough to make out over by the falcons?"

"No way, not with your mother here." For a moment, her voice was lighter than it had been all night, the alcohol loosening her inhibitions, transforming her into the wife, the woman she used to be. Before she'd made such a stupid, stupid mistake a year ago. At the remembrance, Catherine grabbed Carter's arm to steady herself.

"You okay?" He leaned down so they were eye to eye.

She was not okay, feeling suddenly light-headed and, at the same time, like she wanted to shove an entire brownie down her throat. Instead, she took a glass of champagne from a passing server and shook away the feeling.

"Falcons, you said?"

"Supposedly, there's a birds-of-prey demonstration at the end of the night. They'll swoop across the room and fill us with awe."

Catherine tilted her head. "Wait, aren't falcons a type of vulture? Or is it the other way around?"

"I don't know, but I think we're feeding the poor to them at the after-party."

Catherine giggled, her emotions swaying back and forth like palm fronds as she sipped her champagne.

Carter suddenly turned sheepish and changed the subject by making a confession. "I bid on courtside tickets."

Catherine wagged a finger at him. "Now, Mr. Callahan. We agreed to only bid on items we would both enjoy."

"You'll enjoy having the house to yourself. It's four seats, enough for me to take the girls if I win."

Catherine applauded him, despite the fact that she abhorred the idea of an evening to herself. Hours alone to practice, play and write—to be alone with her thoughts and musings—were no longer welcome. "Well done, sir. Well done. But do you think that a seventeen-year-old science nerd and an inquisitive eight-year-old will actually accompany you to a professional basketball game?"

"I don't know." He waved a hand. "At least Lucy will have fun, and I can let the other two bring a book if they want."

Catherine studied her husband. "They'll probably be happy just to hang out with their dad." Sometimes Catherine wondered if Emily even felt close to her father anymore. The twins were young enough for Carter to redeem the years, but there wasn't time for him to start over with Emily. Throughout her childhood, he'd clocked sixty-plus hours a week travelling across the country for a corporate law firm.

"I know. It's good to be back," he said, nuzzling Catherine's ear. "Hey, lady, want to get out of here?"

She glanced around and spotted Rosalyn by the auction tables, leaning into a well-dressed couple, her hand on the man's arm. By her side stood a petite woman with shoulder-length, highlighted hair and eyes framed by long eyelashes. She wore a gold dress, complete with embroidered feathers and sequined trees running up the side. Her mannerisms mirrored Rosalyn's. That must be *the* much-talked-about Leslie Steele. The puppet and her puppeteer. "What about your mother? And mingling? And the tickets?"

He shrugged. "Mother is surrounded by happy, drunken parents who adore her every move. She sneezes, and they think God has spoken." Catherine took a moment to allow the sharp comment to wash over her like a balm. "Besides,

I'm tired of talking to people I don't care to impress, and the school will charge our credit card if I win. How long did you tell Emily we'd be gone?"

"Two or three more hours, but she said she was going to order in pizza for her and the girls, then watch a movie before they all go to bed, so I don't think she'll care if we're out a bit longer."

"Good," Carter said. "Let's do one of your infamous Irish goodbyes and check into the San Luis till someone calls looking for us."

She ran her palm along his stubbled cheek and stared into his eyes. "What has gotten into you?"

He guided her toward the door. "When you took off those Spanx, I knew I had to have you."

She laughed.

As they slipped out of the building, she spotted Morgan, who appeared to have been watching her. The woman offered a subtle wave, almost imperceptible.

As their eyes met, Catherine suddenly remembered where she'd heard the name of Morgan's son.

Alex Frasier.

Her throat constricted as she followed Carter into the smothering night air.

2

September
Morgan

Moments after watching Catherine Callahan exit like a thief in the night, Morgan Frasier found her date standing near the bar, chatting with two other women who must have been embryonic when he graduated high school. But she had to admit: Robert Steele still had it—that wavy hair, the angle of his jaw, his piercing eyes with specks of gold the color of sandstone. Morgan couldn't blame the women. She'd had a crush on him too, even years ago when she was just a freshman and he a towering senior. Now, she was single again, and he was the top neurologist on the island, a fine catch.

"Excuse me, ladies. May I borrow him for a dance?" Morgan asked.

She could feel the women's laser-like stares cutting into her, but what did they expect with their husbands waiting in the wings? She had a far better chance with Robert, what with her much-discussed divorce a couple years in the past.

"Thanks for rescuing me," Robert said loudly into her ear as she pulled him onto the pulsing dance floor. She was relieved to note that even in her heels—the ones that pushed her to right at six feet—he had a few inches on her.

She smirked. "It didn't look like you needed rescuing there, champ."

He tilted his head back and laughed. "How did I miss that spunk of yours all those years ago?"

"I didn't have all of my *assets* in place quite yet."

A few weeks ago, Morgan happened to run into Robert Steele at a place where she volunteered regularly. She hadn't been in the same room with him in years. Afterward she found herself returning to the days of her schoolgirl infatuation, looking for him around town, imagining things she'd say when they bumped into one another again. She'd followed his career from the periphery of her own marriage and child-rearing, so she knew he was a doctor, had been for over fifteen years. Maybe if she were to contract some terrible disease, she could go to him and he would cure her and they would fall in love and live happily ever after.

Robert's voice broke through her medical savior fantasy. "Shall we make an early departure?"

"What did you have in mind?" she said. She wanted to play coy, but more practically, she had no idea whether or not Alex was out with friends tonight, so she couldn't very well invite Robert back to her house. Dating with a teenage son still at home was so awkward to navigate.

Robert inched closer, his mouth so kissable. "Maybe we could go back to your place?" he said. "Open a bottle of wine? See where the evening takes us?"

"Mr. Steele, I hardly know you," Morgan teased, tilting her head.

He grinned in that boyish, guileless way he had. "What

are you talking about? We've known each other practically our entire lives."

"But only just reconnected. Give a girl a bit of time." Her fingers grazed his shoulder, his neck, his jaw. "I guarantee it will be worth the wait."

Before Robert could further tempt Morgan, she exited the dance floor, feeling his gaze on her still-perky backside.

Morgan drove herself home slowly. She knew she would never pass a breathalyzer if she was pulled over. It would probably be some officer she knew anyway—maybe even the chief of police himself. *Good evening, Whitey,* she would say. *Oh, just a few glasses. Hey, remember that time I watched you down that keg when we were sixteen?*

Galveston was a big, small town.

She made it home and stumbled into the loft apartment, standing for a moment in the eerie silence. "Alex?" She called for her son, but no one answered. She glanced around the kitchen and saw a hand-scribbled note on the granite countertop. *Out. Be back later.* God, she hoped he wasn't with Emily. Any girl—but especially Rosalyn Callahan's granddaughter—was the last thing Alex needed just a few months before graduating.

"Thanks for the details," she muttered before pouring herself a final glass of wine and shimmying out of her dress in the middle of the kitchen. She shook away the thought, turned on the TV for company and let her mind drift back to Robert.

It would have been satisfying to bring him home tonight. She took a sip. My, how her high school self would have berated her for walking away from those eyes and those practiced doctor-hands that knew their way around the human body. A chill ran through her, anticipating the pleasure. She wouldn't be able to hold herself at bay for long.

She picked up her phone with her empty hand and scrolled through Facebook, looking at pictures Callahan Prep parents were starting to post. Her good old friend Leslie Steele was in almost every picture. Look, there she was with the mayor. And now a district judge. Oh, and there she was on the arm of Robert. Morgan squinted at the picture, at the way Leslie's arms draped possessively over his. *Stop it*, she told herself. *He wanted to go home with you, but you said no. Besides, Robert and Leslie are brother- and sister-in-law—surely that must be some form of incest.*

She threw down her phone, sprawled her legs across the sofa and kneaded the cashmere throw with her toes. It was too warm for the blanket, but how good it felt to sink her feet, sore from dancing in heels, into its gossamer threads. Morgan sighed. On late nights like these when the town was still buzzing outside her walls, she missed being married, the companionship of just the two of them, she and her ex, Lionel, curled up on the couch, defying the exclusive world.

Lionel would've brought her home from the school gala hours ago. He would be reading Dickens while she worked on her laptop, designing websites for local businesses. Just a side thing, but he'd encouraged her to have something of her own. She'd assumed that meant he wanted her to feel useful, since their son was getting older. She hadn't even considered that *something of her own* might mean an entire bed, an entire apartment, an entire life.

Before it all fell apart, she and Lionel had each other, their home and their son. That had been enough for her. She sank into the couch as she thought about their quiet evenings and lazy Sunday mornings together as a family. At least Lionel had left the apartment and generous child support when he said goodbye.

Morgan cursed her ex again for falling in love during a business trip on the other side of the world with a Greek woman who, besides being unremarkably plain, was five years older than Morgan.

"Do you know what it's like to have your husband leave you for a homely woman?" she'd whined to Lionel when he'd first confessed to the affair. Sure, it had been a petty, mean thing to say, but it was a pettier, meaner thing to leave your wife, especially after she'd just been through hell.

Whenever Morgan thought about that time in their lives, her arms prickled with tiny goose bumps and her peach complexion flushed as pink as bubble gum.

She'd been on her way home from the morgue, having just identified her mother's drug-riddled body, when Whitey— Chief Whiteside, to some—called on her cell phone.

"I know this may not be the best time," Whitey began.

"You think?" She'd wanted to scream at someone all day, and this seemed almost perfect.

"But I was calling because we're gonna need to talk to Alex about that party over at Leslie and Michael Steele's house a few nights ago."

"Why? Is something wrong?"

Whitey inhaled. "Well...we've got a girl saying that Alex... that he assaulted her...that he...well, to be honest, she's saying he raped her."

Morgan had almost dropped the phone. Later, in her most desperate moments, she wished she had run the car off the road.

Lionel took their son Alex to the station, and when they returned, Lionel seemed stunned.

Alex said nothing, just went straight to his room.

"I think he may have done it," Lionel whispered to her that night in bed. "We have to believe this girl. You know how stupid teenage boys can be."

Yes, she knew how stupid Alex could be, forgetting his homework and leaving his uniform at home, but stupid wasn't the same thing as assault, as rape.

Morgan drank her wine now. She hated it when her thoughts went to those dark memories. Despite herself, the same old doubts from years ago came boiling to the surface tonight, Morgan's mind playing both plaintiff and defendant in her son's case as she re-pieced evidence. Sure, the charges had been dismissed before it even went to trial, but what if Alex had done what the Wagner girl accused him of? *And what if Alex tries something with Emily?*

Morgan bit her lip. Emily Callahan could quickly become a problem. Morgan took another long gulp of Cabernet. She drank only once a month or so, but when she did, she preferred to drink enough to put her to sleep. She was almost there.

3
September
Leslie

"The birds of paradise are inspired," Rosalyn had compli-
mented Leslie upon entering The Grand Hall earlier that evening.

They should be. Leslie had kept dozens of the fickle flow-
ering plants at her home, waiting to see which ones would
bloom at the exact right time, so she could drive them over
just before the auction. "They take four hours to open, and
they last for about a day," the Argentinian horticulturist in
Houston had told her a few days ago, his head tilted in wonder at why anyone would choose to decorate an entire hall
with such an exacting plant.

Of course, Rosalyn knew none of this, or if she did know,
she didn't acknowledge the effort. Instead, the two of them
stood together, Rosalyn contented after a successful function
while something akin to a hammer beat in rhythm behind
Leslie's eyes.

Rosalyn kissed both of Leslie's cheeks as she said good-night on the steps outside. "Absolutely lovely, dear. You really outdid yourself." Rosalyn paused and Leslie braced for the criticism. "Although, we could've done without that dreadful cockatoo in the ladies' room. It about scared me to death."

"You're completely right, of course," Leslie said.

"Things to remember for next time, dear. Regardless, I know we raised more than enough for the new concert hall. Oh, and remember, we'll need to meet Monday evening to discuss that awful left-wing teacher. I cannot believe *that* slipped past HR when hiring. Can't they see everyone's political views online nowadays? Really." Wrinkles creased around Rosalyn's eyes as she sighed, speaking a few final words softly, one hand on Leslie's cheek. "The daughter I never had."

"Glad I could be of service," Leslie said, squeezing Rosalyn's hand.

She meant every word. Still, as soon as the older woman glided into her town car to be driven away, Leslie emptied her stomach of the contents of that night's hors d'oeuvres, now a puddle of yellow muck, into the oleander bushes. She always vomited when her nerves were frayed. Her brother-in-law, Robert, stepped outside, two towering plants in his arms. As soon as he saw her, he dropped the orange-beaked flowers at the curb, rushed to her side and held back her hair. She looked up at him. "I am so sorry, Robert. This is disgusting. Thanks for coming tonight and helping me with the decorations. Michael always did that, before."

Robert shrugged. "Don't mention it. Besides, I've seen you in worse shape."

It was true. Though the two of them hadn't been close while her husband, Michael, was alive, the trauma of losing him—Robert's only brother—to cancer had bonded them. Three years, eight months, twelve days. That's how long Michael had been dead. An eternity. "Have you been feeling sick?" Robert asked. "You need another prescription?"

"No. I think something disagreed with me."

It was a white lie, one she told so he wouldn't worry, but she knew Robert didn't buy her excuse. They both knew this was one of the many manifestations of the anxiety that had been intensifying over the past days, weeks, years. Ever since Michael's death.

"I can't believe we lugged these flowers all the way down here," Robert said, kind enough to change the subject.

"I can't believe that you stuck around long enough to help me load them back up. I thought you were on call this weekend?"

"I didn't drink, and by now I can get by on a few hours sleep here and there," he said. "Besides, I wanted to make sure you weren't abandoned at the end of the night. With your boys gone, I knew you might need some muscle."

Leslie smiled and placed a protective hand on his arm. He was so thoughtful, she much preferred to think about him rather than herself. Isn't that how she survived from day to day? *Who needs a care package? Who needs a pep rally? Who needs an auction?* The needs of her family and her community—Callahan Prep, specifically—fueled her sanity, giving her day-to-day life a purpose.

"I saw all those ladies hankering for your attention," she said. "One in particular—Morgan Frasier? We used to be friends. She graduated the same year as me and Michael."

Leslie's tone was casual, but she'd witnessed Robert and Morgan dancing closely, their reedlike bodies melded together in a way that was highly inappropriate for anyone in their forties. Leslie wanted definitive confirmation that Robert was not interested in Morgan—the woman who had tried to steal Michael from her. Twice. Leslie still hated that her last real fight with her sick husband had been about that woman.

Leslie thought back to the night she had broached the subject with Michael as they were standing in front of their bathroom mirrors, each brushing their teeth. "Why didn't you tell me you were having lunch with Morgan?"

"What?" Michael took the toothbrush out of his mouth. "Who told you that?"

"Seriously? That's your question? Who told me?" Leslie rolled her eyes at her husband and felt her pulse increase as she rubbed cream into the wrinkles just starting around her eyes. "You ate at Yagas, Michael, the one place that we always see someone we know. Angela told me, but even if she hadn't, people talk, and I know *all* the people."

It had been enough of an explanation for her husband, who simply sighed as he pulled off his undershirt and stripped down to his boxers. She'd never gotten used to his post-cancer body, shrunken even after his appetite had returned. "We were just two old friends who bumped into each other and were trying to catch up."

A likely story. Not if Morgan Frasier was involved. Leslie wouldn't trust that woman with a favorite pet, much less her husband. "I was actually planning to tell you, so you could join us next time."

"Next time?" She took off the headband she'd been wearing during her meticulous beauty routine.

Michael looked away and moved toward the bedroom. "I mean, we were hoping to make it a regular, once-a-month lunch."

Leslie laughed. She couldn't help herself. "We? Really?" Her voice rose a pitch. "Michael, think for a minute. Isn't it a little suspicious that rumors of her and Lionel having problems are swirling right around the same time she wants to supposedly reconnect with you?"

"Morgan's not like that."

Leslie wasn't laughing as she threw pillows onto the bench at the foot of their bed. "Do not tell me what she's like. Don't forget that she was my best friend until she kissed you right after we got engaged. I know exactly what she's thinking."

Michael crawled under the covers and patted her side of the bed, inviting her to join him. "We've been over this a thousand times, honey. That kiss was years ago. Besides, she was drunk. It didn't mean anything."

Leslie shook her head and pulled the comforter off him. She would sleep in the guest bedroom if she must. Or make him. "Maybe it didn't mean anything to you, but Rosalyn said…"

Michael interrupted her. "Can we have one conversation without you bringing up that god-awful Callahan woman's advice?"

Leslie was sure the shock registered on her face because he backed off, holding up both hands in a gesture of peace. "All I'm saying is that I think the two of you would've remained friends if Rosalyn Callahan hadn't told you to drop Morgan."

"She didn't—"

"Fine. Then we don't need to have this argument again." He moved toward her, reaching out his hand. His touch was gentle, calming, even though she wanted to stay angry. "Look, if it really bothers you, I'll cancel with Morgan. I'll never see her again if that's what you want, but I think it would be good if we all went out together. Maybe we could make it a dinner, so her husband, Lionel, could come too?"

But there was no next time because the following week, they—she and Michael—learned that his cancer had returned. With a vengeance. Somehow, Morgan was now tangled up in

Leslie's mind with those terrible last months and the last time she'd really been upset with her husband.

Her brother-in-law looked at Leslie now and exhaled as he stretched his arms over his head. "There's not a particular woman I'm interested in. You know I'm so in demand that they all start to blend together."

"Cockiness doesn't suit you." Leslie swatted at Robert playfully, but she took the hint: He wasn't interested in discussing his love life then and there. But she would find out one way or another. She always did.

He changed the subject. "Seriously, though, you going to be okay getting home?"

"I didn't drink much tonight either, had to make sure everyone else was happy, so yes, I'm good."

"The perils of the party planner." His head tilted. "What was Anna up to tonight?"

"She said she was going down to the Strand to grab something to eat with friends, but she texted me an hour or so ago and said she's already back home."

Leslie didn't say what she was thinking, how strange it was for Anna to be home on a Saturday night, how something with her seemed off these past few weeks. Ever since Emily Callahan had stepped through the high, hallowed archways of Callahan Prep this past August and threatened everything Anna had worked her whole life to achieve.

"I'm glad she's home safe. I worry about the two of you in that big house on your own now that the boys aren't there, especially with the Gulf looming only yards away. Anyone could dock their boat a few yards from your porch."

Leslie tilted her head, appreciating his concern. "Everything on this island is only a few yards from a boat."

"I know, I know." Robert waved away the reality of the

strip of land they teetered on. "Remember, I'm only a five-minute call away."

"Unless you're at the hospital saving lives—or at a woman's house till all hours."

"Yeah, yeah." He looked around. "Do you need me to follow you home and unload these plants?"

Leslie noticed the circles under his eyes. Robert needed sleep more than she needed his help. "They aren't that heavy, and I'm stronger than I look."

Michael had always said she was a strong, self-possessed woman; she supposed she'd proven him right by graduating their twin boys from Callahan Prep and raising their only daughter, who was set to graduate in the spring.

"Hey, one more thing, Robert. I think Asher is going to call you tomorrow about setting up shadowing, maybe an internship. He wasn't crazy about his MCAT scores, so he's taking it again. I think he's anxious to learn as much as he can, to feel like he's got a head start before med school, especially since he's graduating college a year early." Thinking about Asher, Leslie smiled.

"I'll be happy to have him, but he needs to slow down a bit, enjoy his youth."

"I know, but try telling him that."

She gave Robert a quick hug, and hustled into the car, knowing he wouldn't leave until he saw her drive away. Yes, her brother-in-law had taken his promise to care for his brother's family seriously.

She would never forget how he found her in a heap on her bathroom floor two weeks after Michael's death, sobs heaving her chest, her body clad only in Michael's robe, her hand holding his razor. She'd put on the old robe because the terry cloth smelled of his aftershave and she'd held the razor be-cause…well, all she'd wanted in the days following his death was to envelop herself in him, and if Michael wasn't coming back, she longed to go to him.

Robert had helped her sit up, then hid away all sharp objects. He'd been so good to her and the kids, moving himself into the guest room for the next few weeks until they all regained some semblance of a new normal.

Here was Leslie, all these years later, pulling into her driveway as swaying palm trees framed her car. Her daughter, Anna, had left the porch light on, and Leslie exhaled, relieved to see that she was indeed home—even if it meant her daughter might not have the exact social life she wanted. Her momentary relief was overwhelmed, however, as Leslie's mind veered back to the image of Robert and Morgan Frasier together, the woman's smooth hips and long legs so close to her brother-in-law's strong, muscular frame. Always the fly in the ointment. Leslie felt sick to her stomach again.

EMILY

I feel exhausted from the hurry and flurry of the past few hours, from all of the hands examining me, from the pricks of the needles that give me fluids and take my blood. Though it may not seem like it, I've been awake.

Okay, not awake-awake like people usually think of the term. Maybe a better word would be *present*. Yeah, present. My eyes are closed, my body still, but my mind is mostly in the here and now even as my body lies dormant.

In ninth grade bio Mrs. Flint taught us the difference between predictive and consequential dormancy, explaining how predictive dormancy happens in anticipation of adverse conditions, while consequential is as a result of such conditions. The organism slows down, almost completely halting development to conserve energy. I guess that's what's happening to me, since I lay here unmoving but somehow aware. I have no memory of the adverse condition that brought me here, but coming to this strange little town was certainly the start.

We arrived on Galveston Island one day before school started, so the first person I really met was Alex Frasier. I can still remember the way I felt that morning, walking under the stone arches of Callahan Prep, a school named after a great-great grandfather I never knew. The teachers fawned over me in each of my morning classes, which inevitably reminded me that my grandmother actually held their careers in her hands. They didn't know that all Grandma really talks to me about—on the rare occasion she talks to me—is how she can't wait to pass on her legacy to me and my sisters. It's like she can't wait to die.

That first day the other students mostly stared blankly at me and then turned to talk to the friends they'd known their entire lives. Occasionally, there would be a finger pointed and someone whispering my name. The *new girl* comments weren't so bad, but after my third class I overheard a couple of girls talking about me while I was in a bathroom stall. I'd gotten my period the day before and my cramps were the worst. I was on the toilet, hunched over, pushing into my abdomen as another wave of pain rolled over me when the two girls started in.

"She's not even that pretty. You have nothing to worry about."

"I know. It's not even that. She just came in here like she owns the place. Did you see the way she's been talking to the teachers all morning? Like she's their best friend."

"Or their boss."

"Right? It's gross."

I could see their feet under the stall as the girls turned to face each other. "Anna, seriously. This school is yours. Do not even think about her. Anyway, you know exactly how to take care of a girl like that."

They left, and I cried in the stall, wishing myself away from this terrible school on this horrid island. I stayed like that for maybe ten minutes as I waited for the ibuprofen to kick in.

Then, I did what I always do: I forced myself back together and out into the hall laced with strangers. I was late to Brit Lit, and it didn't help that the teacher didn't even count me tardy, just smiled and invited me to take a seat in the front row. By lunch all I wanted to do was crawl into one of the inviting library nooks and read something brooding, something that echoed my misery at being exiled to this place through no fault of my own.

I was winding my way to the library with my nose already stuck in C.S. Lewis's *A Grief Observed* when I heard a baritone voice call my name.

"Emily?" I looked up and spun around to see a guy my age with broad shoulders and stocky legs.

"Alex," he said, introducing himself.

I stared, mute. No one my age had talked to me all day. Actually, no one my age had talked to me since we'd arrived this summer.

I stuck out my hand awkwardly. "Emily Callahan."

"I know." He chuckled and I frowned. I guess everyone knew who I was. "You going to lunch?"

I shrugged and held up my book. Anyone in their right mind wouldn't want to step into that massive space reminiscent of the Great Hall at Hogwarts without someone by their side.

"*A Grief Observed*, huh? Sounds like some light reading," he said.

I think I smiled.

"I've got in-school detention today," he added, "but they

let me out to grab lunch and come back. You want to walk with me?"

Despite my questions about why he had detention ("I had a little too much *help* with my last paper," he told me later), I joined him, grabbing a sandwich while I watched him load his tray with pretty much every item the cafeteria offered: pork loin, tomato tarts and steamed broccoli from the hot food line, a panini and chips from the sandwich station, greens piled with eggs and bacon from the salad bar and bread pudding from the desserts.

"Gotta keep up my strength," he said with a grin as we swiped our IDs.

As we walked back, he nodded and threw out *heys* to everyone we passed. He was obviously well-known and well-liked, and for some reason, he liked me. Seeing a friendly face like that on my first day only made it about one percent more comforting that my parents had dragged my family to this Southern town exactly 2,268 miles from my real friends, my real school, my real life. But I guess one percent is one percent.

4

October
Catherine

Catherine really hated coming with Carter and the kids to her mother-in-law's house, but this massive dark brick monster of a place had become the weekly gathering spot for the Callahan family. It was their *Saturday summoning*, she liked to tease her husband. The oak paneling and the pine floors did little to alleviate the sensation of folding inward, and sometimes as she stood with her five-foot-two frame at this high door with its gaudy wood carvings, she imagined the house imploding, gulping her and her family down in one final swallow.

"It's good of the two of you to finally join us," Rosalyn said in a piercing voice. She was speaking from behind a maid who opened the door and stepped back to blend into the furnishings. Rosalyn ignored the maid's presence entirely. "You left early from the gala."

"Oh, didn't we say goodbye?" Carter stepped across the threshold, planted a kiss on his mother's cheek and then looked past her, squinting as if trying to remember the evening. Catherine was certain he recalled every second of their time at the San Luis. The crisp sheets, the frantic entwining, the rush of endorphins. She almost blushed.

Rosalyn didn't seem to notice as she handed her son an envelope. "You won the tickets—and the house in Maui for a week."

"But we didn't bid on…"

"Consider it your half-birthday gift," she spouted, already moving on to the children. Catherine had the sudden urge to hide the twins behind her, but stopped, reminding herself that it was just that one time. Just that one time years ago when Rosalyn took one of her children without asking and disappeared. Rosalyn rolled her eyes at Olivia as she squatted to study a tree roach that lay dead in the corner. In Catherine's short time on the island, she'd found that even the priciest establishments couldn't keep the creepy-crawlies out of Gulfcoast living. Next, Rosalyn turned to Lucy, who was playing a game on her phone, an item Carter had insisted on purchasing for each of the girls when they first arrived, claiming that their daughters might need them here.

"Give me one good reason our eight-year-olds need a phone," Catherine had demanded.

"I don't know. Olivia might need to figure out quantum mechanics, and Lucy might need to search 'How to bury the body of a playground bully.'" He knew their girls well. Olivia absorbed knowledge like a sponge, asking question after question, and dear Lucy, she was determined that no injustice be executed on her watch. No teasing, no cheating, no lying. In Lucy's world, everything wrong would be made right.

Rosalyn summoned a maid to collect the tree roach and held out her hand for Lucy's phone. "Hand over that dreadful contraption, darling." She took the device and placed it in a decorative bowl that probably cost as much as Catherine's first-year salary as a professor. Despite having her phone confiscated, Lucy squeezed Rosalyn's midsection tightly in a hug while Olivia looked up from her squatting position.

"I brought my bugs, Grandma."

To Rosalyn's credit, she didn't recoil.

"Don't worry," Lucy clarified for her sister. "They're plastic this time."

"What a relief, dear." Rosalyn stretched out a hand to pull Olivia to her feet while Catherine reached out to grab at her girls' shoulders. She couldn't help herself. "Run along to the kitchen, and tell Marie you're both ready for your chocolate chip pancakes. I'm sure she'd be delighted to hear all about your…insects," Rosalyn said.

The girls darted away while she turned her gaze back to Catherine. "And where is my eldest granddaughter?"

"She wasn't feeling well today. Headache," Catherine said and wished she could claim such an excuse.

"Oh, how horrid." Rosalyn glanced at Carter. "Shall I send Dr. Montague over?"

Catherine spoke for him. "No, Rosalyn. It's just a headache."

The older woman's eyebrows rose and her lips pursed. "Well, then. I'll have Marie make a care package for her. But do let me know if you change your mind."

"Thanks, Mom. She'd like that." Carter's tone of voice sometimes changed around his mother, shifting a degree or so toward his childhood self. It made Catherine cringe, and in moments like these, when they were forced together once a week to act like a big happy tribe, Catherine was reminded that it was her own fault that she and Carter and their girls now lived here. She supposed coming to the family home each week was her penance.

Andrew, her brother-in-law, and, Sarah, her sister-in-law, had arrived earlier, and as they started mixing drinks, Catherine thought of the moment last semester when she'd been caught plagiarizing one of her previous students' work.

"What have you done?" Ali, her longtime writing partner, said as she entered Catherine's office at Woodhaven University, sinking into the chair across from Catherine's desk.

Catherine, seated at the upright piano in her office, had been playing through a particularly difficult stretch of the score they'd been working on together for the past year. She attempted levity, not knowing yet that her friend and colleague already knew. "Hello to you too."

Ali leaned in, cheeks pink with frustration, eyes full of unanswered questions. "What the hell were you thinking, lifting a section of the score? Do you realize that this implicates me, calls into question all of the work we've done together over the past fourteen years?"

With those words, Catherine's carefully constructed career tumbled into a pile of rubbish. She stared at the ground, not knowing what to do or say. She wouldn't waste time denying the truth, but she would attempt to explain her reasoning. Closing the door behind them, Catherine lowered her voice.

"Who else knows?"

Ali rolled her eyes and shook her head. "Who do you think? The dean of fine arts, the president of the university, the student whose work you stole. Fucking everyone knows, Catherine. Why? Why would you do this?"

Catherine rubbed her forehead as she fell into the chair next to Ali. "I don't know. It wasn't exactly intentional. I wasn't thinking. Remember when we had that deadline from Tamburelli Productions? It was right after Carter's father died and then my father…passed away a month later. I was distracted. It was all too much."

Ali's face registered no compassion.

"I just couldn't think, couldn't write anything new. I would sit at the piano, and all that came out were the familiar pieces, so I played them again and again. Verdi, Mozart, Stravinsky, all of their work was so masterful, and I felt like an imposter. I contacted Tamburelli, but the company said they couldn't extend the deadline, that they already had our opera on their production schedule." Catherine was on the verge of tears. "Then, I remembered that one of my doctoral candidates had written that instrumentation for a recitativo a few years ago. You remember when I showed it to you? We both knew that she had that *thing* that can't be taught."

Ali nodded, but her eyes remained hard, two metallic-gray orbs.

"That student wasn't doing anything with her musical compositions—from what I could find on the internet, she went on to be a part-time church music director somewhere in a small town in Indiana. The piece was just sitting there in my files. I planned to use it as a springboard, just to get started, but then the thematic material fit so well, I thought I could just adapt it..." Catherine puffed out a breath. "I know I don't have an excuse, but that student's material is less than a tenth of the entire opera. I told myself it wouldn't matter in the scheme of things. I thought I would contact her before opening night, maybe reference her in the acknowledgments?"

"Great plan. Really, ingenious." Ali almost laughed. "Except you forgot one thing—it's plagiarism if you don't get permission or give credit from the start. You have to know that after teaching all these years." Ali stood. She couldn't keep still with the anger spilling out of her. "It's the principle of the thing. No school will ever employ a professor who's lifted work, and no production company will trust you to compose again. Ever. And, I've not only lost my collaborator. I've lost my friend, all because you 'got stuck.'" Ali wiped at her eyes. "I know you've been grieving. I've been asking how I can help, if I can bring over meals, if I can take the girls, if you need anything."

Catherine knew all this, but she hadn't known how to let Ali bear some of her burden, take on her responsibilities. People's parents died all the time, and they went back to work, kept living.

"How did everyone find out?"

Ali ran a hand through her hair. "It was a fluke. When you sent the first batch of the score to the printing company, apparently one of their guys was looking through the files before finalizing them. He's a violinist on the side, and he'd been hired to play in the ensemble at your student's recital a few years ago. He went home and scrounged around in his old scores and found that the section in your piece matched that one almost perfectly. He alerted the composer—your student—and everything snowballed from there."

Ali moved toward Catherine, compassion starting to crowd out the anger. "Why didn't you come to me? Why didn't you let me help you? We could've figured this out. I would've sat at the damn keyboard myself and plucked out a subpar melody. Who cares if this isn't our masterpiece?"

Catherine's eyes widened. *Who cares?* Didn't every writer, musician and artist care whether or not their current work was *the* masterpiece?

"I didn't want to let you down."

"Yeah, that worked out well, didn't it?" Ali stared at Catherine for a few seconds more and then exited, closing the door behind her.

The next few days were spent in hushed, closed-door meetings, in apologies, in her termination, in packing up her things, in making plans to escape her shame and humiliation, shame and humiliation that she knew would extend to her children in a college town as small as Woodhaven. By the end of the week, Catherine and Carter had decided that they would go back to Galveston, Carter's home. He'd always said he'd like to live there again someday, and with his father's death, it was good timing to help with the family business holdings—his family could always use a good lawyer and he was tired of working for someone else. Catherine's mom had been dead for years, and with her father's recent death and no siblings, she had no other directional pull. Carter's family it would be.

Rosalyn interrupted Catherine's thoughts. "Are you all right, dear? You've gone white as a sheet." Rosalyn didn't wait for a response. "Carter, stay here and speak to your brother. He has some new cockamamie business idea. Something about selling skateboards to the indigent, so they no longer need buses. Please reason with him."

Andrew started to protest as Rosalyn turned to Catherine. "Dear, I simply must speak with you."

"But, Mother…" Carter started, glancing at his wife. He knew that he was never, under any circumstances, to leave Catherine or any of their girls alone with his mother.

The last time Catherine had been cornered in this very home was years ago just before their engagement party, when Rosalyn had scooted her into an adjoining room where the family doctor waited to take a blood sample to make sure everything was in "tip-top shape." The slightest issue—anemia, Vitamin D deficiency, thyroid levels—could lead to the most horrible outcomes, Rosalyn had told her at the time.

Catherine had darted out of the house as fast as she could with a shocked Rosalyn staring after her, wondering why a woman wouldn't want to be in the best physical and mental condition possible during her childbearing years?

Afterward, Carter had tried to explain the complexity that

was his mother, droning on about how his mom had always been concerned about health, almost obsessively. She even had a personal doctor—Dr. Montague —on speed dial. Carter tried to convince Catherine that in Rosalyn's mind, the lab work was intended as a gift.

Catherine hadn't believed it then and wouldn't believe a thing that woman said now.

This time, Rosalyn shooed away her shamefaced son while Catherine's gaze remained glued to his receding back. The older woman guided her into the senior Callahan's office, the one Carter's father had used as an escape from his wife before she killed him a year ago. Okay, so maybe she hadn't literally killed him, but Catherine could list ten reasons why living with Rosalyn would be bad for anyone's health.

The two women sat down across from one another, and Rosalyn leaned forward and touched her daughter-in-law's hand in an awkward gesture of affection. Catherine startled. They were not the kind of in-laws who touched.

"Now, Catherine." As Rosalyn spoke, the faint lines around her lips grew more pronounced, and Catherine caught the whiff of narcissus and coffee, not a good mix. "You know that we have a reputation to maintain at Callahan Prep."

Dear Lord. Catherine wished she could flop back into the upholstered chair, close her eyes and sleep through the next half-hour lecture.

"I have personally ensured that only the highest caliber of student is admitted to our institution, and while I know that Emily has the potential to be the quintessential Callahan Prep scholar and student leader, I have not yet seen that come to fruition. She has not joined any student committees. She is not taking an interest in student government. She's not even participating in social events. Emily has a name to uphold. *We* must set an example for everyone else in our community."

For the flicker of a second, Catherine considered arguing with her mother-in-law, reminding her that this small academy was unimportant to everyone on the planet except a handful of Galveston socialites who lived and worked and played together in this tight-knit community, feeding off one another's anxieties and fueling one another's insecurities. She couldn't remember a single instance of a friend or acquaintance in Woodhaven, Oregon, ever referencing Galveston as "The Oleander City," much less remarking on an inbred little school called Callahan Prep. For 99.9 percent of the world, this academy and this town were not a thing.

"Yes, Rosalyn," Catherine said instead, her eyes glancing toward the door.

"I assume you've been keeping track of Emily's grades? I noticed she has an A- in BC Calculus, and I'm sure I don't need to remind you that I've helped countless of our graduates enter prestigious colleges. I'm certain that..."

Catherine cut her off. "She's in the second month of her senior year, and she's already received early acceptance to the climate change program at Columbia."

"You do realize a college admission can be rescinded?" Rosalyn cleared her throat and started again. "As you know, Emily could be a Harvard legacy, her grandfather and great-grandfather having attended, and though her accomplishments are very remarkable at her *previous* school..." Rosalyn loved commenting on the public schools that Catherine's children had attended their entire lives; they were the ones where all Woodhaven faculty kids went, but you would think she was referencing a penitentiary. Public schools were, after all, state-funded. "Well, dear, the rigor of Callahan Prep is not to be rivaled, and an A at another school might as well be a C here."

Catherine clenched her jaw and willed herself to remain composed. "Emily is fine."

Rosalyn wet her lips and waited a beat. "What with Emily's recent stressors—the move, the loss of both of her grandfathers, your...job change, I just want to make sure you are being attentive."

Attentive? Attentive? *I've been nothing but attentive*, Catherine wanted to scream. *I moved my family all the way to this godforsaken place, so they could have a fresh start without their friends—or total strangers—whispering about their mom everywhere they went.*

"I'm sure Emily is simply adjusting to the new curriculum," Catherine said. She hadn't checked her daughter's grades, she realized, and now that Rosalyn mentioned it, perhaps she had noticed a shift in Emily, the girl who used to enjoy study sessions with her friends and long talks with her mother. The kid who when she was twelve asked to sit in on French classes at the university because she could only take one language at a time in middle school and she already adored Spanish. The daughter who loved hanging out with her family on Friday nights. That kid. Catherine tried to think back to the last time Carter had popped a huge batch of popcorn and the five of them had huddled in the living room to watch *The Princess Bride* or *Back to the Future*. Huh. They'd had no such evening since the move over the summer, and Emily hadn't said a word about it.

Rosalyn continued. "I must be frank. I don't want to see such a remarkable young woman throw away all of her chances at success to focus on something so controversial."

"Hah!" Catherine couldn't keep from blurting, "Something controversial like climate change?"

"Well, yes, dear. Even the leading scientists don't know what to think, and besides, the Lord says that He will return before all that nonsense has time to take place."

Catherine raised her eyebrows at Rosalyn, who seemed

completely serious, as if she herself had studied the topic at length rather than overheard such jargon on Fox News.

"We both know Emily will not need to work, and if she plans to return here after graduation... I mean, really, she could do so much more if she were to focus on French literature or even the visual arts," Rosalyn said. "Wouldn't that be nice? To have an artist in the family?"

A giggle sprang to Catherine's throat as she realized the direction of her mother-in-law's thinking. *Yes, wouldn't it be nice to have an artist, a real artist, in the family? Not someone who churned out fancy tunes for a pittance like you did, Catherine, for your entire career.* She lifted a hand to keep in the crazed laughter. Catherine could overlook the slight on herself, but did Rosalyn even know her own granddaughter?

"Science or religion, that's what I want to study," Emily had told them last year after researching schools and areas of study. "This program allows me to take scientific data and apply it to do something good and necessary in the world, a combination of the two." Catherine didn't understand the affinity for either subject, but she certainly respected her daughter's choice. Rosalyn was oblivious.

Maybe it was the slight headache from the drinks Carter had taken for them from the minibar last night, or maybe it was another derogatory reference to the fine public schools where Catherine had sent her children. Maybe Catherine was just fed up and needed a do-over, to set a precedent for this new life lived in close proximity to Rosalyn Callahan. Regardless of the reason, Catherine stood up and spoke deliberately, her words for the first time in a long time tinged with heat.

"Rosalyn, I'm finished here. Emily is fine, better than fine, and she certainly doesn't need pressure to live up to some unrealistic expectation her grandmother puts on her. She's going to Columbia and she's studying climate change, which is not at all controversial to normal people. But, if she decides to take a year, study abroad, go to community college or become a lifelong barista, I will support her, and I invite you to stay the hell out of *her* business."

As she ended her unexpected speech, Catherine followed Rosalyn's gaze and realized that they had an audience. Andrew and Sarah, Carter and a maid all were at the door. Olivia stood apart, eyes wide and a finger twirling a curl on the left side of her face. A head peeked from behind Carter's waist. Lucy.

"Mommy said a bad word," Catherine heard Lucy whisper.

"We heard yelling," Olivia said bluntly.

Carter covered his daughters' mouths. "Go, sit, eat your pancakes—both of you." He came to his wife and reached out his hand in a dignified way to escort her from the room. "Can I get you some food?"

"I was only trying to help," Rosalyn said to the onlookers as Carter led his wife into the dining room where a full buffet waited.

"I am so sick of her *help*," Catherine sputtered as Carter handed her a plate loaded with lobster eggs benedict, bacon and a petit four. So the lady knew how to prepare a spread. Big deal.

"Here, eat this. You'll feel better."

"I'll feel better when she finally leaves us alone," Catherine said in a strained whisper. "Surely you don't agree with her assessment of Emily and her future?"

"I didn't hear the entire conversation, but I'm sure you know best, Cat."

It wasn't quite the glowing endorsement she would've liked, but it would have to do for the moment because the family was gathering around the table one by one. The girls came over and hugged her neck. "It's okay, Mommy," Olivia said, patting her arm as Lucy kissed her cheek. Her girls. How they loved her.

Rosalyn walked into the room and smiled as if nothing was amiss. As the matriarch sat, she extended her hands and raised her face as if to look God straight in the eye. "Let us bless the food," she said. Other heads bowed and Catherine gave Olivia a look to let her know that despite her own mother's behavior, Olivia had better put down her fork until Grandma finished. "Thank you, Lord, for this opportunity to gather together once again as a family, concerned for one another, seeking the best for one another, working together to make life in this world better for those around us. Bless this food, bless our home, bless this island. Amen."

Catherine took a swig of the mimosa that had appeared at her left hand.

"Why do you always say, 'Bless this island,' Grandma?" Lucy asked as a melted chocolate chip drizzled down her chin.

Rosalyn smiled one of her rare smiles reserved for her sons and grandchildren. "You know that my Grandfather Callahan, your great-great-grandfather, followed the call of God and moved to this island right after the 1900 storm to rebuild the city."

Olivia's eyes narrowed, questioning the claim. "God helped one person fix the entire city?"

Lovely. That's what her girls needed to believe: that the Callahan patriarch *and* God rebuilt an entire city, just the two of them.

"Not exactly, but he founded Callahan Prep Academy and rebuilt the Episcopal church where we attend service—well, some of us attend—every Sunday—" a look from Catherine to Carter "—and he ensured that the city had a bank and a credible newspaper."

A newspaper the family still owns, Catherine wanted to add but didn't.

Lucy looked around at the mahogany-paneled dining room. "That's a lot of stuff to do. Is that why you got the biggest house?"

Catherine choked on her mimosa. She too had been shocked the first time she'd stepped foot in the magnificent Callahan mansion, a behemoth structure that sat proudly on Broadway, the once-upon-a-time promenade that had rivaled the streets of Paris and New York before The Great Storm.

Carter's brother guffawed. "Nope. That's from having a shit-ton of money."

Rosalyn glared at Andrew even as his wife playfully slapped at him. Everyone knew she had only married him for said "shit-ton."

"We do have many financial resources, Lucy and Olivia. Always remember that *you* are Callahans and as such must help watch over Galveston and ensure that the city, the school, the people are the best that they can possibly be. You two, Emily and any children your uncle someday has will carry the Callahan legacy forward. We are the shepherds for these sheep."

Catherine looked around frantically for a drink refill and kept her mouth shut for the time being. Dr. Catherine Rubisi was not about to let Rosalyn brainwash her children into full-fledged Callahans. Over her dead body.

5

October

Morgan

Morgan had always known that in this town at this school, protocol was everything. If a Callahan Prep mother wanted to give a donation to the school, she gave it anonymously before promptly calling her best friend to hint at the amount: "We know the school needs to refurbish the chemistry lab, and it only costs ten grand, nothing compared to what those young minds will be able to learn." The sign for the So-and-So Family Chemistry Lab would then be placed outside the new wing by the start of the next school year. And when a Callahan Prep mother wanted to volunteer, things had to be done in a certain way. There were acceptable outlets for her efforts: plan an event for the Ronald McDonald House, organize a beach cleanup twice a year, take a shift at the annual book fair.

Morgan had decided to break the mold.

"Mom, can you bring snacks for club later this afternoon?"

Alex asked. "It's my week, and it's right after school, so I won't have time to grab anything."

"Since when did you join a club?"

Alex didn't make eye contact. "It's the Astronomy Club. I don't know, it sounded interesting."

Morgan stifled a chuckle. She imagined her tall son in Astronomy Club, towering over the kids applying to Ivy Leagues. "Could you be joining this club for the same reason that you've been out every night this week studying?"

Alex shrugged and tucked into his cereal bowl.

"I actually can't today," Morgan said nonchalantly. "I have an appointment."

He rinsed his bowl and put it in the sink. "What appointment?"

"You know, an appointment," Morgan said evasively. "How about I order a delivery from Whataburger instead?" This would appease him and all of his friends who couldn't go a week without a chicken mini.

"Yeah. Thanks." He grabbed his backpack and started out the door.

"Bye," Morgan called behind him. She watched his car exit their building's parking lot, then dashed out the door behind him.

A few minutes later, Morgan walked into the premises of the clandestine appointment she'd kept every week for the past few years at Let the Little Children Residential Center. Its name was innocuous enough for a place where children with parents who were addicts were cared for by kindly volunteers and nuns who didn't wear habits and chain-smoked in the parking lot. Returning here—to a place that looked too unkept and smelled too sterile and demanded too much dirtying of hands to be on the unofficial Callahan Prep volunteer list—had become habit for Morgan since the death of her mother and the end of her marriage. Let the Little Children gave Morgan a chance to rebalance the scales of her own mother's addiction.

Morgan nodded at Ellen, the receptionist who carried the marks of years of methamphetamine use in her broken smile.

"Good to see you again, Miss Morgan."

"You too. How are you today?" Morgan was always surprised by the compassion she herself had for addicts. Every addict except her mother. Too close to home, as they say.

"Better than I deserve," Ellen answered.

The sentiment was a familiar one, one that her mother would say when she was clean and attending Narcotics Anonymous.

Morgan still remembered coming home as a child from Callahan Prep, where she was on scholarship, to find her mother passed out for the fourth successive day, the bottle of the month nearby. At seven years old, Morgan was already tired of the routine, but she placed a glass of water next to her mother's bed and stared out the window until she woke. If she woke.

A few weeks, a few months later, her mother would be the one to wake her up in the morning, singing "You are My Sunshine." She would strip back the curtains and open the blinds as if life was good, and she would stash away the bottle until the next time she weakened in her resolve. It had been like that for as long as Morgan remembered—days when she had a mother who might be warm and affectionate, caring for her daughter's needs, and then days when her mother succumbed, her true self collapsing into the oblivion of a high that Morgan could never enter into. This is the thing Morgan would never say out loud, her guilty musing: sometimes when she looked at her son, she wondered if her mother's bad genes had skipped a generation and landed on him.

Morgan pushed aside the thought, put on her smock and sanitized her hands, wandering the long, well-lit hallway to the nursery that housed the youngest admissions. By now she knew the routine. She made small talk with one of the hurried nurses and then received her directives.

"If you'll feed Joy, then I'll check Johnny's blood sugar."

"Sure," Morgan said, looking down at the babies and glancing over their wristbands. Some infants came in with names; others were simply temporarily assigned. "No problem."

She began mixing formula with distilled water. The babies she cared for each Monday, babies like Joy and Johnny, were too young to comprehend their own trauma. She knew their conscious minds wouldn't remember the withdrawal of the drugs from their tiny central nervous systems, but she also thought that their subconscious would probably always carry the memory of that first craving. It should've been for mother's milk, not a substance to quench a mother's addiction. This made Morgan angry.

The first time Morgan had held an infant withdrawing from heroin, she wanted to throw the fragile creature back into the crib and run from the residential center. The baby boy wouldn't stop trembling despite the fact that she had swaddled and cuddled and snuggled him, rocking him back and forth at a steady pace and wandering around the infant nursery for two hours. His mewing was high-pitched and squeal-like, so unlike the gentle whimpers or angry bellows of her own infant son at that age. Had Morgan sounded like this when she was born? Had she trembled from head to toe? Did her face have raw patches? Did she sleep for only ten or twenty minutes at a time like some of the most challenging babies did? Or had her mother kept herself clean for the duration of the pregnancy, pushing aside the desire for a high in order to give

Morgan the best chance at a good start? Morgan wasn't sure. She'd never been able to bring herself to ask.

When she'd run into Robert—Dr. Robert Steele now, someone she knew from back in her school days—here a few weeks ago, she'd said quietly, "Please don't tell anyone you saw me."

He hadn't asked any questions, but even if he had, Morgan couldn't have told him the truth: that if people associated a cause like this—caring for children of addicts—with her, then they might also put the strange and disparate pieces of her child, teen and even adult years together. They might figure out that Morgan's family life had not been what it seemed. They might judge her, or worse, pity her.

Her husband, Lionel, had once helped shield her from that kind of scrutiny: a nice home, a nice husband and a nice son had made her entire life seem so *nice*. But then she'd lost the husband, and her son carried the weight of not-so-nice rumors. It didn't really matter, she supposed. She'd never been able to convince the other women on this island where she grew up but never quite belonged that she was anything other than the girl with the strange mom, the girl who had tried to take Leslie Steele's man years ago.

Now, as Morgan watched Robert walk in with his "Dr. Steele" name badge around his neck, she thought it might not be so bad if word of her volunteering were to get out, especially now that the two of them were talking...or whatever they were doing.

"I had fun on Friday night," he said as he checked baby Joy's pulse. The infant girl stared fuzzy-eyed at the ceiling as her tiny fist found its way to her mouth. Morgan checked the temperature of a bottle.

"Me too," she said.

They'd had dinner at his place and enjoyed themselves thoroughly afterward.

"Maybe we could have fun again? Tonight?"

She tried to play it cool. "I'd like that, but why don't I bring dinner this time?"

Robert raised an eyebrow. "You cook?"

The baby between them fussed and Robert recorded the pulse. Morgan held the infant close and smiled as she answered. "No, but I'm great at ordering Chinese."

"Sounds perfect," he said.

She looked at him. "Yes, perfect."

EMILY

Back in Woodhaven, I always thought of myself like a gray wolf, fitting into the pack seamlessly since I'd literally been born into it. But these past months in Galveston, I've felt more like a black rhinoceros, my last name making me too large and too noticeable while I remain completely out of place, the environment inhospitable to my survival.

As days and then weeks passed at my new school, I realized I was becoming more and more asocial—not antisocial, which is by choice. The herd, the one that my ancestors literally founded, had rejected me.

I'd noticed the leader of the Callahan Prep herd on my first day: Anna Steele. I couldn't have missed her. She was the one leading the pledge at the beginning of each school assembly. She was the one front and center at pep rallies, kicking and bouncing and flying through a series of choreographed moves, all in a tiny blue-and-white cheerleading skirt. She was the one signing in volunteers at the mandatory beach cleanup service day, and she was the one who led the school body by example, completely ignoring my existence every chance she got. Except when she talked behind my back, I guess.

In whispers and side comments, I soon came to understand how essential her approval was at this school. *You've got to run any ideas for the dance by Anna*, one person would say. Another would counter with, *Anna would never go for that and you do not want to piss her off.* Those were the fairly innocuous ones. But there were other sound bites, ones I caught as I walked down the hall, sat at my pottery wheel or ate my lunch.

"Do not even look at him, Sydney. You know what happened to the last girl who was flirting with Anna's guy," I heard one girl advise another.

"That was just coincidence."

"Was it?"

I shivered and fled to class, where I could deal with things I could understand: equations and formulas rather than the bizarre social dynamics of this teenage ecosphere.

The one person who seemed somehow beyond Anna's sphere of influence was the boy named Alex. I ate lunch in the library alone most days, but a few weeks into my sentence, I was surprisingly relieved to hear another friendly *hey* when I was assigned my lab partner during the last class of the day. It was Alex. I nearly groaned, but then I looked around and saw my other options, one of which was Anna. I'd take him.

Quickly, I saw that despite the jock vibe he had going, this guy could keep up. Not that he was the one in our partnership to take the lead, but he could record the findings, ask solid questions and throw out correct answers often enough. He was funny too, but not in the traditional high-school boy way, telling crude jokes and making fun of the teacher. Instead, he must've memorized the cheesiest jokes he could find, depending on the dissection for that unit.

"What do you call a sheep covered in chocolate?"

"I don't know," I said, not looking at him as I made the first incision across the pink-white muscle of the sheep's heart.

"A Candy Ba-a-a-a." He even vibrated his voice for effect.

"Oh, no."

"What? Did you cut in the wrong place?"

"No, that joke!"

"Okay, here's another. How do sheep in Spain say Merry Christmas?"

"No idea."

"Fleece Navidad."

"Make it stop," I said, backing away from the heart. His jokes were so awful that I couldn't keep from laughing. He laughed too, full-throated and deep. Too deep for the lightness of him.

When he ran out of puns, I would tell him trivia I'd gathered over the years about whatever organ we were studying.

"Did you know that flatworms don't have hearts, but earthworms have five?"

"So, what do flatworms do without a heart?"

"Diffusion."

"Like the oxygen or whatever flows wherever it needs to go?"

I shrugged as I peeled back part of the aorta, and he measured the length of the valve. "Pretty much, and to clarify, an earthworm heart isn't anything like this one with all the chambers. It's five basic pumps, aortic arches they're called. But still, five."

Alex didn't seem as excited as me about biology facts, but he looked at me in a way that made me think he enjoyed hearing me talk.

To be honest, it kind of scared me. I'd never seen that kind of look from a boy. Intense. Intent. I willed myself to keep my gaze steady with his, not to look away, to show him that if he could hang with me, then I could hang with him.

Soon, we were spending several hours a week outside of school together, though because of the workload of Callahan Prep, this meant we often met at the library to study after his football practice. After school, I would drive Lucy and Olivia home and help make dinner while trying not to glance at the clock. Mom caught me a time or two.

"Do you need to be somewhere?" she would tease. I didn't say, *Yeah, back in Woodhaven*, like I wanted to. I remained the good daughter, honoring my mother as they'd taught us in youth group. Alex made that easier to do.

After dinner, I would usually either head up to the attic to study—if Alex had a night game—or to the library to meet him.

"I concentrate better outside of the house," I would say as an excuse sometimes. It's not that I was trying to hide Alex; I was trying to hide that he was the *only* friend I had made.

In Oregon, I had a handful of friends, girls I'd known since pre-K and a couple of guys who shared the same interests as me. Astronomy Club, Quiz Bowl, Confirmation Class, that kind of thing. Making friends over time—from birth until seventeen—had been something I'd never thought about: *You like science, so do I. Let's be friends! You have questions about God. So do I. Let's figure it out together.* Making friends as a kid was that easy. But not here. I knew if I didn't start bringing people home, my mom would eventually notice, and part of her being okay with this move was me being okay.

Now, lying here, reflecting, remembering and unmoving in my dormant state, I sense that somehow having Alex as my only friend and Anna as my silent enemy may have brought all this about.

6
December
Leslie

Some time ago, during her husband's lingering illness, Leslie stopped sleeping through the night. On any given evening, she would lie down around 10:00 p.m. and wait hours to nod off. Five hours later, almost to the minute, she would wake with a sudden start as if someone had been holding a bag over her head. Regardless, the next day she would tackle life head-on, planning events for the school and running errands for her kids and trying to improve this small island that was her entire world.

Other Callahan Prep moms would ask her all the time, "How *do* you get so much accomplished?"

Sleeplessness, she wanted to scream. Instead, she would say something more palatable, like, "I keep a tight schedule and write everything down in my calendar." Which was also true.

The other moms would nod as if their heads were spring-loaded. These women.

Leslie could put on the makeup and wear the clothes and coordinate the events, but she knew what she was doing. She knew that she played the part for two very practical reasons: to avoid collapsing into a nervous breakdown and to hold her family together. Keep moving, keep going, keep doing, doing, doing. That was the Leslie Steele way—her schedule and her kids motivated her to get out of bed each morning. She knew she should be grateful that Michael had arranged everything—using family money and his life insurance policies—so it would be possible for her to continue as a full-time mom after his death, but with Anna's graduation quickly approaching, sometimes she wondered frantically what came next.

Leslie was trying not to think about all this as she checked her rearview mirror and switched lanes. She was on her way up to the school.

"Hey, Siri, call Asher." The phone rang and rang before going to a voice mail that had never been set up.

She hung up, frowning. She hadn't heard from her son Asher, who was away at college, today. Maybe she should call the RA in his dorm? Or maybe not. She didn't want to be *that* mom. Or maybe she did. It was so difficult to decide how to parent these days. She thought, as she had for some time, that the term *helicopter mom* carried an unnecessarily negative connotation. Helicopters weren't just for hovering; often enough they saved people.

Like the time that she took Asher and his twin brother, Sawyer, to the turtle hatchery when they were three years old. Leslie was full and round, due with Anna any moment, but the boys were fighting constantly, the way brothers do, and she had to get out of the house.

As she waddled around the sticky, airless barn, Sawyer ran from bin to bin, peering over the edge at loggerhead, hawksbill and leatherback sea turtles. Asher remained by her side, his head tucked behind her waist.

"Why don't you go look with your brother, Asher?" she'd said as she prodded him forward and tried to untangle herself from his tight grip. All she wanted at that moment was not to be touched, but Asher shook his head while scooting closer to her.

"What's wrong?" She attempted to bend at the waist and found the movement awkward. By the time she was able to angle herself to meet Asher eye to eye, his wide brown eyes were teary.

"It's not safe," he finally whispered.

She looked around. "The turtles can't get out, baby, and besides, the owners wouldn't let kids in here if it wasn't safe."

Asher shook his head adamantly. "Not the turtles, Momma." He lifted one arm to point at his brother. "Sawyer said he'll feed me to them."

"What? Why would…?"

She followed the small pointing finger just in time to see Sawyer look at the two of them with a smugness that belied his three years.

Leslie still shivered, thinking about that look all these years later. Of course, the boys grew out of this strange and fraught toddler stage, but as they aged, they took turns fighting in new ways, with fists and words. Sometimes it was Asher and Sawyer against the world; other times, the two were only against each other. Leslie was always on guard, wondering when she would need to swoop in and save one brother from the other. She never took any of the kids back to the hatchery again.

Leslie inhaled for four seconds and exhaled for seven as she stopped at the light on the Seawall and looked out over the tumbling waves. Asher was just busy. Studying. Sleeping. During finals, students needed all the studying time and sleep they could get, right? She'd spoken with him only yesterday, but he had coughed several times. What if his asthma flared up again? What if he'd been rushed to the ER by his roommate? What if he'd been found unconscious, his lips turning blue as they had when he was only a few minutes old? What was his roommate's name? Jay? Or Jason? She should've made him write down the numbers of everyone—from fraternity brothers to acquaintances to favorite professors—at school, but she was trying so hard to let him live his life. The phone mercifully rang.

"Hey, Mom, what's up?"

"Oh, nothing." Leslie covered the microphone while she released a shaky breath. "Just checking to see how you're feeling today...you know, with that cough."

"I told you, I was choking on my soda. I swear I would tell you if death was knocking at my door." Asher laughed as if such an image could be funny.

"Don't joke," Leslie said, attempting a light laugh, but tears sprang to her eyes instead. Asher had always been the one she cried over even though she'd chosen his name because it meant "happy," which was all she wished for him.

From the moment he was born, the doctors who rushed Asher to NICU didn't think he would survive; his APGAR score had been a whopping 2 to Sawyer's glowing 8. While Sawyer opened his eyes and looked around peacefully at the sights and sounds of his new world, Asher fought to breathe on his own for nearly a month. Leslie remembered the desperate feeling of having to leave him at the hospital each evening, knowing she must get home to Sawyer, her other infant, the twin son who also needed her. But not as much.

Leslie cleared her throat. "Have you heard from your brother?"

"Nah, not since we got that postcard from him a few

months back. I tried calling a couple of times, but you know Sawyer never answers."

Leslie sighed. "Why does he even have a phone?" She tried to picture Sawyer wandering the surf on a nearby peninsula just a ferry ride away, but she could never actually conjure him in that place, particularly since he hadn't told her exactly where he was living on Bolivar. Not that she would be able to bring herself to go see him anyway. Not after their last real conversation. Leslie hated that memory and shifted her attention back to Asher.

"I'm glad to hear you aren't coming down with a cold. Please call me—or text me—if you need anything. You know Austin is only a three-hour drive from here. Less if it's urgent."

"Okay, Mom. I gotta go study." Asher sounded distracted, almost dismissive of her concern.

She tried another question just to keep him on the line and hear his voice. "You'll be home Friday night for the Christmas party?"

"I'll be there. Hey, if you speak to Uncle Robert, tell him that I'll see him that following Monday morning at 5:00 a.m. at his office."

"You aren't taking any time off between semesters?"

Asher sighed as if explaining his thought process to a child. "You know that the more experience I get, the more of a head start I'll have next fall."

"I'd just hoped we could spend some time together." Leslie tried to hide her disappointment. "But okay, I'll let your uncle know."

"Oh—and I'll tell him later, but it looks like I'll be able to start work full-time early next May. Second-semester professors give papers instead of finals, so I'll be finished on campus by the end of April."

Five more months until her son was home again for good.

She couldn't keep the smile out of her voice as she said good-bye. She listened to him hang up and then turned onto the street of Callahan Prep.

As she got out of her car and looked toward the shore, she thought back to seeing her sons and their younger sister, Anna, snake-dancing their way down this street, their arms intertwined with their peers while she and her husband, Michael, watched from the sidewalk. Every spring in a ritual as old as the school, the students lined up alphabetically and by grade level, winding their way from Broadway to the Seawall in a zigzag. It was a silly tradition that prefaced all the other senior graduation celebrations: a parade, a picnic and an after-party at an undisclosed location. This year Anna would be a senior, but Michael hadn't lived long enough to see their daughter celebrate.

This year, Rosalyn had decided that the festivities would be held at The Monterey Club and end with a bonfire on Jamaica Beach, and Leslie wholeheartedly agreed. Sometimes, though, she imagined herself stomping one foot and saying *No!* to Rosalyn just to see what would happen. It wouldn't be pretty.

Leslie carried her bundles inside.

"Good morning, Mrs. Steele," the receptionist greeted after she buzzed her into the ornate white-stone building.

"Morning, Donna. How's the new puppy?"

Donna Howard rolled her eyes. "Chewing on the furniture and my shoes."

"Have you tried those all-natural chews that Dr. Spignet carries?"

"No, I'll have to ask him next time I take her in." Donna looked around to make sure no one would overhear. "Listen, I heard some of the kids saying that Anna is a shoo-in for Winter Queen this year. Congrats to you for raising such a fine young lady."

She batted away the compliment. "There are plenty of beautiful girls who will be nominated, I'm sure. Besides, she was already crowned homecoming queen." Leslie had placed her own twentysomething-year-old crown on her daughter's head.

"But none having the beauty and the brains and the heart like your Anna. I still can't believe she's the last Steele at Callahan Prep. You must get Asher to settle down on the island so he can send some Steele babies to pre-K here in a few years."

Leslie noticed the omission of Sawyer's name, noticed the way the woman glided past his existence. Even his alma mater—though, to be fair, Sawyer had only graduated at the mercy of the headmaster—didn't have high hopes for that son. Leslie shook her head modestly, and Ms. Howard's face turned grim. "The only one who would stand a chance against your Anna is that Callahan girl Emily, but surely the kids know better than to vote for her just because of her last name. Anna's been a pillar of the school and her community her whole life, and bless her heart, Emily may be a good girl, but she didn't grow up here." Donna lowered her voice to a whisper. "She's not really one of us."

Leslie tried to keep the fire out of her eyes and the edge out of her voice. "I'm sure everything will work out fine."

Surely, this community would know better, this community that had brought their family casseroles when Michael's cancer came back four years ago, this community that held her hand and hugged her children at his funeral, this community that overlooked the petty indiscretions of boys being boys, this community who believed their citizens over outsiders.

Leslie had always fit like a cushioned yolk inside the shell of this community.

"I still remember when that crown was placed on your head all those years ago, Leslie. It's inspiring to see Anna walking around, the spitting image of you."

Leslie squinted at the clock behind Donna's head and thought out loud, "Is Anna still in her free period?"

She really didn't need to ask. She knew Anna's schedule as well as her own.

"The bell just rang," Donna answered.

"Oh, well, that's all right. I just came to drop off these decorations. I was going to see how her government test went."

"I'm sure she aced it."

Leslie smiled at the woman's confidence. It would be strange to no longer have an official connection to this place next year. She bit her lip and rubbed the back of her neck at the terrifying thought.

"Are you all right, Mrs. Steele?"

"Hmmm?" Leslie was jostled back to the here and now. "Oh, yes, of course. I realized that I forgot some of the snowflakes I cut for this year's mums. I'll check at home and bring them back tomorrow." Leslie said her goodbyes and scooted back to her car.

Within seconds that lost feeling of being too far out to sea swept over her again. Her chest tightened. Her hands grew cold and clammy. She pulled out the paper bag she kept in her glove box and breathed hard and fast.

"Hey, Siri, call Robert," she gasped, waiting as she huffed into the bag. As soon as she heard him on the line, she took a gulp of air. "It's happening again."

Robert immediately shifted into a soothing tone. "It's okay, Leslie. Take your time and listen to my voice. You are here in this moment. This moment is enough. Breathe in, breathe out, breathe in, breathe out."

He breathed with her and issued directives in his throaty doctor's voice until Leslie could once again sit fully upright and lean back into the headrest. He must have heard the movement. "Close your eyes," he instructed. "What color do you see?"

"Brown," she said. *Like the Gulf. Like the sand.*

"Okay. Brown. Let the brown settle around you. Let it wash over your head, your face, your hands…" Robert's words were soft and warm, breaking the cycle of irrational fears that backed her into a corner so readily these days.

A few moments later, she took a deep breath, opened her eyes and looked around the parking lot. She was herself again. Capable and confident and prepared.

"Thank you," Leslie sighed into the phone as she started the car.

"No problem. I think that was a new record, calmed you down in less than five minutes. Well done." Thank God for her brother-in-law. "What started it?"

"I don't know, maybe thinking about what I'm going to do with myself next year when Anna is away at school and I'm no longer *Mom*."

"You know they'll always need you to be Mom—all three of them."

She appreciated that Robert included Sawyer. "I know, but it won't be the same."

Robert exhaled. "Yeah, I guess that's true."

She wanted to change the subject. "Busy day?"

"Not too bad. I rounded this morning, and I'm going over some imaging now."

"I talked to Asher a few minutes ago. I swear that boy isn't interested in anything except planning his future."

"He is driven, that one. Reminds me a little of Michael, except he was more interested in saving souls than saving lives." There was a chuckle in Robert's words. "I guess I'll see Asher first thing Monday morning?"

"He'll be there," Leslie said with reluctance. "Hey, do you want to grab dinner with me and Anna tonight?"

Robert paused for a second too long. "Actually, I think I may have a date."

Leslie's stomach churned. "A date?" She tried to cover her concern with a joke. "I can't believe you've found someone worthy of your attentions. Who, pray-tell, is this lovely lady?"

"One of the Callahan moms I hung out with at your auction. Morgan Frasier. You should know her pretty well, right? Her son's name is Alex—he might be a senior with Anna."

"Oh, right, of course I know her." Leslie feigned delight. "Morgan and Michael and I were in the same class at Callahan Prep. Alex is our star left tackle. Rumor has it that..." She paused a moment, cringing at the truth that she and the other Callahan moms had decided to ignore: rumor has it that he nearly raped a girl a few years ago. "Rumor has it that scouts were showing up at home games just to watch him." She didn't mention the other rumor, though surely Robert, even with all of his hours at the hospital, hadn't failed to hear it.

"I didn't think you went in for town gossip," he teased.

"Only when it's necessary to know. Anyway, enjoy your date. Let us know if it gets canceled." She could only wish. "Anna and I are planning to pick up tacos from Gaido's."

"Will do."

Leslie pulled onto the Seawall and looked out to where the muddy gulf met the cobalt sky. Maybe she would take a drive down to Jamaica Beach, put her toes in the sand. Maybe she would throw off the mundane, purposeless activities she used to fill her day.

Ha. Who was she kidding? She still had a menu to confirm for the Winter Dance and invites to send for the next Merry Moms luncheon. It was December, and she still had a respectable to-do list for at least another five months.

7

January
Catherine

Catherine sat at the piano annotating a copy of Beethoven's *Moonlight Sonata*, the arpeggiated chords of the final movement played *Presto Agitato* ("Like bees buzzing around a hive," she'd explained last week to her new fifteen-year-old private music student, the only one of her half a dozen pianists who could handle a piece of this caliber).

The first time Catherine had played *Moonlight* herself before an audience, she'd been in her second-to-last year of college. Her professor, Dr. Faber, had watched her practice the piece for three months, criticizing her and admonishing her until the technicalities—the fingering, the pacing, the intonation— was perfect. Almost anyway.

"Something is missing," her bearded instructor mused, staring into the carpet as he paced while she sat speechless at the keys. "I will think on this," he finally said, dismissing her.

When she returned the next day, Dr. Faber played the piece

for Catherine, and as his fingers brushed the keys, she could hear the difference: his hands didn't toil as hers did. Instead, they worked in a synchronous partnership, so that despite the fact that she knew the score backward and forward, knew the ideal placement of each finger on each key, Catherine could not decipher where his left hand began and his right ended. She worked on *Moonlight* for another three weeks, practicing that piece alone for two hours a day, and still she couldn't accomplish what this man who had lived a lifetime could do.

Her professor sensed this, and in his thick French accent told her, "Do not be discouraged. You must go out and experience the world—love, fight, lose, win. Then you will come back and revisit Beethoven with maturity. You will peel back the layers, make the notes jump from the strings." He'd said the words with such tenderness, as if her innocence rather than her incompetence was actually the thing keeping her from playing as Beethoven had intended.

As she held the sheets of *Moonlight Sonata* all these years later, she realized that her new student was a test for herself—if this kid could play the piece with real emotion rather than simple technical acumen, then Catherine would never attempt *Moonlight* again. She held her hands over the keys, tempted to try the song, now with a husband, three children and a career behind her. After a few faltering starts, the movement of her hands came back as if she'd played it only yesterday, but halfway through, she found tears springing to her eyes. She was still missing that *something*.

Blessedly, her phone interrupted, pinging with two notifications. The first was an emoji-filled email reminding her about "Merry Moms @ The Monterey." She'd received several such reminders from Rosalyn—along with pointed looks—about these invites throughout the past months, and though Catherine hadn't deigned to open those, curiosity tugged at her this time. "You are cordially invited Wednesday afternoon at 1:00 p.m. for a quick bite at The Monterey Club to discuss the spring semester goings-on of our very own senior Callahan Cats. We would simply adore it if you could join us. XOXO. Sincerely, The Merry Moms. P.S. *By Invitation Only Please.*"

She weighed her options: ready distraction at the risk of Rosalyn's insufferable approval versus sitting here with a sonata that had never brought anything but disappointment to Catherine.

The second ping was from Morgan—this one a text. Hey, lady. We have one of those ridiculous grade-level meetings. Please say you'll be there. Catherine clicked to enlarge the image, a hastily-made flyer with gothic font spelling out MOMMIES & MUFFINTOPS with the address and time. Catherine startled herself by chuckling. Maybe she could use this distraction, even if she had been resisting it for so long. Morgan, even with all of her inside connections to the cookie-cutter moms on this island, had become a surprising friend over the past few months.

She'd texted Catherine a couple of days after the auction and they'd met at MOD Coffeehouse to grab a cup of coffee. "You know, all of the cool moms stick with Starbucks, or if they want to go local, they hang out at The Busy Bean."

"Really?" Catherine studied Morgan to see if she was joking. "That's the actual name of a coffee shop?"

"Yep, it's on the first floor of the big residential tower where Broadway meets the Seawall, near the Monterey Club. The tower has a team of twenty-four-hour concierges at the residents' beck and call. I dropped off Alex there for birthday parties when he was in elementary school, and I know that a couple of the Centennial Families still live there."

"Centennial Families?"

"Oh, I forget how fresh and innocent you are!" Morgan

laughed. "Those are the families who've attended the school for at least four generations. They honor them at graduation every year and make sure to give them first dibs on the board seats, that kind of thing."

"That definitely does not sound real. Or right."

Morgan shrugged. "A tiny town where a precious few have most of the money equals some abnormal and exclusive traditions."

"So, you're like a half-centennial family? Only two more generations to go?"

"That's right." Morgan nodded and took a sip of her coffee. "And I guess this means that you are officially a Centennial Family without even knowing it."

Catherine couldn't keep the disgust out of her voice. "No. Never."

"Fair enough. Here's to *not* being one of those moms." Morgan offered up her cappuccino in a toast and then narrowed her eyes. "How would you classify yourself?"

"I don't know." Catherine thought for a moment. "I guess I'd say that I'm a lady who likes coffee and Mozart." Though it definitely was more complicated than that. For the first time, Catherine wondered whether she might have found someone with whom she could share the real story, the full story.

After that, Morgan and Catherine started walking together a couple times a week, sharing anecdotes about who they saw around town, Morgan catching Catherine up on all of the people she was meeting for the first time. They talked about their favorite childhood books—*Little Women* and *The Secret Garden*—and current tastes in films—dark comedies, for sure. They told stories about their kids and Carter and Robert and even Lionel. The only topic they tended to avoid was Alex's past.

Catherine let her hands rest against the piano keys and

glanced at the clock. It was past noon. The kids were at school, and who was she kidding? *Moonlight Sonata* hadn't changed in two hundred plus years, and it wouldn't change in the next few minutes.

Catherine sensed the hush as soon as she entered the private room at the back of The Monterey Club. The Callahan family probably built the building she was standing in, but in the weeks and months since arriving, not once had she desired to step inside this exclusive club, despite the fact that she and Carter were apparently full-fledged members thanks to his mother. *Emily will need to socialize*, Rosalyn had said as she handed them key cards to the locker rooms.

"Welcome! Welcome!" A woman stood up and moved toward Catherine with open arms. Leslie Steele was dressed impeccably in a tennis outfit that surely had never been blemished with a drop of sweat, and her hair was swooped over her shoulder into a lovely long braid. "So glad you could join us. I'm Leslie Steele, Anna's mom." Even though she'd avoided the official introduction for as long as she could, Catherine knew who Leslie was. Everyone knew.

Attempting to escape the embrace, Catherine stumbled backward, but Leslie caught her. "Oh, must set you to rights." The way Leslie spoke, that staccato punctuation of each separate word, reminded Catherine of her mother-in-law; it was unsettling.

Leslie's hand rested on Catherine's shoulder as twenty-five pairs of eyes bored into her. The twenty-sixth pair belonged to Morgan who sat at the very end of the table, a seat between her and everyone else, as if she were waiting for someone to join her. Catherine started toward her friend, but felt the slightest pull on her shoulder, so slight that she wondered if she had imagined Leslie's touch.

Morgan nodded once as if to say she was fine, raised her glass of water and toasted Catherine's entrance with wide eyes. Morgan was wearing her best Callahan-Prep-Mom face, her lips pursed, her eyes bright, her smile one-sided, but she'd missed the memo about the tennis or yoga ensemble and instead sported skinny jeans and a simple gray V-neck. She looked comfortable and beautiful and above all of this nonsense. Catherine wished the two of them could escape this pending melee.

Alas, Leslie had the fleshy part of Catherine's arm in hand, the woman's face unflinching as she smiled stiffly across the room at the moms who looked hungry, not only for information about her. No, they also looked literally hungry. They all had that fresh scrub of a facial and the sallow cheeks of the carb-less.

"We'll give you a chance to meet everyone later, but we were about to discuss the location of the senior getaway. Rosalyn has generously provided us with a short list of options, and we need to finalize details soon." Everything about Leslie screamed *fortissimo*, the musical notation for *very strong*. This woman gave the orders, and everyone else fell in line.

After Leslie ushered Catherine to the seat at her right hand, a host of waiters descended on them, moving the starving women from course to course every seven to ten minutes: a salad with minimal dressing, a tiny bowl of lobster bisque, a petite plate of grilled shrimp and vegetables, and a coin-sized cookie with a dollop of chocolate mousse. As the servers ushered the women through their meal, a cacophony of voices arose.

Leslie spoke directly to Catherine, loudly enough for everyone to hear but quietly enough to make the words seem strangely intimate. "Now, as a Callahan mother—both literally and figuratively—you are automatically one of us, so feel free to jump into the conversation."

One of us. One of us. It was a terrifying mantra. Catherine attempted a smile while also looking for Morgan, whose aloof behavior might show her how to navigate this strange situation, but her seat was now empty.

"I simply adore the idea of Atlantis," one woman offered.

"But they do the beach all the time," another piped in.

"Bev, you know our beaches are a far cry from the white sands of the Bahamas."

"I'm just saying."

"What about a cruise?"

"You remember, Rebecca, what happened when the class of 2017 went on a cruise?"

"Oh, yeah…well, I'm sure we wouldn't lose a kid this time."

Leslie leaned toward Catherine to clarify. "They didn't actually lose her." She turned back to the group, trilling, "Let's not scare away our visitor, ladies. She won't let her daughter anywhere near us." Other women laughed conspiratorially.

Another mother, waving her hand as if she was the only one with reliable intel, jumped in. "It was the oldest Wagner girl, the one who somehow got into the school even though I heard she was at the bottom of the waiting list. Probably paid someone off—or worse. Apparently, she'd been partying all night and the last time someone saw her she was hurling over the side of the ship, so they all naturally assumed she'd fallen overboard."

"Would've been her own fault," a woman with platinum-blond hair added. "The whore spent the night in a crewman's bunk—a thirty-year-old at that."

"I'll tell you what, though, nine months later that eldest Wagner girl was inexplicably absent during the holidays. 'Studying abroad,' the family said. They moved off island shortly after that."

"That mother was such a drama queen." The blonde woman

looked to Morgan's empty seat and lowered her voice. "Remember the awful incident with that same family's youngest daughter right before they moved? They accused one of our best players of forcing himself on her even though she'd been drinking all night."

A silence fell for a millisecond, but it was enough for Catherine to notice a subtle shift in the room. A few of the women were obviously uncomfortable at the mention of the accusation. They were clearly speaking about Alex. She hoped Morgan was out of earshot, but need not have worried.

"It's fine," the woman called Bev told them all. "Morgan told me she had to leave early for some meeting or appointment. You know how flighty she is. Can't rely on her for anything. But honestly, her son isn't really the one to blame. Boys can't help noticing an attractive girl."

"Hey, if you've got two alcoholic girls in the family, I think it's time to examine your parenting. I say, good riddance to the Wagners."

"Didn't they move up north somewhere after Rosalyn Callahan kicked them out?"

Catherine's eyes widened, and Leslie attempted another intervention. "Ladies, ladies. This is completely off-topic. We must plan where our children will spend their final big fling before taking the plunge into adulthood."

Keeping her face neutral had never been Catherine's strong suit, and at that moment she was fairly certain her eyeballs were about to pop out of their sockets. She'd expected a gathering of mothers commiserating about the tedious application process or planning prom, not casually reminiscing about the time a student almost fell overboard before hooking up in a man's berth. Or a casual reference to an assault allegation against Alex, the kid hanging out with her own daughter.

Catherine took a gulp of water. It was fine, she told herself. All charges had been dropped.

A lady who hadn't yet spoken touched her hand gently. "Catherine, may I call you Catherine?"

"Of course," she choked.

"Dawn," she introduced herself, a hand to her heart as if the honor were all hers. "Where did the students in Oregon go for spring break?"

"Oh, well…we didn't have class trips as such." These were faculty kids at a small liberal arts university, she wanted to say.

"Really? How did the kids have one last adventure together?"

They didn't. They prepared for the real life of college or work. During her senior year back in Woodhaven, Emily would've paired up with a faculty adviser to complete an independent study addressing the effects of climate change on Portland's homeless population. It had already been approved. The only real "event" besides academics and graduation would have been prom. Catherine supposed that her daughter would've spent prom night in a hotel room with a few of her girlfriends and slept away the next day at home. Did that count as a trip?

"They were busy volunteering," she said. "And, of course they focused more on planning…um…prom?"

Heads nodded around the table as if this were both an acceptable and a logical response. Their next big event to plan.

Leslie smiled knowingly at the group. "That will be quite a night for our kids as well. Why don't we table this discussion until a few of us have had the opportunity to do a bit more research? But, remember, we'll need to make a decision soon in order to get the best rates."

Like these women cared about the best rates or making a decision. Leslie—or Rosalyn, more likely—would obviously choose for them. With that, the meeting was adjourned, exactly on the hour.

The floor shook as twenty-five women stood to their feet and gave air kisses to one another before flying out the door. Catherine stood along with them, mesmerized and suddenly concerned at how quickly she could become one of the lemmings if she let herself.

Never.

EMILY

I remember when I threw fits as a little kid and my dad would say, *If you'll stop crying, then you might actually have a chance to start smiling.* Although I can neither cry nor smile right now, I have been attempting to think of the things in my life that make me the most happy: the roses back in Oregon, pinks and reds and yellows unfurling their velvet petals each spring in preparation for Portland's Rose Festival; Lucy hugging me every morning before we go our separate ways at school; Olivia following me around the beach, squatting to watch the sand crabs burrow into clumpy mounds; Alex's furrowed brow as I lean over and help him calculate the mass of an element molecule.

Unfortunately, these happy thoughts inevitably jumble with my most unhappy ones, like when Mom told me we were moving. I was so angry. The face-heating, heart-pounding, palms-sweating, urge-to-punch-the-wall kind of angry.

THE NIGHT SHE WENT MISSING

I'd never felt like that before, and I'll never forget when Mom walked into my room, Dad brooding behind her. She put her hand over mine and told me that we were leaving Woodhaven.

"For my senior year? You're taking me away from my friends, my school, our home? When I only have one year left?"

I tried to keep my voice calm even though white-hot emotion was already bubbling beneath the surface. It didn't work. My voice rose and my hands shook.

"This is because of what you did, isn't it, Mom?" I stared into my mother's watery eyes, but she couldn't maintain my gaze. "You stole your student's work, passed it off as your own, and just because you lost your job, we all have to leave?"

Like a child, I wanted to stomp and scream, but I kept myself from that much at least.

Mom wiped at her eyes and stared at the ground as Dad stepped forward. He'd been speaking for the two of them a lot lately.

"We both think this is best for our entire family," he said, his voice firm, but his eyes warm as always. "You know that Grandma would like to have us closer, especially with your grandfather gone now."

I shot Mom a look—the fact that Grandma wanted us there should be enough to keep Mom away.

Dad continued. "She's the only grandparent you have left now." He looked to Mom as I shifted my glance back and forth between them.

I took a deep breath and forced up some sort of prayer, frantic and disjointed as it was. Then I spoke. "I don't want to go," I said simply, bluntly, my shoulders rolling forward. A silence settled between the three of us. Then, I had an idea.

"What about Megan? Maybe I could live with her family for my last year of high school?"

Seconds later, Mom, a full sob escaping from her, ran from the room. I stood up to follow her, to tell her it wouldn't be that bad, that I would come to Galveston for Christmas. I didn't want to hurt my mother, and I really didn't mean to make her feel worse than she already did, but this would be my last year at home anyway. Then college.

Dad put out an arm to stop me.

"Mom doesn't have to work," I tried instead. I could feel my voice take on a pleading quality, and I didn't like the sound. "You're a fancy corporate lawyer, so I know it's not a money issue. We could stay here. Just one more year. Please, Dad. Talk to her. Please."

All he could manage by way of explanation was a shake of the head and five words: "Mom needs this right now." No, she did not need *this*. She needed *us*, and she had us. Here, in Woodhaven.

But the logical part of me, the part I prefer, knew what he meant: that Mom had taken care of my dad and me and my sisters for years, and after completely disgracing herself, she could no longer face seeing the same people at the grocery store, at parent nights, at the stoplight. This was a small town, even smaller when the college students went home on break, but that sense of community is exactly what I didn't want to leave.

"It won't be that bad," Dad tried, rubbing my shoulders and folding me into a hug. "I'll be around a lot more, and you'll go to the same school that me and your grandmother graduated from." Great. "We're waiting to tell your sisters until tomorrow, but we wanted you to have a night to process everything."

That night, I didn't call Megan. I didn't cry. I didn't shout and scream like I wanted to. Instead, I did what I always did, stuck to my routine as a sort of lifesaver. I went for a run to let out my frenzied energy; I took a shower, and I crawled beneath my covers with a flashlight to read.

Still, over the next few months, I would have to use the breathing techniques our school counselor taught during her talks about our bodies, hormones, stress, relationships, sex. I'd never thought I'd have to use those practices, but I also never thought I'd have the dark thoughts I was having—about making my parents regret this decision. So I could barely contain myself a few months later, after I started my senior year at Callahan Prep, when Mom had the nerve to ask me about the one friend I'd made here in our new home.

"Are you sure he's the right kind of guy for you to be hanging out with?"

She seemed more like herself than she had in a long time, cooking dinner and obviously trying to make the conversation sound normal.

But I knew what she meant, and it rankled. Alex was the only good thing about living here, my only friend, the only reason to get out of bed in this awful town some days.

"The right kind of guy?" I repeated back to her.

Mom checked the pot of boiling water as if we were discussing nothing of significance. "I remember hearing your grandmother discussing...actually, gossiping about the accusations against Alex a few years ago. It stuck with me because you'd started high school, and it was so scary to hear about a girl attending a party and coming home after..." She was struggling to find the words. "After having been violated by another student."

I shrugged off her concerns. He'd already told me all of this. "I've read the police transcript, Mom, and Alex showed me the texts that cleared him. He wasn't the guy."

"You know that I trust you." She turned to face me. "You're

a good judge of character, but I don't know if you're seeing things clearly this time."

I could feel the meaning behind the words: How does a nearly eighteen-year-old girl know whether or not a boy is innocent of a crime like that? Weren't good girls inevitably drawn to the wrong kind of boy? But Mom couldn't exactly forbid me from seeing him, especially after she was the one who brought us here, forcing me to start again. I wouldn't give up Alex.

8

January
Morgan

Morgan ran up to Catherine in the parking lot as soon as that asinine Merry Moms lunch ended. "Hey, lady. You want to grab some real food?"

"Yes, thank God. I'm starving. Where did you disappear to and why didn't you take me with you?"

"I come to those lunches just to see what's on the agenda and if I really need to be there. But since Alex isn't going on that god-awful trip, as soon as the ladies' conversations started down that track, I was out of there. Sorry I couldn't grab you. Leslie had you in her clutches."

Morgan didn't add the two real reasons why Alex wasn't going: one, she needed to save every penny, and two, she didn't trust her son. Or maybe she did. She could never decide.

"I don't think Emily will want to go either," Catherine said before raising an eyebrow. "So, thanks for abandoning me."

"I knew you'd be fine. They love anything with the word

Callahan plastered across it, and that includes you." Morgan gave a lopsided grin. "I'll take you to the best restaurant on this island to make up for it. Deal?"

"I guess. I'm desperate after that so-called lunch."

"Good. That's how I like my friends—desperate and hungry. I'll drive."

A few minutes later the two women sat in worn-out, straight-back chairs at Shrimp n Stuff, sharing a plate of fried shrimp and hush puppies between them.

"Is this anything like the schools in the Northwest?"

Catherine laughed. "Uh, no. But my kids didn't attend private school, so maybe that's part of the difference?"

"Here at this school, everyone knows everyone else's business and wants to control how you go about that business. Sometimes I kick myself for sending Alex to this school, for living in this town. I know what it's like, but I can't seem to escape the pull. Maybe I thrive on suffering," Morgan said wryly. She took a swig of Texas Leaguer and changed the subject. "What's going on with our two kids? They've been spending every free moment together."

Catherine wrinkled her nose. "I know. This isn't like Emily at all. She's out every night, studying she says. But she's always been such a great kid, has never broken curfew by even a minute, so I don't feel like I can really say anything."

Morgan leaned back into her chair and stretched out her long legs. "Well, they're definitely studying. Alex's grades have never been this good."

Catherine leaned forward, conspiratorially. "I have to confess—I made Carter follow her one night to make sure she was actually going to the library."

"You didn't." Catherine looked shamefaced, but also proud of her motherliness. "And?"

"No surprises. She was at that library like she said." Catherine shook her head. "She's been like a mini-adult from the time she was five years old and started telling me about the melting ice caps."

Morgan snickered. "That's more than I can say for Alex. That child didn't say an intelligible word until he was four. I think it may have set him up for the reputation of the dumb jock at an early age."

Catherine made a face. "Morgan, that's terrible."

She shrugged. "I know, but that's how it is here. If you're a boy, you need to be good at football or making money. His dad was good at the money part thankfully, and then Alex became the best offensive lineman this town has seen in decades." Morgan popped another shrimp in her mouth. "Which was surprising since neither his dad or I were athletic. We couldn't help him with sports, and every time we tried to help him with math or science, he cried because he wanted to play outside."

Catherine shifted. "Does he ever see his dad?"

"Not in a couple of years." Morgan cleared her throat, but couldn't keep the disappointment from her voice. "Lionel was a decent father for most of Alex's life—made all the big games, that sort of thing—but I think he decided he had the chance at a do-over and took it. He decided to stay in Greece once he remarried, but we're semi-friendly now when we have to be. I guess I don't complain because he agreed to sign the loft over to me, and he pays enough child support that I can be a stay-at-home mom until Alex graduates. That clock is ticking, though."

A do-over. How simple and clean-cut she made Lionel's leaving them seem.

"And how are things going with Dr. Robert lately?" Catherine asked as she took a sip of water. "Remind me how you two know each other."

"He's amazing." Morgan couldn't keep herself from a dumb

grin. "I met him originally back in high school at Calla-han Prep. He was older than me—in Carter's class, actually. Robert was already a heartthrob back then, but also a bully sometimes." Morgan looked upward, trying to conjure up the Robert she knew from her past, the one the other kids some-times called Robby. "I remember when his brother, Michael, and Leslie and I were hanging out one time at Michael's house, and Robert came home angry about some test grade. He took a bat to this massive oak tree outside, but Michael brushed off the reaction, said it was just how his brother let off steam. Robert was harmless, and for some reason, even that brooding teen angst seemed sexy to me. But then he went away to col-lege and med school for eight or nine years before completing his residency in Boston. By the time he came back to town, I was all grown-up with a kid in tow and a husband at home."

And a mother usually high out of her mind, Morgan could've added.

Catherine shifted in her seat. "Wait. I think you buried the lead. So you and Leslie Steele used to be friends? The crazy one who hangs on every word Rosalyn says?"

"The very same." Morgan gave a knowing grin.

"Huh. That means you two have known each other a long time."

"Unfortunately." Morgan noticed the inquisitive set of Catherine's brow and realized she couldn't leave a statement like that hanging. "Leslie and I met in preschool. We bonded over having the same backpack and stuck together from then on. I actually lived with her family for part of our sophomore year while my mom…went on a trip for a few weeks."

Morgan averted her eyes, but only for a second. "But I messed up everything one night during our senior year when I got black-out drunk and kissed her boyfriend, Michael, Rob-ert's younger brother. I tried to apologize, to make things right, but after that, I became her archenemy. I went away to college a few months later, met my husband, Lionel, and eventually we settled here. I always said I wanted to raise a kid on the island, though I wonder every day why I wanted that so badly."

"Maybe because of your own childhood memories?"

Morgan almost laughed at the thought. "I don't know. Maybe. I do have good memories of growing up with Leslie and her family. Her parents were a sweet couple—you know, the churchgoing kind that asks about your life and seems to actually care about the answer. I don't know where Leslie got her ambition from, but she's always been like that. In third grade, she became the teacher's pet. In eighth grade, she became the lead in choir. In tenth grade she became the editor of the yearbook. By senior year she was valedictorian and homecoming queen and everything else you can imagine. I'm sure Carter remembers all this. He was back and forth from college and then law school when his mother started grooming her. Leslie was probably at their house every time he came back to the island, and if I remember correctly, I think Rosalyn even tried to set up Carter's little brother with Leslie at one point."

"Oh, God." Catherine shook her head in wonder. "It seems Rosalyn and Leslie had no choice but to find each other. The universe wanted them together."

"Yeah, I guess so." Morgan put an elbow on the table and leaned against it. "Rosalyn was always at the school, planning events and volunteering. After all, her father was the head of the board, and Andrew and Carter were students there around that time. So Leslie and Rosalyn became best buddies, despite the age difference. By the time Leslie and I parted ways, Rosalyn was somewhere between a friend and mother to her."

"Did Leslie leave Galveston to go to college, too?"

"Nope. She got a degree from Galveston A&M, something

to do with marine science and saving dolphins, but she never used it. She married Michael Steele—his family was almost as rich as the Callahans—and started a family."

Catherine took the last hush puppy. "And you? Where's your family from originally?"

"Who knows?" Morgan shrugged. "My mom grew up in some small town in Louisiana, ran away when she was sixteen, and hooked up with my dad one night shortly after arriving in Houston. He only lasted a couple of months, and she moved to Galveston. She always said she came to the water because seeing the waves every day calmed something inside of her. I guess I kind of feel the same. Me and Alex are both BOIs—this place is in our blood."

"BOIs?"

"Born on the Island. It's what locals say to show who the real insiders are."

"Ah. Then did you work on the island after college?"

"Only for a few months, but when Alex came along, I stayed home for maternity leave, and I realized I quite liked the kept-life. I mostly volunteer and cater to Alex—at least for a few more months." Morgan remembered how good her mom had been after Alex's birth; her grandson seemed to redeem her. Morgan had stayed home to bask in that goodness, that family togetherness. But it didn't last. It never did. Maybe Robert could help change that. "What about you?"

"I've always wanted to work," Catherine said. "That's how me and Carter met, actually. I was in grad school and working backstage at a small musical theater company in Portland. Carter came in one afternoon because his coworker's girlfriend was in the matinee. Carter was in multistate corporate law, a pretty prestigious gig, but he was wearing jeans and a Nirvana T-shirt." She smiled at the memory of a younger Carter Callahan. "After the show, he stuck around to chat. That night we grabbed lobster rolls at a place I knew, and since I'd grown up in the city, the next day I took him to more local haunts. Within a few weeks, we were pretty much inseparable, and six months later, he proposed at the top of Multnomah Falls."

"That had to be beautiful."

"The falls are prettier than anything I've seen in Texas so far, but I know it's a big state, so I'm trying to give it a chance." Catherine grinned. "Anyway, I was so glad Carter showed up when he did. My parents were retiring to Italy, so I didn't have family in the States anymore."

Morgan noticed a wistful look flicker across Catherine's face.

Catherine struck a lighter tone. "Too bad that family was the Callahans."

"I really thought you just taught piano lessons." Morgan studied her friend. "I didn't realize you were into actual productions."

"I've done a lot of things," Catherine said vaguely. She cleared her throat. She had her own topics she obviously didn't want to discuss today either.

"So why come back to Galveston?" Morgan asked.

"The usual reason—family." Catherine hesitated. "Initially, Carter got his undergrad at Stanford to defy his mother's dreams of Harvard—back when he was a semirebel at heart. But then, he decided he liked the West Coast and decided to go to law school in Oregon—to study in the mountains and fresh air, he said. Even though he traveled a lot for work, every now and then—especially in recent years—he'd talk about moving back here someday. He thought Texas would be a good home base for us."

Catherine wasn't quite meeting her eyes anymore, so Morgan decided to let things rest. She'd try a different tack. "I'm excited about Alex's opportunity with UT. He's been dreaming of playing college ball for years. What's Emily planning to study?"

"Climate change."

"No wonder Alex is into recycling all of a sudden," Morgan said. Then there was a pause, one of those silences that must be filled in the early days of friendship. "Listen, I know we haven't really talked about it, and I don't know how much you've heard, but—"

As Morgan trailed off, uncertain what to say next, Catherine picked up the thought. "It's all right. Emily and I discussed everything a while back. It sounds like Alex was unfairly accused." Her words were certain, but her tone was not.

"He was. Definitely." Morgan's heart beat a bit faster. "Look, he's not a perfect kid, but he's a gentle giant. I swear. You can trust him." She gauged Catherine's reaction. "Anyway, all that's behind him now, and though he doesn't say much, whenever he mentions Emily, she sounds like a wonder."

Catherine smiled. "I have to say I agree with that."

After bringing up the subject of Alex, an awkwardness settled between them even as they debated who would get the check. Catherine finally insisted, and Morgan let her.

Moments later, Morgan crawled behind her steering wheel, lost in thought.

Who was she kidding? No mother of a daughter would like the idea of an accused rapist hanging around her kid, guilty or not.

No way could this friendship last.

9

February

Leslie

"Were you able to locate the truffles to make that wine and butter sauce?" Leslie asked Pauline, the caterer. Sometimes when Leslie heard herself speak to people, like to Pauline that evening, she wondered if she sounded as vapid to them as she did to herself.

I promise I care about more than canapes, she wanted to cry out in those moments.

"Yes, everything is perfect, Mrs. Steele. Don't worry about any little thing."

"Oh, and be sure to…" Within a few minutes Leslie would have no idea what she'd told Pauline to do, but that didn't matter. It was on someone else's to-do list by that point.

Leslie was throwing her event of the season, the Steele Family Mardi Gras Celebration. Never mind that she was raised Southern Baptist. It was a Galveston island tradition, and Leslie kept the well-oiled social scene running smoothly.

The most important people would feel the surf breeze blowing through their hair while they drank Chianti and ate lobster rolls and listened to live music. She'd hired Well Done Catering, a dozen servers and, of course, the Mr. Brad Paisley. Rosalyn would be so impressed. There would be absolutely nothing to criticize. Nothing.

Leslie darted from room to room, fluffing pillows one last time and moving votives from one table to another, before scampering to her bathroom. She needed to touch up everything about herself before her guests arrived.

As she examined the deepening wrinkles around her lips and her eyes, she noticed the prescription her brother-in-law Robert had written for her on the bathroom shelf, a generic version of Xanax, something to help her when the anxiety intensified into a full-blown panic attack. She hadn't resorted to taking one yet, and still held out hope—a ridiculous hope, she knew—that the panic attacks would subside on their own after all this time, if she could just stay busy enough, distract herself enough from the fact that her youngest, Anna, was graduating; that her son Sawyer had been AWOL from the family for the past three years, that the other one, Asher, wasn't yet home for good, and that her husband, Michael, was gone forever. Dead and gone.

"Keep the medication on hand," Robert had suggested. "Just in case."

In case of what? In case she finally began to lose her mind? In case she fell so far into her own fears for her family's future that there was no coming back?

She brushed the ominous thoughts aside and scoured the bathroom for the perfume that Michael had given her every Christmas. A floral note with a hint of citrus. Anna had probably taken it again. That daughter of hers was always taking her things.

She bustled upstairs to grab the bottle from Anna's bathroom, and as she came back down the stairs, she noticed again the bare spot on the wall. She kept only a couple of pictures of Sawyer around the house, mainly so visitors wouldn't ask questions about why he was missing, but a few months ago she'd removed the twins' high school graduation picture after Anna offhandedly remarked on Sawyer's bloodshot eyes.

"I doubt he even remembers his own graduation." Anna had laughed, but such a realization was not a joke to Leslie. Had her son been high at his own graduation, the graduation she had fought for? The principal had almost lost his job over that debacle, but for God's sake, Sawyer's dad had died just five months earlier. How could you keep any kid from graduating regardless of how low his grades had fallen or how many days he had skipped school? Especially when generations of his family had attended the school and his father had served as the school chaplain for more than a decade. Sure, Sawyer's grades had plummeted, and sure, she could barely stand the sight of him after what he'd done, but if she had any say, Michael Steele's son would graduate from his prep school alma mater on time.

For days after Anna's words, Leslie's mind circled that evening from every angle. When she closed her eyes to sleep, she would see Asher's tentative smile that didn't quite reach his eyes, hear Anna's loud voice compensating for the quiet in the house, remember Sawyer's conspicuous absence from anything except the most necessary of activities. Leslie had assumed that they all simply missed their father—and that Sawyer felt guilty, no doubt. But even if Sawyer hadn't been the one to help Michael kill himself on New Year's Day, she knew her husband probably wouldn't have been in any state to attend their graduation the following May.

A couple of months before that fateful January 1, Robert,

who was unofficially overseeing his brother's care, had explained that Michael's speech might become impaired and that his memory might deteriorate rapidly. But even though Michael could no longer speak their names, a light would spring into his eyes when any of them walked into the room. Sometimes Michael would stare at Leslie as if trying to communicate his love and the unintelligible truths of the universe before he began to sob uncontrollably.

"The tumor is most likely pressing against the temporal lobe now," Robert had explained, watching tears stream down his brother's face.

Michael had always been sensitive, giving years of service as chaplain to Callahan Prep, his alma mater, while ample money from his inheritance supported their family's lifestyle.

Even before Michael could no longer speak, Sawyer stopped speaking most of the time. The fall semester of his senior year, he would go to school, come home, sit next to his dad until midnight, stumble into bed and then get up and go back to school. Or not. After she received the third call about truancy in late October, Leslie snapped.

"Are you trying to kill your father? The cancer isn't working fast enough, so you're trying to finish the job?" Leslie had thrown her hand over her mouth, and Michael had looked at the floor, unable to voice his trapped thoughts.

Not long after, Michael was dead.

Sawyer had been the last to see his father alive, and Leslie blamed her son every day for that fact. No wonder Sawyer was high a few months later at graduation. It was the only way he could live with the guilt.

As Leslie stood staring at the blank space on the wall and wondering whether or not anyone would notice that a picture was missing, the doorbell rang. She frowned. Guests weren't scheduled to arrive for another half hour, but Leslie pushed her shoulders back like the gracious hostess she always became when the moment necessitated.

"Ah, good evening, Alex." She told herself to smile at the broad-shouldered young man in front of her, but she couldn't quite fake it. She'd known him almost since he was born, at least from a distance, though with his expansive frame, she wondered if he had ever actually been that small. "I heard that you'll be signing with UT officially next week?"

He dipped his head politely. "Yes, ma'am."

Leslie couldn't keep herself from studying him for a moment. He looked so unlike his parents, skinny Lionel and tall, willowy Morgan. *Morgan, ugh.* She caught herself staring as Alex's eyes met her own. Those weren't the eyes of a rapist. Surely.

At that moment, Anna interrupted, darting down the stairs.

Leslie glanced over her shoulder at her daughter, who was wearing a purple halter top that hugged her breasts and skinny jeans that hugged her rear. She'd adorned her braided hair with inexpensive gold beads to add a touch of the Mardi Gras spirit. Anna was far too sexy without seeming to try, and Leslie had the sudden urge to lock her in her room.

"Hey, Anna," Alex said. "I came by to drop off your jacket—you left it in my car after our study session."

Leslie eyed the two as Anna approached him. Hmm…what had happened here? Anna had mentioned a study session, but she hadn't mentioned that Alex had been with her. He didn't seem at all like the studious type.

"Oh, thanks, but I could've picked it up at school tomorrow." Anna's eyes darted to her mom nervously. Anna wanted her to leave. *No, thank you,* Leslie thought.

"I was also going see if you can hang out with us at Natalie's tonight. I know most of the island is going to be at your house, so I thought you might want to escape. A few of us are watching a movie." He shifted on his feet. "Actually, Emily's making us study first for AP Bio."

Anna couldn't keep the disappointment from her eyes, and Leslie knew that the annual shindig, one she'd missed hosting only once—the year after Michael's death—was far less appealing than hanging out with her friends. Even with live music, the crowd was simply too old for Anna's tastes.

Despite her better judgment, Leslie offered a suggestion to make herself seem reasonable. "Why don't you stay here and help me greet everyone and then you can slip out in an hour or so?"

A smile spread across Anna's face, and Leslie wondered if she should rescind her offer. She didn't want her only daughter getting into a romantic relationship with Morgan's son, regardless of the promising athletic future Alex Frasier had before him; she certainly didn't want to share her daughter with Morgan Frasier in any way, shape or form.

She needn't have worried because Alex clarified his thinking, to Anna's obvious disappointment. "Me and Emily are going to meet to grab a burger first. You won't miss much."

"Oh, that's okay." The light in Anna's eyes dimmed. "I don't want to interrupt anything."

"No, Natalie asked me to invite you. Kyle and Jordan and Luke are gonna be there too. You should come."

Anna looked to her mother for a moment, and Leslie nodded.

"Okay. I'll see how it's going here, and I'll make it if I can," Anna told him, taking her jacket as Leslie turned away.

Alex was obviously interested in Carter Callahan's girl.

Even while Leslie felt relieved, her heart sank for Anna.

Emily Callahan was disrupting everything.

EMILY

The only time I can actually remember riding the ferry was a few months ago, in January. Alex and I had decided to explore Bolivar before heading back into spring semester in a few days. It was cold, and the sea spray coated our skin and hair. For as long as I can remember, I'd been terrified of open water—something to do with an early viewing of *Jaws*, Mom speculated—but I was determined to overcome this fear now that I lived on a strip of land surrounded by salt water.

Alex smiled and shook his head as he drove onto the ferry and then noticed the supplies I'd thrown in the back of his truck. "What is all that?"

"My gear." I'd brought a small cage, a bag filled with two pairs of gloves and several specimen bottles as well as a backpack with food and drinks (and a small flotation device that would expand in seconds, but I didn't exactly want to advertise that part). "You said we would go exploring, so I came prepared."

"I can see that."

Alex turned off his truck and then got out and walked to the edge of the boat. I followed him tentatively and peered over the iron railing and into the dark water. I shivered. I knew I would need to get used to being on the water if I ever hoped to make it to the Galapagos to study someday, but instinctively, I reached for one of the hanging life jackets, latched it across my midsection, and held on to the orange fabric like a safety blanket.

I hadn't grown up on the water like the kids here, and the unsteady rocking of the waves made my stomach roll. As we looked out over the channel, Alex reached his long arm around me. He stayed like that for twenty minutes, anchoring me until we reached Bolivar.

10
February
Morgan

Morgan Frasier and Robert Steele were finally taking their relationship public. At his sister-in-law's Mardi Gras party, no less. This was her chance.

Her phone rang. "Hey you."

Robert's voice sounded gruff. "Morgan, I'm so sorry."

Morgan's stomach flipped. She knew what those words meant. She'd heard them many nights when she'd been married to Lionel and he'd call to say he had to work late.

"Uh-huh." She could hear Robert's footsteps on the linoleum floor of the ER.

"I didn't think I would be called in, but a woman had a stroke and…"

Morgan wanted to throw the phone, but how could she? This wasn't her ex staying at the office to broker a deal, if that was true at all. This was a doctor saving lives. Besides, his dimples, his caramel-colored eyes, his do-gooder heart had captured her in a way she hadn't expected after all these years.

"All right, all right. Enough of your feeble excuses," she teased. "I'll see if I can be a third wheel with Carter and Catherine."

She heard his feet stop, and he lowered his voice. "Maybe I could see you after the party? I should be done in a couple of hours unless I get another emergency, which isn't likely. Most people save their tumbles and aneurysms until after Lent officially begins."

"I imagine Alex will be out with friends all night," she said. At a less mature time of their lives, they might've been more subtle. In a childless era, she might have said, *Your place or mine?* In her current state, she simply said, "Call me when you're ready, and I'll come over."

"Hey, wear that black lacy-thing under your dress."

She giggled like a teenager, but her voice was warm. "I already am."

Morgan knocked at the door of Catherine's understated Victorian home, and her friend rushed out, not even calling a goodbye.

"In a hurry?" Morgan asked, laughing.

"The twins are both in bed with the stomach flu, and I've been with them nonstop for the past forty-eight hours. Carter got in an hour ago from a two-day-long meeting with customers in Atlanta, and I told him I'm leaving. Let's go."

"Poor girls. Poor you. Did Emily come down with it too?" Morgan couldn't imagine having three kids. One had about done her in these past few years.

"Not yet. For the past few days, I've quarantined everyone to their own rooms, and she's out tonight with friends."

"That's good. I guess she's at the same party as Alex?"

"Yeah, but honestly, I've been too busy cleaning up throw-up to ask for details."

Morgan was relieved that Catherine didn't seem at all concerned this time about their kids spending time together. Desperation will do that. She had a sudden thought. "Hey, why don't we play hooky from the party and drive into the city for a fancy dinner instead?"

"What about Robert? I figured he was meeting us there?"

"He had a hospital emergency come up."

Catherine crawled into Morgan's Audi, a leftover from her marriage to Lionel. "I like the idea of dinner, but not so much of driving for an hour and waiting for a table. Maybe we could check out something on the Strand?"

"Perfect." Morgan steered the car in the opposite direction of Leslie Steele's mansion-beach-house and headed toward a night of drinks and conversation.

"Do you think Leslie will be mad? We did RSVP."

Morgan couldn't care less. "She won't even notice. Her house is always packed—she invites all of the Galveston politicians, priests and pastors, newspaper journalists and every parent at school. She'll have plenty of company, and remember, I'm an obligatory invite anyway."

Morgan knew that when Alex graduated, she would officially be *persona non grata* in this town's social scene—unless she ended up with Robert.

Catherine leaned her head back and closed her eyes for a moment. "Rosalyn will definitely notice my absence. She'll call Carter as soon as she sees we aren't there. Or she might just send her car to pick us up. She's nuts."

"Her grandkids are sick. What does she expect?"

"For us to get a nanny so we can make an appearance. It's what she would've done."

"Well, I think you've proven by now that your family is different than the family she raised."

Catherine smiled faintly. "Yeah, I guess so."

"I know so. I'll get a couple of cosmos in you, and you won't feel an ounce of guilt for the rest of the night."

"You know, if I hadn't met you, the past few months would've been one long trek back and forth from giving piano lessons to picking up the girls to the weekly brunch at Rosalyn's lair."

Morgan laughed. "That's not quite how I would describe the Black Beast."

It's what most of the locals called the dark brick Callahan house surrounded by a wrought iron fence, sitting on prime Broadway real estate.

"Tonight, all I want to do is relax and recharge before I go home to at least two sick kids and eventually a sick husband. He usually gets whatever they have and somehow needs twice as much attention."

"I think we can make that happen."

Catherine changed the station.

Morgan shook her head as the sounds of a piccolo emanated from the speakers.

"No thank you," Morgan said, taking control of the radio, scanning away from the classical station where voices spoke in dulcet tones about cadenzas and second movements and contrapuntal technique. "Give me TLC or Spice Girls any day."

"You're kidding me? Are you a Miley Cyrus fan too? *Put my hands up, They're playing my song?*" Catherine threw her own hands up.

"Hey, no shame here. You like to listen to a bunch of dead classical guys who didn't even write words to most of this crap."

"Crap? Uh, no. You have to admit that what they wrote was actually music."

"You give a shout-out to Katy Perry, and I'll give one to Beethoven."

"Hey, I can appreciate *good* pop music. Lady Gaga, Adele, Ed Sheeran, Sia. These people write their own songs, which I totally respect." Catherine turned toward her. "Why don't you pick a song and then I'll pick a song and we'll see which is actually the best music?"

Catherine plugged in her phone to the USB port as Morgan caught the glint in her eyes and narrowed her own. "Wait—aren't some of your 'songs,' like, a half-hour long?"

Catherine demurred as she selected a piano sonata. "Did you know that Handel and Bach both went blind at the hands of the same crazy ophthalmologist? Their 'doctor' was very into fanfare, so he performed operations in town squares. Of course, the quack was gone before the patient had a chance to recover—or realize they'd been permanently blinded."

Morgan cringed. "How do you know that?"

Catherine shrugged. "I taught music history for years. I used tidbits like that to keep my students riveted." She continued more seriously, "That doctor actually makes me think of Rosalyn's Dr. Montague. Have you heard of him?"

"I think so. Doesn't he have that retreat center on the West End?"

"That's him. He's been her personal doctor for years, and she funded that retreat center. Half the time, I wonder if he's crazy too or if it's just her."

The thing about Catherine, Morgan thought, was that she didn't bullshit. She didn't share readily, but when she did, she said it like it was. Morgan looked over at her briefly, trying to take the temperature of the conversation before asking the question she'd always wanted answered. "Is something wrong with Rosalyn? All I've heard is that she's really health conscious."

"I've got my own list of possible mental health issues." Catherine smirked. "But no, she's not really crazy, at least not in the way you're thinking. Although, a few years ago…" Morgan drove on, and Catherine paused a moment, looking out the window into the Strand filled with dimly-lit restaurants and bright stores. "A few years ago, she took Lucy."

"She took Lucy, your daughter?" Morgan's eyes widened. "What do you mean? Where did she take her?"

Catherine raised an eyebrow as if she still didn't believe her own story. "We never found out. We were here visiting Carter's family for Christmas, and the twins were only nine months old. I put them to sleep upstairs in the nursery at the top of the house. That room had always seemed dark and creepy to me, but Carter said he had fond memories of running around up there with his little brother and the nanny. Rosalyn had decorated it to the nines in preparation for our visit—giant stuffed giraffes, zebra-print baby blankets, framed animal sketches." Catherine squinted as if seeing the scene. "I kissed them each good-night and sang 'Hush Little Baby' before falling into my own bed, exhausted from traveling thousands of miles with three kids. I didn't wake up until I heard Olivia crying over the baby monitor in the middle of the night. I went upstairs and Lucy was gone."

"Oh, my God." Morgan placed a hand over her heart. "What did you do?"

"I called the police. Carter's father didn't want to, said vaguely that once a long time ago his wife had experienced an *episode*, whatever that meant. But I wasn't about to wait. Chief Whiteside, the father of the current police chief, was still at the house the next morning when Rosalyn showed back up, barefoot and shivering, with Lucy and a diaper bag in her arms. As soon as I opened the door, Lucy grinned and reached out to me.

"Thankfully, the weather was in the fifties, and my baby had on a huge coat. She even seemed like she'd been fed and changed. When Carter and his father took Rosalyn into the office to question her with Chief Whiteside, it was like she was coming out of a daze. She finally told them that the last thing she remembered was seeing a man who looked like someone from her past lurking outside the mansion, said it must have 'set her off.' She wouldn't say more, only that she had to see the family doctor—Dr. Montague—right away. We never found out where she went or why."

"Did you think about pressing charges?"

Catherine was silent for several beats. "Against his mother? No. But I told Carter I never wanted to see his mother again, that I wouldn't trust her to be in the same room as my kids, and I made him book us a flight home the next day on Christmas Eve. But we couldn't press charges. I mean, we could have, but from what Carter eventually got out of her, his mother genuinely didn't remember anything about those missing hours. She said seeing that man lurking had startled her so much that she took one of her pills before bed to help her relax, and when she awoke a few hours later, she was at our front door with Lucy in her arms."

Morgan was clearly shaken as she pulled up into an empty parking space. "How does the gossip mill not know this story about Rosalyn Callahan?" She turned to face Catherine, who only shook her head.

"Well-kept secrets can stay well-kept if you have the power. I doubt the police or reporters would defy Callahan orders to keep quiet. Besides, don't most people here go out of town to some luxurious resort for winter break? A few missing hours was not news by the time school was in session again."

"I guess, but that is one story that a few mothers at the school would love to sink their teeth into." Too bad Morgan didn't talk to any of them, she thought as the two of them walked into Mario's with its twinkling lights and inviting bottles of wine.

The remainder of the evening was spent in storytelling and tipsy laughter, but over the next days and weeks, Morgan would replay in her mind the conversation about Rosalyn, wondering about the woman's polished persona: a woman in control of one of the most prestigious private schools in Texas; a woman who had been married to the island's only billionaire before his passing; a woman who lunched with the editor of the oldest newspaper in the state; a woman who during the last hurricane had stood at the San Luis, hair perfect and nails manicured, next to Houston's top meteorologist, smiling reassuringly into the camera as Galveston's mayor and police chief urged immediate evacuation. This woman had it together. Or so it appeared.

11
February
Catherine

Catherine woke up the next morning with a headache from the three bottles of wine she'd shared with Morgan.

Only a few hours after Catherine poured herself into bed, Carter was awake, showering and shaving. "Mother wanted us to go to the 7:00 a.m. Ash Wednesday service, but I told her you would need to stay with the twins and I have an early meeting."

"Thank you," Catherine mumbled from beneath the covers. "How are Lucy and Olivia?"

"Much better. They didn't have a fever all evening, actually."

"That's good." Catherine squinted into the morning light. "What time did Emily get home?"

"What do you mean?" Carter applied aftershave and began donning a tie. "I thought she was spending the night with her friend?"

"She didn't tell me that." Catherine sat up, rubbing circles in her forehead to relieve the slight pounding. "Did she ask you?"

Carter shrugged. "No. I just assumed, since she always stayed over at a friend's if she was going to be out past midnight."

"Midnight?" A hammer was starting to pound at the edges of Catherine's temples. Besides Alex, which friends did Emily have on the island? Catherine's heart skipped, but she told herself it was probably nothing. Just a miscommunication. She and Carter had barely talked between him getting home and her going out with Morgan, and Emily was still getting dressed for what she'd called a "hang-out" when Catherine left the house last night.

"That was when she had friends whose families we'd known forever. But regardless, she's never stayed out on a school night," Catherine said as she peeked into Emily's room and then wandered into the kitchen to turn on the coffeemaker. She stood in the dark with her phone and called Emily. It went straight to voice mail. Probably still asleep, but where? With whom? And even if she was with a friend, wouldn't she be getting up for school soon?

Catherine told herself she would not overreact. Not yet. Instead, she texted Emily, hiding her nerves behind cheerful words: Rise and shine, sleepy girl. You have school at 8:30, and your grandma wants you to go to service with her at seven if you can make it.

Emily wouldn't want to miss the service, even though Catherine had never encouraged that kind of thing. Growing up herself in Portland with lapsed Catholic parents, Catherine hadn't taken an interest in God, but she could still remember the first time her daughter had started asking religious questions.

"Who made me?" Emily had asked when she was four years old.

"Me and your daddy," Catherine answered matter-of-factly.
"But who made you?"

"Grandpa Rubisi and Nana."

"And who made them?" And on and on the questions had gone until finally Catherine said, "God. God made you."

Emily had smiled at the answer and looked into the gray Oregon sky. After that, the questions had only grown. For whatever reason, Emily was drawn to the complexities and nuances of Christian theology, forcing Catherine to try to answer questions she had no interest in understanding. Still, as a good mother, she helped Emily look up the difference between transubstantiation and consubstantiation when she was in eighth grade, the same year her daughter had asked to attend confirmation classes. Catherine had always assumed that her bright kid would see that religion was supposed to be at odds with science—really, Catherine's field of study in classical music had much more of a traditional spiritual bent—but in Emily's mind, her understanding of the universe served to empower her faith, not diminish it.

Yes, Catherine was certain Emily would want to attend service even if it was with a grandmother she barely knew, but by 8:30 a.m., Emily still wasn't home and had not checked in. Catherine called her daughter's phone so many times in quick succession that voice mail now picked up after only one ring. She phoned the school. They knew nothing.

By 9:00 a.m. she called Carter, who'd left the house for work and was already in his meeting. "Emily isn't answering her phone."

Catherine heard him excuse himself and leave the room. "She probably woke up late at a friend's house." He was still on that line of reasoning. "Have you called the school?"

"Yes, she hasn't arrived."

"Did you try that girl who was having the party? Nancy?"

"Natalie," Catherine corrected. "Not yet, but you know Emily has never been a light sleeper. Can you track her phone? You're faster at that stuff than I am."

"Sure." A couple of minutes later he called back, his words more urgent now. "It says her phone is out on East Beach. I'm heading that way now, but go ahead and call the police station and ask for Whitey—Chief Whiteside. He knows me. Tell him to meet me out there. Just in case."

In case of what? "Should I come? I can bring Lucy and Olivia."

"No. Not yet. Let me get out to the location and talk to Whitey. Stay put in case she comes home." Carter stopped for a moment, his breath ragged over the line. "I'm sure there's an explanation. She's a teenager, right?"

Catherine couldn't respond. Yes, Emily was a teenager, but until this year she hadn't ever really behaved like one. Even then, Emily's frustration at the move and her occasional moodiness upon arrival had been the worst of it.

While her husband looked for Emily, Catherine put on a movie in the living room for Lucy and Olivia, who weren't recovered enough to go back to class yet, as if nothing was wrong. In the kitchen, she turned on Rachmaninoff and began chopping ingredients for the girls' soup later that day, but she couldn't even finish a carrot.

She found Natalie's number in the school directory and called that first. The sleepy voice that answered gave Catherine a rush of hope. Another kid who had missed school. "She's not here," the girl mumbled. "Left around midnight, I think?" Catherine swallowed past the lump lodged in her throat. At least it prevented her from screaming.

"Are either of your parents home, Natalie?"

The girl cleared her throat, obviously attempting to sound more awake and mature. "Dad's at work and Mom's probably at the gym. You can try calling her, but she usually doesn't have good reception."

Catherine pushed back her shoulders and took a deep breath. This was all she had to work with for now. "Did anyone else spend the night there last night?"

"Yeah, I mean, a couple of people. Anna, but she left early to go to some church thing, and Celeste is still here asleep. I'm sure Emily left around the same time as the guys—right after the movie." The girl paused a moment as if waiting for her to respond, but Catherine didn't have words. "Mrs. Callahan, is everything all right?" The girl's voice sounded suddenly awake. "We weren't doing anything bad, I swear. We watched a movie. Emily even made us study first."

"Yes, yes, it's fine. I'm sure she's out for a run," Catherine lied, badly. "Last night did Emily happen to leave with anyone?"

"I mean, she went out the door with Alex, but I assume that she drove herself home."

Alex? Morgan's Alex? Catherine inhaled. "One more question, Natalie. Can you give me a quick rundown of everyone who was at your house last night?"

The girl hesitated. "Yeah, I guess. It was me and Celeste and Anna, and then the guys were Alex, Kyle, Luke and Jordan."

Catherine turned on her professor voice. She could not end this phone call sounding frantic or the news of a missing girl would be all over the island within the hour. "Thank you, Natalie."

Catherine hung up, looked through the senior class list, and called the mother of each kid that Natalie had mentioned, except for Anna. Catherine didn't feel like explaining to Leslie why she'd missed last night's party, and anyway, Leslie was probably still at church. Hadn't her husband been a chaplain or something years ago? Three of the parents didn't answer, and the others hadn't heard anything out of the usual from their kids. This wasn't some raucous party at least, she reassured herself.

Catherine found Emily's laptop and got the password correct on the first try: Momwant$mypassw0rd. She couldn't help but smile when she read that one. They'd always required an open-electronics policy, so they could check anything at any time. She hadn't used this one in years, had no reason to, but Emily had kept the old password.

She combed through text messages that came through to Emily's computer: a couple texts were from old friends back in Woodhaven, the kids who'd grown up spending almost as much time in the Callahan house as their own. Megan, Alicia, Carmen. She went ahead and texted them from her daughter's phone. Hey, this is Mrs. Callahan. I'm looking for Emily—have any of you heard from her in the past couple of days?

With the time difference they didn't answer for another hour, but when they did, they knew nothing. Sorry, Mrs. Callahan. Hope everything's okay. The last time they'd heard from Emily had been three days earlier on a group chat about Megan's college decision. Nothing out of the ordinary as far as Catherine could tell.

As Catherine tapped her fingertips against the kitchen table, Carter called. She answered on the first ring. "Did you find her?"

"Her phone was in her car," Carter said.

Catherine released the breath she'd been holding. "Thank God. Where is she?"

Silence hung over the line for a moment. "We still don't know. Her car looked like it'd been abandoned. Her phone was inside."

Catherine swallowed. "What does that mean, Carter?"

"We don't know anything really," he answered stoically.

"Don't panic. Not yet, okay? I'll talk to Whitey, make sure they're getting fingerprints and doing whatever else they need to do. I'll call you as soon as I know anything. Just stay there in case she comes home."

"Okay," Catherine forced herself to say, choking back tears she refused to cry. Emily could walk in at any moment. She could.

"I love you," Carter said.

"Yeah. Love you," Catherine muttered, hanging up and turning back to Emily's computer. This device contained the only clues she had right now.

She checked social media, which Emily didn't visit often, but maybe there would be a clue. TikTok. Twitter. Instagram. Nothing since yesterday when she'd taken a couple of pictures: the first a close-up of a minnow darting in the surf, and the second, the sunset over East Beach, the caption reading "Light it Up." In the bottom corner of the snapshot was a boy in the distance. She squinted. It was Alex Frasier.

Catherine took a deep breath and called Morgan. She needed to know what Morgan knew.

She answered on the second ring. "Hello?"

"Hey, it's me." Catherine struggled to keep her tone light. "I was wondering if Alex saw Emily leave the party last night? Or if he was with her?"

"Oh, um. He's in his room, still sleeping. Let me check."

The sound was muddled for a minute until Catherine heard the deep tones of a teenage boy's mostly monosyllabic answers. Then, a series of unintelligible words.

Morgan was back. "Catherine?"

"Yeah, I'm here."

"He said that they left Natalie's house at the same time last night. Emily told him she wasn't feeling good, but would text him later. She'd taken her own car, and he was parked behind her, so he left first… Wait a second, he's going to check his phone to see if she's texted."

Catherine waited, walking the ten steps it took to move back and forth across the kitchen again and again. She was about to jump out of her skin when Morgan finally spoke. "He doesn't have anything from her, but he's going to text her right now and tell her to call you."

Catherine knew her husband would receive that message, since he now had their daughter's phone in hand. She took a deep breath and spoke, each word deliberate. "Are you sure Alex is telling you everything he knows?"

Silence. Then, "What do you mean?"

"You know what I mean, Morgan. With those accusations a few years ago, I can't help but think that he may…know more than he's saying."

Morgan spoke forcefully this time, a Mama-Bear tone leaping into her voice. Each word was clipped. "He told you what he knows. He's not lying."

"This is my daughter, for Christ's sake," Catherine said, her voice rising.

"I'm sorry," Morgan tried, "but I know he wouldn't do anything to—"

Catherine hung up before she could finish. Briefly, she considered driving to Morgan's house, pulling Alex out of bed, and demanding answers. In the same breath, Catherine told herself that she had no reason *not* to believe Alex, no reason except that he may have already hurt another girl years ago.

She decided to try Leslie next, damn the embarrassment of missing the party. But the call went to voice mail twice. Catherine pressed her fingertips into the keypad one after another as if striking keys on a piano. Fuck. She needed answers. She needed to breathe. She needed to think. Now.

Catherine and Carter had always agreed that in times of

crisis, they would call his mother only as a last resort. This, she realized, was one of those times. Catherine inhaled and counted to five. Perhaps Emily had contacted her grandmother. Maybe she and Rosalyn had planned a secret brunch after the Ash Wednesday service? She knew she was grasping at straws, but no longer cared. She had to make the call.

"Hi, Rosalyn, I was calling to see if you've heard from Emily this morning?"

"Why? What's wrong?" Rosalyn's pitch had already risen an octave from its normal resting place.

"Nothing, Rosalyn." It wasn't nothing, and Rosalyn was family after all. For better or worse. "Actually, she didn't come home this morning—well, last night—so we've been trying to get in touch with her. Carter used the 'Find my Phone' app and tracked it to the farthest end of East Beach."

Saying these words out loud made her voice catch. Catherine bit her tongue to keep from crying. She would not get emotional, not while speaking to Rosalyn, but the alarms were roaring in her head. Her sweet Emily, her girl who still liked *Momma* to scratch her back while she told her about her day, her intelligent girl who hadn't needed reminding about homework since third grade, her beautiful girl who didn't notice heads turning because she was too busy studying the natural world around her. This girl would not act so irresponsibly. Something was wrong. Catherine buried the phone against her chest, so Rosalyn couldn't hear the tiny cries escaping. Breathe. Breathe. Breathe.

As Catherine attempted to steady herself, a memory rushed back, something Emily had said to her the first day they'd arrived in Galveston, the two of them leaning against the railing of the front porch, looking down the street into the heart of the Silk Stockings District at homes that had survived the destruction of the 1900 Storm. Emily suddenly looked up. "The sky feels too open, Mom."

"What do you mean?"

"I don't know." Emily had looked around. "I think it's because there are no mountains to break up the horizon."

"Don't say that to your father," Catherine teased. "Apparently the wide-open sky is a *thing* to Texans." She wouldn't know. She'd grown up in Oregon and had loved Portland and Woodhaven and all the other surrounding northwestern towns. The mountains anchored her.

"There's all this water." Emily crinkled her nose. *"Water, water, everywhere, Nor any drop to drink,"* she recited from some poem she'd memorized in middle school.

"I think that's supposed to be a feature of any island. Lots of people love this place. In fact, I read that even though only 60,000 people live here, there are about 200,000 people on the island on any given day. More in the summer." Catherine couldn't believe she was trying to talk this place up.

"I don't get it." Emily looked straight up. "Don't you feel like you might… I don't know, get swallowed by the sky?"

"More like carried away by the undertow." Catherine moved on to more practical matters, leaving her daughter's philosophizing behind. "I know you don't like to swim, but you and Lucy and Olivia know not to go out onto the beach without a buddy, even though you'll be eighteen in a few months, right?"

"Yes, Mother." Emily rolled her eyes and put on her singsong voice.

Catherine swatted playfully at her daughter before grabbing her into a full-on hug.

"M-o-o-o-o-m!"

"What? You're my kid, so I get as many hugs as I want. That's why I birthed you."

Emily laughed and struggled to free herself before planting a light kiss on her mom's cheek. "I'm going to unpack my room." It was the first time she'd laughed, really laughed, in weeks.

Before she turned to go, Catherine had taken Emily's face in her hands. "You know your dad and I love you?"

Emily nodded, her expression turning serious, darkening.

"And you know that we thought it was best for our entire family to come here? That we didn't make the decision rashly?" Emily nodded again, but Catherine could tell her daughter was thinking so much that she wouldn't let herself say. She was too busy trying to be a good kid. For God, for her parents, for her own conscience. Sometimes Catherine wished Emily would just go ahead and lose it.

"Oh, my God!" Rosalyn screeched now, and Catherine pulled the phone away from her ear.

"Rosalyn, you haven't heard from Emily, have you?"

"No, but I'll call Whitey and demand he get a search party together immediately."

Catherine almost appreciated her mother-in-law's commanding personality in that moment. "Call Carter first. Chief Whiteside was meeting him out on East Beach." She would let Carter deal with his mother, as she always had.

"Yes, dear. I'll take care of everything."

Catherine hung up and tossed the phone across the room. She heard Olivia's weak voice. "You okay in there, Mommy?"

Catherine sank to the floor. She was not okay and might never be okay again. The tears came fast and ferociously. She couldn't stop their thunder, her chest heaving as if it were turning itself inside out. Moments later, two pairs of hands were on her face, her neck, her hair.

What's wrong?

It's okay, Mommy.

Are you sick now too?

Where's Daddy? You want me to call him?

The touch of her younger daughters brought her back to herself. She wiped her nose and her eyes on her forearm and swallowed the remaining cries. She would pull herself together for her girls, and as she waited, she would turn on all the lights in the house and will Carter to bring their daughter home.

PART II: THE SEARCHING

"There is a time for everything, and a season for every activity under the heavens:
...a time to search and a time to give up...a time to be silent and a time to speak."

—*Ecclesiastes 3*

12
February
Morgan

The call from Catherine had rattled Morgan, resurfacing all of the old doubts and anxieties from the past. After she put down the phone, Morgan stood unmoving for several seconds. Then, she forced her son out of bed. It wasn't that she was concerned about him missing school—most Callahan Prep kids missed the first couple of classes on Ash Wednesday, either for religious purposes or because of the revelries of the previous evening. No, she wanted him out, so she could search for any indication that he might be involved in Emily's disappearance. She needed to reassure herself.

"Time for school," she said, throwing clean clothes on top of Alex.

"Did Emily call her mom?" he asked, his voice gruff with sleep.

Morgan ignored the question. "Come on, out the door."

Alex threw her a look, but she knew he would do what she said.

A half hour later, the conundrum lay in how to look through her son's room without disrupting the ordered chaos he had created: balled-up socks and boxers in one corner, school papers and books scattered across his simple desk, a pile of cereal bowls on his bedside table. Alex had always been the kid who knew if you touched his stuff. *Did you eat one of my chips?* he would ask his father, peering with one eye closed into the full bag of Lay's. *Did the maid wash my lucky socks?* he would ask his mother, who had indeed asked the maid to launder them but had also instructed her to leave them out in the humid air to slow dry, so they would retain a slight stench. Somehow Alex always knew, and for this reason, she kept her hands tucked at her sides as she scanned his room. A prick of guilt poked at her, but this was what parents did. At least *good* parents.

She started at the most obvious place: his iPad, leaving the tablet in place and tapping potential passwords into the screen. He'd changed it again, as he did every month or so. *Dammit*, she muttered, her thumb going to her lips, her thinking stance. She eyed his desk, but all she saw were half-finished assignments and an outline for some paper about Iago's homosexual undertones in *Othello*. Well, then.

Lifting the corner of the mattress only a few inches, she found a T-shirt that had been compressed into a blob of starchy cotton, and rifling through his closet, she spotted a small bag of pot. Her hands grew clammy as she held the bag, and she swallowed back the fear that lodged in her throat. This was how it started; he was her mother all over again. No, she couldn't think about that now. She shoved the weed deep in her pocket. She would dispose of it properly—down the toilet—later.

Her final chance at inside information was the built-in

bookshelf. She used a finger to pull back each book—most of them old school texts or important novels she hoped he would someday read—one at a time until she came across a leather-bound journal. Morgan removed it, mentally marking its place on the shelf. The first few pages were filled with Alex's distinctive handwriting, all capital letters so small and leaning that they didn't shout. His teachers had attempted to break him of this antiquated capitalization back in second grade.

"He's quite capable of correcting the issue, if only he would apply himself," Mrs. Cleary had informed her at the parent-teacher conference.

When Morgan had asked Alex why he persisted in this vein, he had a quick answer. "Isn't every letter just as important as the other?"

"Yes, but sometimes we have to make the people who matter happy. Mrs. Cleary is the person who matters right now, got it?"

He had refused to conform.

Morgan opened to a section where he'd tucked loose-leaf pages, the edges sticking out so that she could only read a word or two, so tantalizing in their obscurity. Fine, she would just skim them. Her eyes scanned the pages. Several lines were punctuated incorrectly, and the language was raw and unfiltered:

I HAVEN'T EVER FELT THIS WAY ABOUT ANY GIRL… I HOPE WE GET TO BE ALONE TOGETHER TONIGHT… WHEN I THINK ABOUT HOLDING YOU MY HANDS WON'T STOP SHAKING… I HAVE SOMETHING TO TELL YOU BUT I WANT TO WAIT UNTIL THE RIGHT TIME… SOMETIMES I THINK I CAN TASTE YOU EVEN WHEN WE ARE APART.

Morgan's throat constricted. They were all addressed to Emily, and the further she read, the more unnerved she became.

*I DON'T KNOW HOW TO TELL YOU HOW I FEEL,
SO I FOUND THIS POEM. HIS NAME IS e.e. cummings—
HE WRITES IT JUST LIKE THAT. THE OPPOSITE OF
ME—HA! HERE IT IS:*

> *"i like my body when it is with your*
> *body. It is so quite new a thing.*
> *Muscles better and nerves more.*
> *i like your body. i like what it does,*
> *i like its hows. i like to feel the spine*
> *of your body and its bones,and the trembling*
> *-firm-smooth ness and which i will*
> *again and again and again*
> *kiss, i like kissing this and that of you,*
> *i like, slowly stroking the…"*

Oh, God. She might throw up. Morgan put a hand over her mouth and swallowed several times, attempting to keep her stomach at bay and dislodge the images. Finally, she threw down the missives, wishing she could shake away the words as easily. A mother should not read such words penned by her own son. But her son should not be penning them, right? Were these love letters to Emily Callahan? Or something darker?

First the weed. Now…this? Each of these alone would be enough to keep Alex from graduating, especially with the way Rosalyn Callahan ran things. No one could know. Morgan would protect her son from himself, whatever the costs.

She looked down at the pages scattered on the floor for several moments, no longer caring if she didn't place them back in exactly the right spot. She and Alex were beyond such things at this point.

EMILY

Without meaning to, I made an enemy as soon as I arrived at Callahan Prep, maybe as soon as I stepped foot on the island. I didn't know this until the day students were voting for homecoming queen and somehow my name appeared on the ballot. Let me assure you that a homecoming nomination would never have been on my radar back in Woodhaven. There, I was the smart, quirky kid who might have been nominated for Most Likely to Succeed but never for any popularity title.

The afternoon of the vote, I went to my locker and found a note.

To: Emily Callahan
This isn't your school regardless of your name.
Go back home.

I wasn't scared, but I was intrigued and frustrated. I thought the unwanted attention I'd garnered on first arriving was waning. Apparently not. I folded it and stuck it in my backpack. I would think about it later.

By that point Alex and I were hanging out most weeknights at the stone-walled library on Broadway. This was probably my favorite place on the island, besides the surf where I could explore sea creatures. I loved getting lost in the stacks, the thousands of books, some of which hadn't been checked out since the 1950s. The Reading Room was open to anyone who wanted to research the island and its artifacts and only required an appointment to wear the white gloves and comb through original photos taken in the aftermath of the 1900 storm, lists of refugees who had fled from Poland to Galveston in the late nineteenth century, and political ephemera labeled with my family's name. The Callahans were never mayors or city council members, but somehow we were always endorsing the winning candidates.

I showed the note from my locker to Alex that evening at the library. "Any idea who this could be from?"

He read the few words. "I don't know, but if I had to guess I'd say it's probably Anna Steele. She'd be the one person not crazy about the fact that you got nominated for homecoming queen and could actually beat her."

"That's ridiculous. No one here even knows me."

"Yeah, but your name is kind of on the building."

"So?"

"Who your family is means a lot in a place like this."

"Even with the students?"

He shrugged. "Not as much, but yeah. It still matters." He gave me a lopsided grin and held up his hand with his finger and thumb a few inches apart. "Besides, you're a little cute, kind of sweet and pretty hilarious. I might vote for you."

"Don't you dare." I rolled my eyes, but really, I liked the compliment. Alex was the first boy to say those kinds of things to me, the first boy I wanted to say those kinds of things to me, and the way he looked at me made me think they might be true. At least to him.

"For real, though, me and Anna kind of had a thing this past summer, so that could also be part of the problem."

My heart skipped. I hated the way I couldn't keep my body from responding to him, sometimes blushing and stuttering against my will; other times, my stomach flipping and my hands growing clammy. These physical reactions went against all of the ways I wanted to respond—with a cool logic, an even steadiness, the way I approached every other area of life. Alex defied my logic.

"You had a thing?" I tried to sound unconcerned.

"Yeah, it only lasted a few weeks. I was working as a life-guard at The Monterey, and she was there a lot with her friends. Got a job there eventually. We started hanging out after work, but when school started, we went back to normal life and I met you and…whatever. It fizzled out. We're still friends, there was no big explosion or anything."

"Are you sure Anna knew that whatever it was ended?"

"Yeah. I mean, she hangs out with the preppy kids, and I'm more of a jock anyway. I think she's talking with Stewart now. He's one of those rich nerds."

I punched Alex lightly on the arm. "Isn't Callahan Prep filled with rich nerds?"

"Yeah, I guess, but you know, Stewart is one of those rich nerds who keeps track of his parents' net worth and the stock market. That kind of thing."

We left the conversation there while I dove headfirst into the study of the endocrine system and he tried to rewrite Hamlet's soliloquy into modern English. I didn't think about the note again until I received the next one months later, in the same handwriting, warning me to keep away from Alex.

That one, I pored over in my attic nook before I finally tore it up in frustration, never telling anyone else about this unknown person who wanted me gone.

13

February

Leslie

Leslie received the call from the wife of Chief Whiteside an hour or so after the Ash Wednesday service. Though Whitey had been an anemic, spineless boy for most of his life, his father and grandfather were the police chiefs before him. In this town, those credentials were enough.

"Emily Callahan is missing." The voice squealed at having a scoop to tell the nearly all-knowing Leslie Steele.

"Missing?" Leslie froze. "What do you mean?"

"Emily didn't come home last night after some get-together, and she hasn't been seen since midnight," Whitey's wife clucked in a Louisiana cadence. She wasn't from around here, but didn't know—or didn't care—that she really shouldn't be the one to call Leslie with this news. "Though why it took her parents until this morning to figure that out, I will never understand. Emily's daddy went looking for her and found the girl's car in the surf at the farthest point out on East Beach.

Her wallet, backpack, cell phone—all inside. The doors were locked and her keys gone."

Though the voice didn't say so, Leslie could hear the undercurrent of universal judgment. Some people weren't meant to be parents.

She felt a jolt of guilt at a memory: years ago Leslie had been ushering her own kids, then six-year-old twin boys and three-year-old daughter, out of the pool at The Monterey when an acquaintance had stopped to talk. It had been one minute, maybe two—a simple "Hello! We're so glad Michael took the job at the school. Isn't that so sweet of him to want to be chaplain?"—but when she turned to gather the kids, one of them was missing. Sawyer had plunged silently beneath the pool, the surface still and calm as if hiding precious treasure. *Nothing here to see*, the water breathed.

Leslie dove in, designer swimsuit and all, leaving Asher and Anna to watch on the sidelines. When she pulled her son from the water, still clutching the toy he'd gone in after, Sawyer coughed and sputtered. While Leslie did her best to hold back sobs, onlookers gathered around, whispering their disapproval at her mothering. Fifteen years later, Leslie remembered that feeling of a child missing, a child almost lost forever. She clutched at her chest now and reminded herself that all of her children were well. They were fine. Fine.

"Are you there, Leslie?"

"Oh, yes. I was thinking about that poor girl and her parents," she fibbed. Then an idea came to mind. "Anna and I can help coordinate a search effort." Leslie had no idea how to coordinate a search, but it couldn't be that different from party planning, right?

"I knew you would say that. Rosalyn called Whitey earlier, and I told him, I said, *Leslie will be on it!* He's expecting to hear from you."

Leslie had sat on the pew behind Rosalyn just that morning at service, both of them receiving their ashes with the priest's intonation—*You are dust and to dust you shall return*—both oblivious as to what this day actually held.

This time, Leslie would come to Rosalyn's rescue.

Leslie found Anna in her room; she'd decided to stay home from school after the service. She had a cold and wanted to catch up on a research paper, so she was hunched over a mound of textbooks, a cup of coffee on the desk beside her.

"Hey, anything interesting happening at school today?" Leslie wanted to see how much information was already out there.

Anna narrowed her eyes. Leslie knew that look, the one that wondered why her mom was being weird. "I don't know. Obviously I'm not there. Why?"

"You know Emily Callahan?"

Leslie caught Anna rolling her eyes. "You know I know Emily. She's the one who might beat me out for valedictorian, remember?"

Leslie didn't acknowledge the comment, though, yes, she was very aware. "They found her car out on East Beach."

"So? She's probably out bird-watching or whatever it is she does. A lot of kids don't usually go to school the day after Mardi Gras."

"What I mean is that they found her car with all of her stuff inside, and they think she's missing."

"Missing?" Anna stared, incomprehension etching her brow. "Where would she go?"

"I don't know, but I'm about to call Whitey. She was at the party you went to last night, right? The one Alex invited you to."

"Yeah, but she left around midnight, and I slept over at

Natalie's. I had Asher bring me clothes because I didn't want to drive home."

Leslie knew why her daughter didn't want to drive, but that would remain an unspoken acknowledgment between them. Every high schooler drank sometimes.

"I thought Emily was going straight home, but she and Alex did leave at the same time. Maybe she was doing something out on East Beach." Anna raised her eyebrows. "Or someone."

"Anna Steele, really," Leslie reprimanded. Anna shouldn't say such things even if she was thinking them. Even if everyone was thinking them. Leslie pushed forward. "Hey, have you seen your brother today?"

"Wasn't he going to leave at, like, 5:00 a.m. to get back for some class he couldn't miss? You said he just came home for the party."

"Oh, yes, that's right." Leslie placed a hand to her forehead. "Well, I'm glad he was available to bring you what you needed."

Anna glanced from her mother to her books and back again, obviously wondering if this conversation was finished. Leslie knew her daughter needed to get some research done, but she also knew that their family needed to coordinate a search and rescue.

"I've got to go to The Monterey," Leslie said. "We're going to work on putting together some search parties, be the hands and feet for whatever Whitey needs us to do. You'll need to make an appearance."

"Why don't they trace her phone?" Her daughter had not listened well.

"I told you. Everything was inside the car."

"Aren't there any tracks in the sand?"

"I don't know, Anna." Leslie sighed. "I assume that the tide washed up around the tires."

"That's so weird."

"Right now we all need to be good citizens and help out the Callahans."

"Fine." She closed the book in front of her. "What do I need to do?" That was her Anna. Leslie knew her daughter would come around if she understood the severity of the situation.

"Let your entire class know that we're meeting at The Monterey right after school. Tell them to bring flashlights and wear solid shoes." Leslie was going by what she'd seen on television, but that sounded right. "I'll call Gaido's and ask them to bring a variety of tacos for... I don't know, what do you think? A hundred people?"

She hadn't seen that part on TV, but she wasn't one to issue an invitation without providing something to eat.

Anna pulled out her phone. "Maybe 150 to be safe? That covers half the senior class plus a bunch of parents."

This might be a bigger shindig than Leslie's party last night. Leave it to the Callahans to upstage her.

"Thanks for pulling all this together," Carter said, frowning, as soon as Leslie approached him at The Monterey. His wide eyes wandered to the news crews setting up in the ballroom while his right hand tapped restlessly at his side. He was a bundle of contradictory emotions. Impatience and frustration, gratitude and concern oozed from him. And something else. Leslie narrowed her gaze. Guilt? Her heart beat faster as she watched him pace.

But of course Carter would feel guilty. What parent wouldn't after failing the number one parental requirement: keep your kid safe? It was what Leslie lived for, the air she breathed, the water she swam in. A rush of sympathy washed over her. Carter—someone she'd known forever—was suddenly living every parent's nightmare. It could just as easily have been her.

Chief Whiteside waved to Leslie from across the room. He looked so official in his pressed uniform compared to the Whitey she'd known almost her entire life. A younger female officer circled him, listening to him talk on the phone.

"I'm finally putting my efforts to good use," Leslie told Carter with a self-deprecating grin. Even though they'd never been particularly close, she remembered his face at all of the important moments in her school years. She also remembered how Rosalyn Callahan had often thrown her and Carter's brother, Andrew, together at parties or to plan school events. How strange that this man could've been her brother-in-law instead of Robert. "We couldn't sit by and simply wait for…" Leslie didn't know how to finish the sentence. For Emily to walk in the front door? For her body to wash up?

Carter attempted a smile, but it came across more like a grimace. "Catherine's at home with Lucy and Olivia. We're trying to wait to tell them that Emily is missing. Hopefully, she'll be back soon, and we can forget all of this." He heaved a sigh and then motioned absently to the cameras and the microphones. "They made fast work, didn't they?" He lowered his voice as he cursed. "Damn media."

"Yeah." Leslie spotted a few reporters she knew, but most of them were strangers from off island. There was nothing cable news loved more than a pretty missing girl. Leslie gulped back the lump in her throat. "It could help us find her faster," she offered.

"I guess it's one of the *perks* of being a Callahan," he mumbled, running his hand through his hair. Poor man. He needed a strong cup of coffee.

Leslie handed him a large map of the island to help her stretch out on a table as Whitey sauntered over.

"Leslie, good to see you. Looks like you came prepared."

"I've marked and numbered all of the entryways onto East Beach on photocopied maps, and I have Philip's Hardware delivering extra flashlights and batteries. I figured you could point out the exact location of the car and indicate the best places to search."

Whitey glanced over at Carter, already apologizing for what came next. "The next twenty-four hours is crucial to finding Emily, so as many feet as we can get walking the area, the better. We already have boats combing the water."

Leslie was glad Whitey hadn't said *dredging the water*; it would've sounded so final.

"When a good crowd gathers, I'll speak to the volunteers, tell them to look for tracks and to kick away the sand in any… any mounds, any dunes. Thirty of my officers will be out there, close enough to hear a call should anyone find anything. I've notified the coast guard as well. They'll be searching by sea and then join us tomorrow on land if we haven't made enough progress. Catherine is at the house in case Emily comes home?"

Carter nodded, but his eyes were empty.

As the men looked like they were about to disperse, Leslie leaned forward. "I called Rosalyn on the way here," she said in a low voice so reporters wouldn't overhear. "She doesn't want any press conferences right now. I'm sure she knows best."

"She said as much to me, too, never been one to want the media involved," Whitey added knowingly. He looked to Carter, as if for permission.

Carter nodded stoically.

"All right, then. I'll await word from her before we make any announcements," Whitey said in a more official tone. "We'll convene in a few minutes and start sending people out in groups of three, but I don't want anyone wading into the water after dark. We don't want to lose someone else."

Lose someone else, Leslie repeated to herself.

The words would play on a loop inside her mind for the next few hours. *Lose someone else. Lose someone else.* She'd already lost several people in her life—one way or another—Michael, Morgan, Sawyer and now Emily Callahan. She, they, this town could not afford to lose someone else.

Leslie had the urge to call Asher and Sawyer, to make them come home from wherever they were, whatever they were doing. She wanted all of her children under her roof tonight. She wanted to feel like she could protect them from the world, even if it was only a false sense of security. A lie.

14
February
Catherine

Nine years earlier when Catherine was bulging with two new lives instead of one, she began sleeping in short increments, one or two hours at a time. Because of her new sleep patterns, she also began remembering her dreams. Her most recurring one she referred to as *the marble dream*. She even wrote a short piano piece, dissonant and jumbled, with this same title. *I dreamt about the marbles again*, she would tell a yawning Carter, who understood exactly what this meant. In her dream, Catherine delivered not one, not two, but three healthy girls. She adored her trio with their tiny pinpricks of blue eyes and porcelain hands and feet. There was only one problem: they were all the size of tiny glass balls, and as such, she kept misplacing them. Once, the marble babies slipped beneath the crack in the seat as she tried to buckle them into the car; another time, they fell into the strings of her piano, trapped and crying for help. Though the dream sounded silly years later, at the time she would wake in a cold sweat, terrified at the thought of losing one of her babies.

Lucy and Olivia had recovered from the stomach flu, and she wanted so badly to take them out to search for their sister, but it had been less than a day and she hadn't yet told the girls the truth. Even after the two of them found her weeping on the kitchen floor, she simply said she wasn't feeling well. While they assumed that their older sister was at school, Catherine tried to envision the moment that Emily would walk through the door.

"I got lost," Emily would say, even though such a thing was not possible on this gridded island. Or perhaps, "I was running away, back to Woodhaven." Catherine would take that. At this point, she would take anything if it meant her daughter was back home.

While the twins ate dinner—sourdough bread coated in butter and a bowl of vegetable soup—in front of another kids' show, Catherine sat at the kitchen table, watching the news on her phone. She found herself gazing into the dark surf only a few miles from where she sat. As people searched for her girl, she listened to the reporter repeat Emily's name again and again on live television.

"Teams of three and four are scouring the beaches out here tonight, searching for signs of Emily Callahan," the reporter said, the camera panning the shoreline. She could see the lights from the boats far out on the water. "It has been reported by an unnamed source familiar with the investigation that police have found no usable fingerprints inside the car. We've also been told that any footprints would have been washed away by the early morning tide. The good news is that there appears to be no sign of struggle or foul play."

Was that good news? Wouldn't it be better to have some sign that her daughter had tried to escape, not simply walked into the endless void of the sea? Catherine no longer knew what would be best. She squeezed her eyes shut, trying to imagine what Emily must have been thinking last night after that party.

I'll go for a run. No, she would never be so irresponsible.

Or maybe, *I'm too wasted to go home.* Maybe she'd been drinking and felt embarrassed to face her parents with their high expectations?

Catherine tried to imagine Emily drinking to excess, but couldn't envision her daughter in such a state.

Maybe Emily's thinking was more along the lines of, *I'll meet up with him and then head home?* Oh, God. This was Catherine's great fear. What if Emily had been out with a boy? What if that boy had harmed her? What if that boy was her friend's son? *Alex Frasier.* Catherine tasted bile every time she thought about him with Emily, the two of them. Together.

Morgan had texted her several times, but each word only made Catherine more suspicious, angrier.

M: Alex and I are going to The Monterey to join the search.

M: He asked to go as soon as he got home from school.

M: He said he won't rest until he finds her.

The words were only a plea of innocence, one that Catherine couldn't buy. She didn't reply.

Catherine's phone rang. It was a Woodhaven area code. She'd deleted all of her contacts since the move, but she thought she recognized the number.

"What the hell is happening, Catherine? Are you all right?" It was Ali, her writing and composing partner for so many years.

"No, of course not," Catherine cried. "I'm a complete mess."

"Emily's missing?" Ali's normally calm voice was shrill.

"Yes."

A sharp intake of breath. "And you didn't tell me? No phone call? No text?"

"I hoped she would come home before news got out. How did you hear?"

"Facebook. There's apparently a Find Emily Campaign already going strong." Ali's voice choked on her tears. "Oh, my God, Catherine. What do you need? I can be there on the next plane tonight."

Catherine couldn't ask this, not even of one of her oldest friends. "There's no need for you to come."

"Like hell there isn't. We've known each other forever, whether or not you'll return my calls. Emily is my goddaughter, and this is way bigger than any issues the two of us have."

Catherine wanted to hang up, wanted to shrink back from this call, but she knew Ali was right.

"What are the police saying? How is Carter holding up? Lucy and Olivia?"

"The twins have had a stomach flu, but are doing better now. I haven't told them what's going on yet. I'm still hoping that this will all end before I have to tell them." It could become the big family secret—that time Emily went missing and no one talked about it. Catherine would take that kind of family dysfunction too. "Carter's out with the search parties, and I'm here at home." Catherine teared up again. "It's so hard sitting here waiting for something to happen…for someone to tell us what they know."

Alex Frasier. The name rustled through Catherine's mind like an unwanted breeze. Her breath caught in her throat as she tried to hold back a sob. "I don't know why, but I feel like I'm the only person who can find her."

"It's the uterus."

A laugh escaped despite herself, and Catherine threw a hand over her mouth. They'd always joked about how for some reason the two of them were the only ones in their families who seemed to be able to find anything. "I guess it's the working uterus," Ali had said one day, and the saying stuck.

"Of course you feel that way. Any mother would." Ali was quiet for several seconds. "Listen, I already texted Carter and got your address, so I'll be there first thing tomorrow."

"No."

A slow exhale. "Why not, Catherine?"

"I know you're in production right now, am I right?"

Silence on the other end.

"Production for the opera we were supposed to be debuting together," Catherine said. "They need you, and your family needs you. I know from past experience that they haven't seen much of you lately, and you can't do anything here that you can't do from there. I want you to stay and finish what we started—what you fixed after my mistake. Just be thinking of us, okay? I promise to call as soon as I know something more."

"Are you sure? I want to be there for you, for Carter and the girls."

Catherine wiped her eyes on her sleeve. "I know, and that means more than you know. Stay for now, though, and I swear I'll call you as soon as I need you here."

Catherine hung up and went to find Lucy and Olivia sleeping on the couch in front of their show, wedged foot to face. She fell to the rug in front of them, pulled a blanket over herself and closed her eyes. She would dream about finding her girl, and when she woke, maybe Emily would be home.

EMILY

Until seventh grade, the creation of the cosmos had all been technical: Big Bang, black holes, evolution, humans. Then, I read the poetry of Genesis: *In the beginning, when the earth was formless and empty, darkness was over the surface of the deep.* This language drew me into something bigger, something beyond the science that I already loved.

Behind the darkness of my closed eyes this verse comes to mind again, and I envision the deep, the Hebrew word *tehóm* signifying confusion, chaos, disturbance. I looked it up one time.

Alex would chuckle when I told him things like that, make some kind of pun, something like, "Girl, that's so deep." I can see him smiling as he says the words in his singsong way with his pursed lips and a slow shake of his head, like he's a '70s hippy come to life to contemplate the surprises of the universe with me.

The first time he did that, I thought he was making fun of me, and I turned away, chewing the side of my lip. I hadn't hung out with boys much back at home, not beyond the ones I'd toddled around with since we were in diapers anyway, and figured maybe most guys—or most people—didn't like being told facts about spider crabs and pelicans and the tide.

"Hey, I'm kidding," he said. I studied Alex, his face mimicking my own, his eyebrows tilting downward. "Really, Emily. I like it when you tell me stuff like that."

"You do?"

He nodded. "Yeah, of course."

But it wasn't an *of course*. Somehow in this new town at this new school—which, unfortunately had my last name plastered everywhere I looked—my new peers didn't seem to appreciate the way I asked questions, the way I gave answers in class. There was always a snicker from the corner or an eye roll from across the room. *Arrogant know-it-all*, a girl in BC Calculus muttered under her breath at me one day. *Teacher's pet*, someone else said when our English teacher handed back papers and had me read mine out loud to the class as an example. I was mortified. I suppose being with the same people from pre-K to eleventh grade in Woodhaven hadn't prepared me for the fact that people at this new school might not understand me. And I might not understand them.

But me and Alex, we somehow understood each other despite how different we seemed, and I liked that. I wanted that. I needed that.

"Hey." After a couple hours, he would peer over the stack of books between us at Rosenberg Library, his eyes without pretense or guile. "I like hanging out with you."

I would feel myself blush. I liked hanging out with him too, but could never say it that directly.

"Thanks," I would mutter instead, and he'd look down

at his book for a few more minutes before he lifted his head again.

"Want to grab a coffee and walk on the beach?"

I would finish reading the page I was on, and he would wait patiently. I couldn't say no to him, didn't want to, so off to the Strand and then down to the water we would go, chattering away until I had to be home. But they weren't one-sided, our conversations. While I told him about biology and climate change, he explained football plays and positions in minute detail.

"Am I boring you?" he would ask sometimes. But he never was. I soaked up everything he said like a sponge, partly because I was so lonely and partly because I'd never met anyone who I wanted to hang out with so much. We were friends, but maybe something more. Maybe something good.

15
Early March
Morgan

According to the FBI, anywhere between thirty and forty-five thousand juveniles went missing in any given month. In the last year of recorded data, October and May were the most likely month for a kid to be taken. Morgan had looked up statistics, had memorized data, but she was already getting tired of digging, tired of thinking. Of course her son wasn't involved in all of this. Emily had simply fallen off the face of the earth or been buried somewhere beneath it. Shit, shit, shit. She couldn't begin to imagine what Catherine must be going through, but being on this side of a missing person was its own kind of hell.

After tromping through the sand for the past five days, Morgan's legs ached, though she would never complain to Robert as he accompanied her home in the wee hours of the morning. Alex had gone to a late dinner with a few friends, the same ones who'd been with Emily the night of her disappearance. Morgan tried not to let it bother her that he could still eat like a horse at a time like this.

"She's got to be out there," Alex had told Morgan earlier that day, clenching his fists as they walked through the heavy sand. "It's my fault, Mom, and I have to find her."

"This is not your fault," Morgan whispered, looking around to make sure no one was in earshot. "Just because you drove away from the party thinking she was right behind you does not place the guilt on you. I don't want to hear you talking that way again."

No, what she wanted was for her son to keep his mouth shut. She wanted to make sure no one thought about the accusations three years earlier. She wanted to keep the police from snooping around his relationship with Emily, which he swore was only friendly even after Morgan confronted him about the letters she had found.

"I didn't give them to her because... I don't know. It was complicated." Alex had averted his eyes, his hand going to the back of his neck, but Morgan pushed until he finally shouted, shutting her down. "It was a stupid crush, but I swear nothing happened! Can you just fucking believe me?"

Morgan had nothing left to say to him after that.

A crush was fine. Normal. The problem was that this had been a crush on a girl who had gone missing. Why couldn't Alex have liked any other girl?

It was late now, and Robert kissed Morgan on the forehead as he walked her to her building. "You want me to come up to your place? Is Alex home?" Robert had been alternating between volunteering at the children's facility, pulling shifts at the hospital and helping with the search. The man did not stop.

"Can I take a rain check? All I want to do right now is sleep until tomorrow afternoon," Morgan said, stifling a yawn.

"Yeah, I could use a good night's sleep too." The look he

gave her was a weary one. "You heard that they canceled school for tomorrow? Leslie was telling me about it."

Morgan nodded. The school had sent out an email saying they wanted kids to have time to visit with the school counselors, psychologists or chaplains without thinking about academics. "I know. That school hasn't closed for anything other than a Category 4 hurricane. I remember wading through a foot of water to get to school more than once as a kid. But Emily is the great-great-granddaughter of the school's founder."

Robert leaned against the stair rail. "You don't think they would do the same for any kid?"

Morgan lifted a shoulder. "Maybe."

Definitely not, she thought. She remembered an assembly in ninth grade in which all students were informed by *the* Rosalyn Callahan that Morgan's math teacher, a tiny woman with kind eyes, had died—they didn't use the word *suicide*—before being dismissed to first period with the platitude to stop by the counselor's office as students had need. Otherwise, business continued as normal with teachers stepping in to cover the dead teacher's classes like clockwork for the remainder of the year.

"How's Alex holding up?"

Morgan skirted the question. "I haven't seen much of him. We've been out searching, but in different directions." Alex would catch up with a few of the guys from the team who were missing school to volunteer for search parties, and the boys would run ahead, eventually fading into the horizon. Just a day at the fucking beach.

Morgan paused, considering how much she should disclose. Robert seemed like someone who wouldn't unjustly accuse her kid, and he'd stuck with her this long despite all the rumors she knew he would've heard. Robert seemed decent, and Morgan was tired of carrying the weight of the questions all on her own.

She approached the subject tentatively, put out feelers for how he might react to a real conversation about her son. "Alex is quieter than normal." *Which isn't hard to be*, she almost added. Instead, she said simply, "I do think he and Emily were...close."

Robert tilted his head. "Yeah?"

She took a deep breath and then her words tumbled out all at once. "He's been hanging out a lot with her this year, which surprised me at first because I expected that Emily would be fairly straitlaced, not the kind of girl he'd like. Plus, I'd heard through the rumor mill that she was destined for Columbia or maybe even Harvard. I love my kid, I really do, but even I realize he's only going to college because somehow he ended up with the genes to play football. He's not dumb, but he doesn't apply himself."

"That's harsh." Robert threw his head back and laughed. "Way to believe in your son." But then he looked at Morgan and changed his expression. "Sorry. I didn't realize you were serious. I haven't heard a parent talk so bluntly about their child—well, not outside of Leslie talking about Sawyer. I apologize. I lose my filter after about twenty hours without sleep."

Morgan bristled at the comparison to Leslie.

"Hey, I'm sorry." Robert leaned in and gave her a long kiss. This man cared for her, she was sure, and more importantly, he wasn't immediately suspecting her son.

She put a hand to his cheek. "Fair enough. Go home and sleep. I'll call you tomorrow and check on you. I heard Whitey say that he's calling off the volunteers in a few hours. It's been five days of searching, and wandering back and forth across the beach isn't accomplishing what he'd hoped it might."

Robert leaned in to kiss her one more time, and Morgan kissed him back, feeling guilty for the thrill she enjoyed at this man's touch, all while Catherine's daughter was still out there somewhere. Missing.

★ ★ ★

The next morning Morgan woke to cabinets and dishes banging. Alex. She emerged from her bedroom, eye mask propped over one eye. "Can I help you find something?"

"I'm looking for a clean bowl." His eyes were dark and deep-set, rings circling them. She knew he hadn't been sleeping well, but it was finally catching up. The sink was piled with dishes because they were down to a maid only once a week. Morgan stomped to the counter and began scrubbing a bowl.

"You know, this isn't difficult. I bet you could've already finished your cereal in the time you took to crash around the kitchen."

Alex glared at her.

"Seriously. Why are you so angry..." she narrowed her eyes at the clock. Morgan knew she must look a sight "...at 7:00 a.m.? You're supposed to be asleep."

"I just got home."

"What?"

"I was out walking East Beach. Looking."

"Alone?" Shit. Was he trying to seem guilty?

He was shamefaced. "Yeah."

Morgan wanted to reprimand him, to tell him that being out at all hours was stupid. Not because it was dangerous; they both knew that a big guy like him could wander almost any-where he wanted, anytime he wanted without threat of bodily harm. No. It was stupid because it was noticeable, could draw the wrong kind of attention. "No news, I assume?"

"No."

Morgan opened the refrigerator. "Sit down. I'll make you eggs and pancakes."

Alex didn't say a word, but he slumped into the chair and laid his head on his folded arms like he had each morning of kindergarten before he'd gotten used to the routine. His hair fell across his face, and Morgan heard him sniffling. She started the griddle and walked over to rub his back. "It's going to be all right, son." She rarely called him "son," but she had the urge to throw her arms around him, rock him back and forth, comfort him like a mother should be able to comfort her boy.

Alex shook her off. "It's not going to be all right. She's dead."

Morgan froze. She felt as if he had thrown her into the wall. She stumbled backward as he raised his hands and looked around at nothing, as if trying to grab words out of the air. "I mean, I don't *know* that she's dead, but don't all those TV shows say that the first twenty-four or thirty-six or forty-eight hours are the time to find a missing person? If you pass that window, it's over. They're most likely gone. Dead."

His eyes widened and his mouth turned down, the tears starting to stream. He was on the edge, but the edge of what, Morgan wasn't sure. He attempted to speak through the mounting gasps and the rushing tears. "Mom, she-she-she was different from the girls here, didn't care about…being the prettiest or…or having everybody like her. We were… we were…"

Though it had been twenty years and counting, Morgan remembered the intensity of first love with Lionel. A real, tactile sort of experience. All-nighters on the phone, each one sharing secrets and silliness and eventually waiting for the other to doze off. This was the bond of youthful relationships that could only be broken by the gravity and problems of adult life.

Morgan attempted to finish the statement for him. "You were close?"

Alex shook his head. "No. We were in love."

"We? Emily was in love?"

He looked at his mom as if surprised by the question. "I mean… I think so. We never said as much, but she understood me, she trusted me, she thought I was smart, she wanted to hang out with *me*, not because I play football, but because she liked *me*. She talked to me like I was her equal instead of some dumb jock."

Morgan wanted to scream, *That doesn't mean she was in love with you, you stupid boy!* But she couldn't bring herself to hurt him that way.

Instead, she tried, "Didn't you tell me that she just wanted to be friends?"

He sat down, heavy in his chair. "I don't know anymore."

Morgan sat with him, patting his back, his shoulder. When his breathing steadied, she rose silently, going through the motions of cooking his breakfast. He finished eating without another word, still teary-eyed, and she forced him to bed, ignoring the acrid odor of his man-boy room. After shutting the door on him, she made herself a cup of strong coffee and finished washing the dishes, keeping her hands busy while her mind circled.

Alex was in love: the boy who wrote love letters that nobody read; the boy who was so big and broad that people automatically suspected him; the boy who could as easily be guilty as innocent.

As the bubbles in the sink melted into suds, Morgan reasoned out the best course of action for herself as his mother. If word got back to the Callahans or the police that Alex had been in love with Emily Callahan, they would definitely suspect him of being involved with her disappearance. For Christ's sake, Catherine already did.

Though she'd never responded to Morgan's texts, they had seen one another at The Monterey on the third morning of the search.

"How are you?" Morgan said the words earnestly. She really did want to know, but feared the question would somehow come across as insincere.

Catherine stared back coolly. "How do you think I am?" There was an iciness in her tone that Morgan had never heard before.

Morgan lowered her voice, glancing around. "I've been saying prayers for Emily while we search."

A corner of Catherine's mouth turned up as she leaned into Morgan's face. Her breath smelled of sleeplessness. "Are you also praying that your son will tell you what he knows? Or that you'll finally be a good mother and make him do the right thing?" Catherine shook her head. "Until then, do not say my daughter's name. Not even in a prayer."

"He knows nothing" was all Morgan could manage. *Dear God, let that be true.*

If the police got involved now, Whitey would ask something like, "Didn't your son have some trouble with a girl a few years ago?" He would narrow his eyes, asking the question as if they both didn't recall details of the charges the Wagner girl had made. The charges, Whitey said at the time, couldn't be proven, but Morgan thought it just as likely that they may not have been investigated fully. Whispers circulated. Some said rape kits sometimes went missing; others, that the girl didn't go to the police soon enough to provide a useful DNA sample. No one except the police knew for sure.

For the first time, Morgan recognized her desire for Emily's return for what it was: utter selfishness. If Emily returned, she would finally be able to set to rest her concerns about Alex's involvement with the Wagner girl three years ago. She would finally have the peace of mind that all mothers deserve when thinking of their children. She would finally know that Alex wasn't a rapist, wasn't a murderer, wasn't a filthy degenerate.

16
Late April
Catherine

"Come to bed, Cat," Carter whispered to her through a haze of dreamlessness.

"Huh?" That one word was all she could manage.

Carter sat on Emily's bed next to his wife's constricted frame. "Come to bed. You've been sleeping at the piano, on the couch, or here since she disappeared. I need you next to me."

It was true. Weeks had passed since their daughter had disappeared, and for some reason Catherine couldn't bring herself to sleep in her own bed, as if she didn't deserve real rest until her daughter was back under her roof, safe and sound.

Catherine smacked her lips. Her throat was parched. She took in her husband, his disheveled hair, his sunken eyes. "How are the girls?" *The two we have left.*

"Sleeping soundly."

Earlier that night they'd finally told the girls that their sister wasn't just missing. Most likely, Emily would not be coming home. Ever.

How Lucy had sobbed and how Olivia had run to her room, crying muffled sounds into her pillow. It seemed, from the comments of well-intentioned people, that the girls had expected Emily to magically reappear at some point. Like when they were babies, one had started crying and then the other.

Carter looked away. After they'd told the girls and lay on the twins' bedroom floor until Lucy and Olivia fell asleep, the two bereft parents had sat on the couch side by side, unmoving. Finally, he'd stretched out his arms, wrapped himself around Catherine, and confessed that he still carried the guilt of being the parent in charge on the night when their daughter hadn't come home. He should've known she hadn't come in, wasn't in her bed asleep. He should've known where she was. Catherine couldn't help but agree.

"I think the worst is passed," Carter finally said. Catherine repeated his words in her mind. The worst is passed; the worst is past. Either way you wrote it, the statement wasn't true. Not by a long shot.

Returning to school after Chief Whiteside gave up the official search had also been difficult for the twins.

"It's good to restore normalcy," Rosalyn had said when she came over to tell Carter and Catherine that it was time for Lucy and Olivia to go back to school.

"There is no normalcy for them, not until their sister comes home," Catherine replied, her jaw clenched. "They aren't ready." It had been only two weeks at the time. Lucy was crying herself to sleep every night at bedtime, and Olivia was wandering into Emily's room at all hours and picking up mementos to hold while she stared aimlessly.

Catherine hadn't been able to look at her mother-in-law, who stood there with her unwrinkled pantsuit and clear complexion. Carter had told her that he'd seen his mother crying, once at her house and once at The Monterey, but Catherine refused to believe it, especially not when Rosalyn was trying to push the twins back into something they clearly weren't ready for.

It was Olivia who had finally shaken Catherine out of her stubbornness. "I do miss Mrs. Hogan," she said quietly, her eyes downcast as if she were ashamed.

Rosalyn had the nerve to send a knowing glance Carter's way.

"You do?" Catherine pulled Olivia in front of her and gently lifted her chin. Olivia nodded, and Lucy came to her knees and leaned against Catherine. "Lucy, do you miss your teacher too?"

Lucy shrugged. Catherine knew that her girls didn't want to upset her. It sickened her to admit that Rosalyn might be right.

Despite Catherine's hidden tears as she dropped them off the next morning and the next and the next, they'd done fairly well. Lucy sometimes wanted to stay inside for recess, and Olivia often visited the nurse with a tummy ache, but otherwise, their grief came in unexpected waves followed by time to play or do homework or cuddle with Mom or Dad. But that had been when there was still hope.

Now, Catherine lay in Emily's room, everything just as it had been on the night she went missing, and rotated her neck back and forth. "I came in here for…for something."

"I know." Carter looked at his feet, his eyes glazed. "You miss her."

"No… I mean, yes, but I was hoping I'd find something. I looked through all of Emily's school stuff again, her nature logs and her boxes, the ones she hadn't unpacked yet. I found some old journals, but nothing recent. You said a few days ago that you emptied her locker at school a while back?"

"The police did, but I was with them. There were textbooks and a couple of notebooks."

"Notebooks? What kind?"

Carter shrugged. "Calculus notes and a blank one."

"Nothing else?"

"No. I'm sorry, babe. I can help you look through her boxes in the morning, but I really need to sleep to think clearly. You do too."

Catherine nodded. He was right, of course. She held his hand and then squeezed. "I'll come soon, okay?"

Resigned, he looked at her one more time before turning from the room.

Catherine couldn't shake the feeling that there was something here in her own home, something that she must be missing.

"Give me something, Emily. Let Momma know where you are. Where else should I look?"

Catherine thought about the many nights that Emily had gone to study at the library or…where else? Where else? Suddenly, she remembered the one other place Emily might've left pieces of herself. The attic.

Most of the boxes up there were storage, but Catherine recalled what Emily had said to her the day after they moved in. She'd been helping Catherine sort boxes: Christmas ornaments in the front for easy access and Catherine's boxes of compositions in the far back corner to collect dust.

Emily had stopped and sat down in the window seat in the eave of the house. She curled up against a giant stuffed monkey sticking out of one of the boxes.

"You look cozy," Catherine had said.

"I forgot all about Mr. Monkey." A rare smile fell across Emily's face.

"He's the perfect size for that nook," Catherine said.

Emily studied the space for a moment. "I would've loved this attic as a kid, the perfect reading spot." Afternoon sunshine streamed through the window as if spotlighting Emily. "Don't tell Lucy and Olivia about it, okay?"

That was understandable. Those two were a force, taking over every room they entered with their toys, books and art supplies. Emily needed her own space. Over the next few months, Catherine would hear Emily shifting around up there from time to time, but she hadn't thought much about it. Until now.

Catherine pulled down the attic steps. She tugged at the cord to light up the dark, dusty space and was surprised to see boxes moved around into a makeshift desk. There were several throw pillows, collections of shells and driftwood, and three scattered cups of half-drunk tea. On the desk were a series of photo booth pictures, taken on the Strand no doubt, of Emily and Alex striking various poses and seeming incredibly comfortable, touching and wrapping arms around one another. There were three books—one by Richard Dawkins, one by Stephen Hawking and one by C.S. Lewis. Oh, her girl, a galaxy of contradictions and complexities.

Glancing around the desk, Catherine's eyes landed on what must have drawn her here: torn paper, wadded up and scattered as if pieces had been thrown without attention to where they landed. Catherine picked them up, unfolded them, and began rearranging them.

He's not what he seems, the words read. *For now, he's sweet and charming, but wait until he turns on you, fucks you and leaves you lonely and sad. Last time, the girl ended up moving away. People said she was pregnant, had to drop out of school, give her baby away. All because she was with him that one night. This will not end well. I'm warning you. Stay away from Alex. Go back home.*

No signature.

Catherine gasped and let out a shriek. Carter came running.

17
Late April
Leslie

"Thank you all for coming on such short notice," Chief Whiteside said to Leslie and Anna along with the other parents and kids assembled at the police station. Leslie glanced at her daughter. Most of the teenagers looked groggy, but not her Anna. Good girl.

"What is this about, Whitey?" Leslie demanded, trying to make him nervous. Everyone knew that Whitey didn't have his father's eagle eye for reading people or his grandfather's way of coaxing the truth out of witnesses. Coming from a family of cops, you'd think he'd be better at this sort of thing.

"We…uh…we were going over some new information and wanted to speak with each of the witnesses about what happened the night Emily Callahan went missing."

"You've interviewed them once already," Leslie said on behalf of those gathered. "I don't think that a few more questions about something that happened more than seven weeks ago is

going to jog their memories." Whitey quailed as Leslie continued, "Should we call our lawyer? Are our kids in danger here?"

He cleared his throat. "Bear with me, okay. No one is on
trial. We're only trying to figure out everything we can to
help the Callahans determine what happened to Emily."

"So, Catherine wants this?" Morgan sounded circumspect.
Weren't she and Catherine friends? And she knew nothing
about this? Leslie frowned and noticed several of the parents
taking out their phones.

Whitey sent a pleading look her way. She knew he didn't
want information getting out right now, didn't want lawyers
swarming his station. He put out both hands in surrender.

"All right, then," Leslie said, standing. "Let's humor him
and put away our phones. For now." She eyed him. "Besides,
we have nothing to hide."

"Thank you, Leslie." He turned to the other parents and
took a deep breath. "We'll have you and your kids out of
here in no time. I promise no one here is a suspect. Does that
sound reasonable?"

A couple of heads nodded, but most of them seemed wary.

Anna spoke up, lifting a hand. Leslie raised her eyebrows
but allowed her daughter to speak. "I don't mind telling you
what happened again, Mr. Whiteside."

Whitey smiled in appreciation and relief. "Thank you,
Anna. Would you mind going with Officer Cortez?" Whitey
turned to the parents once again. "Just a quick conversation."

Without waiting for permission Leslie followed Anna into
the interrogation room, ready to intervene if necessary.

Leslie sat up straight next to her daughter. She figured that
Rosalyn—and maybe even Catherine and Carter—was watching on the other side of the one-way mirror. There was no
way it was legal, but that didn't matter on this island.

Whitey turned his attention to Leslie while Officer Cortez settled into the corner. Leslie could just see the female officer in her periphery. "I'm gonna allow you to stay in here with Anna, but I have to ask you to stay quiet while I ask her questions," Whitey said. His voice almost had authority in it.

"I understand."

"Okay." He turned to Anna and mopped at his brow. "Thank you for helping calm things down out there. Can you go over with me again when you arrived at the party and what you noticed throughout the evening, particularly anything connected to Emily?" He leaned back and rubbed his eyes, a notebook in front of him.

"I got there late because my mom had her Mardi Gras party," Anna started. Next to her, Leslie nodded, but kept quiet. "So, when I got there, Natalie had ordered pizza and the guys were getting ready to watch some awful horror movie, but we convinced them to go with a superhero film instead. Compromise, you know?"

"So, you all watched the movie?" He glanced at Cortez, who remained still, head tilted, watching.

"Well, not *all* of us."

Leslie noticed Cortez shuffle in her seat. This must be new information. Leslie's hands began to sweat as Whitey took the cue.

"What do you mean not *all*?" he asked. "Who was not in the room with you?"

"Kyle said he was going to get something to drink, to turn it up, and would be right back. He came back a half hour later with a keg and a bottle of rum." Anna had yet to look at her mother during this exchange. No wonder. But it might not be a big deal. So there was underage drinking? That wasn't much of a surprise in a tourist town where everything shut down at 6:00 p.m. from October to March.

"We won't be handing out arrest warrants anytime soon," Whitey joked. It fell flat, and he cleared his throat. "Was anyone *not* drinking?"

Please say you, please say you, Leslie thought, even though she already knew the truth.

"Alex didn't drink, I don't think, and Emily only had a cup or two," Anna said.

That was surprising.

"Anything out of the ordinary happen after kids started drinking?"

Anna shifted uncomfortably and looked at the floor.

Leslie couldn't keep herself from stepping in. "Anna? You don't have to answer anything that you—"

Whitey sent her a look, but it was Cortez's hand on Leslie's shoulder that actually silenced her.

Anna continued. "It's just...after we started the movie, some people seemed like they might hook up before the night was over."

Hooking up. Leslie hated that term. Didn't all adults? It could mean anything from meeting up to making out to an actual sexual encounter. She almost missed the days of her parents' cheesy lingo, when they called things by more descriptive names: necking, petting, even first base, second, third.

"Which means?" Whitey leaned forward.

"I don't know... Natalie said she could heat up the hot tub, but no one jumped on that. I did see Alex laying on the couch behind Emily." Anna looked uncomfortable again as if she were a kid tattling. "They were spooning underneath a blanket."

"You think they might've been up to something in front of everyone?"

Leslie tried not to cringe at Whitey's question. Teenagers.

Anna shrugged. "It was just weird."

"Why?"

Leslie raised her eyebrows. Did Whitey seriously need to ask *why*?

Anna scrunched her nose in the way she had as a kid whenever she saw a dead bug. "Would you want someone doing *that* in front of you?"

Of course not.

"And what is *that*?" Whitey asked.

"I don't know. Feeling her up?" Anna stared straight at him. Oh, my. Was her daughter trying to make this grown man blush?

Whitey paused at the description. "I suppose that would be...weird. Did you notice anything else about Emily?"

"Toward the end of the movie, she got up and left the room, and Alex went after her. They were gone for about twenty minutes. Long enough for...you know."

Ah. Leslie really didn't want to piece together what Alex and Emily might have been doing in those twenty minutes. She couldn't even imagine how Rosalyn might be feeling on the other side of the glass, facing something she couldn't control.

"And when they came back, did they seem—" Whitey was grasping for a way to say it. "Did they seem disheveled?"

Anna's eyes darted to Leslie for a moment, and she gave her daughter a subtle nod. "I don't know. I went outside to call my brother to bring me an overnight bag. He was home for Mardi Gras, and I didn't want to drive, you know, after I'd..."

"Been drinking?"

Anna nodded.

"Right," Whitey said. "Did you see Emily leave?"

"Yeah." Anna thought for a moment, furrowing her brow. "Actually, I don't know. I just remember waiting outside for Asher. I guess I wasn't really paying attention, though."

"Why not?"

"I was... I was upset, crying." Leslie was surprised to hear this. Why would her daughter be crying?

Whitey leaned back. "Crying?"

"Yeah, it was silly. For some reason, when I drink, sometimes I get emotional. I'd had a tough day at school—a bad grade on a test." She put out both hands, showing she was hiding nothing. "You know how it is." Leslie knew well how stressed her daughter had seemed this year, but she figured it was normal. Senior year, college applications, all that mess.

Cortez shifted again, and Whitey pressed on. "Did you see Alex leave the party?"

"Yeah, I'm pretty sure about that. He left and then Emily—" Anna squinted as if peering through a haze. "Actually, I think Emily sat in her car for a while. I figured she was texting or something, but it was dark. Asher pulled up, and I grabbed my bag and ran inside."

"Then you did not actually see Emily drive away?"

"Well, no, but I mean, she must've. Her car was parked out on East Beach, right?"

Whitey paused and looked at his notes one more time. "Right. Well, I think that's all."

Leslie let out a sharp breath she hadn't realized she'd been holding.

Anna looked straight at Leslie for the first time. "I'm sorry I was drinking, but I'm totally responsible. I swear. That's why I didn't drive myself home."

Leslie leaned forward and squeezed her daughter's hand. "I know. We can talk about it later."

"Thank you, Anna," Whitey said, motioning toward the door. "And thank you, Leslie, for your support out there."

"Of course, Chief Whiteside," she said, raising an eyebrow to remind him that she knew him first and foremost as Whitey, the boy who couldn't get a girl to go with him to prom. "Of course."

EMILY

Months ago, Alex told me that his friends thought we were sleeping together even though he swore to them that it wasn't like that. Still, they teased him, like they'd teased him about Julie Wagner. He told me all about the accusations the first time he drove me out to East Beach as we were watching the sun set from the flatbed of his truck.

Alex said that three years earlier he heard he was being accused when his friend Kyle texted him. I've been around Kyle a couple of times outside of school, and I'll just say that he doesn't have too much happening beyond partying and girls. *He's a cornerback. Too many concussions*, Alex once joked about him. But to Kyle's credit, those texts ended up being the thing that finally cleared Alex. Legally anyway. Alex keeps a screenshot of the exchange on his phone just in case he ever needs it again, and while we were out at East Beach and he was telling me the whole story, he opened up his screen to show me.

Kyle: heard you got some last night

Alex: What?

Kyle: you fucked that girl. what's her name? julie?

Alex: Wasn't me.

Alex said that he spent a few minutes deciding whether or not to send that last response, but figured he should after his health teacher's *talk* earlier that week.

It's not like it once was, boys, Coach V had told Alex and the other ninth-grade boys. When Alex did his impression of the coach, he paced in front of the flatbed, hunched over and with a banana in his hand. *Guys all over the country are getting accused of crap because a girl has a few drinks at a party… Like they didn't enjoy it. Anyway, if you're gonna do her, make sure she isn't drunk. Oh, and you better wrap it.*

"He did not say that," I protested.

Alex straightened up for a second. "He did. I swear he did. And then he sat down and ate the entire banana in front of us. It was so nasty."

I shuddered. I couldn't even unpack the Freudian nature of that entire exchange.

"I think somebody with money complained to your grandmother, 'cause he was gone a few weeks later. Well, sort of," Alex clarified. "They still let him coach, since the football team was on a winning streak that year."

So that's why Alex texted Kyle, *Wasn't me.* He said he wasn't about to get in trouble for something he didn't do. He'd been at that party, he'd been drinking, and he knew everyone else had too. That included Julie Wagner, but he swore he was never even alone in the same room with her. Next, he showed me screenshots of the police reports that cleared him. I took the phone, zoomed in and read over them. Then I studied him for a moment before turning to watch the red-gray S-curves of the birds against the darkening sky.

"Did you know that the tricolored heron can travel a bunch of different ways? In groups of two, six, twelve, one hundred."

"Wait," Alex said, confused. "Don't you have any questions for me? Anything else you want to know?"

I considered, looking over the surf a few feet away. "You were pretty thorough, and I can already see that you're not that kind of guy," I told him. "I've never been nervous for a second around you. Not once. About anything."

He wiped at his eye. I returned to the herons, so he wouldn't feel embarrassed. "So, if I was a heron, I'd definitely stick with the group of twelve. You've got enough of a flock to offer protection, but you can still break off and hang with a couple of heron friends or your mate. Did you know that both the male and females incubate the eggs? They both feed them too…" I saw him hang his head and felt suddenly self-conscious. I was babbling on about birds while he was obviously having a moment. Sometimes I wasn't great at reading cues.

"Sorry. I'm talking too much," I said. "I've just never seen a tri-colored one in the wild."

"No. It's good. I like it." He wiped at his nose and looked up with me. "What do herons eat?"

"Mostly small fish, but sometimes frogs, salamanders, lizards or spiders. They're patient hunters, hanging out perfectly still, eyeing their prey before they swoop in." I realized how predatory it sounded all of a sudden and turned back to the water.

He stepped out of his sandals and into the surf. "Do you mind if we walk awhile?"

I followed suit. Alex took my hand and interlocked his fingers with mine as we walked ankle-deep into the sandy warm water.

18

Late April
Morgan

Morgan was walking down a narrow hall at the police station, looking for the restroom, when she crossed paths with Catherine. Morgan had been waiting two hours for Whitey to call Alex back. All that time, he'd been watching his friends stream in and out of the interrogation room, some taking much longer than others. Her son being last did not bode well in Morgan's mind.

She considered ignoring Catherine. *Keep walking*, she told herself. But she just couldn't. Morgan skipped the niceties. "You asked Whitey to bring in the kids? Again?"

Catherine stopped in her tracks. "I did," she said matter-of-factly. "I found something."

"What does that mean?"

Catherine huffed out a breath. "Just tell Alex he better tell the truth in there."

Morgan was tired, and she hated that Catherine relentlessly

pursued the same line of reasoning, a line that always led back to Alex. "What the hell, Catherine? He already answered all of their questions once. He's been torn up about Emily." She forced herself to lower her voice. "I hear him crying at night."

"Oh, yeah? Torn up? Crying? Tell that to my eight-year-olds who don't understand why their sister hasn't come home. Last week Olivia asked me what the word *suicide* means because she heard two teachers talking about Emily." Tears were starting to well in Catherine's eyes. "Since arriving on this island, Alex has been the person Emily spent the most time with. Even if he didn't hurt her, I can think of plenty of things he might know and not be saying."

With that, Catherine turned her back on Morgan and walked away.

"Okay, Alex," Chief Whiteside said, leaning back and crossing one foot over the other. The man's voice sounded tired. "We've pieced together most of the evening. We know there was some drinking, and we have a pretty solid order of who went home and when. Looks like Luke drove Kyle and Jordan. Celeste and Anna stayed the night with Natalie. That leaves you and Emily. Can you set the scene for me when you left the party?"

Morgan swallowed back the lump in her throat. *He is innocent*, she reminded herself. Maybe thinking it would make it so.

"Yes, sir." Alex licked his lips and took a deep breath. "I saw Anna waiting on the porch. She looked upset about something, so I asked her if she needed a ride, and she said something about staying with Natalie. She was kind of—" Alex looked at his shoes. "Anna was kind of drunk, so I figured she needed a minute and then would go back inside. I was parked behind Emily, so after I made sure she was in the car,

I backed up and drove away. She was coming right behind me, I was sure."

"You put Emily in the car even though she'd been drinking and you hadn't?"

Morgan shot Whitey a look.

"I knew she wasn't drunk. She had one beer at the beginning of the movie, said that sometimes her parents gave her wine with dinner, so this couldn't be that different. I think she kind of wanted to fit in, be normal or whatever. I'm sure she wasn't drunk, but…" He paused.

Officer Cortez spoke next. "But what?"

Alex shook his head. "I don't know. She seemed kind of distant, but I figured she was in a mood or something. You know how girls get sometimes."

Whitey chuckled even though Morgan knew that Alex hadn't intended to be funny. Officer Cortez and Morgan were not laughing.

"Okay. That actually brings me to my second question," Whitey continued. "What was the nature of your relationship with Emily Callahan?"

Do not say you are in love with her, Morgan pleaded silently.

"We were sort of dating," Alex said.

Dating? The room suddenly felt very warm.

Alex caught the look on his mom's face. "I mean, it was mainly group things, you know," he clarified. "Emily didn't want to be in some complicated relationship when she was leaving for school in a few months, but she was a good friend. We hung out most nights, sometimes on the weekend when she wasn't doing stuff with her family or didn't need to study on her own."

"And you were there together that night?"

Alex nodded.

"What did that mean to you exactly?" Chief Whiteside

paused for a moment, and Morgan could see that he was weighing how to continue. "Did anything physical happen between you and Emily?"

Morgan took a quick breath.

"No, I mean, not really. Why? Did someone tell you I did something to Emily? 'Cause I would never make her do anything that she didn't want—"

"No, no." The chief leaned forward and put both hands on the desk. "Alex, I know this has to be difficult. You were accused of messing with that Wagner girl years ago, and you're afraid that's going to come back to haunt you this time, am I right?"

Morgan wondered if there was a right answer to this question. She had to jump in. "That's not fair, Whitey. You can't bring up something he didn't even do and expect to—"

Whitey extended a hand to stop her.

"I didn't touch that Wagner girl, and I swear I have no idea who did," Alex interrupted. "It was dark, and there were probably forty people at that party years ago. I wasn't even upstairs when it happened."

Chief Whiteside nodded and looked from Morgan to Alex. "We know, and you were cleared of all charges. There's no need to rehash dead ends, and I'm not holding you as a suspect, okay? But there was some mention of you and Emily disappearing for about twenty minutes at some point that evening."

Alex shrugged. "Yeah, we went off to talk. Emily was acting weird about halfway through the movie, like she wanted to get away from me, or maybe like she was sick. I don't know. She kept looking away from me and holding her head, and I was trying to figure out if I'd done something to upset her or if she needed me to take her home. She wouldn't tell me what was happening, so we mostly sat in silence the rest of the time." He sighed. "She was kind of distant then, but she usually liked it when we…when we were together."

Officer Cortez again. "And by together you mean…"

For Christ's sake, Morgan wished people would quit assuming that her son did whatever the hell he wanted to girls. "He would never hurt Emily."

"I wasn't fucking her, okay?" Alex cut in, his jaw clenched as he said the words. Morgan's spine went rigid.

"All right. Calm down now, Alex," Whitey said. "We only want to make sure we've left no stone unturned."

Alex took a shuddering breath, and Morgan placed a hand on his back. "I think we're done," she finally said, looking from Whiteside to Cortez.

They both nodded, and a few moments later, Chief Whiteside spoke in a low voice. "Thanks, Alex. That'll be all."

Morgan guided her son from the room.

19
Late April
Catherine

After all of the teenagers and their parents left, Catherine finally made her way out of the police station. She and Rosalyn had watched the questionings together behind the one-way glass, the older woman tutting and shaking her head and generally driving Catherine crazy. Whitey debriefed with the two women for an hour afterward, only to finally conclude by saying, *As you can see, we still don't really know anything new.*

Carter was at home with the twins, and as Catherine drove in that direction, thinking back over the not-quite-confessional words she'd heard, she decided that she had one last stop to make. She had unfinished business.

When she showed up at Morgan's loft, Catherine knew she must look awful with her stringy hair and red eyes, but she'd already run into Morgan that evening and frankly, Catherine didn't care. She couldn't remember when she'd last showered or ironed clothes or put on makeup, none of those simple actions that once seemed routine and necessary. She hadn't seen her daughter in weeks, and that evening through the glass she'd watched each pathetic interview going nowhere. It was like watching a failed conductor, the instruments playing random notes.

Whiteside was supposed to find out what happened to her daughter. He was supposed to find out whether or not Alex Frasier was to blame, but Catherine would no longer leave this up to the police. She used the building's entry code that Morgan had given her months ago, took the elevator to the top floor, and began knocking frantically at her door.

Morgan answered, her eyes squinting into the hallway light. Catherine had no idea what time it was, didn't know how long she'd listened to Rosalyn rant to Chief Whiteside and Officer Cortez.

"Catherine?"

"Can I come in?"

Morgan opened the door. As if she had nothing to hide. "It's practically the middle of the night."

"Is it?" Catherine looked around the apartment. She'd been here several times in the past—to drop off a book, to pick up Morgan for dinner, to go with her for a walk around the Strand. "I need to speak to Alex," she said, starting toward his room.

"He's sleeping."

"I know he's sleeping," Catherine said, stopping. "The entire damn island is sleeping, but I need to see him. Now."

Morgan stepped in front of her. "All right, but let me wake him up first."

A few moments later a kid-man, rubbing his eyes with balled fists and stretching his back to his nearly six-and-a-half-foot frame, sauntered into the living room. "Mrs. Callahan?"

Catherine hadn't mentally rehearsed her next move. She'd

been too eager to get here, to find out the truth. She looked down at her phone, opened the picture of the letter she'd pieced together and shoved it in his face. Something Whitey wouldn't do. *Be patient*, he'd kept saying. She was done being patient.

"What is *this*? Who wrote it?"

Alex took the phone and read the words slowly before handing the image off to his mom, his eyes pleading for her to fix this for him. *Not this time*, Catherine thought as she waited, the tension tightening her chest.

Morgan finished reading and spoke, her voice shaky. "Where did you find this?"

"Torn up next to Emily's makeshift desk in the attic. I found it yesterday."

"So that's why Whitey called everyone in again." Morgan reached out a hand to her son and kept her voice low. "Listen, a few years ago, Alex was… I mean, you already know he was accused of some things that he didn't do. We talked about it, remember?" Catherine certainly remembered. "Since then, his name has been cleared completely, but some people…the rumors never completely went away."

"I know what he was *accused* of, and even though you like talking around that accusation, it sure as hell sounds a lot like rape." Catherine bit her lip to keep from crying. She tasted metal.

"I'm sorry, Catherine, but he's my kid. And he's innocent. I know… I mean he wouldn't actually do something like…" Morgan's voice trailed off, and Alex shifted uncomfortably.

Catherine glared at Morgan. "Do you have any idea who wrote this? Do either of you know?" She stepped toward mother and son. She needed an explanation. "I need to speak to whoever it is. Tonight." At least Alex had the decency to shift his eyes away from her. She continued. "Listen to me carefully. Emily is a girl who practices math problems for fun, who memorizes the migratory patterns of birds. She does not make enemies, especially not because of a boy, so whoever wrote this has something against you, not her."

Alex obviously recognized the validity of that argument. "I don't know. It could be one of the girls I dated."

Catherine couldn't help herself. She let forth a laugh, nearly a cackle, that sounded foreign even to her. "And how many would that be? Have you been sleeping with the entire school?"

Morgan stood between them, but Alex took the verbal punch like a man and answered. "No, I mean it could be…" He frowned. "Maybe Anna?"

Morgan turned her head to Alex, eyes wide. "Anna. As in Anna Steele?"

"Oh, you didn't know about your son's extensive love life?" Catherine said, sarcasm sharpening her words. "Figures."

"We had a thing for a couple of weeks last summer," Alex interrupted. "Nothing serious. It wasn't a big deal, but Anna might've said some other stuff like that to Emily at some point."

Had a thing? Said some stuff? What did that even mean? Catherine saw red, and her voice rose an octave as she moved only inches from the boy's face and spoke each word deliberately. "Tell me the truth. Were you sleeping with my daughter? Did you hurt her? Is Emily missing because of you?"

If Alex said yes, Catherine might kill him. Seriously, she could put her hands around his throat, press against his carotid artery, choke him until the blood vessels in his eyes burst. Isn't that how it worked? His face would redden and then turn eggplant before settling into a nice gray pallor. She could do it. She would do it.

Alex took slow steps backward, both hands out. He was crying. The nerve. "No, no, no. I swear I didn't touch her, I didn't do anything to Emily. Why does everyone think…?"

He ran his fingers through his hair, pushed his shoulders back, and met Catherine eye to eye.

"Mrs. Callahan, I love your daughter. She might not have felt exactly the same way, but I swear I would never, ever hurt Emily. I wish I had waited that night, followed her home, made sure she was safe. I feel guilty all the time because I drove away and left her there. If I ever see her again, I'll tell her all this, tell her how sorry I am, and if you or Chief Whiteside or whoever figures out that somebody had a part in her disappearance, I swear, I'll help you kill them."

His pupils were dilated. This boy was full of his own fury.

Catherine sank back. She wanted her daughter, she needed her daughter. That's all. The air deflated from the room around her. There was no compass to guide her. She was utterly adrift as silence rolled in like an island fog.

When she finally collapsed, Morgan caught her. Then there was that long inhalation, the buildup to animal-mother wails tearing from her throat. Catherine was a screeching mess, the grief that had gnawed at her for weeks escaping in a new way, a louder, more violent rending. Something she could only experience without her other two children underfoot.

Alex fled from the room, his teenage-boy-self undone, unsure how to react.

Seconds, minutes, perhaps hours passed. Catherine couldn't tell, but Morgan stayed next to her, a hand on her shoulder. She was the one who answered the phone when it rang.

"It's Carter," Morgan said, glancing at the screen as she placed it on the floor where Catherine had fallen. Morgan accepted the call and put it on speaker. "Catherine Callahan's phone."

"Catherine? Are you there?"

She managed a guttural response, but didn't move from her prone position. It was too much effort. Morgan spoke for her. "This is Morgan, but she's here, listening."

"Hey, babe. I know you were out at the station, but when Whitey called just now, he said he hasn't seen you in a couple of hours."

"She's been with me the whole time. We've been... talking," Morgan offered as some sort of explanation.

"I'll need you to come home as soon as you can, okay, Cat?"

Catherine lifted her head. Something was wrong with his voice, some terrible undercurrent in the way he was approaching her too gently, too cautiously. She managed to find words. "What is it? What's wrong?" She swallowed back the sobs that weren't finished with her yet. "Why did Whitey call?"

Carter coughed back something and took a deep breath. "They...they found Emily's keys. They were in her..." He cleared his throat. "They were in her jeans. It... They were found on East Beach. Some early morning surfers called it in. I need you to come home, Cat. Please."

Then, he began to cry.

"I'm sorry, Mr. and Mrs. Callahan," Whitey said as he sat across from Carter and Catherine in their living room at 4:00 a.m. Rosalyn hovered nearby. The past hour of Morgan driving Catherine home and Carter bringing her inside had been a blur, a haze of sights and sounds that couldn't be happening to her because her daughter was not dead. She wasn't.

Rosalyn spoke up from behind her, and Catherine wanted to cover her ears. "Tell it to me straight, Whitey."

Whitey glanced at the floor, his brow furrowed. "I wish I had something better to tell you. I do. Even if Emily survived the waves and made it back to shore, we should've seen some evidence of her tracks in the sand that night. But no footprints? And then her keys and part of her clothing washes up? At this point, I can't call it anything else but..." His eyes fell back to the floor. "I can't call it anything else but a drowning."

"Oh, God, Cat." Carter let out a cry. "It's my fault. I moved us here, and I was the parent at home that night when she…" He couldn't finish the statement.

Catherine took his hand and shook her head. "But Emily knew how to swim. And she would never go into the water at night—not…not by choice."

"Yes, ma'am. I understand." Whitey sighed and looked down at the notebook he'd brought. "But after all this time and the lack of other sufficient evidence, it appears that Emily went out into the Gulf of her own accord on the night of her disappearance. Maybe she'd had more to drink than those kids knew, or maybe she got the idea in her head to take a late-night swim. Kids are impulsive, especially teenagers." He sighed. "I'm so sorry."

Sorry. Everyone in this town, they were all so very sorry.

"Thank you, Whitey," Carter said softly as he reached around his wife and tucked her into his side. "Mother will show you out."

Catherine's limbs were heavy, too tired with the living she had to do, the living her daughter would never do again… except… No, Emily wasn't dead. She wasn't. Maybe if Catherine stayed still enough for long enough, time's coil would unwind and she could sink into oblivion until her daughter returned. Then all would be well again.

"Catherine?" Carter was speaking, and it took all her effort to turn her face to him and blink. His eyes were wet and his body crumpled forward. "Catherine…what do we… How do we… When…?" His eyes were frantic with questions for which she had no answers for.

Rosalyn walked back into the room. "Leave it to me. I'll take care of all the details."

"No," Catherine said, and Carter's arm tightened around her. "Emily could still be out there."

"You heard Chief Whiteside," Rosalyn said too evenly. "We must accept reality."

Catherine shook her head. "No, I would feel differently if she were really gone. I'm her mother. I would know." She turned to Carter. "Wouldn't I know?"

He didn't say a word, just shrugged as if he didn't have any of the answers either.

"Catherine, I understand that this news is devastating, but it's been weeks—more than two months—since she went missing."

"I know how long it's been," Catherine said. "I've been aware of that fact every second of every day."

"Then you must know how much we all need some sort of closure," Rosalyn said bluntly, though she did finally seem to have a single tear. "Think of Carter. Think of the twins."

"I don't want closure," Carter whispered.

"No," Rosalyn said firmly. "That's not exactly what I meant. Of course, none of us wants this to be the end, but we must trust the evidence—or lack thereof. We must find a way to say a proper goodbye."

Catherine tasted salt and realized that tears were streaming down her own face. She blinked. "Why, Rosalyn? So you can throw a big funeral? A party like the town has never seen."

Carter stepped between Catherine and his mother. "Catherine, that's not fair," he tried gently.

She knew it wasn't fair, but she didn't care. None of this was fair.

"It's all right," Rosalyn said before turning on her heel and leaving both of them in their grief. "Like I said, I'll handle all the details."

A few days later Catherine arrived at The Grand 1894 Opera House with Carter in her wake and her girls flanking each side. She was wearing an old dress she'd pulled out of her closet with barely a glance. It could be torn and stained and she would not care. This service was all Rosalyn's doing.

Rosalyn had come to their home only that morning to tell

them that everything had been arranged, and they were expected at the church in a few hours.

"What does that mean, Mother?" Carter had asked, his words tremulous.

But Catherine knew. Catherine had always known that Rosalyn would do something like this, something so hurtful that it could never be undone. Now, her husband knew it too.

As Catherine had stood in the kitchen in her robe, dishrag in hand, midwipe, she'd almost laughed at the absurdity of it all. "You planned a service for Emily, didn't you? Even after I told you not to."

"What did Grandma do for Emily?" Olivia asked, jumping to attention and holding her cereal spoon aloft.

"Where is she? Can we see Emily?" Lucy asked, hopefully. Her eyes darted around the room as if expecting her big sister to pop out at any moment.

Catherine realized she would have to explain why their grandmother was inviting them to their sister's memorial service.

"Get out." It was all Catherine could say, but her tone was hard enough to make the older woman flee.

"The service is at two o'clock," Rosalyn threw over her shoulder as she ran to her waiting car.

The next few hours were spent with Carter, debating whether or not they should attend.

"Are you seriously considering this?" Catherine had asked her husband.

He sat on the edge of their bed, his spine curved and his head in his hands. "I don't know. I can't believe she—"

"Let's not talk about what we can or cannot believe your mother did. For God's sake, it's done now, and in two hours and twenty-three minutes, this town will be laying our daughter to rest. Without a body. Without her family present."

"Unless we go," he said, his eyes shamefully meeting hers.

"No. I cannot give that woman the satisfaction of—"

"Think about it, Catherine. I mean, don't think about Mother. Think about what people will be whispering behind Lucy and Olivia's back if they don't attend their own sister's memorial? You know how parents talk and how kids repeat everything they say. Especially in this town, at this school. It will be unnecessary questions, unnecessary drama for them, as if they haven't had enough in the past few weeks."

"But your mother—"

"I know. I know." Carter stood and moved toward Catherine. He folded her in his arms. "This is so wrong that she can never make it right, and we never have to forgive her. But I don't want our girls to suffer for something their grandmother did."

"We haven't even told them that Emily…" Catherine swallowed hard. "I mean, we told them that we didn't think Emily would ever come home, but we never said the exact words. We never told them that Emily is definitely…"

He sighed. "We have."

"What do you mean?"

"We have told them. Yes, not in those exact words, but they know she's…gone. Lucy asked me two nights ago if she should pray for Emily's soul. Something she heard in religion class at school."

"And last week Olivia made a list of everything she wants us to have in case something happens to her," Catherine remembered. "She left her bug collection to you."

Carter wiped his wife's eyes gently with his thumb. "I say we tell the girls the truth, or at least the highlights. Grandma wanted to plan a service to honor and to think about their sister, but the four of us can hope that Emily is still out there, somewhere."

Catherine hated that her husband was right, hated Rosalyn for putting them in this situation, hated herself for moving her family here a year ago in order to hide from her own stupid mistake. If only she could rewind the clock, she would've stayed and suffered any amount of disgrace to keep her daughters safe.

At the memorial service in the opera house now, Carter touched the small of her back and led Catherine to the far right row where she'd agreed to sit. *I'll enter as soon as the service begins and exit as soon as it ends*, she'd said. And her hands would never let go of her two remaining daughters.

As the priest took his cue from Rosalyn and moved to the pulpit to begin the terrible proceedings, Catherine thought back to one semester years ago when she had conducted a senior seminar called "Life & Death in Harmony." She'd begun the class with songs of birth, like *Cradle Song* by Johannes Brahms. As she and her students listened to the music while following the score, she couldn't keep herself from mouthing, "Go to sleep, go to sleep, go to sleep my little darling." She'd never been much of a singer, but she remembered placing her baby girls next to her on the piano bench as she played the tune for them. Within seconds of the piano's soothing vibrations, their crying would cease.

By midsemester, Catherine was asking her students to deconstruct the bridal song, Johann Pachelbel's *Canon in D*. She told them about how the piece had been lost and forgotten from the seventeenth century until 1919, and then they analyzed the structure. "Remember that a canon imitates and repeats one major theme throughout. Do you hear how the violins speed up before moving into a steadier pace and then finally to a halting end? What do these changes remind you of?"

"The stress of life," one of her students had answered.

"The stages of life," another corrected.

"Exactly. We are born, we live, we fall in love—whether

it is with a person, a vocation, an idea—and then life slows down once again as we near the end."

Emily's life had not been anywhere near the end. If she had endured a lingering illness, if she had been in a car crash, if she had given her life to save a child from drowning, if she had affirmatively and definitively died in any number of ways, Catherine would have agreed to plan the service. She would have selected pieces that she had taught in that very seminar, pieces that both mourned her daughter and sought to bring comfort to the mourners. Perhaps she would have selected Chopin's *Funeral March*, which was played at his own funeral despite the fact that some critics wondered whether or not he had actually mastered the sonata form by the time he wrote that piece. Perhaps she would have used the plentiful Callahan money to hire an entire symphony to play Tchaikovsky's finale, entitled aptly *Pathétique*, from The Symphony No. 6 in B minor, the final notes void and despairing due to the lack of resolution.

The problem for Catherine was that, to her, this was an empty ceremony full of meaningless pomp and fanfare, another required social obligation for many of the Callahan Prep families who knew nothing about her daughter. She wanted to force her way to the stage and shout, *Get out, all of you. You didn't even know my bright, beautiful, silly girl.* But she had two sets of hands to hold, two sets of eyes to dry, two girls to get through this awful day.

One of the girls tugged at her hand. She couldn't remember which one was on which side. She looked down. Olivia.

"What is it?"

Olivia was pointing to the back of the venue where there was a rustle.

"That man is saying something," Lucy whispered from Catherine's other side.

Catherine watched the man dressed in dark green coveralls appear like a beacon in a sea of black suits and dresses. He held a baseball cap in one hand as he ruffled his hair, obviously self-conscious in this grand assembly. He was walking down the center aisle directly to her. Rosalyn started toward him, but Catherine stepped forward first, dropping her girls' hands for the first time.

"Yes?" Catherine asked, her heart beginning to speed up.

"We found her, Mrs. Callahan. We found your daughter. Emily. She's alive."

EMILY

When I turned seven years old, my parents allowed me to get my first pet: a rabbit I named Martha Phoebe Sowerby. I'd just read *The Secret Garden* for the first time, and the real heroine of that story seemed a fitting name for my cuddly rabbit. Except I soon found that Ms. Sowerby, as I affectionately called her, wanted nothing to do with my cuddling.

My parents had neglected to read up on the preferences of rabbits, and after Ms. Sowerby went limp in my arms, lying feet up for a quarter hour on several occasions, I logged into my dad's laptop and discovered the term *tonic immobility*: "Despite the fact that the animal appears at utter and complete rest, the respiration and heart rate of the furry creature denotes actual fear for its life. It is defending itself against a perceived predator."

All these years later as I lie here, I ask myself, am I somehow doing the same?

★ ★ ★

I smell the scent of Old Spice before I hear my dad's voice. I think my lips tilt up in a smile, but it's probably my imagination.

"Scooter," he whispers, the nickname he's called me ever since I refused to learn to ride a bike at six years old, insisting I would happily stick to the scooter as my choice of transportation.

He leans over and brushes my hair to the side of my face. He's crying. My dad never cries.

The last thing I remember is the men pulling me out of the water, but an ambulance must've brought me to the hospital because I hear beeps and drips and muted voices. There's no rush of an ER, and I can tell I already have an IV in my right hand. The cool liquid pumps through my veins and I taste a metallic flavor.

"I'm here, Emily," Mom says, and I feel something inside of me relax. "I'm here, and we're going to find out where you've been."

She is determined, her tone as hard and unflinching as the agate and jasper I collected from the Pacific shores as a child. Dad bought me my first tumbler when I was nine, so I could polish the stones. I loved the rumbling of the rocks scampering past one another, smoothing away hard edges until I could hold shiny pieces of the earth in my palm.

Mom bends over me, and I breathe in the flower scent of her hair as she touches my cheeks with cool fingertips, like water droplets on my skin. Those fingers that she held over my own as she placed both of my thumbs at middle C and taught me my first faltering notes.

"I won't leave. I'm here." Mom must turn to my dad because next she whispers, "Carter, are her eyelids fluttering? Do you think she can hear us?"

"Maybe," he answers with a sniffle.

I know I've been missing, but that's all I know. I can't open my eyes, move a muscle, or speak, but relief washes over me as soon as I hear my parents. Wherever I've been, now I'm home.

I can tell by the tapping feet and swishing skirts that they've brought Lucy and Olivia with them. My baby sisters. Back at the house, Mom has a giant picture hanging in our foyer of nine-year-old me holding one of them in each arm as I sit atop an upside-down planter in our backyard. Lucy, a pound smaller than Olivia, looks into the camera with big eyes and a round mouth while Olivia gazes upward at the sky. Things were so much simpler back then.

Today, Lucy's hand wraps around mine while Olivia stands near enough that I can hear her breathe.

Olivia speaks first. "Why does she have that bruise?"

"The nurse said they think she hit her head, and Chief Whiteside believes that she may have fallen and that's why she was floating unconscious in the water," Mom answers. "It's only been a few hours, but they're trying to figure things out at fast as they can."

"Are you sure she didn't jump?" Olivia waits for an answer, but no one says anything for a long moment.

Lucy takes a sharp breath. Though Olivia's question is blunt, I know she's just trying to piece things together. Like me. I can almost see her thin brows turning down like a searching caterpillar.

"We don't know a lot right now, like where Emily has been since she went missing," Mom says. "But we're going to find out everything, I promise."

I hear a stranger's voice mumbling, asking my mom to step outside for a moment. A pause and then dad steps in to explain things to Lucy and Olivia.

"The man who found Emily said that she was wearing a

life jacket from one of the ferries—you remember how nervous she gets around water?"

Olivia giggles. "She was a scaredy-cat."

"Don't say that," Lucy says, defending me. "She always told me it was because she was so sweet that she might melt."

How I wish I could scoop both of them onto this hospital bed with me.

"Chief Whiteside told us that the problem is that the ferries don't have cameras onboard," Dad continues. "So he's going to ask the people in charge of the bird cameras on Pelican Island—where the ferry passes—to look at their footage. It could take a week or two for them to discover something, though. Does all that make sense?"

"Kinda," Lucy answers.

"I want to go to Pelican Island," Olivia declares.

Mom's scent wafts back into the room, and she speaks quietly. "Carter, we need to talk." My mom's words are simple, but I can hear the tremor in them. I want to remind her that she no longer needs to be afraid, that I am all right. "Girls, why don't you take my phone and go sit in the hall and watch something for a few minutes?"

I can hear them bickering over Netflix versus YouTube as they leave.

A voice, weak and whispering and almost familiar comes into the room. The strong scent of hand sanitizer accompanies it. "Dr. Steele wanted me to remind you that it's best to keep all visitors to a minimum for now."

"We're her family," Dad responds. I can feel his words biting the air.

A few moments later, the rapid staccato of another set of footsteps enter the room.

"Good evening, Mr. and Mrs. Callahan. I'm Dr. Robert Steele." His voice is soft as well, as if no one wants to interrupt my solitude. "What my nephew Asher—my intern, actually—is attempting to communicate is that we don't know for sure the amount of trauma that Emily has experienced, so we want her to rest as much as possible over the next few days in hopes that she'll regain consciousness and tell us what she can remember."

Dad speaks again. "Okay. So what do you know so far?"

"She seems to be in a coma, and though we aren't giving her much—beyond mild pain relievers and, of course, the IV—she has remained unconscious since she arrived." I feel the doctor's hand cover mine. "The good news is that Emily could awake in a few minutes, but it may also take several days, possibly weeks, though that would be surprising. As far as injuries, they are numerous, but minor." He pauses and flips pages—my chart, I assume. "She has a protrusion on her head, a few scrapes on her legs, minor bruising across her left hip, some…"

But Mom won't wait for the doctor to complete his list of ailments.

"Carter, she's pregnant."

PART III: THE UNRAVELING

*"There's the scarlet thread…
running through the
colourless skein of life,
and our duty is
to unravel it,
and isolate it,
and expose every inch of it."*

—Sir Arthur Conan Doyle, *A Study in Scarlet*

20
The first of May
Catherine

"Have you considered rape?"

Catherine was taken aback by Rosalyn's question. Had she heard correctly? Rosalyn sat unmoving, her shoulders pulled back as if with a wire, seeming almost impassive. Just the facts, please. Whitey stood across from the two Callahan women in the conservatory, a viewing room for Rosalyn's prized oleanders.

Catherine had been at the hospital for the past couple of days, dozing in the chair next to Emily's bed, when Carter called. "Mother is asking Whitey to reopen the investigation, and I thought you might want to speak to him directly. Why don't you let me and the girls come up and sit with Emily while you go?"

Carter was right. She did want to speak with Chief Whiteside directly. She would also appreciate an apology from both

Rosalyn and Whitey for not trusting her maternal instincts, instincts that told her that Emily was alive. But instead of an apology she would take their renewed determination to find where her still-unconscious daughter had been.

Whitey's cheeks reddened at Rosalyn's question, and he swallowed hard. "I hadn't given it much thought to this point. I guess I was relieved to see her home again."

Rosalyn squinted and Catherine watched the officer wither under her gaze.

"Chief Whiteside, what Rosalyn is trying to say is that…" Catherine stopped as Whitey shook his head ever so slightly and Rosalyn raised one eyebrow. Apparently, no one was allowed to speak on behalf of the almighty matriarch.

Rosalyn pretended she hadn't heard Catherine's interruption. "Given that my granddaughter is unconscious and has been missing for close to ten weeks, it is our duty to determine where she has been and with whom—at least until she can tell us herself. Since I am confident that she would *not* be involved in lewd acts of her own volition, the question is a natural one. Thus, I'll ask again—Chief Whiteside, have you pursued the idea that my granddaughter may have been raped?"

Whitey put out his hands. "Mrs. Callahan—" He paused, his eyes darting from Rosalyn to Catherine. "And Mrs. Callahan—" He obviously didn't know where to look. "You know that we came up empty-handed at every turn with her disappearance."

"Yes, I am fully aware of that fact," Rosalyn acknowledged, leaning toward him. "I expect this investigation to be more fruitful."

Catherine slowly inhaled. She had to reach this man in a way that Rosalyn couldn't. "Chief Whiteside, we know that the hospital isn't able to identify any evidence of violence after so much time has passed, but is there a way to figure out where she might have been all this time? Who she might've been with?"

Whitey stood and started pacing in front of the floor-to-ceiling windows, gripping his hat in his hands. "I went out to the harbor with two of my men today, cordoned it off like a crime scene even though all we've got is a life jacket that has some very rough fingerprints that appear to be her own. I spent a good half hour with Dr. Steele, running through every scenario, trying to see if there are any tests we can run at this point. I don't think there's a stone we're leaving unturned."

"We are all aware that too much time has passed to check for DNA remnants on my granddaughter, but there are other tests," Rosalyn reminded him. "You could test the fetus."

"You've got to understand that even if we could pinpoint the exact DNA of the…" Whitey appeared at a loss for words as he moved his eyes from one woman to the other again. "The DNA of the…the fetus, it's not like I have a database of DNA samples back at the office."

"What about evidence from previous cases? Surely, you have a registry of potential offenders," Rosalyn said. "I haven't looked at the police files for quite some time, but there must be something helpful you can use."

Whitey shook his head. "Remember how we tried to get permission a few years back to start collecting DNA? We wanted to request samples from kids we pulled over, guys with DUIs, ladies who were…less than reputable, but the voters didn't approve it."

Since when would that stop Rosalyn? Catherine wondered.

Rosalyn cleared her throat. "What about the case three years ago with the Wagner family?"

"That was never conclusive, ma'am."

Rosalyn tucked her kitten heels behind her and rolled her eyes. "I am well aware of that fact. I did some digging and found out that your office somehow mislocated the swabs the girl gave?"

Whitey stopped pacing. "We can't reopen that case, but even if we could, it's a dead end just like this one was. But now that your granddaughter—and daughter—is back, that's something to celebrate." A lopsided grin settled on his face as he looked hopefully at the women. They stared blankly back at him.

Rosalyn spoke slowly. "Yes, Emily is back, but she is unable to communicate why and how she is carrying a child. Have you no brain in that thick skull of yours? This is not the time for a party."

Whitey's face fell. "I know, I know. That's not exactly what I meant. It's…" Catherine saw him wilt again under Rosalyn's stare. "Mrs. Callahan, Texas law doesn't collect DNA unless someone has been officially convicted of something, and I can't exactly go door-to-door asking for cheek swabs."

"My God, man. Why not? This is Galveston. We are an island unto ourselves, one of the places where such things can still be done if the press doesn't report on them, and since I own the press, it will not be reported."

Catherine almost laughed at the absurd truth of Rosalyn's statement.

Rosalyn pinched the bridge of her nose and closed her eyes. "Whitey, stop your endless pacing, sit down and listen closely." The older woman pursed her lips and thought for a moment. "I will not repeat the story I am about to tell you, and if I ever catch word of it floating around this town, I will denounce you as a crazed maniac and strip you of your title and position. Do we understand each other?" Rosalyn turned to Catherine and simply added, "This affects Carter too, so I know I have your confidence."

Whitey gulped and sat down like a schoolboy about to receive his catechism.

Rosalyn began. "Nearly forty-five years ago, I was young and dumb and a little in love with a man who had been staying with my family for some time. He was a business associate of my father's. Such a gentleman he had seemed when the two of us went walking on the Strand, attended the Knights of Momus Ball, enjoyed dinner at The Monterey. He was my father's right-hand man, though several years his junior. The perfect age for marrying—established, but not yet tied down." Rosalyn examined her cuticles as she recollected. "This man lived here for several months, working at the refineries during the week and attending events with my family each weekend. He was supposed to be a man of the future, brilliant, you know? And my father had tasked him with bringing the Callahan refineries into the modern age." Rosalyn sighed deeply, as if giving up part of her very soul with the story. "The two of us became...close.

"We began spending each evening together, so much so that my mother teased me about wedding gowns and my best friend secreted away *Brides Magazine* from the library shelves so the two of us could pore over the pages late into the night. I remember that summer after my senior year as one of anticipation, like my destiny was shifting with the tide. I had enrolled at Radcliffe for the fall, but Mother had reminded me on numerous occasions that I would have no need for a college degree if the right man came along. I became certain that the right man was Everett Montgomery."

Whitey frowned as if trying to recall the name, but Rosalyn waved him off. Catherine was surprisingly intrigued, the need to know how this might relate to Emily keeping her in her seat.

"Everett wasn't here long enough for his name to become well-known, but at the end of the brief time he was in Galveston he began making plans, talked about purchasing his own home on the island, toured several high-end listings. Mother and I came to expect a late-summer engagement and Christmas nuptials. The historical buildings downtown would be laced with white lights, and I would wear a long-sleeved, cream-colored gown with a mink wrap.

"The night I expected him to ask for my hand, Everett drove me to the shoreline at the West End." Rosalyn swallowed as if the words were becoming harder to say. "We stared over the water, the moon bright enough to make out one another's profiles against the starlit sky. He held me and told me how he'd been waiting to… Well, his eyes smiled, but his fingers clenched my arm, and I realized that he might leave a bruise. I tried to laugh him off as I pulled away, but he pushed me to the ground, his hands wandering…" She took a deep breath and cleared her throat. "I couldn't move, so I tried to pretend I was somewhere else, someone else. He was on top of me, pushing at my skirt, and the last thing I remember is the gristle of the sand in my molars. After that, everything went dark."

It was Catherine's turn to stare at her hands. Her mother-in-law was suddenly an actual person, real flesh and blood.

"Suffice to say, I married a man of my parents' choosing— my second cousin, Henry Callahan—weeks later in order to avoid a scandal." Rosalyn nodded at Catherine, who tried to keep her face as blank as possible. "And yes, Carter was born seven months later."

Catherine tried to keep her face neutral. This woman had just handed her and Chief Whiteside raw information. Rosalyn continued. "For years, even though I couldn't remember all the details of what happened at the shoreline, I thought it was my fault. Why didn't I fight? Why did I freeze? Why couldn't I remember things clearly? Later, under the care of Dr. Montague, I learned the proper terminology. I dissociated, or more precisely, I experienced dissociative amnesia caused by a...a traumatic event. That's why I didn't remember Everett bringing me home or going to bed or staying there for days. I pieced all that together later. My mother assumed I was ill, and the next thing I recalled was her sitting at my bedside with a family physician taking my pulse. By then, Everett was gone, and mother assumed we had quarreled. When she realized I was with child, she accused me of seducing a decent man, and I never told her otherwise."

Rosalyn looked to Whitey. "Based upon my experience, I don't know if Emily will remember what happened to her, so it is essential that you do the intensive investigative work. Do you understand me?"

"I think so," he said, his eyes downcast.

Catherine interjected with her own clarification. "You're saying that if Emily underwent trauma, she might not remember where she's been even after she wakes up?"

"Dissociative amnesia can take hours, days, weeks, months, even years of a person's life," Rosalyn said. "A victim may even go into a fugue state and wander for a time."

Realization hit Catherine. "Is that what happened to you when you took Lucy?"

"I thought I saw someone who looked like an older version of Everett wander past our home. It made me anxious, so I took some sleeping pills to calm my nerves and help me sleep." Rosalyn studied the floor. "That must have triggered it."

Then, Rosalyn exhaled, collected herself and placed the guarded expression she always wore back over her face. "Whitey, what I'd like you to determine is twofold. Take out a pen and write this down."

The man jumped to attention as Catherine struggled to comprehend the story her mother-in-law had just shared. Carter's father—the one he'd grown up with—was not his biological father. And this dissociation, this trauma at the shoreline. What if history had simply repeated itself?

Rosalyn spoke again. "First, what event triggered Emily's disappearance?" Whitey wrote the question and then looked up like a good student. "Second, what predator took advantage of my unwitting granddaughter?"

He choked and then scribbled away before stammering. "And—you...you...you think that a kid on this island had something to do with her disappearance?"

Rosalyn placed a finger to her temple. She was obviously ready for this conversation to come to a close. "Something happened the night Emily went missing, something that triggered the episode, the wandering. Those kids have been rather tight-lipped with you, only saying she watched a movie with a few friends, but I know there's more. I know you can dig deeper."

Please, dig deeper, Catherine implored silently.

"We interviewed all of the people who were at the party, Mrs. Callahan. Twice," Whitey said. "You both saw the second interviews through the interrogation window. It was a bunch of kids studying, watching some movie, a bit of drinking."

"I assure you that's not *all* it was," Rosalyn said, her voice rising for the first time. "A girl doesn't disappear because of a night out with friends. Pardon my language, but something scared the shit out of her, Whitey, enough to send her out of her own mind, and I need you to find out who or what it was. You do whatever you need to solve this case, and the Callahan family will do whatever we can to keep you out of trouble and in your current position as police chief. Do you understand?"

"Yes, ma'am." Whitey looked around the room, presumably for the nearest exit while Catherine stared at the older woman who had deeper secrets than she had ever realized.

★ ★ ★

Back at the hospital, Catherine glanced at the music composition notebook Carter had brought her. Reluctantly, he'd left her alone and taken the twins to pick up dinner. She, of course, hadn't told him what she'd learned from his mother. There was no emotional energy at the moment for him to process this new truth about his biological father. Later. After all this was over. Maybe.

When he'd handed her the pages before leaving, he gave her a kiss on her forehead and said, "For when your mind is reeling and you can't sleep." He knew how charting the contrapuntal lines on the page stilled her in a way that nothing else could.

She hadn't written a single note since her fall from grace, but Catherine would never forget penning her first melody in a plain, plastic-bound notebook like this one during Intermediate Music Theory. If she sat at a piano at this moment, she could pluck out the musical phrase she had written, the repetitive theme so simple to her professor but opening a world of sound to her.

Years later, Catherine's favorite personal composition became a fugue that she set as the focal point of an opera based on the life of Johann Sebastian Bach.

"Masterful," one reviewer had written.

"Strikes the right tone between Bach's Baroque genius and twenty-first-century experimentation," another wrote.

To Catherine, the fugue—a style in which several instruments interweave one basic melody in a combination of ways—was as complex as a fusion of flavors to a chef. Her thesis advisor had said it well: *A fugue is to Western music as the sonnet is to Western literature.*

Twentieth-century Russian composer Igor Stravinsky had been her idol as Catherine worked toward her doctorate, his double fugues a thing of wonder: the way he blended two themes seamlessly, the way the variety of tonal voices symmetrically mimicked one another. Looking at the empty notebook as she sat near her daughter's hospital bed, Catherine told herself that someday she would be able to write again.

Then, she started to feel sleepy.

Startled awake by beeping, Catherine jolted from her five-minute nap with a tune in her mind. She glanced at Emily, still unchanged, and hummed the melody. *Bah, da, da, dee, da-da.* She scribbled the notes in A minor, the most somber of keys. The melody began on the keynote before leaping to the seventh. The next note dropped a half step before falling down two whole steps and rising back to the dominant. *Bah, da, da, dee, da-da.* It wasn't much, but it was more than she'd written in a long time.

If only she could approach her daughter's disappearance like she had once written her songs, what could she find? She thought again of the fugue, the repetition of lines retelling the same story again and again, but in a new way with a new voice each time. What stories did she know that might help inform the here and now?

She knew that a few years ago at Callahan Prep, a girl accused a boy—a boy that her daughter had spent the past few months getting to know—of rape. She knew there were three options for what happened to the girl named Julie Wagner: Alex did it, it never happened or the blame had been misplaced.

She knew that her daughter's grandmother had once separated from herself in order to survive a trauma. She knew that years later, Rosalyn had been triggered again and wandered away with Lucy.

She knew that as of the past year, her family was living a new story in which the plot and setting had shifted drastically. She knew that despite the changes, she remained a mother, and mothers protect their children, regardless of the costs. Mothers find out the answers to the unanswerable questions.

Catherine glanced at her beautiful daughter, grateful to have her here and alive. Then she looked around the room and out into the hall. She'd been waiting for an opportunity to inspect her child, to see if the medical professionals had missed anything. The compulsion to look Emily over from the top of her head to the toes of her feet was reminiscent of the night of her daughter's birth when Catherine had unwrapped the bundle and examined every finger, the soft bump of each elbow, the smooth shoulder blades and the round caps of her knees.

Quick and efficient, Catherine closed the door and moved around Emily's bedside, running hands and eyes over her daughter's extremities: her spine, her belly, her scalp, behind her ears. There, she stopped. She felt along Emily's jawbone and then back into her hairline. Something wasn't right. She lifted back the earlobe, indented from wearing earrings for the last eight years. The tender skin behind her ear rose and puckered, unnoticeable to the casual eye, but Catherine shone the light from her phone along the three-inch strip of uneven terrain and gasped as she saw a piece of art: in black-and-white etching was a tattoo of a striped lighthouse with a clock in the center and two minute birds flying from a low window. Though in miniature, the picture was intricate and specific in such a way as to make her feel this must be a real place.

She pushed the call button and tried to calm her voice when the nurse arrived moments later.

"I need to see the doctor. Now."

"Dr. Steele is not available, but I can refer you to another doctor if this is an emergency," the nurse said flatly.

This was not acceptable. Catherine decided to play it the way another person carrying a generations-old name might.

"As I'm sure you realize, this is regarding Emily *Callahan*. I am her mother, and I need to see Dr. Steele. Now."

"I understand, but unfortunately…"

Catherine glanced down at her phone. "Fine. I'm certain I can get the number I need from my mother-in-law, Rosalyn Callahan."

The nurse's mouth fell as she remembered exactly to whom she was speaking. Carter's father had been on the hospital board for twenty-five years, and his mother still contributed generously to sustain the pediatric wing that carried the Callahan name. "I'll ring him. He'll be here shortly."

Catherine searched her mind for any mention of lighthouses or tattoos, but neither had ever been a subject of discussion with Emily. If she had asked for permission to get a tattoo, Catherine would've reluctantly agreed. Her daughter would research the cleanest and most talented artist within a hundred-mile radius, and Emily would select a work of art, a quote, a mantra so profound that she would want to wear it on her body for the next seventy to eighty years. But she was sure they had never discussed it.

When Dr. Steele arrived moments later, polished as always, Catherine shone a light on the tattoo. He bent forward and looked behind the earlobe, obviously confused. "I apologize, Mrs. Callahan, but I'm not sure why we're looking at your daughter's tattoo. There doesn't seem to be an infection. Can you fill me in here?"

"My daughter does not have a tattoo."

He looked back at the artwork, trying to follow her logic. "You mean you didn't know your daughter has a tattoo?"

Catherine shook her head, though she supposed he was technically correct. "My daughter did not have a tattoo before she went missing, and now she has a lighthouse behind her ear, a very unique lighthouse from the look of it."

Dr. Steele placed his palms upward. "As I said, it's not infected, so I'm not sure what you want me to do with this realization. We certainly can't remove it."

She reached a hand to her forehead and rubbed at the creases etched there by the experience of the past few weeks. "I don't want you to remove it, Dr. Steele. I want you to tell me how long it's been there and what it might mean."

He let out a quick sigh and examined it once again. "I don't know much about tattoos except what one of my nephews taught me by getting a very unfortunate skull on his left shoulder the night after his graduation, but I think that the redness and the slight indent of the skin indicates it may be fairly recent."

"So, in the past few days?"

He nodded. "At least the past couple of weeks."

"Where could she get a tattoo nearby?"

Dr. Steele shrugged. "A number of places, I suppose. You know that the island caters to tourists who come to escape real life. Unfortunately, that often means drunken requests for body piercings and tattoos."

Catherine shook her head again. "That's not Emily. If she did this, she had a purpose, a reason."

"Well, it does look like the Bolivar lighthouse, though it's no longer striped these days. The salty air is hard on buildings. One of my nephews—the one with the skull tattoo, actually—has been working out on Bolivar. You might contact him?"

"Yes, of course, where is it? I'll drive out there today."

Dr. Steele glanced at his watch. "You'll need to take the ferry, so I would wait until after dark. The traffic backs up from about 4:00 to 8:00 p.m." He wrote down the name and number of his nephew. "He probably won't answer his phone, but as far as I know he's still living and working out there. His name is Sawyer, Sawyer Steele, but if you happen to speak with his mother, please don't say anything about where he's living now. He doesn't want many people to know."

"Thank you."

Catherine called Carter. He and the girls would wait with Emily while she searched the one lead she had after all these weeks of waiting. They would not tell Rosalyn or Whitey. For now.

Bah, da, da, dee, da-da, she heard again in her mind. For the first time, she could hear the eerie melody of this island faintly calling to her. She would follow wherever it led to find out where her daughter had been.

21
May
Morgan

"You'll see for yourself, but she's doing well," Robert told Morgan as they passed in the hallway of the neurology wing. His nephew shadowed behind him. If Asher hadn't been hovering, maybe Morgan would've folded herself into Robert, maybe she would've found a space to steal a kiss, maybe she would've finally released the tears she'd been holding back, tears for her son and this girl whom she hadn't really known, but who had become such a part of her life.

Instead, Morgan squeezed his hand, the simple gesture unable to convey all that he meant to her. Robert came to her mind when she least expected—while picking up her groceries, while running a warm shower, while going for her morning run. It seemed a quiet love had crept in while the two of them changed diapers at the children's center and wandered the shores looking for Emily. But Morgan wasn't here to see Robert right now; Catherine had called and asked her to come.

Morgan wasn't sure what to expect, but she felt she owed it to her to at least show up.

She knocked three times before entering the room. Though the air was stale and antiseptic, it had also taken on elements of the girl sleeping there: a stack of books on the windowsill, a bunch of balloons tied to her bed, cut-out pictures from a science magazine.

Morgan took in Emily's thin frame. How does one acknowledge the lifeless daughter in the room? Catherine met Morgan's eyes briefly before turning back to Emily and brushing her hair behind her ears.

"All of her vitals look good," Catherine finally said. "The MRI is clear, but she does have a bruise on the back of her head. Dr. Steele says it's a waiting game now, that we should expect her to wake up anytime." She leaned down and kissed her daughter's forehead. "You hear that, baby girl? You can open those eyes any time you're ready."

Morgan couldn't imagine seeing her child, big and tough and full of energy, incapacitated like this. She couldn't imagine calling Lionel to come and wait for his son to awaken.

Carter walked into the room, carrying drinks and candy. Lucy and Olivia were at his heels, peering cautiously from behind their dad. "Movie night," he said, shaking the peanut M&M's box.

"Carter thought he and the girls could hang out with Emily while we take care of a couple of things," Catherine said too brightly. "Here, girls, why don't you each sit on one side of Emily's bed, so she knows you're here with her." Catherine placed a hand on Emily's forehead. "I'll be right back, okay?"

The heart rate monitor sped up a few beats, and Catherine kissed all three of her girls before pulling Morgan into the hallway.

Morgan spoke first. "Hey, are you okay? What's going on? I haven't seen you since the memorial service and even then…"

Catherine put out a hand as if to stop her. "Look, I didn't call you so we could fix our friendship, and full disclosure, I'm not convinced that Alex wasn't involved in Emily's disappearance."

Morgan steeled herself. She had not come here to rehash these accusations. "But—"

"No, Morgan. Don't try to convince me right now. That's just where I'm at, and I need you to know," she added, not unkindly.

"Then why did you call me?"

"I called because we're probably the two mothers on this island who most want to know the truth about Emily. I want to know where she's been and how she got pregnant, and you want to clear your son once and for all."

Morgan's eyes widened at the revelation of Emily's pregnancy. "I'm listening."

"I think I finally know where to start looking, but we need to go to Bolivar Peninsula tonight. I'm too nervous to go on my own, Carter is with the kids, and there's no way I'm asking Rosalyn to come with me." Catherine leaned forward. "Are you in?"

"I'm in," Morgan answered.

22
May
Leslie

Leslie couldn't remember when she'd first started suspecting that Anna knew more than she was saying—not that Anna was guilty of anything per se, but she had initially lied about the alcohol, hadn't she? They all had. Perhaps that was why Leslie snuck into her daughter's room and stole her phone. She needed quick reassurance. That was all.

Anna had fallen asleep with her phone in hand, but this wasn't Leslie's first time monitoring one of her kids. She gently slid the phone from Anna's fingers, replacing it temporarily with her own. Then, she fled the room and put in a pin number, the one that secretly allowed her to access all of her daughter's recent posts and texts as well as her search history. She'd downloaded the software before giving Anna the phone last Christmas, but she'd wrapped everything back so nicely in the original packaging that her daughter had no idea.

Leslie poured herself a glass of water and began her search

in the dim kitchen light. She would keep it to ten minutes just to be safe. As she scrolled through Anna's search history, she thought back to the night of the incident with the Wagner girl three and a half years ago.

The Steeles had hosted the varsity football team, the cheerleaders and a handful of tagalongs at their home to celebrate a big win over their archrival, the Westover Buccaneers. Leslie provided all the fixings: brisket, baked beans, fried okra, corn bread, coleslaw, rolls, peach cobbler with Blue Bell ice cream. All catered, of course.

Though she didn't say so, all she could think about was how that game was probably the last big one that Michael would watch his boys play. The knowledge of her husband's impending demise was probably why she hadn't noticed the beers and wine coolers that a couple of the players slipped into the party.

Leslie couldn't remember the specifics, but she knew she would've heard the cheering and laughter from the kids in the great room and said something like, *Listen to those kids! They sure are having a good time.* Michael would've attempted a grin, shrugged his shoulders and sunk back into his recliner, trying to stay awake until a respectable hour when he could crawl into bed with his pain pills and sleep away the constant aching behind his eyes, the unquenchable fatigue that ransacked his body. Blissfully unaware of anything unseemly happening beneath her roof that evening, Leslie would've tried to strike the balance between playing a good hostess and giving the young people their privacy.

Despite being unaware of the party's goings-on, Leslie vividly remembered the next morning, wandering through her kids' rooms, carrying a laundry basket, tossing in items they'd left on bedroom floors: a mound of Anna's socks, a few of Asher's undershirts, a pair of Sawyer's shorts. As she was cleaning out her son's pockets, she felt a wad of fabric and realized she was holding a pair of black, lacy panties.

Leslie didn't mention the find to Michael, who had enough problems by that point. Teenage sex happens, right? Her boys were almost eighteen, and they'd both been schooled on how to be careful. She wasn't worried, so she threw away the panties and didn't think about the incident again until she received the call from Whitey a few days later.

A girl had made an accusation about something that happened at the Steele home on the night of the party. Whitey was calling as a friend: Did Leslie know anything?

"No, of course not," she had lied automatically.

"I figured as much. You know how these kids can be at parties—hooking up and whatnot. I wanted to make sure you didn't notice anything out of the norm."

"Just a good meal and kids having fun, as far as I know." Leslie's hands began to sweat. Lying didn't become her.

"The family requested a rape kit when they took the girl to see the doctor, but it had been a couple of days, so we don't know if it'll be conclusive."

"Oh, my." Leslie knew it sounded as if she was concerned for the girl, but to her shame, that wasn't what caused the catch in her voice. "Can she identify the young man?"

"No, that's the thing. She was pretty drunk," Whitey said. "The girl woke up and realized she'd been taken advantage of."

Leslie paused and then rushed her words to compensate for the silence. "Please know that I'm happy to help in any way I can, but it sounds like the justice system is doing its due diligence."

"We've got it under control. Could know something definitive by the end of this week," Whitey said. "I'm getting ready to send everything off to the lab."

"Best of luck, Whitey, and if I hear anything—gossip or otherwise—I'll be in touch." And she would have normally.

She didn't think of herself as a woman who hid mischief, but she was a wife and mother who needed, at that time of her family's life, to keep the peace while her husband died. His last few months would not be spent watching Sawyer march back and forth to court for a stupid mistake.

It had to be Alex, said everyone, including Julie Wagner. After all, Alex was the biggest guy on the varsity team—and the youngest, the most immature. And didn't one of the other girls at the party see him leaving the room where Julie said it happened? Yes, it was definitely Alex. At one point in her own grief and pain during the following months, Leslie had almost started to believe it herself.

It wasn't until after Michael's death that she'd asked her son Sawyer the tough questions about that night. Sawyer had stumbled in at 2:00 a.m., and Leslie had clearly had enough of his stupidity.

"How could you let that boy take the fall for you?"

"What are you talking about?"

"Alex. His reputation is ruined because of the accusations Julie Wagner made." Leslie tried to keep herself from shouting. "But it was you and your irresponsible partying, wasn't it?"

Sawyer narrowed his eyes and shifted his balance as he swayed slightly. "Julie?"

Leslie suddenly realized that if he had been this wasted on the night of the attack, he actually might have no memory of what he'd done. That made it even worse.

"Don't know a Julie," Sawyer slurred. "She hot?"

Leslie grimaced. "You can't keep doing this, Sawyer. You've got to clean up your act."

"I'm not acting, Mom." Those were the last words he said before falling face-forward into the couch, passed out.

Asher was already away at summer school, so Anna found

Sawyer in the living room the next morning. "Guess Sawyer had fun last night," she muttered.

Leslie knew she shouldn't let Sawyer stay under her roof, setting that kind of example for his little sister, but she'd lost enough. She couldn't very well kick out her own son, could she? She needn't have worried. Within a month, Sawyer was gone, out somewhere on Bolivar, finding himself.

Leslie returned her focus to Anna's phone. Her daughter's search history was clear and her posts were innocuous. Good. Leslie began scrolling through her daughter's texts. She went back as far as the day after Emily's disappearance, saw Alex's name, and took a jagged breath as she read the words.

Anna: OMG. Did you know Emily never went home last night?

Natalie: Her mom called this morning looking for her. i was so out of it.

Kyle: what did she want?

Natalie: to know who was here last night, what time Emily left, that kind of thing.

Celeste: what did u tell her?

Natalie: I told her who was here.

Luke: you think her mom thinks we did something to her

Natalie: no. wtf?

Kyle: you just wish you did something to her, Luke.

Anna: where do you think she went? my mom said her car was parked out on East Beach

Kyle: Prob to mess around with Alex. You on here, A?

Jordan: he's prob working out. Gotta make the recruiters happy.

Kyle: this is gonna be just like freshman year when they called everybody in and asked us a bunch of questions. shits going down. i bet alex was with her.

Anna: I was on the front porch and saw him leave alone. She was still in her car when I went inside. Mom is organizing search. Can you let people know? I'm supposed to get the word out: 6 pm Monterey

Celeste: I'll send out an email to the senior class

Luke: not gonna lie. i was pretty drunk but me and kyle and jordan left first, so we are clean. Alex, you're the only one they might have something on, so text us when you get this. I'll head up to the gym and see if he's there.

Natalie: I don't think anybody actually believes we were involved.

Anna: Not with her car found out on East Beach with her stuff inside. No tracks around, mom said. Ya'll come to Monterey, okay? I don't want to be the only senior out there looking for her just because she didn't have any friends.

Kyle: Alex was friendly enough with her. Ha ha.

Celeste: Somebody better find her or she's gonna wreck our senior year

Anna: Just be there. All of you.

23
May
Catherine

When Morgan and Catherine approached the lighthouse an hour later, it was cloaked only in the light from the stars. The outline of the tower appeared like a slender knife cutting through black velvet. As they approached the tower and their eyes adjusted, the details of the structure—the clock, the low-hung window—became visible.

Morgan stretched her neck to one side. "Is it leaning?"

"I think so." Catherine pulled out her phone and looked at the photo of Emily's tattoo again. "How did someone get this three-inch tattoo to look so much like the original?"

"I don't know, but that structure has definitely seen better days."

They looked around and spotted a table with a lantern. A slatted wooden sign read Tickets for the Ghost Tour, May 1– August 31, and a scrawny kid with wire-framed glasses, the ticket seller presumably, looked up from her book.

Catherine took the lead. "Hi there. Can we speak to your mom or dad?"

The girl, who must've been only six or seven years old, was as mute and staring as a statue, the only sign of life her slow blinks as she gazed at them.

"Maybe a grandparent?" Catherine asked as Morgan took out her wallet. "How much for tickets?"

The girl looked away.

Morgan spoke. "Okay, kid. Here's twenty dollars. We're going into the lighthouse, all right?"

The girl watched Morgan set the money on the table and then returned to her book.

Catherine stepped inside first and called up. "Hello?" She heard movement above and called again. "We're looking for the owner of the lighthouse."

"Who's there?" A husky voice came from above them. "Ghost tours wait down below."

Catherine wanted to scream. She did not want a ghost tour. She wanted information about her daughter's whereabouts for the past ten weeks. Her fingertips reached for the cool stone as she wandered up the circular staircase. At the top, her eyes adjusted to a faint glow from scattered lamps. "My name is Catherine Callahan. I'm looking for news of my daughter, trying to find out if she came this way."

As she reached the top of the stairs with Morgan trailing behind, a woman crouched before them, wearing stained overalls a size too big and thick-soled brown boots. Glass panes that were coated with muck and grime were scattered all about, and the woman's hands were coated with suds. Her white hair stood on end as she looked up at her visitors.

Catherine held out the senior photo of Emily that she'd carried around with her in a plastic sleeve inside her wallet since she went missing. "We were hoping that you might have seen this girl—Emily. Emily Callahan."

A flicker of recognition, Catherine was sure of it.

"I don't know her."

"Please, Ms.—"

The woman looked from Catherine to Morgan, her mouth unsmiling, before she creakily stood to her feet. "Who'd you say you were again?"

"I'm a mother looking for news of her daughter. She was found in Galveston harbor a few days ago—alive," Catherine clarified. "I need to know if she spent any time here, even passing through."

The woman lifted her chin, considering. "My name's Delphinium Miller, but Phin is what people call me." She went back to her knees, wiping down the windows, though certainly no real light shone through them anymore. This lighthouse had been decommissioned more than two decades ago, from what Catherine had found online. Phin continued talking while she worked. "How do you know that the girl wants you to find out where she's been? Seems to me if people go missing of their own accord they don't usually want to be found."

Catherine bristled. "My daughter did not go missing *of her own accord.*"

Morgan stepped forward. "Emily is pregnant," she blurted and then held out a hand to Catherine as if to assure her that the abrupt admission must be made. The woman stopped the circular scrubbing motion for a few seconds. Morgan continued, "Is that your granddaughter down there? With the glasses? Wouldn't you want to find out everything possible if she went missing?"

Phin pinned Morgan and Catherine in place with her glare. "I'll invite both of you to leave my grandbaby out of this particular situation." She stood, wobbling for a moment on the uneven cement landing. "Listen. I may have seen your girl around here, but I don't feel at liberty to say much more until Sawyer gets back."

"Do you mean Sawyer Steele?" Morgan asked.

"That's his name. Sawyer's been a godsend these past couple years. He's out checking the crab traps, but he should be back in the next hour or so if you want to wait." The older woman threw her wet rag into a bin and motioned for the two of them to follow her back down the stairs and into the house hidden in the darkness a few yards away. Phin's granddaughter, her book and a flashlight in hand, followed them wordlessly.

"Logan, get these ladies some iced tea while Granny shows them where they can sit and rest a while. I don't think we'll have any ghost visitors this time a night anyway."

Catherine couldn't tell if Phin meant tourists or actual ghosts, and she shuddered at the thought. This remote place on the edge of the sea, unlit and untended, seemed like it would invite spirits.

"Have a seat." Catherine looked around at the high-back Victorian chairs. "Logan isn't gonna say two words to you, but she's all right. Misses her momma and daddy. Sawyer came along when I was wondering how we would manage the crabbing and the shrimping by ourselves, just an old woman with a toddler in tow."

Morgan took the reins of the conversation. "Do you know Sawyer's family? His mother? Leslie Steele?"

Phin shook her head and settled across from them, her knees creaky as she seated herself. "Can't say I've met her, and he don't talk much. None of us do, but we look out for each other. To tell the truth, I was sorely afraid I might lose him to the mainland the day after... Well, I reckon' he'll tell you about all that if the spirit so moves him."

Logan brought in iced tea and a plate of cookies, glancing

over at her grandmother for permission. Phin signaled with a terse nod and a hint of a grin, and Logan grabbed a cookie for each hand and wandered into the recesses of the house.

Catherine had the sudden urge to hurl questions at the old woman, to hurry her along, but she sensed that their invitation into this home had only come by means of a kind of submissiveness on their part, a willingness to wait if that's what was required. The pace was slower here, almost like they'd stepped back in time: the low-set corner couch, the yellow-tinged lighting, the thin strips of dark hardwood. Had her daughter spent time here? Sat on this chair? Drank from this glass?

Catherine couldn't help herself. "How long have you lived out here?"

"My family's owned the lighthouse for generations. I helped maintain the place until the government no longer had need of it, but we keep it up for the tourists now." Phin leaned back and stretched her arthritic hands. "You know, those old ladies who travel around looking at all the lighthouses? They'll come, and a handful of nights in the summer, we'll get some younger visitors with our ghost tours." Phin's face returned to an unexpressive stare. "Well, I've got some work to do, if you'll excuse me." The old woman stood again, patted her pockets as if missing something, and disappeared down the hallway where her granddaughter had walked.

Morgan looked around. "What is this place?"

"Sounds like it could be where Emily has been for the past ten weeks, and if so, I need to know everything about it."

Catherine wandered around the room, searching for anything that might indicate Emily's presence. Other than the seats, a dark desk and an upright piano in the corner, the room was sparse. Not even a television or computer in sight. These people must almost live off the grid. "What do you know about Sawyer?"

"He's a twin, three years older than his sister, Anna. I used to think the boys were identical, but the older they got, the more different they looked. Sawyer seemed like a pretty normal kid until his senior year when his dad died, and he kind of fell off the deep end." Morgan paused for a beat. "To be fair, though, I think Michael was probably the normal parent in the family."

"What kind of trouble did he get into?"

"Mostly skipping school, drinking, smoking pot, Alex told me. But I wonder if the kid was just trying to escape the expectations of the island. You know, get away from the comparisons to his brother, from the label as the 'kid whose dad died.' Asher went the other direction, throwing himself into busyness and achievements just like his mother." Morgan moved toward the kitchen and bit her lip as she took in the stained cabinets. "Well, shit. Might as well really look for clues. It doesn't sound like that crazy lady plans to come back."

Morgan began shuffling through drawers while Catherine sank into a kitchen chair and closed her eyes, mentally scanning through the past few days and weeks. *Give me another clue, Em. One clue.*

Morgan inhaled. "Look at this." She was holding a sketch of a girl's face, the eyes penetrating. Her hair hung full and free over her shoulders. "This is Emily, right?"

Catherine fingered the drawing, tracing the outline of the jaw and the smile creases around her daughter's eyes. That was her girl.

"Yonder he comes," Phin said, reentering the room. "Ah, I see you found the portrait. That's good." She shuffled out to meet the young man in the darkness, to warn him most likely.

Minutes later, Catherine took in the boy, almost a man, standing before her. He looked similar to Asher, the college student who'd been shadowing Dr. Steele, but she wouldn't have said they were identical. This boy was the exact same height as that one—maybe five-nine—but he had a mop of brown hair growing wavy over his ears. His lips were thin and his eyes wide-set like his brother, but Sawyer's frame was broader. His sleeves were rolled up, and his biceps were full and round, probably from setting and opening the traps scattered around Bolivar. Sawyer's appearance looked like the young man at the hospital had been cloned and then toned up with hard work and plenty of sunshine.

"Ms. Phin says that you wanted to see me about a guest we had out here for a few weeks?" He spoke and his voice was dark and somber, reminding Catherine of a bass clarinet. She realized that she'd only heard his brother speak a handful of times, but Asher's voice was lighter, a French horn. Sawyer's question was more direct than Catherine expected, but how glad she was that he got straight to the point.

She cleared her throat and held up the picture Morgan had found in the cabinet. "How do you know this girl?"

Sawyer's eyes lit and his lips went into a half grin. "Emily?"

Hearing her daughter's name startled Catherine. "She has a tattoo of a lighthouse that looks like the one here, and she was found in a life jacket floating in the harbor a few days ago. I want to… I need to know what happened to her."

"Is she okay?"

Catherine considered how much to share. "Yes," she said simply.

Sawyer inhaled and paused, looking at Catherine and Morgan's faces. "All right. I just have one condition. If I answer your questions, I want to see her."

Catherine calculated: This might be her only chance to find out where her daughter had been.

"Deal," she said.

Phin refilled glasses of iced tea while Sawyer changed into clothes that didn't carry the stench of seawater. A few minutes later, he sat across from the two women.

"So, what do you want to know?"

"When did you meet her?"

"I was about to drive out to Rollover Pass to change the traps when I saw this girl wander onto the bank of the road between the asphalt and the salt water. She looked like she was lost, so I pulled over to make sure she was all right."

"Was she? I mean, did she look like she'd been…" Catherine paused and looked to Morgan.

"Did she look like she'd been attacked?" Morgan finished for her.

"I couldn't tell for sure, and she didn't offer any details." He looked to Phin. "Right? Not even after she'd been here a few weeks. I could see that her hair was messy and her eyes were—I don't know, confused? She was wearing a long shirt or maybe it was a short dress. She didn't have on shoes, but she wasn't…she didn't have any bruises or…or blood."

Thank God, Catherine sighed. "That's the shirt she was wearing when she disappeared, but her jeans from that night washed up on the shore a week or two ago. Any idea how they got from her body into the water?"

Catherine stared at Sawyer, the penetrating power of a mother wanting more information.

Sawyer avoided her eyes, but answered. "I don't know, but that morning she wasn't wearing jeans and didn't have a purse or backpack, so I didn't think she was a hitchhiker. She looked tired, but when I spoke to her, she didn't seem particularly scared or anything."

"What did she say when you pulled over?" Catherine bit her lip.

"She didn't say much. I asked her what her name was and where she was trying to get to, and she told me that her name was Emily, and she needed help. I thought she meant that she needed food and a place to stay."

"A place to stay?" Catherine's throat caught on the words. "She had…has a home."

"I didn't know." Sawyer put out both hands. "She never said."

"Sawyer was trying to be helpful." Phin took a step forward. "He brought her to me and asked if we could put her up for a couple of nights until she sorted out a more permanent situation. I fed her breakfast and gave her some of my daughter's old clothes, and by the end of the week, Emily already fit in like she'd been here forever." Phin nodded toward the back door. "She helped plant the raised garden out back that you can't see 'cause it's too dark, and she's the one who helped me start cleaning the lantern panes. That's what I was working on when the two of you arrived."

"Why didn't you ask about her past? She's eighteen years old. Barely an adult." A sob threatened to escape from Catherine's throat. "We were terrified. You can't begin to understand."

Phin put out a hand to stop her. "Listen, I've lost both Logan's momma and her daddy, so I think I can imagine what you were going through, and I'm sorry. But we only knew what your girl told us. She told us her name, but beyond that, she didn't seem like she wanted—or was able—to talk much about the past. I'm not sure if you've noticed, but we aren't a real chatty bunch. We like to let people be."

"Phin took her in like she took me in a couple of years ago," Sawyer said. "Gave me and then Emily a place to stay and something to keep our hands busy, keep us out of trouble."

"Emily isn't the kind of kid who gets herself in trouble." Catherine was undeterred. She stood. "Sawyer, we need to take a walk."

He turned to Phin, questioning.

"I don't think she's much of a threat, if that's what you're wondering," Phin said plainly.

Morgan moved as if she were coming too, but Catherine

stopped her. She needed to know every detail and didn't think Sawyer would talk if he had an audience.

"After you," Sawyer said and then followed Catherine out into the blackness of the night.

"Sawyer, I need to know what your relationship was like with Emily. I need all the details—good, bad and ugly. Do you understand?" Catherine could barely make out his profile, but she somehow felt him nodding beside her. She hoped she could sense whether or not he was telling the truth as well.

"Me and Emily didn't have too much to do with one another that first week she was out here. She slept a lot, and Logan stayed by her side. She had a bad headache when we first picked her up and seemed to have trouble remembering much of anything except her name. Phin kept her fed and let her rest and then told me one morning that she'd be joining me on my errands, said it was time for Emily to learn that this wasn't a charity home." He chuckled lightly. "That's how Phin is. She gives tough love."

"So Emily worked with you?"

"Yeah. I taught her how to check the traps, and she seemed to already know a bunch about wildlife even though she couldn't remember simple things, like her phone number or address. She cracked me up with how she'd rattle off facts about crabs and birds." That sounded like Emily.

"And she never talked about her family?"

He shrugged. "No. All she said was that her family used to live in Oregon. She seemed really confused when I asked her for details. Maybe something happened before I picked her up."

That, among other things, was what Catherine was afraid of. "And did you…did you become close to Emily?"

Sawyer cleared his throat. "Yeah, I suppose."

"How? When?"

He stopped and turned toward the sound of the lapping waves. "I don't know if I can say exactly."

Catherine was growing impatient. "Try."

"Yes, ma'am." He paused, considering. "I guess it was the second week she was here, but to be honest, you kind of lose track of time out here when every day is spent about the same as the last. Emily was handling the blue crabs and the stone crabs like an old pro. After the first couple days, she'd learned to bait the throw line and could spot the berry crabs, the ones we can't keep during spawning season. I gotta say I was impressed. I'd never seen someone take to the sea creatures so fast. That day when we...we connected, I guess you could say—"

Catherine's eyebrows rose, but thankfully, he couldn't see her in the dark. Connected, he'd said? What did that mean? But if she pressed for more information now, Sawyer might quit talking. She kept quiet.

"At the end of her second week here, I decided to take her out on the North Jetty, one of the best places to collect quarry. It was early March, a cold day and windy as everything. Nobody else was out there when we walked to the farthest point around 6:00 a.m., and I was showing her how to locate and check one of our smallest traps when I lost my footing. Next thing I knew, Emily was on her belly. She'd grabbed me by my jacket hood and was holding on for dear life while the waves tried to throw me into the rocks. I don't know how long it took me to get back to dry ground—maybe ten minutes—but I was shivering like I'd been dropped in a bucket of ice. Emily sprang into action and took care of everything. She drove me home and got me in a hot shower and made breakfast. I guess it was like a damsel in distress except in reverse."

Sawyer chuckled at the memory, but Catherine wasn't smiling. This boy had been with her daughter for two and a half months and hadn't alerted any authorities. She was not amused. "And after that?"

"After that, we were friends. She started telling me about her sisters and she borrowed every book she could find from Logan about sea creatures and she made dinner with Phin every night. She became one of us. And then—" He stopped midstride.

Catherine wanted to tell this boy that Emily was not and never would be *one of them*. Instead, she said, "We told Phin already, but I think you should know. Emily is pregnant." Catherine paused to gauge his reaction.

"But how? What do you mean? When—?"

Catherine measured her words carefully. "Sawyer, did you take advantage of my daughter?"

"No. I mean, no, ma'am. I would never... I mean... I loved her." His voice cracked. "I do still...love her, I mean."

Catherine narrowed her gaze. He loved her? What was it with these boys—first Alex, now Sawyer—fawning over her daughter? Emily had never even dated anyone back in Woodhaven, though to be fair that could've been because she'd known most of them since birth. She called her daughter's innocent eyes to mind. Would Emily sleep with a boy who she thought loved her? Maybe. But Sawyer and Emily had known one another for all of ten weeks at best. Ten weeks! Besides, Catherine had always expected her daughter's faith would prevent that kind of thing. That was one of the perks of having a religious kid.

"Sawyer, I've heard things about you. I know you have a less than reputable history with drugs, with alcohol, and I need to know if you were ever under the influence when you were with her." She tried to sound generous as she added, "Maybe you don't remember..."

"I swear I've been clean since Phin took me in. You can ask her."

"All right. I will," Catherine said matter-of-factly. "So when did you last see Emily?"

"It was the night that we drove out near the Bolivar ferry docks where I first picked her up. We were looking at the stars, and we…we kissed. And it was like as soon as I touched her, her eyes went wild, like she didn't know me or…or like she was scared of me."

He stared down at his feet as Catherine's throat constricted. Her daughter did not often feel afraid; Emily had too much knowledge and too much faith for fear. If this boy had made her feel threatened, then she had reason to be. What was Catherine missing?

"The next morning, she was gone," he said. "She only took what she'd brought with her."

"When we found her, she had on a life jacket from the ferry."

He shook his head. "That's not what I expected. I thought she'd headed back to her family in Oregon, but she didn't leave a note or anything. Phin told me to be patient, that we would hear something soon enough." He turned his gaze to Catherine. "But I guess you were only a boat ride away this whole time."

Just as Emily had been for those ten weeks. Why hadn't Emily contacted her? Had she really not known that her family was only a dozen miles away? Had she really been that separated from reality?

"I'm going to be straight with you, Sawyer. The police will pull you in for questioning, and they will likely come out here to visit with Phin and take a look around, but before they start all that, I'll keep my word. You can follow us back to the hospital and see Emily."

"Hospital?" Sawyer sounded genuinely concerned. "Is she... Is Emily hurt?"

She stared at him for a long moment; she hadn't realized that he knew nothing of her daughter's current condition. "We told you that we found her floating in the harbor, but I failed to mention that she's been unconscious since the fishing boat picked her up. We have no idea when she'll wake up."

Sawyer struggled to catch his breath at first, and when he finally looked up, the tears in his eyes—barely visible in the moonlight—surprised Catherine. Tears or not, his name would remain on her short list of suspects, right above Alex Frasier.

"Take me to see her," he said. "Please."

She would. And she would be watching him the entire time.

24
May
Emily

Someone new is in my room, the open scent of salt water wafting in with him.

"Hey, Emily. It's Sawyer." I know that voice, but I can't picture him. He leans so close that I can feel the heat from his skin. I think of Alex and the way he could tuck me into the warmth of him. I don't know this heat. Or do I?

Flickers, the spark of a memory, begin. A hazy road, this same voice saying, "Are you all right?"

In my memory, I stumble forward and look around, uncertain of my surroundings. My head pounds in the light of early morning. I don't know how long I've been walking, but my mouth is dry and my feet sore.

"Whoa. Careful."

Road, water, salt grass as far as the eye can see. Except for this boy and his truck. He follows my gaze to the horizon, and his brow furrows. He's puzzled about something just like

I am. I stumble again, and he moves to catch me. I don't run. I can't. I'm tired, so very tired. I wish I was at home in Woodhaven, laying on our couch, falling asleep while my family watches *An Affair to Remember*.

"Is there somewhere I can take you? Family I can call?"

I move my head, but I don't know if I'm nodding yes or shaking no. "Oregon," I finally answer, the words coming without a thought.

"Hmmm…that's not quite in driving distance," he tries to joke. When I don't laugh, he studies the asphalt. "How about this? I'll give you a ride out to a lady I know—Phin. She'll help you sort everything out."

As I step one heavy foot and then the other into the cab of his truck, the memory stops as if someone presses pause. Then, it's that endless black chasm again.

The boy whispers now in my hospital room, his voice halting every few words as if he's holding back tears. "You remember driving out early…to watch…to watch the sun rise over the water? You said…you said it reminded you of the first lick of an orange sherbet pop." He has an easy laugh full of whispers and promises.

I can't decide whether I want him to stay or leave, but Mom's hands are on the other side of me, gripping me, tugging me back to her.

"And remember that cake you and Logan made? You forgot the eggs and it turned as hard as a rock, but we dipped it in coffee and ate it anyway?" He sighs. "Logan's been asking about you, in her way. Wants to make sure you didn't go away forever like her momma and daddy. I told her you'd come back to us soon enough, but I had no idea that…"

He breaks off and sniffs a few times, backing away from me. Logan? I have no idea who or what he's talking about, and frustration rushes in, heating my face and making my monitors beep, but I drift off into my memories and let them deal with my physiology.

Suddenly, I'm wandering in the forest at the base of Mt. Hood the day I learned about the Alpine snow gum in our fourth grade plant unit—the *Eucalyptus pauciflora*. Mrs. Hall explains how this evergreen was transplanted to Portland from the mountains of southern Australia and remains important in Oregon because it offers shade to the lavender and cistus plants. I stand next to the squatty, striped trunk of the tree while she tells us how the snow gum can withstand a variety of conditions. She speaks with eyes full of a contagious excitement. *The seeds need heat—like fire—to implant, to burrow into the earth.* She holds up a cone and shows us the resin coating it. *When the fire melts the protective layer, the cones open, releasing the seeds so more snow gums can grow. Until that happens, these cones may lay dormant—asleep—for years, waiting for an event to open them up, so they can plant their seeds and grow new life.*

My mind climbs back to the present, to this boy who is not Alex, to this boy who brushes a stubbled cheek against my hand, to this boy who ignites memories. Something tells me that Sawyer may be my fire, or he may be the fire that burned me.

As a nurse comes in and quiets the beeps, I try hard to squeeze my mom's hand, to tell her that I am inside here, listening and thinking and wondering along with her, to tell her that I wish I could wake up and help her find out what happened, to tell her that I need her to keep searching on my behalf.

Though my mind pleads with my fingers to move, my body refuses to cooperate, so I remain alone inside my mind until I hear Mom mutter *That's enough* before ushering this familiar stranger from my room.

I wish I could call Sawyer back to me. For better or worse, I think he's the flicker that may spark me back to life.

25

May
Leslie

At the end of the school day, Leslie met Anna at her car. They were on half days for finals, and while most schools didn't require seniors with solid grades to take the tests, Callahan Prep demanded excellence from start to finish. Anna had taken two long exams that morning, and light blue rings now shaded her eyes.

"Hey, Mom. What are you doing here?"

"I was picking up the card that everyone signed for Emily. I wanted to put it with the orchid I'm taking up to the hospital. You want to ride with me?"

Anna hesitated, so Leslie gave her an out. "If it's too much for you…"

A half hour ago Leslie had wondered if it was too much for herself as she'd hovered over the toilet, releasing the contents of her stomach. But she'd cleaned herself up and pressed onward as always.

"I mean, I should probably go, right?"

Leslie looked her daughter up and down. *Yes, you should go.* "It's up to you," she said instead.

Anna looked up as if waiting for an answer to fall from the sky. "Fine, I'll go. Will Asher be there?"

"I suppose."

Asher seemed to spend every moment at that hospital with his uncle. He was even talking about missing his own upcoming college graduation, a ridiculous idea after how hard he'd worked. Leslie would see about that.

A few minutes later as the two Steele women stood outside the neurology wing, daughter behind mother, Leslie heard the cadence of familiar voices rising and falling. Her boys, here at the hospital, together. She could hardly remember the last time she'd heard Sawyer's voice. Instinctively, she started toward them.

"Slow down, Mom," Anna called. Leslie hadn't even realized she was picking up speed until her daughter tugged at her arm, but she couldn't slow down. They turned a corner and almost slammed into her sons, both of her sons.

When Leslie dropped the orchid, the wide ceramic bowl splashed against the tiled floor, spraying shards and fragments from the pot as well as a layer of dirt and roots.

The Steele family, gathered together unexpectedly, examined the mess before looking from person to person. How long it had been since they'd all been in the same space, Leslie thought before she and Asher began speaking at once. Sawyer stooped down to pick up the sharp pieces, and Anna's shoulders slumped forward as if she wished she could blend into the wall.

"Mother—" Asher started.

"Oh, my God. Sawyer, where have you been? And don't tell me—" Leslie said at the same time, her motherly concern colliding with her frustration at this boy who had done so much wrong but was still her son.

"He came to check on—"

"You have no idea how scared I get when I think of you out—"

"If you'll give him a minute to—"

"Were you planning to miss your only sister's graduation? How can you—"

Robert approached the four of them, startling Leslie mid-sentence. "Can you all keep it down? This is the neuro wing, not the psych ward."

The rest of the Steele family did not laugh.

Leslie pulsed her hands and attempted a deep breath, but it was as if a vise had clamped itself around her heart. A cold sweat crept from the back of her neck to her forehead, and the room began to tilt on its axis. She sank to the floor, conscious, but heaving for air, blessed air. She felt Robert's hands push her head between her knees, and for a split second she was glad she still did yoga three times a week; otherwise, she would've never been able to get into the pose.

"Ask a nurse for a paper bag," Robert's voice instructed, floating above her.

"I'll get her water," Sawyer's voice said.

"I'm fine," Leslie attempted as her brother-in-law rubbed circles into her back until her breathing returned to near normal. A few minutes later, she raised her head and attempted to stand. The movement made her dizzy and bile rose in her throat.

"Let's wait another minute, Mom." Sawyer spoke again. He had called her *Mom*. For the first time, she examined him, his long hair and chiseled jaw. He was becoming a man and looked more like Michael than ever.

Leslie's eyes darted behind him as heads peeked out from

a nearby room. Catherine Callahan. And, oh, no. Rosalyn emerged from the room and slowly walked toward her. Leslie had not expected to see the woman here today, didn't know if she could stomach seeing her, not in this disheveled state, not after the emotions of seeing Sawyer for the first time in years. She'd always wanted—no, needed—to project back to Rosalyn that image of confidence and authority, to show the older woman that she could carry on the traditions of Callahan Prep and orchestrate the social structure of the island. Where were those anxiety pills when she actually needed them?

Rosalyn's lips smiled, but her eyes remained aloof. "Do we need to get you a room, Leslie?"

"I think our patient is better," Robert tried awkwardly. "How is Emily? I was about to come and see her."

Rosalyn glared at him in a way that made it seem as if he were personally responsible for her granddaughter's state. "You should know better than anyone. Still sleeping, Doctor."

After arriving home from the hospital, Anna went straight to her room, obviously not wanting to rehash the afternoon. They hadn't even made it in to see Emily, instead handing over the card to Rosalyn and making a quick getaway. Leslie took a pill and rested for a couple of hours, but as soon as Asher entered the house, she tromped into the kitchen. She needed to know if Sawyer's return had anything to do with Emily Callahan. She watched Asher make himself a sandwich and then tossed out her first question.

"Why was Sawyer there? To see her?" she asked.

"Who?" Asher questioned between bites of a peanut butter sandwich. All her son ate was hospital food, cereal and sandwiches.

"Oh, Emily? He said she was out wandering around Bolivar weeks ago. Apparently she was pretty confused, couldn't even tell him where she actually lived."

"Where did he take her?"

"To where he's been staying—that old lighthouse."

This was news to Leslie. "Did he know that Emily was missing?" She held her breath for the answer.

Asher shook his head. "No. You know how the Callahans keep the island press away from their family, and even if the story was on the news or out on social media, Sawyer isn't into that kind of thing. It sounds like he's pretty disconnected. No television or internet."

"But the lighthouse had to be within the police-search parameters," Leslie countered. "Was she there with him the entire time?"

"I guess, but it makes you wonder, huh?" Asher raised an eyebrow.

"Wonder what?" But her palms began to sweat.

He sighed. "Mom, she was at a nonfunctioning lighthouse for weeks, a place completely unplugged."

"What do you mean unplugged?"

"Off the grid. No electronics, no electricity except what they generate on their own. Apparently, when he wasn't setting traps, he was working on the property, restoring the lighthouse, installing solar panels, that kind of thing. The woman who owns the place lost her daughter and son-in-law a few years ago in a boating accident and went a little nuts. She's been managing on her own since then. I'm sure she thought she'd hit the jackpot when Sawyer strolled up one day, free manpower in exchange for room and board. And I'm sure Sawyer was thrilled when this girl wandered into his life. Saw his chance to finally get a girlfriend."

Leslie frowned as Asher continued.

"Remember the last time he tried to get a girl?" He gave her a pointed look. "She ended up moving away."

"Who?" Leslie hoped Asher wasn't saying what she thought he was saying.

"Julie... Julie something."

"Julie Wagner." Leslie tried to stay calm, unfolding and refolding the dish towel in her hand.

"Yeah, that's her," Asher answered.

It felt as if a dense fog had just rolled in, her mind stumbling through the thick murkiness of the truth. One son was confirming her worst fear about the other: It had been Sawyer who took advantage of that girl years ago, and now he'd found another girl to prey upon, a Callahan at that.

"Who is this woman that Sawyer has been living with? I want to speak with her."

Asher placed a hand on her forearm. "Mom, if you couldn't get Sawyer to call you back, how do you expect to get him to put you in touch with this lady?"

"I'll drive out there and—"

"Sawyer's planning to head back to the ferry after visiting hours tonight—if Emily's family lets him see her again, which I doubt." Asher finished the last bite and took a sip of Red Bull. "Anyway, I'm supposed to meet a couple of med students to hang out, but Sawyer said he was going to head over here and say hello. If I were you, I would talk to him about all of this."

Asher took off, and Leslie sat down to wait.

It was another half hour before Sawyer walked in, the prodigal son returned.

But Leslie was not the parent with open arms. This meeting brought her back to another late-night conversation in this very room. It was a week after Christmas three years ago.

Sawyer's eyes had been red-rimmed and puffy, and Leslie had felt numb as she stumbled from the downstairs bedroom where her husband had spent the last month. Moments earlier, she'd found Sawyer standing over his father, his dead father.

Sawyer's voice had cracked. "This is the way Dad wanted it."

Leslie had swallowed back her tears. "How do you know what your father wanted? How and when he wanted to...to go?"

Sawyer's eyes were questioning, uncertain. "He wrote down what he wanted before he...before he got to the point that he couldn't even say his own name. I'm sure he talked with you about how he wanted this to end?"

Sawyer had looked at her, as if pleading for absolution. *Please tell me this is what Dad wanted. Please comfort me.*

Leslie wanted to, but she couldn't. Yes, her husband had told her that when he became fully and finally incapacitated, he wanted to go. *No lingering*, Michael had said before he could no longer speak, but she never thought he actually meant it. Who in their right mind would want to leave their family while breath remained in their lungs?

"You know he wasn't thinking clearly when he wrote that," Leslie sputtered.

Her husband lay in the other room, his soul flown from his body, his eyes eternally closed while Sawyer's eyes turned metallic.

He looked at his mother with a penetrating gaze so like his father's. Over the fireplace, she had a picture of the two of them deep-water fishing at an annual Boy Scouts event. Sawyer's spirit, his mannerisms were a carbon copy of his father's, and that's why she wanted to forgive him even after he'd done the unforgivable. She even wondered fleetingly if she should thank him for doing the hard thing that she could not bring herself to do, but instead, she'd pushed Sawyer further and further away.

Sawyer had tried a different argument. "You know Uncle Robert couldn't administer the medication. It had to be someone other than a doctor."

Medication? Could one rightfully call drugs used in assisted suicide a medication?

"Uncle Robert could lose his license, and even if he didn't and word got out, his patients would never look at him the same. This way it looks like Dad passed away peacefully, in his sleep. Here, at home."

As her son said those words, Leslie experienced for the first time that awful feeling of terror that had become her companion ever since. Leslie couldn't take a deep, solidifying breath, her heart pummeled her rib cage, her stomach lunged and her knees weakened. Of course, she'd heard of panic attacks, but she'd never experienced the sinking sensation, that feeling that she might truly be dying at that very moment. At least she would join Michael, her one consolation.

Sitting at the same kitchen table years later, she took a long drink from her Cabernet. "What are you doing back on the island?"

Sawyer smiled an awkward grin. "Good to see you too, Mom."

"You know what I mean. After everything that happened with that Wagner girl and the drugs and your father…"

Sawyer sighed. "Can we please not do this right now? I especially don't want to talk about Dad tonight."

"We will talk about him and all the other…things. I tried to speak with you about all of this years ago before you fell off the face of the earth, but you wouldn't call me back, wouldn't even come see me," Leslie said, her tone harsher than she'd intended. She didn't know how to approach him after all this time. "Surely you've grown up enough by now to take owner-ship for your actions."

Sawyer sank into the chair across from her. "Where's Asher?"

"He went out with some friends, but he'll be home in a couple of hours. He has to get up early to round with Robert tomorrow morning."

"Figures."

"What does that mean? Your brother is responsible, tak-ing his future seriously. What have you been doing with your life?"

As she said the words, she stepped toward him. Part of her wanted to reach out, to wrap him in her arms, to tell him they could start again.

"After everything with your dad, you lost all sight of your potential. You could've done something meaningful with your life instead of living at some lighthouse that doesn't even work." Leslie surprised herself by tearing up. "Your brother told me."

"God, Mom." He stood and brushed a hand through his hair. It needed a good trim. "I can't do this right now. Emily... My... She's laying there unconscious."

"*Your* Emily? Is she pregnant with *your* baby? Yes, the whole island knows of her...condition. Did you do to her what you did to that Wagner girl?"

Frustration leaped into his eyes, but his tone remained stoic. "That wasn't me."

Leslie could feel the redness rising to her cheeks. She was angry with her son for so many things: for lying to her, for hiding his drug use, for helping kill his father. If only he would tell her the truth, the full truth for once. Her fingers clenched the rim of the wineglass as she tried to control her emotions.

Sawyer stared into her eyes until she had to look away.

When he spoke, his voice was forceful. "You want to talk about what happened with Dad? Fine. I came in and found Dad already breathing erratically. He'd taken the drugs that Uncle Robert had given him. Dad was in so much pain, Mom. You saw him. He was ready to go, but I actually tried to save him. I was about to call 911, hoping they might have something to reverse the effects, when Dad reached out one last time and pulled my head to his chest. He couldn't say it, but I knew he'd chosen the time to end things. I didn't tell you all of this back then, couldn't let you think of him as taking his own life. He was a chaplain, for God's sake. That's why I let you and everyone else in this family believe the story you wanted."

Leslie wiped at her tears with the palm of her hand.

"And yeah, I smoked weed and drank for a while to medicate my grief, but I'm sober now, and I would never hurt a girl. You know that."

Leslie didn't know that. She'd thought this whole time that he'd been the only one to blame for Michael's death, an ending she hadn't been ready for. Michael could've made it to the boys' graduation, maybe even through the summer. And maybe Sawyer was still to blame. He hadn't called 911, after all. Regardless, this information changed nothing. She was sure that Sawyer was somehow involved in Emily Callahan's disappearance.

Biting her lip, Leslie tried to keep from spewing all of this at the child who had lied to her, abandoned her and humiliated her. The child she still loved, despite it all.

She glanced at him one more time before turning off the light. "You can stay here if you need to," she said over her shoulder. It was all she could bring herself to offer.

He stared at his boots, worn and scuffed, and shook his head. "No, I need to get back home."

26

May
Morgan

Whitey's voice startled her as soon as she put the phone to her ear.

"Morgan? We're gonna need you to come down here and pick up Alex." With one eye open, she examined her surroundings, reminding herself that she'd ended up at Robert's apartment. After her excursion to the Bolivar lighthouse the night before, she'd needed to be with him. They'd eaten a late dinner and come back here for a drink, among other things.

"Wait. Where is he?"

"At the station on Thirty-First."

Her heart hammered, the rhythm hard and fast as a techno beat. "What did he do?"

"Come down, and we'll explain everything."

"On my way."

Whitey's voice lowered to a whisper. "As a courtesy to you,

I'm keeping him out of a cell and in a holding room, but you'll need to speak to me before you see him."

Without waking Robert, Morgan threw on her clothes and slipped out into the early-morning hours, the air already hot and sticky despite the breeze.

Minutes later she was seated before Whitey. Again. "What's this about?"

"We got a call a couple hours ago. There was a disturbance at one of the bars, one that supposedly serves only sodas to minors."

"The Anchor?"

That place had been a popular hangout spot when she was a kid. Morgan remembered the night that she and Michael were there, listening to a local band while Leslie was at the school decorating for some event. It had been a rough couple of weeks for Morgan, dealing with her mother. By that point, she was waking her, dressing her, driving her to work and picking her up at the end of the day. She had no idea how her mom functioned in the in-between hours. To let off a little steam, Morgan drank a couple more than usual, sobbed incoherently on Michael's shoulder for a half hour and then, without a thought, kissed him. She thought he probably kissed her back, which made the ordeal all the worse. It was stupid, a mistake, but one that Michael had confessed to Leslie the next day, forever ruining the two girls' friendship.

Here Morgan was, in this police station because of another stupid mistake made at The Anchor.

"Alex was part of the disturbance?"

Whitey sighed. "Alex was the disturbance. Apparently, he has some kind of issue with one of the Steele twins and gave him a pretty good pounding."

"Which one?" Morgan hoped it wasn't Asher, Leslie's favorite. She could not deal with that woman tonight.

"The one that's never around."

Sawyer. Thank God. "What were they fighting about?"

Whitey shrugged. "What it's always about—a girl. Neither one would tell me much."

"Who all was there?"

"Asher was hanging out with some friends when his brother came in, talking about having just one drink before he boarded the ferry back to Bolivar. After a couple of rounds, your boy appeared on the scene, and within minutes, he was punching Sawyer. Asher jumped into the fray at some point."

Morgan cringed. She knew her son's strength. "How bad was it?"

"Asher's fine—just a fat lip. But one of the ER docs is taking a look at Sawyer over at the hospital. From what I could see, this'll be nothing more than a black eye, maybe a broken nose. The kid's gonna be sore for a while, I can tell you that, but it coulda been worse. Honestly, it's probably nothing one of the boys couldn't get on the football field in a rough-and-tumble game."

Morgan knew this truth well. Alex had exited games with a variety of injuries over the years: concussions, a dislocated shoulder, a torn ACL. All for the love of the game.

"Can I see Alex?"

"Yeah, I told him you were on your way and that he got lucky that the Steele boys didn't want to press charges. Apparently, Sawyer just wanted to get back to Bolivar."

Morgan frowned. Hadn't Sawyer been dying to see Emily?

"I also told Alex that he's gotta stop getting himself in these messes," Whitey said. "He's about to graduate and go off to school, and I don't want to see a good kid like him wind up on the news because he's in the wrong place at the wrong time. Trouble seems to follow him wherever he goes."

"You don't have to tell me," Morgan mumbled.

★ ★ ★

When Morgan and Alex pulled into the parking lot after a silent ride home, a car was waiting. Leslie. Shit. The two women hadn't been alone in the same space for…well, more than two decades, and tonight was not the night for a confrontation.

"Go inside and get an ice pack for your hand," Morgan said to Alex as she eyed the woman standing on the sidewalk. Alex brushed past Mrs. Steele, his eyes fixed on the ground.

"Your son doesn't look the worse for wear," Leslie said after watching him close the lobby door. Her tone was rocky, unstable as if she'd been drinking.

Morgan nodded, wiping clammy hands against her leggings. "He said Sawyer didn't fight back. Just took the hits."

Leslie leaned against the hood of her car, crossing her ankles, like she was trying to appear natural, at ease. Instead, she tilted slightly to one side. "I'd just fallen asleep when Asher came home and woke me up to tell me about the fight. Apparently, Robert is at the hospital now with Sawyer, but you probably already knew that."

Morgan didn't know that, but she brushed the comment aside. This wasn't the time to get into her love life. Instead, she offered an olive branch. "I'm glad to hear that Sawyer's going to be okay. There will be consequences for Alex."

"I don't know about okay," Leslie huffed. "That boy may wind up in jail someday."

"Sawyer?" He seemed like a decent enough kid to Morgan, but what did she know? For years she hadn't been able to determine the guilt or innocence of her own son.

Leslie nodded and took out a cigarette. Morgan remembered Leslie smoked on two types of occasions back in the day: when she was nervous and when she was elated. Morgan could guess which one this was.

"So…you're not angry about what happened at the bar tonight?"

Leslie stared into Morgan's eyes, holding in a drag before releasing the smoke along with her answer. "No, not mad, not at that."

Morgan stepped closer, closing the distance between them. With the smoke and the May heat and the scent of Leslie's shampoo, nostalgia hit her like the casting of a spell, a spell that took her back to the days when she could confide in Leslie, when they could share the best and worst of themselves— everything except Morgan's mother's addiction. *That* she'd never shared with anyone except her ex-husband. Morgan sometimes wondered if the silence may have been the first crumbling brick in the ruins of her friendship with Leslie. If only Morgan could cross the chasm between them, the chasm opened by her unwillingness to confide about her mother's drug use and widened by a drunken kiss decades ago—an unforgivable act of betrayal in Leslie's mind—then maybe they could reconnect. Leslie was an all or nothing kind of girl with everything in her life: from school dances to bake sales to friendships. By not initially sharing her mother's illness, perhaps Morgan had signaled that she was not all in.

Leslie put out the hand that wasn't holding the cigarette. "Listen. Tonight, the confrontation between our boys made me think, made me start digging around in the past."

"That's never a good thing."

"Maybe, but I… I need to know something." Leslie took a deep breath. "What was going on between you and my husband before his last cancer diagnosis?"

"Nothing, Leslie. I swear. Nothing at all. We reconnected, met for lunch once, that's it. The last time I heard from him was when he called to tell me that the cancer was back."

Leslie rolled her eyes. "For Christ's sake, he was *my* husband. He didn't need to tell you that or anything else. I don't know why you could never give up chasing after him."

A surge of frustration gave Morgan a hit of courage. "I wasn't chasing him, and I think that deep down you know that." She narrowed her eyes, trying to read this version of Leslie Steele. She wasn't the same person she'd been all those years ago. "You want to use me as a scapegoat for any problems you ever had in your marriage? Fine. But I swear that nothing was going on between me and Michael. Ever. It was one stupid kiss."

Leslie spat a low chuckle, the sound spoiled and dark, as if something inside her had been festering for far too long. "Don't give me that crap. Our last fight was about you and him and whatever move you were trying to make. It was because of you that I doubted my husband, *my* Michael. Of course I knew the two of you met—this is a small town and I'm well-informed—but I also knew that a woman like you doesn't get together for lunch or coffee without a motive. The timing was ideal. You were about to lose your husband, and you wanted mine. You've always needed someone to make you feel loved, what with your mom being nothing more than a junkie."

Leslie took a final drag, looked at a stunned Morgan as if she knew she'd hit her intended mark. Leslie stomped out the cigarette, climbed into her car and drove toward the dark ocean.

27
May
Emily

Seven days. That's how long I've been lying here.

In Genesis after God finishes the heavy lifting of creation, the writer says, *On the seventh day He rested from all His work.* The Hebrew word for *rest* is *shabbat* and can also translate as *cease, desist,* or even *celebrate.*

Lying here with all the time in the world, my mind winds backward like a movie reel in reverse. I picture God's spirit hovering over the deep, His voice speaking into the darkness: *Let there be light.* Everything evolving over billions of years. Then finally, after all the work, He rests.

Last spring back in Oregon, my final paper in Ms. Thakkar's math class was on Chaos Theory, an idea first penned by Mr. Edward Norton Lorenz.

Mr. Lorenz was both a mathematician and a meteorologist, and he basically gave those of us interested in climate change the foundational tools needed for our field of study. In addition to all that, he gave us Chaos Theory, which states that a tiny change (like rounding a decimal point to .507 rather than .507127, as he did in his sequence modeling of weather patterns) can have a massive impact on the final outcome. You may have heard of the term "butterfly effect," which he also coined. The way I explained all of this to seven-year-old Olivia when she asked me to read my paper to her was like this: if a butterfly flaps its wings in Argentina, it could eventually lead to a hurricane in Galveston.

Something happened the night I went missing; one small change affected the outcome of my life's trajectory. This small change could have something to do with Alex. It could have something to do with Anna. It could have something to do with Sawyer. It could be all or none of them, but Chaos Theory tells me that at least one change disrupted my life and brought me to this new place in time, and I only need one small change to bring me back to myself.

Grandma has come to visit, and I hear her ask, "Would it be all right if I had a few minutes alone with Emily?"

My mother doesn't say anything, but I feel her eyes on me, assessing. I know all about what happened with Lucy, when Grandma wandered off with her, but with all my tubes and wires, she wouldn't get far. *It's fine*, I want to tell Mom. I don't know my grandmother well—I haven't been around her enough—but I've never been afraid of her. She loves me in her way, the way of gifts and expectations and admonitions.

"I'll grab a cup of coffee and give you a few minutes alone," I hear Mom mumble, and we all know she'll only walk down the hall for two minutes and counting. She doesn't even close the door behind her. Quickly, Grandma shuffles around the room.

"Emily, my darling girl, I'm here to help," Grandma says,

speaking in low, melodic tones. "It's a little something Dr. Montague acquired for me."

Mom wouldn't approve, I'm sure. But I'm also pretty sure that my grandmother wouldn't do anything to hurt me, so I wait, curious to see what she has in mind. Like a twisted science experiment.

For several moments, Grandma rubs oil into the soles of my feet and for several more, she wanders around my bed, the scent of her White Diamond perfume telling me where she is at any given moment. She rustles my IV bag and something cold lights up my veins. Then, she sits. I can almost see her proper posture, folded hands, feet tucked behind her just so.

When Mom returns with coffee, I find myself staring at both of them, eyes open, my head tilted forward, hungry as a bear out of hibernation.

"Mom," I finally manage, my voice weak from lack of use.

"Emily." She drops her coffee in the trash, runs to the side of my bed and covers me with kisses, like she did when I arrived home from my first day of kindergarten. "Oh, my God, you're awake."

I offer a faltering grin, my vision still wobbly from Grandma's ministrations. I'm awake.

28
May
Leslie

She was really dying this time, her heart clenching and un-
clenching every three seconds while the room spun around
her. She'd already thrown up once.

This is anxiety, she told herself. *It's not a heart attack. It's not
a heart attack.* She stumbled to the medicine cabinet and fum-
bled with the pill bottles. First, a baby aspirin just to be safe.
Then, her benzodiazepines. As she emptied the contents into
her hand, her fuzzy vision honed in on the disparate tablets,
the walls pushing in as she counted. One, two, three. Three
Xanax pills. The rest of the bottle had been replaced with
circular tabs of generic Advil, an obvious and paltry effort to
mislead her. Christ. Leslie rubbed the heel of her palm against
her forehead. Anna had been taking her pills again, but this
time it had been more than one or two. It had been a handful.

I'm so stressed about this test, Anna would say, and Leslie
would give her a pill.

I don't know how I'm going to sleep tonight, Anna would whine, and Leslie would tell her to grab one off her nightstand.

Leslie supposed that her daughter had eventually presumed an open-bottle policy, but what was she doing with so many? Selling them? Snorting them? Her heart beat faster and she struggled for a deep breath.

With the anxiety threatening to turn her lungs inside out, Leslie swallowed two of the remaining pills and one more for good measure. Then, she decided that speaking to Anna about her irresponsibility could not wait. She'd already discreetly called the lawyer on behalf of one of her children, the one she couldn't seem to manage; she would not be forced to do the same for Anna, who probably had the contraband with her, maybe even in her system right now. And at her first job, no less. What the hell was she thinking?

Leslie drove the three miles to The Monterey, her brain already feeling the blessed relief of dopamine calming her rapid heart rate and leaving her with lightness, a sensation she adored. The effect, combined with the adrenaline coursing through her, was absolute magic. Sometimes she'd wondered why she waited so long to start taking them. The benefits— calm, clarity, quiet—far outweighed the risks—anterograde amnesia, dissociation, a lack of inhibition. Foolishness. She'd never experienced a single one of these.

When she entered the club, she got to the point. "I need to see my daughter."

"Hey, Mrs. Steele," the receptionist greeted her. Everyone here knew her name, and that's the way she normally liked it. But not today.

"Where is she?"

Another girl about her daughter's age stepped forward, somehow understanding the vague question. She must have that angry-mother look. Good. "I saw Anna out by the pool, restocking the towels."

Leslie didn't say another word as she marched past the white columns and through the spacious dining room, glittering with crystal chandeliers. She was aware of the familiar gazes of acquaintances and neighbors sweeping over her. A couple of them called a *hello*, but she had a central purpose and would not be distracted.

Leslie approached her daughter, took her arm and started with her toward the door. "Anna. Come. Now. We're going home."

Startled, Anna dropped the fluffy towel she was holding and squinted into the sunlight silhouetting her mother. "Mom? What's going on? Is everything okay?"

"No. Everything is certainly not…okay." The words were already loosening in her mouth, like ice melting across her tongue. "You've been taking my pills…even though you have absolutely nothing…nothing to be stressed about." Did she slur the last few words?

"What are you talking about?" Anna leaned forward and sniffed her mother. How dare she! Anna glanced around the pool, obviously embarrassed as she lowered her voice. "Have you been drinking?"

Leslie searched her mind for her own volume control and couldn't figure out where she'd placed it. She began to giggle, but caught herself and popped a hand over her mouth. This was a serious matter. "My prescription. It seems that I have either contracted dementia, or you, darling, have been stealing my pills."

Anna's face whitened to the color of the pristine marble flooring inside the club's foyer. "Mom, let's talk about this later. I'm at work."

"This cannot wait, my dear." Leslie's eyes widened as she

thought of something. She leaned forward as if confiding her own secret. "Did you drug her, so your brother could get her out to Bolivar and hold her captive for weeks on end?"

Leslie's arms were heavy, like they'd been weighted with sandbags, the kind they used when preparing for floods. She remembered the last big flood that had damaged their home. Hurricane Ike in 2008. For weeks they'd been without electricity. In August, no less. It had been hot, so hot. Just like she felt now. She began unbuttoning her shirt as fast as Anna could stop her. "Were you afraid she was going to steal your spot at Callahan Prep, or with that Alex Frasier?"

Leslie lowered her voice, conspiratorially. Or at least she tried to. "I must admit, I thought she might!"

"God, Mom." Anna looked around frantically at the small crowd gathering. The members of The Monterey had probably never seen a drama quite like this unfold and certainly not from one of the most prestigious families on the island. Fine. Let them look. Let them see the real, the amazing, the Leslie Steele.

"That's crazy. Of course I would never... I think we need to talk about this at home. Alone." Anna paused, rubbing her hand against her side for several beats. She was nervous. Maybe she should be. "Mom, how many Xanax did you take?"

Leslie ignored the question and instead tried to say that this kind of conduct did not become a Steele. She tried to tell her daughter that it was one thing to commit an indiscretion, but another thing entirely to be indiscreet about it. Leslie wanted to say so many hard-to-catch words, and maybe she did say them out loud, loudly enough for the birds to carry the sound to the four corners of the earth. Behold, Leslie Steele, the protector and defender of her family, the mother who could do it all even while her husband's flesh festered and rotted in the ground.

She felt the sudden urge to vomit. Had she already vomited? She turned toward the pool and emptied what remained. Coming up for air, Leslie took in the crowd, a people so confused and helpless without her to coordinate their every move. She gave them a majestic wave before turning back to Anna and finally whispering, "What *have* you and your brother done?"

Suddenly, a fire lit her daughter's eyes. Leslie actually saw the sparks. How shiny!

"What have we done? Mother, are you seriously pointing fingers right now?"

"Whatever do you mean, Anna?"

"You're the one who wrote those letters to Emily, warning her to stay out of the limelight. First, when she was running for homecoming court, and later, when you wanted her to stay away from Alex."

"That was to protect you, you ungrateful bitch," Leslie hurled as she raised a hand to slap her daughter, but her palm fell back limply against her side. She fell back with it.

Her daughter stood over her. Was Anna yelling? Cursing? At her own mother?

"Do you not understand how fucking embarrassed I was when everyone heard about those notes and thought that I had written them, that I cared that much about something as stupid and insignificant as homecoming queen? Or a boy? I am not you, Mother. Thank God, I am so not you."

"But you work so hard, dearest. And you deserve to be happy." From her prone position, Leslie made a sound that was halfway between a screech and a groan. A sob rose in the back of Leslie's throat. She wanted to lie down, that's all. Couldn't everyone leave her alone for a few minutes and let her sleep? Did no one understand that she hadn't had a proper night of rest in the three years since she laid her husband to rest? If she could only close her eyes for a few moments, then she would get up again and plan another damn party for these insufferable people.

Anna's face was sour, her arms crossed, her eyes still burning. "You mean *you* worked hard to get me to this place. I couldn't care less about any of the idiotic Callahan Prep traditions."

Leslie opened her eyes wide, fighting against the darkness that tempted to pull her under. "It's what your father would've wanted."

At the mention of Michael, a silence settled over the pool area, no one moving or uttering a sound for a hushed moment.

Then, Anna broke in. "Yes, I've been taking your pills, okay? They help calm me like they help calm you, except for today apparently. And yes, I had a couple of them on me the night that Emily went missing. I crushed them up and dropped them into my drink after I got to Natalie's to help me relax after helping host your ridiculous party, and to…" Here, Anna faltered, realizing something for the first time. "Oh, shit."

Leslie watched her daughter begin to levitate. Didn't she have the loveliest curls of ribbon shooting from her head?

"What if I accidentally switched the drinks?" Anna finally said in a panic as Leslie trailed off into the blissful darkness of sleep, a smile on her lips, leaving her daughter standing with a heap of bleached towels scattered around her and an array of phones lifted and aimed at both of the Steele women.

29
May
Morgan

Three days had passed. Morgan knocked on Alex's bedroom door, but there was no answer. She opened it a crack and saw the lump of his full frame, facing the wall beneath the covers. He'd been like this more often than not lately.

"Hey, hon. I'm sure that Emily would like to see you."

Morgan had received a text from Catherine earlier.

"She's awake."

It was enough.

When Morgan had called, Catherine answered her questions briefly and succinctly, but at least she answered them. So far, based on Emily's few and scattered memories, Alex seemed entirely innocent. *Emily insists he wasn't with her when she disappeared*, Catherine had said quietly. Morgan could breathe again.

"I don't want to see her," came a muffled voice from Alex's covers.

Morgan took any communication as a good sign and stepped over the piles of socks and underwear and T-shirts to his bed.

"Are you sure?"

"I don't have anything to say."

"Alex... Emily doesn't remember much. She doesn't even remember who's the...the father of her child." She wanted to shout, *But it's not you!*

Silence.

His head finally peeked out from the sheet. "I can't, Mom."

Morgan looked at her boy, so big and vulnerable.

"I understand," she said, sitting on the edge of his bed and picking at a loose thread. She'd tried to act like everything was normal, even though Emily's appearance and subsequent awakening had unsettled their lives almost as much as her disappearance. An ungenerous thought, Morgan knew, but not only did her son seem disoriented since finding out about Emily's pregnancy, but Morgan had also lost contact with Robert, who seemed to have disappeared himself.

"Just busy," Robert said the couple of times she'd managed to reach him between patients. He hadn't even been to the children's center in the past two weeks.

Morgan forced herself to focus on her son. "Whitey called. The police finished questioning Sawyer and that woman he was living with. They didn't find any evidence that the two of them were holding her there against her will, but that doesn't mean that Emily was in her right mind. They think she may have some kind of amnesia. It wasn't *your* Emily out there with them."

He sat up abruptly, cutting her off. "God, Mom. Do I need to spell it out for you?"

Morgan's eyes widened. *Yes, please. Spell it out. I'm so tired of trying to read your freaking teenage mind*, she thought. But instead, she lifted one shoulder nonchalantly.

"Can't you see that either way, whether or not it was on purpose, Emily didn't want me? Whether she knows it or not, in the back of her mind, she would rather run away and hook up with some guy she's never met than be with me."

Anger distorted his features.

"I'm sick of this whole fucking mess, this town. I wish I'd never met her. I wish I'd gone to Greece with Dad when he asked me."

Morgan startled. "What are you talking about?"

"Did I not tell you?" Alex screwed up his features as if in his own pain he found some sort of pleasure in inflicting her with his words. "Dad called right before he told you about the affair and asked if I wanted to move to Greece with him. Guess he didn't like my answer, since he hasn't called much since."

Lionel had tried to take their only son away from her? Morgan felt a rush of anger, but forced herself to brush away the words, to remember that Alex was hurting and might be making up stories, that they both needed to focus on the real issue: Emily. She cleared her throat. "This isn't about me and your dad right now. It's about you and your…friend who needs you. I don't think Emily would be asking about you if she didn't care."

He rolled over to face the wall.

Morgan left Alex to nurse his misery. She considered calling Lionel and cursing out her ex, but really, she didn't care enough to expend the energy. Instead, she drove to the hospital, determined to see Robert, to see if he knew anything more about what had happened to Emily and to make sure he was all right. They had shared more than a bed these past few months: they had shared an emotional journey of loss and hope, one that she could, in part, thank Emily for if it didn't sound so damn self-centered.

As a teaching physician, Robert had his own office, and she decided she would wait there until he inevitably stepped in. She pressed the elevator button for the fourth floor and walked down the long corridor, but as she neared his office, she heard voices inside: Robert was with someone.

"How did this happen?" a male voice said.

"I don't know, okay?" Robert's words were crackling with fatigue and…something else. Frustration? In the few months they'd been seeing one another, Morgan had only heard three of his tones: professional and businesslike, teasing and flirtatious, and the tender way he had with the babies and toddlers at the center. "I thought we were administering the correct dosage," he said. "I can't figure it out."

The other voice raised slightly. "What if she starts to remember?"

"That's highly unlikely," Robert answered. "Regardless of her current state of awareness, if she was suffering from a form of dissociative amnesia, as the psychologist has already diagnosed during the consult, then I'm convinced she won't remember much of anything that happened before she woke up here."

"But what about recovered memories?"

Robert sighed. "You're worrying over nothing. To distinguish between recovered memories and false memories is nearly an impossible feat, and lest you forget, the patient remains under my care, so I can help her distinguish between the two."

"But she has a psychologist treating her now."

"We—the psychologist, me and even her obstetrician—are treating her in conjunction. Trust me. I promised your dad that I would always look out for the three of you, and you know that I'm a man of my word."

Frozen in place, Morgan had to make herself move when Robert stepped out of his office and spotted her.

"Hey, what are you doing here?" His tone was curious, but as caring as always.

Fast, Morgan told herself, think fast. "Oh, I thought I'd see if you had time to grab a quick bite."

It was close to lunch, right? Morgan impressed herself with how naturally the words tumbled from her tongue, like the pecans that fell from the untended trees across the island. Moving toward him so he couldn't see her face, she stroked his back with one arm and nuzzled against his ear. "I've missed you," she breathed.

"I've missed you too."

He was telling the truth, Morgan was sure of it. This man had come to care for her, and now he was mixed up in some awful mess involving a patient. Morgan was certain that patient was Emily, but it had to be a terrible misunderstanding. Robert was the doctor who visited the children of addicts, who cared for his niece and nephews as if they were his own children, who wandered beaches looking for a lost girl he'd never met.

Robert gave her a quick but furtive kiss. "Meet me at my place after I get off work?"

"Sure," she said as he led her to the elevator without another word. She loved this man, and she wanted to believe he was the person she had come to know.

Because of this desire, Robert had Morgan in his grip whether she wanted it that way or not.

30
May
Emily

I am more nervous than my parents say I should be to meet with the psychologist again. I'm up and about now, but our first meeting was from my hospital bed and consisted of mostly a series of quick questions. Still, the woman was nice enough with her big smile, her red-rimmed glasses and her flowy skirt.

"Emily, so good to see you looking well."

"Thank you, Dr. Garza," I say hesitantly.

"Feel free to call me Fran. All of my patients do. It makes things less formal."

I look around at this office of blues and purples and low lighting, inviting to children of all ages. Such a contrast from my room only one floor away where I spent the past week of my life. I wish I wasn't one of her patients, but I'm so grateful to have finally been brought out of my awake-sleep state, my dormancy, that I will do whatever she asks to help me figure out what happened. In the twenty-four hours I've been awake, I've already started keeping a stream-of-consciousness journal—as Dr. Garza requested—though I run into a wall every time I get to the end of that party.

"As you already know right now, we think we may be dealing with a form of dissociative amnesia, and your primary symptom is memory loss that involves an inability to remember personal information."

Memory loss. That's an understatement. Everything after getting in my car to leave the Mardi Gras party is like a blank piece of paper, though occasionally I can spot a faint word or symbol. "But according to…to Sawyer, I knew my name when I met him."

"True. But at the time you didn't remember where you currently lived—Galveston—or how you ended up on Bolivar," Dr. Garza clarifies. "Pieces of your identity and your personal history were missing. You were disoriented, confused. As I told you in our initial meeting, this is often caused by trauma."

I nod and bite my lip.

"Which brings me to a secondary diagnosis, one that is rare, but that can accompany dissociative amnesia," she says as she puts down her notebook. "A fugue state. Have you ever heard this term?"

The only fugues I've ever heard of are the ones my mother plays, the two melodic lines imitating and overlapping. I roll the word around in my mind. *Fugue*, coming from the Latin *fuga*. I savor the word, tasting the letters. *Fuga: to flee. Fuga: to escape. Fuga: to fly.*

"A fugue state is characterized by wandering for a period of time and can be an effect of dissociative amnesia. Studies show that a person can remain present and conscious—though perhaps unaware about where they live or who their family is—without encoding memories. We believe something like this may have happened to you."

Dr. Garza draws a line on a piece of paper and points to the beginning of the line, moving her finger slowly across the page. "This is your normal life, moving to Galveston, making a friend, going to school."

Her finger stops and she draws a large X on the line. "This is a traumatic moment, most likely occurring on the night you went missing."

She scribbles across an inch of the line. "This is the blurry ten weeks you can't remember—the fugue state—when you were disoriented and confused. You could speak and eat and act almost like yourself, but you had none of the normal impulses to go home or to be with your family. In fact, if people ask patients in a fugue state where they live, they often can't—or don't—answer at all, though some may be able to tell their name and their favorite foods or color. Others in this state may assume an entirely new identity and act completely erratically, but this doesn't seem to have been the case with you.

"For you, it's almost like time stood still, and your past life was like a dream. You separated—or dissociated—from your actual identity. This state of dissociation can last anywhere from days to hours to months to years. For you, the period of time was about ten weeks."

Dr. Garza points at another X at the end of the scribbles. "And this is when you most likely hit your head, somehow ended up in the water, and were brought to this hospital. Notice how the line straightens out again. When you were in the fugue state out on Bolivar, your past life in Galveston felt so jumbled and confusing and hazy that you couldn't readily access it, but now that you're out of this dissociated state and back to your normal life, those ten weeks become the jumbled, confusing and hazy part of your past. Do you understand what I'm saying?"

"I think so," I say, my brow furrowed. "When I was out on

Bolivar Peninsula, I couldn't remember my real life because I was separating from my identity in some ways—as a sort of self-preservation instinct against trauma. But now that I'm back to my normal self, it's like the switch flipped back again. I feel like my actual self, but now I can't remember much of anything about those ten weeks out on Bolivar."

"Exactly." She hands me an article. "Your mom says you're an avid reader. Here's an example of dissociative amnesia and the ensuing fugue state in the case of a young woman named Hannah Upp that was reported in *The New Yorker*. We don't know why, but people like you and Hannah—people in fugue states—often gravitate to water. Hannah disappeared three times—the first time they found her south of the Statue of Liberty, floating in the water, and the second time near a dirty creek in Maryland, but the third time...well, the last time anyone saw her, she was in the Virgin Islands."

"She's still missing?" My stomach lurches. "Does that mean something like this could happen to me again?"

Dr. Garza considers for a moment. "Not necessarily. I consulted with your neurologist, Dr. Steele, who said there was nothing anatomically wrong with your brain, so for now we will assume you were operating in this kind of fugue state during the ten weeks you were missing. While we can be watchful, we can't be sure whether or not this might inevitably happen again."

I swallow.

"If this is the case—if you *were* operating in a fugue state—then most, if not all, of these lost memories are likely not recoverable. But that doesn't mean that we won't try."

She stops for a moment to study my reaction.

I think I appear calm and composed even though my mind is reeling.

"I have several treatment options that could aid the process of recovering memories," she says, "including hypnosis, EMDR therapy, mild cranial electrotherapy stimulation. We can discuss these with your parents if we aren't making progress in the next few days and weeks. How does that sound?"

I nod, but say nothing.

"So, I believe that both you and your parents have expressed interest first and foremost in finding out what might have triggered this fugue state, this sort of dissociative amnesia."

"Yes."

"As you already know, we can't test to see if you were drugged that night. Date rape drugs typically leave the system within days, but if you were given a substance…"

"I wasn't." My face heats, and the pitch of my voice rises. I don't want them to think that Alex had anything to do with my disappearance. I'm certain to my core that he is innocent, even though he still won't see me.

Dr. Garza puts out a hand. "We're not accusing anyone here. I'm not a detective, but we do need to recognize that such things do occur, even at the hands of someone we think we can trust. We also need to acknowledge that narcotics can set off an unusual or unexpected response system in the brain."

"Are you saying that a pill could make me forget the past two and a half months of my life? Forget how I got pregnant?"

"It's not that simple." Dr. Garza sighs. "The brain can be a delicate and fickle instrument, a combination of both nature and nurture, genetics and epigenetics, two areas that I know interest you." I'm following her, so Dr. Garza continues. "Think of it like that line I just showed you. For eighteen years your brain moved along normally, the synapses connecting as they should, but then something…" She snaps her fingers. "Something happened to disrupt that synaptic dance. This could be a stressful event—like something as extreme as an attack or something less obvious like a neurological reaction to a chemical. Either or both could set the brain on an unexpected and unintended course like a fugue state."

"I think I understand."

Dr. Garza leans back. "I want you to try to remember as much as you can before that late night/early morning when your car ended up on East Beach. Tell me again what you recall about the get-together at your friend's house."

I tell her the same thing I told Mom, that the last spotty memory I have is getting inside my car, then feeling sick, so sick. The headache hit me about halfway through one of the bug movies. *Spider-Man? Ant-Man?* I can't remember which one. I have the sense that someone—Alex, I presume—was holding me, but he'd never held me like that before. Yeah, a hug, an arm around me, a hand in mine, sitting shoulder to shoulder, but he'd never wrapped himself around me like we were lying that night on the couch—and in front of people too. It's like that girl wasn't me, like I was looking at a snapshot of someone in my body.

Dr. Garza listens without judgment, her hands folded.

"I think I stood up in the middle of the movie. I needed some space because my headache was getting worse. We went into another room, and I could hear Alex asking if he'd done something wrong. But I couldn't find the right words to explain that I didn't feel right. My vision started blurring at some point, and I remember that I wanted to go home, but I didn't want to call my mom to come pick me up. I'd had one cup of beer, and I knew even though she trusts me, she would worry that I might be hanging around the wrong kind of people. Plus, we lived literally five minutes away. I figured if I closed my eyes for a few minutes, then I could drive myself."

Dr. Garza jots a few notes. "That night, did you willingly take any substances? Besides the one drink?"

"No drugs. I've never touched them. And that cup of beer, I

swear it was only the one. My parents have always been pretty open about that kind of thing at home, holidays and stuff, you know? I figured that a glass would just relax me, and it might make me seem more like the other kids at the party." I stare at my hands. "I hadn't made many friends, so it was actually a pretty calculated decision."

Dr. Garza studies me for a moment and then seems to accept this answer. "And what is the very last moment, the final second that you can recall?"

I squint, trying to think. "I remember walking out to the porch, passing Anna, and getting into my car. I saw Alex start to pull out ahead of me, and I think I tried to call out to him, but he probably couldn't hear me. I closed my eyes... Then, it all goes blank."

"And how was your body positioned when you closed your eyes? Can you remember?"

I close them now. "I remember leaning against the steering wheel because my head hurt so bad, like someone was prying open my forehead."

"Do you remember starting the car? Driving anywhere?"

"No. I mean, I guess I drove out to East Beach, but I don't remember any of it. That's where Dad found my car, though."

We both know these details.

"Emily, I want to suggest you try something that may be rather challenging, but I think this could be the most successful form of treatment if you attempt it sooner rather than later."

"Okay." I know Dr. Garza is ranked top in her field; Grandmother wouldn't accept less. And I think I'm willing to try almost anything.

"It's a reenactment. Survivors of trauma sometimes use this when struggling with dissociation. Basically, we retrace your steps on the night of your disappearance as closely as possible in hopes that the physical space might help stir memories.

For you, this would mean starting at the last place you can remember—in front of that home—and ending at the lighthouse on Bolivar, where we know you spent ten weeks. The young man who found you, Sawyer, would have to participate as well if you are both willing." She pauses, gauging my reaction. "If this is something you feel comfortable trying, I'll reach out to him and then set up everything."

I find that I'm clutching the arm of the chair with one hand and force myself to release my grip. "What if…what if I remember something and it's too…it's too painful?"

Dr. Garza leans forward, her eyes compassionate and her gaze steady. "You are so strong already, Emily. Not many young women in your situation would have the wherewithal at this point in their recovery to sit and talk with me like this. I have no doubt that with your support system in place, you'll have the strength to face these memories—if they come. Practically speaking, however, you can be assured that your parents, the police and I will be nearby."

"I'll think about it," I say. But I know I'll do it sooner rather than later. I want to know what happened badly enough.

She takes a deep breath. "All right, then. I'd like to end our session today by having you close your eyes for a moment as you relax into your chair."

I do as instructed.

"I want you to say the first word or phrase that comes to mind when I say a word. I know that some people use word association as a parlor trick, but I want to see if it opens any doors for us to walk through."

"All right."

"Oregon," Dr. Garza says.

"Home," I answer.

"Callahan."

"Family."

"Callahan Preparatory."

"Easy."

"Galveston."

"Isolated."

"Mother."

"Worried."

"Father."

"Anchor."

"Sisters."

"Love."

"Party."

"Lonely."

"East Beach."

"Lost."

"Alex Frasier."

"Friend."

"Sawyer Steele."

"Scared."

Without knowing why, I start to cry.

31

May

Catherine

Waking up to sunlight sprinkling her pillow that morning, Catherine had curled beneath the comforter, nuzzling into a still-sleeping Carter, resting in the fact that all of her children were beneath her roof. Emily was finally home. Lucy's worry lines had faded. Olivia had stopped biting the edge of her thumb. Their world had been made right. Almost.

Now, Catherine watched the blip of the heartbeat on the screen at her oldest daughter's prenatal appointment. This kind of moment should normally be happy, but as she watched the tiny fluttering, Catherine felt more like someone had grabbed her around the throat and begun to squeeze. Emily had already had a tough time at Dr. Garza's office earlier that afternoon, but they didn't want to reschedule this appointment, not when every day mattered.

Eighteen years ago, Catherine's first ultrasound had been so different when she saw Emily's grainy image for the first time. A few years after that, Baby A, Olivia, and Baby B, Lucy, bounced into one another on the screen, startling and scaring and delighting her.

But today, there were no feelings of delight.

"It looks like the embryo is measuring 3.8 centimeters, which puts you at about nine weeks and five days. Because we start dating from your last menstruation, I'm going to set the due date as...let's see, December 29? Looks like this will be a holiday baby." The young technician smiled briefly before undoubtedly remembering the situation that had brought this girl here. "I'll just go get Dr. Hart."

Catherine did the math. That meant conception had occurred almost a month after Emily had gone missing, and if the due date was accurate, she could confirm that the night of her daughter's disappearance had not been the night she was impregnated. Which meant that this was definitely not Alex Frasier's baby. She let out a breath. "I'm sorry you had to see that."

Emily looked at her blankly. "See what?"

"The ultrasound," Catherine answered even as she steeled herself. "Unfortunately, you may have to go through this again when you go for the abortion."

Those were words she never thought she would say to her daughter. No mother did, she supposed.

Emily nodded as she stared out the window high above the Galveston streets, the distant water stretching into the horizon. Catherine had looked up the legal requirements a few days ago, but she'd been waiting for the right time to discuss next steps. With an abortion, they could collect a tissue sample for DNA testing as well as remove the embryo. They could finally determine the father.

Dr. Hart knocked at the door. "Hi, Emily. It's good to finally meet you. I'm glad to hear that you're recovering after your ordeal." The older woman in dark scrubs had a few smile lines around her eyes that made her seem like someone's grandmother. "I know you may have some questions for me, so I'm happy to answer anything you want to ask. After that, we can get you dressed and on your way. How does that sound?"

Catherine already liked this woman who assumed nothing and instead waited for direction from her patient. Emily would certainly have questions.

"I'm getting close to the end of my first trimester?"

"That's right. You have about three more weeks to go."

"But I'm not throwing up or tired. I remember how sick my mom was with my sisters."

Dr. Hart nodded. "Every pregnancy is different, but the fact that the tech saw a strong heartbeat statistically means that you are carrying a viable pregnancy."

Emily swallowed hard. "So, is there a chance I could… could miscarry?"

Catherine's brows furrowed, but Dr. Hart only lifted a shoulder. "It's hard to say. Statistics do vary, but I can tell you that after the first trimester, the chance of miscarriage drops significantly. Some studies say as low as one percent with a single fetus."

Catherine eyed her daughter. Why was she asking *these* questions? Why not get to the point? She, for one, could wait no longer. "We're interested in a referral for a doctor who can provide the abortion. Can you give us that information and tell us what to expect?"

Though Dr. Hart listened as Catherine spoke, she kept the focus on her patient, on Emily. "Is this something *you* would like to know more about?"

Emily gazed up at the ceiling for a moment, and Catherine knew without a doubt what her daughter was doing: praying. Catherine had the sudden urge to shake her. This was time for action, not quiet contemplation. The longer this embryo grew inside her daughter, the faster the window of decision closed.

"Not right now," Emily finally said, reaching for her mother's hand and turning to speak to Catherine as if Dr. Hart wasn't in the room. "I don't think I can go through with an abortion, Mom. It's fine for other people, just not me. I don't think I could get past it."

"But you—"

Emily squeezed her mother's hand with a lightness that reminded Catherine of when her toddler fingers had wrapped around one of her own. She sensed that at that moment, Emily needed her mother's support, not her judgment or her advice.

Catherine swallowed back her arguments as her daughter continued speaking with Dr. Hart.

"I read about an amniocentesis," Emily said. "I want to do that, so I can find out who the father is."

Dr. Hart nodded in understanding. "That would happen at sixteen to twenty weeks. I'll get my scheduler," she said and left the two women alone, silent; mother astonished and daughter eerily calm.

After the appointment, Catherine drove the two of them to East Beach at Emily's request. How she hoped she could talk some sense into her daughter when they got out of the car, revisiting the place where the nightmare began. If this was where it began. East Beach? Bolivar Peninsula? Catherine hated not knowing.

The two of them took off their shoes and put their feet in the warm water, toes sinking in the sand.

"You know your dad and I only want what's best for you. You need to get this all behind you, and the only way to do that is to have an abortion. You're so young, and you have your whole life ahead of you." Catherine sought for another argument that her daughter might respond to. "Even religious people say that in the case of rape…"

"We don't know that I was raped."

"You can't remember losing your virginity, so whatever happened to you qualifies." Though her words were bold, Catherine glanced tentatively at her daughter. Emily seemed so much older since she woke up. It wasn't just the weight loss that had sharpened Emily's features. There was a quiet about her, an acceptance that made her seem beyond her years.

"I don't know, Mom. When Sawyer came to see me in the hospital, I swear I recognized his voice. I'm scared to meet him, but if I don't do it soon, it's only going to get harder."

Catherine curled her toes as the waves splashed her ankles. "Dr. Garza said a reenactment can help some patients regain part of their memory."

"She told me that too," Emily said. "Maybe if I do that, I'll remember more. If this is Sawyer's child, he should have some say in what happens to it, don't you think?"

"When I asked him point-blank, Sawyer said he didn't take advantage of you," Catherine answered. "Though I realize he may have lied."

"He may not have needed to take advantage." Emily looked at her mom. "What if he and I were actually… I don't know… together?"

"No. I can't believe that, not when you'd only known him for such a short time, but regardless, it's entirely your decision whether or not to have this baby because it's your life that will change." She sighed. "As for meeting Sawyer, I don't know, Emily. He hasn't shown up to see you since that first visit when you were unconscious. That doesn't speak well of him." Catherine stepped on a shell that bit into the heel of her foot. She swiped at it, but ignored the pain. "Listen, I know that a part of you doesn't want this…" She struggled for the word.

"This baby?" A light leaped into Emily's eyes. That was the same look Emily had given Catherine numerous times since she told her daughter their family was leaving Woodhaven.

Her daughter's independence, her womanhood was asserting itself. Catherine looked away.

"Fine, this baby. Fetus. Embryo. Whatever. I heard you ask Dr. Hart if there was a chance that you might miscarry. Is that what you're hoping for?"

"I wouldn't be sad," Emily admitted. She was watching crabs burrow in and out of the holes in the sand. She knelt down to scoop one up, and the small creature darted around in her hand, like a pinball machine. "But I can't go through with an abortion. I remember how we learned in biology that the baby's lips and nose are already forming. That's too real. If I was only four or five weeks along, this might be a different conversation."

"Five weeks, ten weeks. It doesn't matter. Yes, maybe this bunch of cells is slowly turning into a baby, but it's not one yet." Catherine felt her face heating. "I don't want to see you throw your life away because you were incapacitated for whatever reason and some pervert attacked you."

Emily placed the sand crab back in the surf and picked up a blue shell, fingering the tiny ridges. Her voice rose over the steady surf, the movement of the waves unrelenting. "This is my choice, Mom, and I need you to respect that."

Catherine reflexively shook her head, but she knew she couldn't force her. In this instance at least, Emily at eighteen was an adult. "Promise me that you'll think about all of this seriously over the next few days. Pray about it, if that helps," Catherine said. "That's how certain I am that your dad and I are right on this one."

The two of them stood eye to eye, both women in their own right, both mothers in that moment.

"I will," Emily said.

"I know you will." Catherine hugged her for a long moment. She would let the issue alone for now.

Catherine's phone buzzed. It was Carter.

Watch this, the text said. Some kid who was at The Monterey earlier today sent this video to Whitey. He and Officer Cortez are on their way over now.

Catherine shadowed the screen with her hand and turned the volume up all the way. Head to head, she and Emily watched the three-minute video of Leslie and Anna's poolside drama. Catherine almost dropped the phone at Anna's fateful words: "What if I accidentally switched the drinks?"

Both were speechless as the screen froze on Leslie, passed out poolside.

"This means—" Emily went pale. "I was drugged but not by Alex, like everyone thought. It was—"

"It was Anna," Catherine finished.

"But why would she—?" Emily's brow turned down as she thought about the ramifications of this new information.

"There's no way that was an accident."

"I don't know. If her mom wrote those notes, if it wasn't Anna, then maybe Anna didn't hate me as much as I thought she did."

"Hate you? How could anyone hate you?"

Emily shot her mom a look.

Catherine shrank forward. "I'm so sorry we brought you here, so sorry for…for all of this. I knew you were unhappy, but I had no idea how bad things were for you. If I had it to do over—"

Emily stared at her hands. "I didn't want you to know, especially after why we had to move."

Catherine stared at her girl and then put an arm around

her shoulders. "Chief Whiteside is on his way over, so we better get back to the house."

"Okay. Just one more minute." Emily turned back toward the water. "Dad found my car out here?"

"Yeah, it was about a quarter of a mile farther down. I went out to the exact spot dozens of times, could probably find it in complete darkness."

As Catherine was thinking about how much she wished her daughter could remember driving out here, how much that memory might help with the missing pieces of the night she went missing, Emily suddenly crumpled forward as if she'd been hit in the stomach.

"What's wrong?" Catherine held her as she lurched forward, a hand pressed to her forehead as she stumbled into the sand. "Are you hurt?"

"No...it's just...it's like I saw something, a flicker, like someone turned on the lights for a millisecond."

"Maybe this is what Dr. Garza was talking about. Going to the place to recover the memories." Catherine crouched next to Emily. "What did you see?"

Emily shook her head as she spoke. "I was in the passenger seat of my car. I wasn't driving."

Catherine sank down into the sand with her. "I don't follow."

Emily took a couple of deep breaths and squinted into the horizon. "Mom, what if I didn't bring myself out here? What if someone took me somewhere else and then drove my car here?"

"But there were no tracks."

"Right. The tide washed them away, Dad said. Maybe that's why the car was parked in the surf in the first place. Maybe it was intentional."

"But for someone to leave your car here, eventually they

would need to go through the sand. There would be prints somewhere."

"Not if he—or she—walked—or swam—far enough down the coastline. Then, other peoples' tracks would act like camouflage."

Catherine looked in both directions. It was possible, though it would've taken significant effort with the dunes, the webbing plants and the stone jetties interrupting the beachfront. If someone went through all of that, then they had something to hide.

"I think I need to do the reenactment as soon as possible. I want Dr. Garza to call Sawyer while all this is fresh. I need to officially meet him, as I am now."

Catherine had to keep herself from shouting, *Hell, no*. But she also knew that at this point, Dr. Garza's suggestion might be the only way to find the truth—short of capturing Sawyer and Anna and torturing them until they talked. That was always an option.

"If that's what you want," Catherine said.

"It's not what I want, but I think it may be what I need."

32
May
Morgan

In the early-morning hours after midnight, Robert drifted off as soon as he and Morgan finished making love. She couldn't sleep, couldn't keep her mind from replaying the past few days. She would begin by thinking about what Leslie had said, how she had blamed Morgan for the problems between her and Michael, and then she would move on to what she'd overheard at the hospital. What exactly had Robert done? And how could this kind, generous soul do whatever it was?

After lying awake and alert for an hour or more, Morgan knew she would not be able to sleep until she knew the truth from Robert. It couldn't be as bad as the scenarios playing out in her mind, so she decided to wake him with tender kisses. He turned and wrapped his arms around her.

"So tired, babe," he murmured into the pillow.

"I know, but it's really important."

He squinted one eye, attempting to see her expression.

What he saw must've convinced him of its seriousness because Robert forced himself upright and took a long sip from the water on his bedside table.

Morgan put out both hands. "Okay, I can't stop thinking about something I accidentally overheard you saying at the hospital."

He cleared his throat. "When? Today? In my office?"

"Yeah."

He rubbed one of her bare arms, and she settled into a pillow against him. Morgan could no longer see his eyes, but maybe it was better that way.

"What did you hear?" Robert brushed her hair back and waited.

She didn't want to be talking about this. She wanted to curl up on his chest and fall into a dreamless sleep, but she had to know the truth. Morgan sighed and looked at the ceiling. "I'm not sure, but I think something about Emily and the correct dosage? Whoever you were discussing it with sounded really stressed, almost panicked."

When Robert didn't say anything, she rolled onto her belly to look at him. A faint smile crossed his face, but his eyes carried a hint of disappointment. "Yeah, my nephew made a mistake, and I was trying to help him make it right."

"Sawyer?"

Robert rolled his shoulders back and stretched his neck, but he didn't meet her eyes. That was answer enough for her.

"How were you helping him make things right?" she asked. "By medicating Emily?"

"You know I don't lie to you, and you don't lie to me. We are who we are, and I think that's why we work so well together."

Morgan nodded, enjoying hearing him talk about how they worked well together. He puffed out a breath of air and rolled onto his side, turning her so that their bodies mirrored one another.

"I'm going to tell you the truth—at least my part in it, okay?"

"Okay."

"You probably already know that many of my long-term patients are taking some pretty strong medications for conditions like Alzheimer's, MS, seizures, Parkinson's."

Morgan would assume as much.

"Well, there wasn't anything technically wrong with Emily when she came in. Her brain scans were clear, and she was functioning normally, except that she was unconscious. She was in what we call a light coma. Based on this, I assumed that she would wake up in a few hours or a few days at the most, but then my nephew called and told me about some things that might be…problematic, that could unjustly implicate him in Emily's disappearance. After hearing that, I went ahead and put her on a low dose of a drug that would keep her sedated for a few extra days while we figured things out. It wasn't that different from what her own physiology was already doing for her."

Morgan's heart beat faster, and she sat up. "Wait. You gave her this drug without telling her parents? Even when you knew it might keep her from waking up sooner?"

Robert sat up too. "I swear to you that it sounds worse than it is. You've heard of medically induced comas, right? This was basically a version of that—it was simply a continuation of what her body was already doing when she arrived. I was hopeful that as soon as we stopped with the medication, she would wake up. It didn't go against protocol. It could even help reset her brain entirely."

Morgan's face screwed up at the idea of resetting anyone's brain, but she couldn't address that now, not in light of the other ethical lines the man she loved had crossed. "Except you totally went against any kind of protocol when you didn't tell her parents."

"Look, Morgan, a lot of doctors don't tell their patients everything. The idea of even letting patients know that they have a disease, especially if it's terminal, only came about in the mid-to-late twentieth century. Otherwise, the decision was solely the doctor's."

He ran a hand across his forehead like he did when exhausted.

"You were keeping her sedated, Robert. That's huge. Any way you look at it, Catherine and Carter needed to know."

"Emily wasn't completely sedated. I told you it was a low dose, I mean really low. She told me in our follow-up that she could hear everything going on around her most of the time. She knew when we were in and out of the room. Anyway, I'm sure she needed the rest."

Morgan stared unblinkingly at him. "Are you kidding me with this, Robert? You know you wouldn't want Anna or one of the boys sedated without your knowledge."

"I'm telling you, it's fine." He watched her stand and start to dress. He looked hurt as he said, "Morgan, don't you trust me?"

That was the problem. She wanted to trust him. But how could she? After telling her all of this?

"I think I need to go," she said, getting up and yanking her dress off the floor and over her head. She looked around for a missing shoe.

"Morgan—"

"No. Look, I just need time to process what you've told me."

Robert sighed. "That's fine. I understand, but I do need you to promise that you won't tell anyone about this. Some people wouldn't understand the complexities involved in a case like this."

Morgan lifted her head to look him in the eye. She couldn't promise that. Even after everything, Catherine was her friend and had a right to know, even if it didn't change the outcome at this point.

"Morgan?"

"I'm sorry. I can't promise that."

Robert stood and put on his boxers and then a shirt before moving toward her. His movements were slow and methodical. "I told you all of this because I thought I could trust you. I thought that we were... I don't know... I thought... I've been looking at rings."

This was news. "What?"

"You have to understand that this thing between us is serious, you and me. I'm in my forties and have never been married, have never found someone who makes me want to be a better man, who makes me feel safe enough to tell you something like this."

He took her hand and sat down on the end of the bed. Morgan's cheeks flushed as he dangled the carrot in front of her. These words were the thing she'd been waiting for, the thing she'd set out to accomplish, her wish being granted. She wouldn't need to worry about finding a real job in coming months or about being left alone when Alex went away to school. If she stopped arguing now, she would have security and companionship. She almost kissed him, but then, he continued.

"But you have to understand that I can't let this knowledge hurt my family, a family that you might become a part of. Not after I promised my brother that I would always protect Leslie and the kids, that I would make sure they have happy lives."

Morgan couldn't keep herself from snorting a quick laugh.

No one, not even the best parent in the universe, could fulfill that promise. Besides, Leslie was a grown woman, capable of making her own decisions, and the kids were practically grown too, whether or not Leslie—or Robert, apparently—wanted to admit the fact.

"What?" He seemed surprised at her response. "Why is that funny?"

Morgan tried to compose her expression. "No, not funny. Just a strange promise, one that can't be kept under the best of circumstances."

Robert shook his head. "I have to try. I wasn't able to save Michael. This is all I have left."

So that's what all this came down to. Guilt, the motivator for many a life purpose.

Robert's eyes clouded. "Morgan, I'm asking you to swear that what I've told you won't leave this room." His fingers found her arm, gripping tightly enough to leave a bruise.

She could feel the heat rushing to her face, but she would not be intimidated. "I told you that I can't promise to keep this secret, Robert. Catherine is my friend, but beyond that, any mother would have the right to know what you've confessed."

He frowned at her, a genuine sadness escaping from his eyes. "Then, I can't let you leave."

33
May
Leslie

Leslie awoke in her bedroom, dark as a tomb, the blackout curtains drawn to shutter the midday light. If her hazy memory was correct, Anna had driven her home after a couple of people loaded her into the back seat of her car. No, surely none of that was real.

Her lips were parched and her bladder full. The clock read noon, so she must've been out for nearly twenty hours. Glancing at the empty pill bottle, she realized she'd taken the last three pills yesterday. Oh, God. Glints and glimpses of the previous day rushed back at her, like looking through one of those View-Master toys she'd had as a kid. She stood up and went to the bathroom, and as she finished, there was a knock at her bedroom door.

"Mom?" It was Asher.

"Come in." For the first time she noticed that she was in the same clothes she'd worn yesterday. She attempted to smile at her son. "Have you seen Anna? I guess I had kind of a rough day yesterday.""

"Yeah, she said that you were pretty out of it," he answered vaguely.

"I'll have to apologize. I probably scared her, though I can't remember everything. I think I accidentally took a strong dose of Xanax."

Leslie's cheeks pinkened. Had it been an accident? Or had she deliberately taken three pills at one time? She knew it was the latter, her tolerance had built up fast.

"Anna will be fine. She's actually already at work."

"I feel like she or I said something about Emily and…?"

Asher jumped in, cutting her off. "Nah. Don't worry about that." He paused a moment, embarrassed for her, it seemed. "Are you feeling better? I came to check on you a couple of times, but you were still sleeping. I also called Uncle Robert to tell him to swing by, but I haven't heard back from him." Asher appeared sheepish all of a sudden. "I took your phone, so no one would disturb you."

"Thank you." She took a long gulp of the water he'd brought her. "But that's strange about Robert. Aren't you supposed to be with him at the hospital today?"

"It's okay, I went up there this morning and waited for an hour, but he never came in, and the office said he's not answering his pages. One of the nurses finally got worried enough to call and ask me if I could track him down. I'm about to go over to his place now. You sure you don't want to go back to bed? You still look exhausted."

"I'm feeling better, actually." She didn't want her son finding his uncle sick, or God forbid, unconscious. Her mind always gravitated to the worst. "I'll come with you."

"That's okay, Mom. I'm sure he's fine."

Why was her son handling her like she was a child? What

had she done yesterday to place him so on edge? "No, I said I'll come."

"Okay," Asher hesitated. "But I'm driving."

When they arrived at Robert's apartment, no one answered, and when Leslie pulled out the spare key he'd given her years earlier, the door still wouldn't open all the way. It was dead bolted from the inside.

"Robert?" Leslie called.

"Uncle Robert." Asher raised his voice. "It's us, me and Mom."

They could hear stirrings from within, a harried rustling as if he were moving something out of the way. "Give me a minute."

He opened the door, and Leslie caught an out-of-place floral, citrusy scent. It smelled like Morgan, the last person she wanted to see this afternoon. Ugh. She couldn't face her right now. They should leave.

"Is everything all right?" Leslie tried to sound concerned, yet casual. She really didn't want to see Morgan waltz past in Robert's robe.

"Yeah. I think I may be coming down with the summer flu, though. Thought it best to stay away from patients today." He coughed into his arm. "You two should probably go, but thanks for coming to check on me. I meant to call into work so as not to set off any alarms, but it must have slipped my mind with this headache."

That wasn't like Robert, the man who kept an entire neurology wing in motion. Leslie knew he was lying, but didn't know why. Despite her desire not to see Morgan, she shoved past the half-open door. Leslie wasn't afraid of a flu, and she didn't like secrets—at least not secrets kept from *her*. As she glanced around, everything seemed to be in order. Except for the pile of dirty dishes stacked in the sink, the place was remarkably clean, not like it had been every other time she'd been here. Robert might be a great doctor, but he was usually a subpar housekeeper at best. Maybe Morgan had been here, playing house.

Asher touched his mother's shoulder. "Looks like everything is good here. We should probably let Uncle Robert rest."

But then she heard it, a quiet thumping coming from the bathroom, steady as a slow heartbeat.

"What's that?"

"Hmmm?" Robert seemed oblivious. "What do you mean?"

"I'm sure it's nothing, Mom."

"No, it's coming from in there."

From the bits and pieces she could recall of yesterday, Leslie knew she might have seemed a little crazy—or maybe a lot crazy—when she showed up to confront her daughter at The Monterey. In fact, yesterday Leslie may have been on the verge of a nervous breakdown. But today she was in her right mind. A noise was coming from the other room, regardless of what Robert and Asher were telling her.

Leslie broke away from her son's touch and her brother-in-law's watchful eyes, and before they could stop her, she was in Robert's bathroom, pulling back the shower curtain to find her once-friend, wide-eyed and muzzled. Morgan's feet, hands and mouth were duct-taped, and a blindfold had slipped from her eyes.

"What the…what have you done, Robert?" Leslie screamed at him as she knelt to rip off the blindfold and tape. She immediately felt the presence of her brother-in-law and son behind her, hovering.

Morgan spoke as soon as she was able. "Something is wrong with Robert. He drugged Emily, and when I wanted to tell Catherine, he kept me here like this. And now—"

As the words tumbled out of Morgan, Leslie looked back and forth from this woman, whom she had known since preschool almost four decades earlier, to Asher and Robert, two of the people she loved most in this world. Her family.

"It's not what it looks like," Robert attempted.

"Are you sure? Because it looks like you kidnapped your girlfriend."

"I'm sure Uncle Robert knows what he's doing," Asher interjected, surprised but perhaps not surprised enough.

Leslie's eyes flickered for an instant to her son. What was he saying? "Stay out of this, Asher."

He stepped back, probably because he'd never heard that tone of voice from his mother.

The years since Michael's death hung between the three of them now, thick as a mist. Leslie was certain that if her husband had lived, they would not be standing in a bathroom with a woman bound and gagged in a tub. Thank God, Morgan was still alive. Thank God, Emily was still alive.

For the first time in ages, Leslie knew exactly the right thing to do, and she was determined to do it.

"Asher, call our lawyer. The number is in my phone. Whatever this is has gone too far, and your uncle obviously needs help. The lawyer can arrange everything."

"I can't do that, Mom." Asher's voice took on a hard edge.

"Excuse me?"

Robert spoke. "He's right. We don't need a lawyer—or a psychiatrist, which is where I'm sure the lawyer would take me. Whitey and his minions would eventually get involved, and we can't have that. It's a misunderstanding, that's all."

"You think I want to drag our family into the spotlight? No, Robert, but this is a new low. You do realize that?"

Morgan remained silent throughout their conversation; she seemed all right with letting Leslie act on her behalf.

Robert continued. "Don't you see, Leslie? I did this to protect your son."

Leslie was taken aback. This? Kidnapping Morgan somehow protected her son?

"How does *this* protect Sawyer?"

Robert hung his head, and Asher stepped forward and pulled Leslie from her kneeling position and into Robert's room.

"No, Mom. It's me," he whispered so Morgan couldn't hear. "Uncle Robert is protecting me."

As Leslie's son spoke the words, her brother-in-law—tears in his eyes—approached her from behind.

34
May
Emily

Mom and I wake up while the moon is still high in the sky to drive to Natalie's house in separate cars. Dr. Garza and Chief Whiteside aren't far behind. This is where we'll start, where I remember that night ending.

I sit in the driver's seat alone and squeeze my eyes shut as I grip the steering wheel. *You want everything to be as close to the actual event as possible*, Dr. Garza told me last night. The problem is that we—me, Mom, Chief Whiteside, Dr. Garza—we're dealing in speculation and assumption rather than actual facts, but it's all we have so it will have to do.

I stay parked against the curb, hoping for memories that do not come. Nothing. Nothing. Nothing. I fiddle with the seat belt and try to listen to the quiet, but after twenty minutes I give up.

I check my rearview mirror for my support system—they are there, only yards from where I'm parked, silently willing me to remember—before I begin the drive to the ferry dock, a trip I don't remember taking. A trail of cars weaves behind me now on the mostly empty streets.

Minutes later the two terminal workers wave their neon flags until I'm bumping over the loading ramp. The moon is full and glowing and a breeze blows back the fly-aways from my ponytail.

I make sure the other cars are behind me now onboard the ferry, but I don't approach them or talk to anyone. I tentatively get out of the car and try to stand against the deck's rail, staring into the darkness of the sea beneath. My stomach turns. Even though I know the others are sitting in their cars on the ferry, no one speaks to me. This is supposed to mirror the night I disappeared. Except for the very real fact that I may not have been alone.

Instinctively, I grab one of the life jackets tacked to the railing; it's almost the same as the one I was wearing when they found me.

Mom finally heard back about the bird cameras on Pelican Island. All they could see on their grainy film was a speck—me—going overboard. Stupidity or a desire to jump? Hopefully, neither. "Just an accident, I'm sure," Mom said as she stroked my hair and originally told me the news. I'm grateful for that life jacket and for the fear that prompted me to put it on. Otherwise, fishermen might've never found me floating in the harbor. I could've been deadweight.

A few minutes later we dock on the northeastern side of the channel, and I get back in my car. I lean into the seat, take a deep breath and try to calm the drumbeat inside my chest, a reaction I can't seem to control. Something feels off inside of me.

I follow the blacktop and wind around the curve of the road until I can see the beach. I park, so Mom can crawl behind my wheel while I scoot to the passenger side as we discussed. If we're assuming that someone drove me at some point, we must recreate that feeling as well.

"Remember that you have us nearby," Dr. Garza reminded me before we began the reenactment. "Your mother will be out on Bolivar with you, and the police and I will be only seconds away. As soon as a memory surfaces, tell someone. Don't repress it. And if no memories come, that's all right. We'll keep trying."

Mom drives aimlessly toward the shoreline, taking paved roads that end in shifting sand. This is the part we really don't know, the path that is as dark as the 5:00 a.m. horizon. She parks and, as agreed upon, Mom steps out of the car to give me a few minutes alone with my thoughts. Dr. Garza recommended that I try a variety of physical positions that might put me back in the moment.

I place my head on arms splayed across the passenger-side dashboard. I stay this way until I feel a dull ache in my temples. But no memories. Next, I lay my seat back and turn my head this way and that. The headache moves forward to the back of my eyes. Nothing. Minutes later, I prop my seat upright again, but in frustration, like a petulant child, I slouch and lean toward the empty driver's seat. My heart begins to beat faster, and automatically, I feel for the door handle—an escape, but from what I don't know.

Hesitant, afraid of what I might see in my mind, I close my eyes. *Breathe*, I tell myself. *Pretend Mom isn't here at the shoreline, that a cop car isn't parked a few yards away, that everyone isn't waiting for the recess of your mind to release its contents.*

My body freezes, my mind empties. I'm suspended like a chrysalis waiting to emerge, like a spider watching her kill. Not really knowing why, I feel for the glove box and open it.

Seconds later, I gasp and throw open the car door.

"It's gone," I scream and Mom comes running at the same time headlights flash in the rearview mirror. "It's not here." My breath is staggered and shallow, and my hands are starting to shake.

"What's not here?" Mom kneels as close as possible without actually touching me.

"The hammer. That little one you bought me when we moved here. Remember?"

Mom nods. "I said you might need it to break glass if you got confused and drove into the ocean. A bad joke."

"I used it, Mom. His hands…his hands, they were everywhere. He'd taken my…my jeans off of me, and I was sick, so sick. But I remembered that hammer and…" I lean forward. I may throw up. Mom catches me. I've got to keep talking, to give these images a voice. "And while he was…he was crawling on top of me, I hit him…on the back of the head."

I shut my eyes tight for several seconds and a tear escapes. "Then I ran."

Footsteps approach and it sounds like the crunch of the sand beneath my own feet that early morning all those weeks ago, when I was running. From him. The tears comes faster, but I keep trying to explain.

"I didn't hit him hard enough to knock him out—it just got him off me long enough that I could get away. He screamed and tried to chase me, but I lost him in the dark."

Dr. Garza steps forward with Chief Whiteside. "Emily. Listen to me. Who? Who is *he*?"

"The intern in the hospital. The one who was with Dr. Steele. His nephew." I somehow manage the last few words. "I think his name is Asher. Asher Steele."

It takes me a half hour to collect myself, but I'm determined to finish this ordeal. Everyone heads back to their cars while

I remove my jeans, self-conscious even though I'm wearing a long shirt similar to the one I wore on that terrible night. I feel exposed as I walk in the direction of the road where Sawyer said he found me.

As the sun rises, it touches the silt-strewn water, turning the browns to oranges and golds. It's sure to be a hot day with the way my hair already clings to the back of my neck. A truck pulls to the side of the road, and as Sawyer emerges from the cab, I flinch.

Looking at him now, I can see that his nose and chin are similar to Asher's, but the way his hair falls over his eyes and the filling out of his arms and shoulders makes him appear completely different. I'm certain I wouldn't have connected the two of them, especially if I'd been in a drug-induced state.

I'm out in the open, just like I was that morning three months ago. Vulnerable. Then, I hear his voice. We aren't following a script, so he can say whatever comes to mind.

"Emily," he says, his eyes taking in all of me—as if he knows all of me.

He wants to kiss me, I can tell. I feel the electricity between us, but I want to recoil.

"Hi," I try, forcing myself to stay in place. *He's not Asher*, I remind myself. It helps that their voices sound nothing alike.

"I've been hoping to see you again, but...but I... I didn't know how to get in touch," Sawyer stammers. "I called my uncle a few times, but he never answered, and when I called the hospital, they wouldn't give me any information. I thought about showing up again, but didn't know how your mom would feel about that." He stops the onslaught of words and motions toward the cars several yards out. "Is that her over there?"

"Yeah." I turn my head. "She's making sure I'm safe."

"Makes sense after everything you've been through." He looks around. "What are we supposed to do next?"

"I think we drive," I say.

We drive in silence with Sawyer at the wheel of his truck for a couple of miles before he speaks again. I try not to stare, but I can't help but wonder at how familiar he seems. His hands. I know those hands. "Do you remember the lighthouse? Phin? Logan?"

I shake my head. "Sorry."

"It's okay. That's what I expected."

He taps the steering wheel nervously with his thumb, a rhythm without music. "The three of us live out there at Phin's place. Me, Phin and Logan—that's Phin's granddaughter. Logan's seven, and you two get along... I mean, you got along really well. You taught her how to tell apart the birds..."

He looks almost shy as he mimics me. "'There's actually no such thing as a seagull, just a variety of gulls,' that's what you told her. We would take her out while Phin made dinner. You two would bird-watch while I sketched."

I try to picture myself out there at the shoreline with Sawyer. "Did you draw that portrait of me that my mom found?"

"Yeah. That was one of them." Sawyer inhales. "You asked me to tattoo the lighthouse behind your ear too." I finger the place where the drawing is, this image that will forever be a part of me, and he switches subjects again. "Logan really wants to see you again. I told her I would say hello."

I don't know how to respond, but this little girl must be innocent in all this mess. "Tell her I hope to meet...to see her too."

"She actually said a few words while you were out there with us. She hadn't talked much since her parents died, and it was really nice how she followed you around wherever you went. She even came on a few dates with us."

"Dates?"

He bites his lip.

"I mean, I guess they were dates. We never actually defined much, just seemed to fit together, you know?"

I don't know, but I nod anyway.

"We'd go out and watch the sunset or we'd map out the constellations from the back of the truck. That kind of thing. It was simple. Easy."

His right hand rests too close as he stops at a red light, so I fold mine in my lap. "There's not much to do out that way, but you seemed happy."

He turns toward me as we sit still. "Emily, I swear we were really happy."

There's a tone of desperation in his words that I don't want to acknowledge. I can't bear anyone else's confusion or disappointment or sorrow, all because of me. "Look, I know this is super difficult for you. I have this history with you, and you can't remember a thing. But I need you to know where I'm coming from."

The light changes. I can ask him to pull over so I can run back to the safety of my mom only a car away, or I can lean into this life I don't remember.

"You can tell me," I decide. This is a vulnerable place for him too.

"It wasn't exactly love at first sight, but after we spent our first long day together a week or so after you arrived, I was... I was hooked. I woke up the next morning, and I wanted to spend every minute with you. I know it probably feels weird to you now, but I know you, Emily." He catches my eye briefly. "You like to eat pancakes for dinner. You like getting up early to walk on the beach. When you see the sun rise, you close your eyes for a few seconds and whisper a prayer. You like to fall asleep with a book tucked under your arm in case you wake up in the middle of the night. Your birthday is January 7, and you've never liked your middle name." *Lillith*, we both say at the same time. "You crinkle your nose whenever you're thinking hard. You love baked potatoes but hate them mashed. You've always wanted a kitten, but one of your sisters is allergic."

This boy does know me, which makes the question I have less intrusive somehow. "Sawyer?"

"Yeah?"

"When did we... I mean, we slept together, right? I'm pregnant with your child?"

He bends his head for a split second. I can't tell if he's sad I don't remember or embarrassed. "Like I said, I fell for you fast."

"Right."

He clears his throat. "It was probably only the third week you were with us. It just kind of happened. We spent the day at the beach with Logan, and when we came home, Phin took Logan on their monthly trip into Houston to stock up on supplies. They stay overnight, so Logan can see her cousins, so it was just me and you. I steamed crab for dinner, and we put a VHS on the old television Phin keeps to watch her movies."

I squint, maybe remembering a detail. "Wait...was it *The Philadelphia Story*?"

Sawyer grins. "That's the one. I'd never seen it before, but you swore by it. Said you watched it with your family."

"I talked about them?"

"Kind of... You talked about being back in Woodhaven with them, but you never told me they were in Galveston." He shakes his head. "I swear. Phin can vouch for me."

I believe him. "And then after the movie?"

"We sat on the porch, drank hot chocolate and watched the fog roll in."

I stare at my hands, willing the scene into place. Something's there.

"And then...we..."

My hands grow clammy as I remember the fire of his touch, how I wasn't afraid, how I wanted him, how I'd never experienced that kind of urgent longing, not even with Alex. I turn to Sawyer and feel the strange sensation of familiarity that I had when he came to see me in the hospital.

"You're not wearing your ring," he says quietly.

"Ring?" I look down at my hands, stretching my fingers.

"Don't worry." Sawyer chuckles at my wide eyes. "It's not like an engagement ring or anything. Me and Logan made it together. She wanted to give you a gift. I guess she sensed that you were leaving soon."

I squint so hard that I can almost see a ring on my right hand. It's made of wire and blue beads the color of the wide Texas sky. Just as quickly, I see that ring in my palm. It falls. I reach for it, and there's a rush of water. I gasp.

"What?" Sawyer brakes and reaches a hand out in front of me. "Are you okay?"

We are parked on the shoulder now, and Sawyer turns his body toward mine.

"I was reaching for Logan's ring," I say. "I was holding it and then it fell. When I reached for it, I must've slipped and hit my head. That's how I went overboard on the ferry that day."

Sawyer inhales and his jaw trembles slightly. "I'm just glad you're okay. Look, I don't know why you left, and I don't know all the reasons you can't remember our time together, but I feel like I can't let you leave today without telling you the truth." He rubs his eye with the back of his hand. "The truth is that I love you, Emily." This boy is braver than I first realized, not the type to hide his missing, his grief or his happiness at seeing me again. His brow furrows as he thinks of how to phrase what comes next. When he finally speaks again, his words are direct. "You're carrying our baby, mine and yours, and that's not something I take lightly. I will be there whenever and however you'll allow me to, for you and the baby. I will spend a lifetime getting to know you and letting you get to know me all over again. If you'll let me."

I look out the window at the structure coming into view, and again, I touch the lighthouse etched into my skin. Some things can't be easily erased.

35
May
Morgan

"Robby, it's Whitey. Can you open the door?"

Morgan heard the voice faintly from the bathroom. Whitey, Chief Whiteside. Shit, if she had to rely on him as her rescuer, she might as well give up now.

Morgan attempted to call out, but the duct tape muffled any chance at finding her voice. Robert had reapplied and reinforced the sticky fabric over her mouth and hands and feet after Leslie's attempt to rescue her. Now, Morgan could move only inches at a time. She wasn't sure if she could make enough sound to get Whitey's attention through the walls.

Morgan hadn't seen or heard from Leslie in several hours. Despite whatever was between them, Morgan couldn't bear the thought of Leslie being hurt...or worse. Surely Robert wouldn't harm his own sister-in-law. And what about Asher? Morgan thought she'd heard Robert talking to him in low tones at one point, but she couldn't be sure.

She wiggled her fingers to keep the blood flowing and listened as hard as she could to what was happening on the other side of the walls.

"Quiet, Mom. Just stay quiet." It was Asher in the bedroom with his mother, but what was he thinking? *Let her scream. Let us all scream.*

Morgan heard Leslie's muffled sob.

A door—the front door—opened.

"Hey, Whitey. What's going on?" Robert asked.

"We received a call from Anna this evening," Whitey said, his voice booming loudly enough for her to hear.

Morgan had lost all sense of time, but if it was evening, then at least fifteen hours must've passed. Robert had come in here twice to give her food and water and to let her relieve herself. Once before Leslie's rescue attempt and once after.

"I'm not trying to starve you," Robert had said, the hint of a flirtatious smile on his lips, when she wouldn't eat the fettuccini he tried to feed her sometime before Asher and Leslie arrived. "Come on. It's my homemade Alfredo sauce."

Her stomach was growling, but she was not about to literally eat from Robert's hand.

But he pressed, almost force-feeding her. When she was three bites in, she tried to keep her voice from shaking as she appealed to reason. "Listen, Robert, maybe I was too hasty."

"What do you mean?" He frowned.

"I mean…" Morgan looked up at him, eyes as innocent and round as she could make them. "I obviously overreacted, and laying…sitting here has made me think about your side of things. You didn't have any choice with the way you had to…to protect your nephew and…"

Robert breathed out slowly as he leaned back into the sink's pedestal. "I'm so glad to hear you say that," he said. "I need for us to be on the same page, to know that we are in each other's corner."

Morgan forced a matching smile. "So, why don't you take off these…" She looked down at her hands, unsure of how to describe the mess of tape binding her wrists together. If she brought attention to this insanity, he might realize what he'd done and keep her like that.

But at that moment, there had been a knock on the door and Leslie and Asher had arrived and interrupted their chat, setting him off again.

Now, Morgan listened to the exchange in the living room, willing Whitey to search the apartment, to hear Leslie's crying or Asher's attempts to calm her. Wait…why wasn't Asher muzzled too? And why wasn't he drawing attention to the obviously dire situation they were in? Morgan tried unsuccessfully to kick her feet against the base of the tub.

"Is everything okay with Anna?" Robert sounded surprisingly concerned as he spoke to Whitey.

"She'll be fine," Whitey said. "She wanted to talk to us about a video that was circulating. It had possible information about Emily's disappearance. Apparently, your niece may have accidentally switched a drug-laced drink with Emily at a party on the night she went missing."

"What? That's crazy." He sounded so sincere. "But if it was an accident, Anna wasn't taken into custody, I hope?"

"No, nothing like that. It sounds like a real mix-up that wouldn't have caused much trouble under normal circumstances, but…well, everyone already knows how things went."

Robert spoke quickly. "Right. Very unfortunate. But thankfully Emily seems fine now. That's what matters."

"Right. Except that Anna also said the pills weren't hers, said she used a couple of Xanax that you gave to Leslie."

"Leslie had been having panic attacks." Robert's voice

shifted. "It's not illegal for a doctor to give a prescription nowadays, is it?"

Whitey chuckled, to Morgan's chagrin. "No, no. But beyond all that, the real reason I'm here is that Anna said she hasn't seen her mother today and that with everything that happened yesterday at The Monterey, she just wanted to make sure that Leslie was okay. We tried calling you and Asher, but neither of you answered, so I decided to stop by."

Robert hesitated for a second too long. Morgan felt a shift in the air.

"I haven't heard from Leslie today," Robert finally said.

Whitey sighed. "Look, I hate to do this at such a late hour, but we also got some information on Asher today. I know you two are close. Do you mind if we come in and talk for a few minutes?"

We? Ah, the lady cop—Officer Cortez?—must be with him. Thank God.

"I mean, I don't think that's a good idea right now. Maybe if you come by my office tomorrow—" Robert was trying to stall, and Morgan hoped Whitey or Cortez would be able to see through his charade. Morgan heard the front door widening, and Robert's footsteps moving toward the bathroom where she'd been kept. Morgan started to twitch as much as the duct tape would allow, and she emitted a sort of a half-hum from her throat. She pushed her feet against the porcelain as she'd done when Leslie and Asher had arrived earlier that day.

Leslie was still crying. *Shut the fuck up*, she heard Asher whisper.

"What is that?" Whitey asked. "Robert, is someone here?"

"It's coming from the bedroom," Cortez said, more forcefully.

"Wait." Robert's voice was rising. Morgan could almost see him blocking the threshold. "You can't do this, Whitey.

No one is here." The officers were closing in. "Hey, you can't search my apartment without a warrant. I know my rights. You can't—"

But then, there was a door being broken in, a tackling in the living room, Robert shouting as he was taken down. Next, Officer Cortez was ripping something that sounded like a giant Band-Aid, and Leslie's voice pierced the air.

"He has Morgan too—she's..."

Morgan heard Leslie suck in air. "She's in the bathroom. Get her first."

Then, Morgan lost it. She cried, whole sobs that held the pain of this day and all the others that had been so hard because of the actions of other people, even people who said they loved her.

A moment later, she was unbound, in a heap with Leslie on the living room floor, their shared trauma pulling them together.

A team of EMTs rushed to her and Leslie's side as the women watched Whitey handcuff Robert, who lay sprawled on the floor.

Morgan looked up. "Wait...what about him?"

Whitey followed her gaze to Asher Steele. "We'll get to him soon enough."

"He was part of this, too," Morgan said. "I heard him telling Leslie to stay quiet."

Leslie's eyes widened, and she shook her head. "I don't know what you heard, but it wasn't Asher. He was trapped in there with me."

Morgan took a hard look at Leslie, who was only inches away. She had her poker face in place. Damn. Leslie was lying, and Morgan wouldn't stand for it. Not after...whatever the fuck had happened here today.

"Hell, no," Morgan said. "I am not letting this little shit get away with whatever it was he did. Robert, you were protecting him, not Sawyer, yes?" She looked back and forth between uncle, mother and nephew. "Am I right?"

Asher stepped forward and put out a hand to silence her. "It's fine. I have nothing to hide. Once I explain, you'll see this is all a misunderstanding, and they can let me—and Uncle Robert—go."

Morgan felt Leslie's back go rigid.

"Asher, you don't know what you're saying," Leslie tried. "You're confused."

Whitey propped Robert against the wall as Officer Cortez started toward the young man, her voice calming. "You're probably right, Asher. Why don't you sit down next to me and tell me what you remember?"

Asher looked around, nodded reassuringly at his mother and uncle, and then sat next to Cortez on the couch as if they were having a simple chat.

"Okay. So, I was at my mom's Mardi Gras party when I got a call from my sister. She wanted me to bring her an overnight bag because she'd been drinking. So I did. But as I was leaving, I saw a girl sitting in her car on the street. I thought it was weird that she was just sitting there with the ignition started, so I opened the door to check on her, you know?"

"That's enough, Asher. You don't need to tell them this," Leslie said. "You didn't do anything wrong."

"I know," Asher said, his voice full of confidence. "That's why I'm telling them."

He turned back to Cortez, whose face was remarkably neutral. "So then I saw that the girl in the car was Emily Callahan. I didn't really know her, but I knew about her from my sister and had seen her a couple of times in a group of Anna's friends. She was totally wasted, like sitting up but passed out, for real. At first, I thought maybe she just had her eyes closed, so I tried to see if she was asleep and wake her up. Since she wasn't very heavy, I moved her over to the passenger seat, thinking I would drive her home, but as we pulled away, I realized I had no idea where she lived. I tried to call my sister, but she didn't answer, so I just kept driving."

Robert sent a look to Morgan as if he wanted her to do something.

Not a chance.

"I want to call our lawyer," Leslie said, intervening.

Cortez smiled tenderly. "I really don't think that's necessary. Your son is just telling us a story." She paused a beat, letting her calm permeate the air. "But it's up to Asher."

He shook his head. "It's fine, Mom. I didn't do anything wrong. I swear."

Whitey spoke this time. "Where did you plan to take Emily?"

Asher looked away, thinking. "I don't know. I didn't have a plan, I swear. She just looked so peaceful with her head resting against the window. Then, she moved around and rested her head on my lap, and I don't know, I guess I thought that she and I, maybe, I don't know... Before I knew it, we were out on Bolivar. Dad used to take us across the ferry, so we could go fishing, spend time together." He looked at his mom. "Do you remember that?"

Beside Morgan, Leslie was stunned silent and across the room, Robert hung his head. Morgan didn't move, concerned that she might break the strange magic that was happening between Cortez and Asher.

"I guess that's what I was thinking about, how great those times had been. I started thinking that maybe I could spend time with this girl, and we could get to know each other.

That's why I was so excited when she sort of came around. I pulled over at one of the pocket beaches, so we could talk."

Officer Cortez again. "Was Emily awake by this point?"

"Yeah, it seemed like it. She looked at me like she wasn't scared of me, just curious, and then we didn't even have to say anything, just started, you know…" He turned away from Leslie and lowered his voice. "We were kind of making out. She was definitely awake by then, so she wasn't doing anything she didn't want to do. I swear, I'm a good guy. You can ask anybody."

Whitey spoke up. "Have you had similar experiences like this? With other girls?"

"No, I mean, maybe." Asher glanced at his mom before pushing his shoulders back, turning to Cortez and taking a deep breath. "It kind of reminded me of Julie a few years ago— Oh, and a girl at UT last year. Those have been my only two girlfriends. Emily was into me just like they had been."

"Are you saying that you had an encounter like this with Julie Wagner?" Cortez asked, her voice remarkably even as she listened to the confession. "And another young woman?"

Leslie sprang to life again. "No, he's not. You are not saying that, Asher. Stop. Now."

"No, I'm not saying that the exact same thing happened with those girls. I mean, I did kind of fool around with them, but they liked it too. Emily wanted me, just like those other girls." His cheeks began to redden as if he was either embarrassed or realizing that things might be harder to explain than he first thought.

"Maybe I should talk to someone?" Asher's eyes widened as he considered the possibility. "Maybe I do need a lawyer?"

"I don't think there's a need for that, son," Whitey answered. Morgan was impressed with how even he kept his voice.

"No more," Leslie tried to tell Asher again, but Cortez nodded at the young man to continue.

"I... I got her... I mean, she took her pants off, and we were about to...you know, but all of a sudden she turned on me, knocking me in the back of the head with some little hammer thing, the kind that people have in their cars in case they need to break the glass." Asher's voice rose. "It was small, but a hammer, for Christ's sake. She went from being all into me and then turned into an angry little bitch." He lowered his voice and seemed suddenly penitent. "I apologize for the language."

"That's all right," Cortez said. "You're doing the right thing by telling us all of this. Why don't you take a deep breath and then explain why you felt angry at Emily and the other girls?"

"I don't know." Asher took a couple of breaths. "I guess I realized that Emily was just a cocktease like the others. Sorry, but girls today are so fucking entitled, all dressed up and like 'come and get it' and then when a guy takes a chance, puts himself out there, they're ready to turn on you. After Emily hit me, I was kind of out of it for a minute. Saw stars, that kind of thing. I had a bruise for a month, a fucking month."

Morgan watched Whitey circle behind Asher, but somehow it wasn't threatening even though Morgan could see that he was in perfect position to pounce if needed.

Officer Cortez kept her cool. "Where was Emily when you recovered from the blow?"

"She was gone. Can you believe that? I helped her, and she just left me out there all on my own. I tried to follow her footprints, and I called after her a couple of times, but she didn't come back. I figured she could find her own way home, so I took the ferry back and drove her car to East Beach where I knew somebody would find it.

"She'd left her phone and backpack in the car, which was fine. I didn't mess with them. But then I saw her jeans and her shoes and realized someone might think something bad had happened. I wiped down the steering wheel, grabbed her clothes and walked down the surf a mile or so, even though there's some rough patches—I didn't want anybody to see my shoe tracks and get the wrong idea. That's when I shoved the keys into the pocket of her jeans and threw them in the ocean." He took a steadying breath. "Anyway, after I walked back to Natalie's house where I'd left my car, I grabbed a few things from home and drove back to school, just like I'd planned.

"I guess Sawyer found Emily and is gonna be some big hero now for supposedly rescuing her. It's kind of ridiculous. None of this would've happened if Emily hadn't been such a slut, but I swear I didn't know she was missing until Mom told me after I'd already been back at school for a few weeks. I'm really a good guy. Ask anybody."

That moment, Whitey sprang to life, and Cortez pulled handcuffs from behind her.

Asher's face registered shock. "Wait, what are you doing? I told you what happened. Don't you see that it was Emily's fault? She brought this on herself."

This time it was Cortez's turn to do the talking. "You have the right to remain silent. Anything you say can and may be used against you in a court of law…"

Too late, Morgan thought as she watched the two officers take Robert and Asher away.

36
May
Catherine

Within the hour Rosalyn issued a summons to Leslie, Morgan and Catherine. Her library. Midnight.

"Welcome, ladies. I know it's late, so I appreciate you coming."

"It's the middle of the night," Catherine stated obviously, disdain lacing every word. She glanced around at the rows of leather-bound books and wondered if Rosalyn had ever taken one off the shelf. "Don't you think we've been through enough late nights recently?"

"I know, dear," Rosalyn said. "That's why I said *thank you*."

Catherine had received her unwelcome invite from Rosalyn via text message right after Whitey had called Carter and given them a final update. Robert and Asher were behind bars, and Asher's confession explained the final missing pieces of Emily's disappearance.

"I really don't understand why the three of us are here," Morgan added, a troubled look in her eye.

Catherine scooted closer to her friend, hoping to communicate so much through that one movement: *I'm here. I'm sorry. It couldn't have been your son.*

Leslie offered no words, her eyes blank. She seemed to be in shock.

"Yes, well, I'll get right to it," Rosalyn said. "I called you because it's crucial that the four of us discuss a few things."

"Asher's innocent," Leslie muttered under her breath. "He has to be."

Rosalyn ignored the statement. "As you all know, my family helped rebuild this town, and because of our history, I feel it is my duty to maintain a sense of…we'll call it decorum among the citizens of this island, particularly those of a certain social standing."

Catherine cringed.

"That said, I've brought the three of you here because we desperately need to clear the air between us before the legal authorities begin to gather evidence to charge anyone involved in Emily's disappearance. I want justice for my granddaughter, but I also want to ensure that this is an open-and-shut case and that no unnecessary names—Callahan, or otherwise—are dragged through the mud. We've largely kept this out of the local media, and I'd like to keep it that way."

"I don't think so, Rosalyn. Let Chief Whiteside, the media, the justice system finally do their job," Catherine said. "I want every single detail about how Emily went missing to be exposed, and I don't care how it's found out."

Rosalyn looked down at her daughter-in-law as if she were naive about the inner workings of this town. "But dear, I am the justice system."

Morgan's expression soured. "I call bullshit."

Rosalyn shook her head. "Let me clarify. The police force, the investigators, the judges do their jobs, but when intervention is necessary, I am not above taking certain measures. Morgan, have you never wondered how the charges against your son were dropped so swiftly years ago?"

"My son provided sufficient evidence to Whitey that he was innocent," Morgan answered.

Rosalyn shrugged. "What is sufficient evidence, after all, except evidence that the authorities deem legitimate? Yes, Chief Whiteside wanted to believe your son, but in one of our weekly conversations about the goings-on around this town, I may have helped nudge him in the right direction."

Morgan's face heated, and Catherine put a hand on her shoulder as if to remind her that Rosalyn wasn't worth the effort.

The older woman took a deep breath and continued, "Ladies, let me start afresh by stating my reason for inviting you here. Look around at the faces in this room."

The women's eyes darted around the room, not quite resting on any one person.

"We are the women who know the most and who are closest to the events of the past few months. We must lay everything on the table and work together to ensure that justice is served."

Rosalyn motioned toward Catherine, who glared at her mother-in-law. "Catherine, let's begin with you. Can you tell these women the real reason for your move to the island?"

"Seriously? After everything that's happened? That's what you want to talk about?"

"Yes, seriously."

Catherine huffed out a breath and took a long pause before acquiescing. Anything to move this along. "Our family needed a fresh start after some things happened at my job, and we thought Carter should help with the business after his father's—"

"Ah, ah, ah." Rosalyn shook her head as she gazed down. "My husband—God rest his soul—died several months before your move, it's true, but things were in good order, and I am fairly competent. You could have chosen *not* to immediately disrupt Emily's academic and social life. You could have allowed your eldest daughter to finish high school, but you suffered a bit more than mild disappointment in your personal career, isn't that right?"

Catherine stood, matching her eye to eye. "Rosalyn, I don't think this is relevant."

"Isn't it? Didn't the reality of your disappointment— No, that's not the best word…let me see." Rosalyn paused. "Didn't the reality of your *disgrace* speed your decision to disrupt your daughter's life?"

Catherine swallowed hard. "I've already faced my guilt in all of this, Rosalyn. You can't add one ounce to it."

"Good." Rosalyn shifted her entire frame toward her next mark. "Then, we'll move on."

"Leslie, dear," Rosalyn began again, placing a hand on her shoulder and smiling down on her. "I've known you for most of your life. By the time you were finishing high school, you had already become my right-hand woman, my hope to take over the social goings-on of Callahan Prep, of this town. Unfortunately, somewhere along the way—most likely because of Michael's unfortunate and untimely death—you lost sight of our primary job. To protect and maintain peace on this island, not only in your family. I care for you, Leslie, and that is why it is so difficult for me to detail the numerous misdeeds of you and your family."

A maid interrupted, bringing steaming mugs of coffee.

Everyone took a cup and paused to consider what was coming next.

Catherine glanced at Morgan periodically to see how she was doing after the day's terrible events. She couldn't imagine how the woman would recover from what Robert had done to her, but Catherine wanted to reassure Morgan that she would be there.

Rosalyn nodded a thank-you as the maid exited.

Leslie swallowed the hot drink in a great gulp, as if the coffee were fuel for the fire within her. "I'm quite aware of my children's flaws, thank you, and my lawyer and I will be handling everything," Leslie said.

Rosalyn swiped with her unoccupied hand as if discarding Leslie's words. "We have no need for the mention of lawyers in a gathering like this, Leslie." She took a slow sip. "In fact, let's start with one of the more innocent members of your family, shall we?"

Rosalyn perched on the edge of her wing chair, coffee in hand, and Catherine was at full attention. This—the temptation of knowledge only Rosalyn possessed—is what kept her here.

"Anna. The diligent girl, who has a perfect GPA, numerous friends and the titles of homecoming and Winter Dance queen. But she also has one little problem—she can't keep her hands out of Mommy's pills. It was these pills that found their way into Emily's red Solo cup the night of her disappearance and set off a chain reaction that left her missing for weeks on end. Does all of this sound accurate so far?"

Leslie pushed her shoulders back, but didn't answer.

"Come, come. Anna has already said as much to Whitey—and on a circulating video, from what I understand. It went... What's the word? Viral, I believe." Rosalyn squinted at Leslie to see if she would admit her daughter's guilt. Not yet. "Okay, if you insist. Then, we'll move on to one of her older brothers, the bright and promising Asher Steele."

Leslie shook her head again. "Leave Asher out of this. He's done nothing wrong. Any confession that Whitey got out of him was coerced, and I'll prove it." Leslie's hands began to work at the fabric of the throw pillow at her fingertips. Catherine could see the anxiety mounting in her.

"No, Leslie. No." Morgan sprang forward. "Asher confessed. You and I heard him with our own ears. How can you sit there and deny it? He helped tie you up, his own mother. What the fuck?"

Rosalyn peered over at Morgan. "Language, dear."

"Uh, no. I will use all the shits, damns and fucks I need to right now. This little fucker attacked not one, not two, but three young women—maybe more." Morgan's face screwed up as she processed the ugly reality again. "It's time to say things like they really are. Julie Wagner was a freshman, and Asher was a senior when he took her into a room in Leslie's house—with dozens of people outside the door—and raped her while she was unconscious." Catherine put a hand to her neck, the reality hitting her anew. "He confessed to something similar during college, and now he's attempted the same thing again."

Silence settled even as Catherine's heart beat faster.

"So it would seem," Rosalyn stated evenly.

Catherine felt a lump rise in the back of her throat. She reminded herself of Emily's revelation out on Bolivar Peninsula. She'd fought Asher off. Her brave girl had incapacitated him long enough to flee. The thought allowed her to breathe again.

Leslie finally stood for the first time to face Morgan, holding the pillow in her arms as if to shield herself from the truth. "Not *my* Asher. He wouldn't do any of those things. It was Sawyer. Asher's just trying to protect his brother."

Morgan looked from Catherine to Rosalyn and back to Leslie.

"Does anyone else see the other terrifying problem here?" Morgan asked. Her mouth hung open for a brief moment, her eyebrows dipping. "This woman. Leslie. She's not only in denial, she's also bat-shit crazy."

Catherine jumped in, finding her voice again. "I want Asher locked up. For life. He has no problem with raping girls and then letting others take the fall for him." Her voice lowered, so the other women had to strain to hear. "I swear, I'll kill him if he gets out of this one."

Leslie's breathing intensified. "You will never lay a finger on my son."

Catherine shook her head and spoke through gritted teeth. "Like how Asher never laid a finger on my daughter?"

37
May
Leslie

Leslie could see that Catherine's eyes were filling.

"This can't be real," Leslie said. Her hands, having released the throw pillow, were pulling and twisting at a strand of her own hair. She needed something to hold, something she could control. "Asher cannot be guilty."

Leslie looked to Rosalyn. *What happened to us?* she wanted to ask the older woman. *You were my friend, my mother. My own parents never understood how the world actually works, but you did. You taught me.*

"Your son—Asher, that is—is in a holding cell, awaiting your visit tomorrow morning," Rosalyn stated almost stoically. "You can call Whitey if you need confirmation."

"He's just a boy," Leslie tried, her gaze going everywhere at once as if she were looking for someone to speak on behalf of her child.

Catherine apparently had seen and heard enough. "Just

a boy?" Her eyes narrowed in on Leslie. "I searched for my daughter for ten weeks. I attended a memorial service I didn't sanction. How can you say that Asher is just a boy? If we'd known to start the search out on Bolivar, we might've found Emily in a few hours, not a few weeks. Before she got pregnant. Surely even you can understand that somewhere between Anna's drug use and Asher's attack, my kid's brain went haywire and sent her into some kind of dissociative amnesia."

Leslie covered her ears. She'd borne so much the past few years, but this was her limit. She could not bear these accusations against those she loved. "It's not *his* fault," she said, trying to keep tears at bay. "Asher went back to school like he was supposed to. He didn't even know Emily was missing until weeks later. If you want to blame anyone in our family, it should be his brother. If he'd kept in touch with his family, if he'd told us he was seeing some girl, then all of this could've been solved a lot sooner. I won't defend Sawyer's actions." Leslie knew she sounded desperate. Because she was. She could not lose another member of her family to heartache, to tragedy, to rebellion. One had to be redeemable.

"Ah, Sawyer," Rosalyn said, letting the name of Leslie's *other* son wander into the room, letting it sit among the women. "Your third child, the family member who may be the only innocent Steele in all of this. Yet, you would condemn him to release the guilty one. I never thought you capable of such disillusionment, Leslie."

Fine, maybe she was disillusioned. Maybe she was mad. Maybe the events of the past few years had finally broken her.

The door creaked open, and each woman's head turned toward the sound. A collective gasp resonated as a fifth person entered the drawing room. Emily.

Catherine rushed to her daughter's side, hugging her tightly before scanning her entire frame; she would probably do that for the rest of her life, making sure her girl was intact every time they met. "What's wrong? Is everything all right? Why are you here?"

Leslie had to look away. The guilt was too much. What had she and her children done to this poor girl? But wasn't Leslie too only a mother trying to protect her child, her Asher, the baby born with the weak lungs, the toddler afraid of the turtles? How wrong could that be?

Emily stood in the doorway, a piece of paper dangling from her fingers. "Grandma, you asked me to come?"

Leslie saw Rosalyn smile as she moved toward Emily. "Perfect timing, my dear," she said, taking both of her granddaughter's hands in her own. "I sent your summons a bit later, so us grown-ups could take care of some other business."

Rosalyn turned to address the entire room of women. "You see, I asked Emily to come tonight, so I could share the final piece of this puzzle, a piece that goes back almost forty-three years. If I had shared my own story—one about a young man who stole my innocence when I was Emily's age—it might have made her more cautious, more watchful. I kept this knowledge to myself at the time, hiding my own struggles behind the appearance of a seamless life. But because of my trauma and ensuing mental health issues over the years I—along with Dr. Montague—have been researching a wide variety of treatments and medications to combat dissociative disorders. In fact, this extensive research is how I knew that administering a dose of Flumazenil might help Emily regain consciousness."

Leslie gasped, and everyone's eyes shot to her. "Flumazenil?"

"Indeed," Rosalyn said.

Leslie felt herself going somewhere else. Back to the late night when her husband had left her once and for all.

Rosalyn interjected. "Leslie recognizes the drug's name because that's what surgeons use to help patients regain consciousness after surgery. Dr. Steele kept a vial at their house with Michael's other medications, in case they ever needed to counteract the sedatives used to make Michael comfortable."

Leslie muttered. "I tried to use Flumazenil after...after Sawyer found his father. But, I... It was too late." She crumpled into herself.

Rosalyn watched Leslie for a moment and then looked to Catherine. "Flumazenil was the only way I could combat the drugs that were in Emily's system, drugs that Robert was administering on the sly. I had received a tip from one of the nurses, but I wasn't sure until I gave Emily the antidote. I rubbed her feet in lavender oil to keep her calm, and then I added the medication to her IV. Within minutes, she was fully conscious again."

Catherine and Emily both stared at Rosalyn, shock evident on their faces. Emily placed a hand on her grandmother's shoulder.

Rosalyn put a hand over Emily's and took a fortifying breath. "To summarize, the Steele family bears the bulk of the blame. Leslie, you wrote the letters warding off Emily. Don't deny it, dear—you apparently confessed as much in that god-awful video. Your daughter drugged Emily, accidentally or otherwise, which started this nightmare. One of your sons attacked my granddaughter and Julie Wagner and who knows how many other young women, a fact that is both appalling and terrifying and cannot be blamed on his father's illness and death alone. And your brother-in-law tried as best as he could to cover up Asher's actions, even if it meant drugging a patient and kidnapping his own girlfriend and sister-in-law. Sawyer may be the only innocent Steele in all of this."

Catherine sniffled, wiping her nose on the back of her

hand. "Innocent? Maybe. But Sawyer *is* the father of Emily's baby. It seems that any way you look at it, we cannot escape the Steele family."

"True," Rosalyn acknowledged.

Leslie could see herself running away, escaping. She wanted to grab each of her children—even Sawyer—and her brother-in-law and bring them to a safe house where they could live out the rest of their days together. Family means everything. Simply everything.

But since that plan was impossible with Asher and Robert already in custody, she would need to figure out an alternate plan, one that would free those she loved. She would contact her lawyer first thing tomorrow—just as Rosalyn had taught her. Leslie forced herself to sit upright as Rosalyn offered a few closing words.

"I think that's everything, ladies. The truth as we know it. Now, we must decide how much to tell everyone else."

38
May
Morgan

The four women—Catherine, Emily, Leslie and Morgan—
didn't flee the Callahan place immediately, wrung out as they
were. Each woman was quiet and contemplative, except for
Leslie who, after emerging from her crumpled state, couldn't
seem to sit in one place. She'd even called Whitey out of a dead
sleep. He told Leslie that she could see Asher in the morning.
That man was finally growing a pair.

For all of them, the revelations had been as heavy as a boul-
der crashing into the sea, but for Morgan and Catherine, the
closure was worth all the weight of knowing.

Sometime before dawn, Morgan pulled Leslie aside, hoping
to reason with her and to offer one last olive branch, especially
after what they'd endured together in Robert's apartment.

"I know this is one of the most difficult things you'll ever
go through, Leslie, hearing people whisper about your son,
watching your family fray at the edges. I would never wish

this on you, regardless of what happened between us. I want you to know that, and I also want to thank you for trying to rescue me from Robert."

Morgan couldn't imagine what that kind of betrayal might do to a person, especially a person who seemed as undone as Leslie.

"This is neither the time or place, but I don't know when I'll get the chance to ask you again, so, here goes. Leslie, this thing between us, this distance, this animosity, it can't be all about Michael, can it? You have to know that I never had any plans to steal him from you."

Leslie's hands stopped fidgeting while she answered. "I don't know anymore."

Morgan sat with that answer until Leslie spoke again, her voice flat and steady.

"At first, I thought it was all about him, but maybe it had something to do with the jealousy I've felt our entire lives."

"Jealousy? What did *you* have to be jealous of?"

Leslie stood, one hand on the mantel, looking out the window beyond the formidable gate surrounding the mansion and into the lights of the few passing cars on the road at the early hour. "You were always so strong, even in the middle of chaos. I was a compulsive and anxious mess even in an ideal situation." Leslie almost smiled. "I was jealous of your way."

"My way?"

"The way you approach life with that if-you-want-it-then-make-it-happen focus. You saw me struggle and study and work my butt off to be somebody that I could be proud of, but everything came naturally to you. I was jealous of the way you didn't care one way or another, like popularity and recognition didn't even matter."

"When your mom is high for half of the month, you get some perspective," Morgan breathed out. Leslie's face relaxed and she finally looked like herself, vulnerable and lovely like she had when they were young. Before all of this. Morgan tried again. "We could try to salvage a semblance of our friendship, for the sake of what it once was and because we live on a tiny island where we'll inevitably run into each other."

Furrows and crevices marched across Leslie's brow as she sank back into her adult self. "Too much has happened."

"But—"

"Let's leave it, Morgan. Let's remember this moment. I'm sorry your son had to go through all of the rumors and inter-rogations for what my... Anyway, maybe I never should've blamed you for trying to steal Michael, but I am who I am, for better or worse. Besides, I don't think you'll approve of how I'll handle Asher's trial—if it gets to that point."

Morgan raised her eyebrows, questioning, and Leslie clarified.

"Your son is safe, and mine will be too. One way or an-other, Asher will be acquitted. He has to be."

"Leslie, you shouldn't interfere in something like—"

She waved a hand as if swatting at a fly. "I will, though. It's who I am." Leslie closed her eyes, rubbing the lines from her forehead.

Morgan stepped away silently, gave Catherine and Emily a long hug, and left the mansion, hoping never to return. All Morgan wanted was to be at home with her innocent son, who would soon be going off to college.

Alex was sleeping with his head turned up and to the side like he'd once slept on her shoulder as a baby. When she sat on the bed next to him, he startled awake.

"Are you okay? I was worried about you, was about to call Chief Whiteside before Emily finally texted me back and told me that you were at Rosalyn Callahan's house."

Morgan couldn't keep from crying then, hearing her son concerned about her. He put one broad arm across her back and held her close. He was maturing, had matured a lot over the past year. He was becoming a young man she could be proud of, one who had endured ridicule and kept his calm through it all—most of the time anyway.

She wiped at the tears and dabbed at her nose. "Does this mean that you and Emily are communicating again?"

He gave a half grin. "Maybe. It's a start, right? Looking for your mom in the middle of the night because you have no idea if someone has trapped her in a bathtub again will bring friends back together."

Morgan laughed. She had to, to keep from crying even more. She looked at Alex and knew she had to say something before the moment passed. This was a night for saying things. "I'm really sorry that I didn't believe you. I mean, really and fully and completely believe you, that you wouldn't hurt a girl. I shouldn't have had any doubts."

"It's okay."

"No, it's not. A mother should know her son well enough to tell whether he is truthful or a liar, and before everything happened, I knew you were one of the most honest people I'd ever met. When you were six years old and busted that statue in the foyer of the school, you confessed right away. Do you remember that?"

"Yeah. I was practicing tackling. Not my best moment."

"You also confessed when you thought another kid cheated off of you on a test in middle school, even though you had nothing to do with the kid's wandering eyes. You've always been a good kid, and I shouldn't have doubted you."

She grabbed him by the shoulder and planted a kiss on his cheek, even though she knew he would protest. "You're my favorite son, you know that?" It was what she'd said to him every night when she tucked him into bed as a kid.

"And you're my favorite mom," Alex said back at her, as he always had.

39
May
Catherine

Catherine and Emily arrived home around 4:00 a.m. Carter, concerned, made Catherine tell him everything before they went to bed, and she did, relaying the entire bizarre summons from start to finish.

Catherine's mind finally rested with all of the puzzle pieces in place, but when she awoke with her husband's arm snaked around her, she couldn't help but shake him off. The two of them had clung to one another like life rafts these past few months, but in a frantic sort of way, as if when they let go, then the vessel of their marriage might sink to the bottom, carrying their children with them.

"What's wrong?" Carter asked through the haze of too-little sleep.

Catherine didn't answer and instead sat at the side of the bed with her head between her hands. He came around and placed an arm across her shoulder. It was meant to be comforting, but she didn't really want him to touch her.

Carter spoke in a soothing tone. "Hey, it's going to be okay."

She looked at him. Did he really believe that everything would suddenly be okay, after all they had been through the past few months? Were they simply to go back to normal, build a new life? Here?

"We almost buried our daughter," she whispered. "Less than a month ago."

Carter shook his head as if trying to dislodge the experience. "But she's safe in the other room, and we finally have all of the answers."

"She has a baby growing inside of her that's going to come out in six months' time." Catherine stared at the wall. "What's the answer to that problem?"

Carter sighed. "I don't know, but we'll figure it out. Remember that she's an adult now, and our job is to support her decisions. That's the one thing you said you've been learning through all of this, right?"

Catherine threw out words before weighing whether or not they were completely fair. "Support her like you supported me?"

Carter eyed her, confused. "I have supported you. We moved here for you."

"Right." Catherine couldn't keep the sarcasm from her words. "And taking over your family's business and being close to your mother again didn't sound appealing?"

"Catherine, you know that I've always talked about eventually coming back to Galveston, but the timing was for you."

"Why?" Her voice grew gruff with the frustration that had been building for the past year. It was all too much and someone had to bear the force of her fury. "Why?" She stood and began yelling. "Why? Especially if you think that what I did was just some silly mistake, meaningless to the real world, meaningless even though that one mistake ended my career."

"It didn't end your career." Carter moved away from her, flailing a hand as he attempted to keep his voice at a steady pitch. "For God's sake, you *can* compose again. People will forgive and forget after enough time has passed. God, Catherine, you've been living with this guilt hanging around your neck, and no one here gives a damn about a stupid mistake you made."

He stared at the ground, thinking. Catherine knew that he was attempting to solve this problem, this final problem of him and her. That's where Emily and Olivia got it from.

"Yes, you made a bad decision, and yes, you were humiliated, but if we've learned anything in the past year, it's that the thing that really matters is *this*—our family, us and the girls." He sat down and pulled her to the edge of the bed. "If it helps at all, know that when you first lost your job, I was furious at you for disrupting our lives, but that frustration was short-lived, especially when I realized how much you were already blaming yourself. But I never—not even one time—thought you were responsible for our daughter's disappearance. Forget what my mother said about your guilt tonight. She's full of shit half the time anyway."

Then Carter smiled a sly grin. He knew that criticizing his mother was always a way into her good graces.

She looked at him through her doubt and tears, the frustration of the past year starting to dissolve. It was like the edge of a glacier that would take time to melt, but for the first time in a while, Catherine knew that eventually they could return to what they had once been.

"That's actually the nicest thing you could say me, Carter Callahan."

★ ★ ★

The next night, the five Callahans gathered around the television to watch *Flight of the Navigator*. Emily cuddled close to Lucy, their feet tucked beneath her favorite blanket, while Olivia pieced together a 3D puzzle at their feet. She was building a spaceship while they all watched the one on television carry a boy far away.

Carter brought out big bowls of his signature popcorn, the kernels popped to life in oil and salted to perfection. As her girls and her husband watched the film, Catherine watched them and thanked God that the five of them were here together in this fragile space in time.

40
A Few Months Later
Emily

Mom and I finally set up our back porch with a swing, a table and a few chairs. We don't have a view of the mountains like we did in Woodhaven, but as soon as my sisters get home from school each afternoon, they ask me to sit out here with them while they pretend to do their homework, the Gulf breeze brushing against our skin. As I watch them read and draw, as I listen to them giggle and sing silly songs, I can't help but wonder how they will remember the past few months when their big sister disappeared, when they sat at her memorial service, when she came back from the dead.

I've read several articles on cases of dissociative amnesia and fugue states like mine, where men and women sometimes even take on a persona other than their real life. One man more than a century ago left his family and settled down, starting over with a new wife and kids. He stayed with them for years before waking up one day and returning to his original home.

Another man's story is in *National Geographic*: he woke up one day in America, speaking the language of his childhood home in Europe and forgetting English entirely. Today, he remains in this same fugue state, waiting. That story made me wince, knowing I could still be lost, waiting.

The most famous case I found was perhaps that of mystery writer Agatha Christie who drove her car into a tree and became "Mrs. Teresa Neele" at a health spa in Yorkshire for several days before her brother found her and came to take her home.

I know that probably neither religion nor science has all of the answers I'm looking for, but one thing I do know is that my own daughter will not be clueless about the potential her brain has to change her life. I'll teach her that the brain is a fickle tool that must be cared for, nurtured and appreciated and that if it ever breaks down, she'll have the support system in place to find her way back home again. Just like I did.

Lucy brings me back to the present, her thin fingers tangled in my hair as she messily attempts a braid. At my feet, Olivia sketches a roly-poly curling and unfurling in the sun a few inches from her pencil case. Dad will be home in an hour, and we'll all eat dinner together. Alex will be here too. His mom is working late tonight at Let the Little Children Residential Center where she's one of the paid coordinators. Alex is home from UT for Labor Day weekend and seems to finally be willing to be my friend again. There's even a girl at school that he said he likes and wants me to meet.

As for the others: The two men who were guilty remain guilty. At Sawyer's suggestion, Anna moved out to live with him and Phin and Logan once Leslie checked herself into a rehab facility. Phin and Logan have welcomed me to their home three times, each time reintroducing me to pieces of myself and helping me remember.

Like he promised, Sawyer has been at every doctor's appointment, and twice a week, he takes me out on the town, despite the fact that as my belly grows, it gets more and more difficult for me to climb in and out of his big truck. He just smiles, patient as he gently steadies my back, holding my arm, stroking the back of my hand with his thumb. He's possibly the most patient person I've ever met, and though I don't expect to ever remember all the details of our first romance, we're making new memories together, memories we'll tell our daughter someday.

I'm both nervous and excited about becoming a mother, but together we'll figure this thing out.

Next week, I'm starting to take some college courses online. I'm not ready to leave home yet, I'm still processing everything that happened. But I'm already corresponding with a professor at Columbia about her work, measuring rising sea levels. She says I'm in a perfect locale to send her data.

In this moment with my sisters, though, I listen to the grinding cicadas and the notes my mother plays from inside the house. *Moonlight Sonata*, a piece full of paradoxes: sadness and confusion, wonder and beauty, innocence and guilt. I hear the stumbling melody and realize something. Mom has never played a piece with this kind of feeling, this kind of emotion behind the faltering notes and stammering phrases. Yes, I'm certain she's never played a song quite like this.

★ ★ ★ ★ ★

ACKNOWLEDGMENTS

Literary agent Catherine Cho was kind enough to pass along my manuscript to my agent Hayley Steed, who saw the potential of this project and spent months giving editorial feedback to shape the story into a cohesive narrative. Thank you to Hayley for answering question after question about the publishing process, for alleviating fears, and for teaching me along the way. Thank you to Georgia McVeigh for helping with the edits, and thank you to the rights team, Liane-Louise Smith and Georgina Simmonds. Thank you to all of the wonderful people at Madeleine Milburn Literary who believed in this book.

Thank you to my editor Kathy Sagan, who took this book under her wing and sent it out into the reading world. She knew the conversations that needed to be expanded and how to make the timeline fluid. I appreciate her work as well as the efforts of all those at MIRA, particularly my publicist Leah

Morse, who took the words on the page and worked their magic to get the book on the shelves.

Thank you to the first reader of this book, Gina Johnson, who read other stories I wrote, saw something different in an early draft of this one, and gave tireless feedback through multiple drafts.

Thank you to Jessica Lee for your friendship from the day we met at the park swings on a church outing. You are my oldest friend and the one I dream of someday living near. You wrote in the margins of this manuscript with three littles running laps around you, and for that, I'm impressed and grateful.

Thank you to Dr. Jenny Howell for reading and cementing feedback into sound bites—that must mean a career as an editor is somewhere in your future. Your friendship and your analysis were so integral to this book.

Thank you to Dr. Tara McDonald Johnson for reading this book even though I told you that you didn't have time. Thank you for your backyard sits and for taking care of all of us when the world crashes down.

Thank you to Angela Wainwright for telling me, in your no-nonsense way, what you liked and could do without in the early drafts. I'm so glad that they put us right next door to each other all those years ago.

Thank you to Carolyn McCarthy for your love of all things mystery and for catching tiny details. Thank you to Kate Lambert and my English department at The Kinkaid School for your personal love of writing, for your collegiality, for helping me teach those never-ending TASS patterns (Pattern 4).

Thank you to Brandi Lucher and Christie Green for your prayers, your listening ears, and your words of wisdom throughout this entire process. You celebrated with me and let me whine when I felt overwhelmed.

I was first inspired to write Emily's story after reading

"How a Young Woman Lost Her Identity" by Rachel Aviv in the *New Yorker*. My students and I read this story together, and my mind began to formulate all the what-ifs. To Hannah and her family: may all that is lost one day be found.

Thank you to Sarah, who—at the risk of being super cheesy—is the sister of my heart. You read an early draft and said nice things about it even though the pages were rife with errors. You've been at my side through the beauty and pain of daily life. So many of the friendships I write are through the lens of our morning conversations.

Thank you to Mom and Dad, Kathy and Lynn Brock, who first taught me to love the written word. You read to me, and in later years, you read what I wrote. My late-night memories of the two of you involve me walking into your room—unannounced, of course—to find you each in bed with a book in hand. Mom loved the historical fiction; Dad, the business books. You thought I was brilliant and beautiful when I was stumbling and awkward, which is what I needed.

Thanks to my siblings, who are woven into all of my stories just as they are woven into the fabric of who I am. Lindsay, I wish I had an ounce of your quiet calm. Thanks for making me "Aunt Kristen." Katie, thanks for letting me be your second-mom and sister and for reading my books and recommending so many great writers whose works I devour. Cody, you're the one I rocked to sleep, whether you remember it or not, and you can't escape my hugs.

Thank you to my three girls for making me "Mom" and for inspiring the three Callahan girls in this story. Macie, your kindness and sensitivity for those without a voice astound me, and your tears are worth it. Thanks for reminding me to love everyone—even when it's hard. Sadie, when you describe the world, it's like putting on a completely different pair of glasses that lets me see staggering details I would otherwise miss. Thanks for trusting me with your questions and feelings. Ruby, you want to try all the things, go out and experience life's adventures, and then come home and cuddle on the couch. Thanks for telling me you love me when we're driving down the road, grabbing Starbucks, and going to sleep.

And finally, to Tim, the guy I said I'd never marry who became the one I never want to live without. You told me "We're okay. You go write" too many times to count. You've been my anchor as we've faced loss, my partner while raising three under three, and my ideal date whenever we could sneak away from it all. Thanks for fighting with me and for me. There are so many wonderful people in our lives, so you know how much it means when I remind you again: you're my favorite person.